Praise for Andrea Bramhall

Ladyfish "is Andrea Bramhall's first novel and what a great yarn it is… fast and fabulous and great fun."—*Lesbian Reading Room*

Nightingale "is a tale of courage and determination, a 'don't miss' work from an author that promises a stellar career thrilling us with her skillful storytelling."—*Lambda Literary*

Nightingale "will move you to tears of despair and fill you with the joy of true love. There aren't enough stars to recommend it highly enough."—*Curve Magazine*

"[I] recommend *Nightingale* to anyone, lesbian or feminist, who would like to read a thought-provoking, well-written novel about the clash of cultures."—C-Spot Reviews

Clean Slate "is a great story. I was spellbound. I literally couldn't put it down."—*Lesbian Reading Room*

By the Author

Ladyfish

Clean Slate

Nightingale

Swordfish

The Chameleon's Tale

Visit us at www.boldstrokesbooks.com

THE CHAMELEON'S TALE

by

Andrea Bramhall

2015

THE CHAMELEON'S TALE

ISBN 13: 978-1-62639-363-9

This Trade Paperback Original Is Published By
Bold Strokes Books, Inc.
P.O. Box 249
Valley Falls, NY 12185

First Edition: August 2015

Credits
Editor: Cindy Cresap
Production Design: Stacia Seaman
Cover Design by Sheri (graphicartist2020@hotmail.com)

Acknowledgements

Thank you to everyone at BSB. Rad, for taking a chance on another of my…slightly unconventional ideas; Cindy, for all your hard work in making sense of my truly atrocious spelling and grammar; Sheri for, in my humble opinion, the best book cover; and to everyone else working behind the scenes. You all rock.

Louise and Kim, your encouragement and beta-reading skills on this project kept me going when I believed this project should hit the bin and nothing else. When I couldn't connect, you both helped me to find my way back to this story, for that I am forever grateful.

And finally, the most important people. My dogs. Just kidding. I mean you. The people who spend their hard-earned cash to buy this book and read it. So, I hope you enjoy it, my friends. Perhaps with a nice glass of South African wine…

To the man who showed me the wonders of the world beyond my own doorstep, and in doing so taught me so much more than he will ever know.

Thanks, Pops.

PROLOGUE

Imogen had always been fascinated by the churchyard with the craggy summits of the Stellenbosch Mountains towering behind the white walls of the beautiful old church. The spires over the doors and rising from the roof were mesmerizing to her. The rows of gravestones stuck out of the ground like teeth erupting from grassy gums. A small hand squeezed hers own, offering comfort. She looked at Amahle. Her hair was braided against her scalp in neat little cornrows, her T-shirt was freshly pressed, and tears ran down her cheeks. Amahle's big brown eyes were so solemn that it hurt Imogen to look into them. Instead she looked up at her father. His eyes watered, but the tears never fell as he bent and picked up a handful of dirt. The minister spoke softly as he proclaimed, "Ashes to ashes, dust to dust." But it seemed that was not enough for Alain Frost. He opened his hand and stared at the dirt on his palm.

"Red. Look at this, Immy." He pushed his hand under her nose. "Look at it. Do you know why the earth is red?"

"No, Papa."

He squatted beside her. "It is red because it is stained with blood." He curled his fingers into a fist. "It's red because it is stained with your mother's blood." He threw the clump of earth as hard as he could against the box as it was lowered into the hole. "No more." He stood tall and turned his head to the sky. "No more, do you hear? I won't let you take any more of them! I've given up enough of my soul for this bloody country and its bloody politics. No more!"

Imogen wished she'd known the answer to his question so she could have stopped him from getting angry. But she could do nothing about that now. Instead she did the only thing her seven-year-old mind could think of, she picked up her own handful of dirt and tossed it onto her mother's coffin as her father turned his back on her and walked away from the graveside. She managed three steps after him before a hand gripped her shoulder and pulled her to a stop.

"Let him go, child," Mbali said, still holding her daughter Amahle's hand. "He must rage against the world in his grief. Let him do so, and then he will return to you."

"But I made him angry."

"No, you didn't. The world has made him angry. Africa has made him angry. You are all that brings him happiness."

Imogen felt failure settle in her chest. "He is not so happy now, Mbali."

"No, little one, but that is not your fault." Mbali draped her arm around Imogen's shoulders and led her away from the grave and back to the vineyard they all called home. Amahle wrapped her small fingers around Imogen's, offering silent support as big fat tears continued to roll down her cheeks. Imogen brushed them away and hugged her before walking the rest of the way home in silence.

When they finally got there, Imogen squinted as the bright sun reflected off the white lime washed walls of the Cape Dutch building with the ostentatious frontage over the huge front door. The cavernous building was deceptive from the front, the traditional façade hiding the extensive work that had been long since completed at the rear to make the main home of the Frost Family Vineyard a building of palatial proportions befitting one of the most prestigious vineyards in the Western Cape. How many times had her father told her that one day this would all be hers? Imogen wasn't sure she could even count that high. He'd walked with her through row upon row of grapes, showing her the subtle differences between each variety that grew from the rich loam and clay earth beneath her feet. She'd wandered freely, in and out of the pressing rooms, the cellars, amongst the workforce, both black and white, and she had known this place was in her blood.

Today the doors were closed, the curtains drawn, and no one but Amahle seemed able to meet her gaze. She went to push open the door to her home only to find it locked, and the crashing noises from inside made her jump. She was afraid to go in. She was afraid of her father.

"Come, child." Cebisa, Mbali's elderly mother, waved her over. Imogen approached cautiously, always a little afraid of the grizzled old woman, her fingers twisted with age and her eyes heavy with sorrow. She placed one of those work roughened hands upon Imogen's cheek and spoke softly in Xhosa, her tongue clicking against the roof of her mouth as she sounded the rapid-fire words. "Tonight, you will stay with us."

Amahle jumped excitedly beside her, and Imogen wished she could feel as happy about the extra time with her friend. But she couldn't. She missed her mother. Two weeks. That's how long it had been since her mother had left the house and never came home. She'd heard words like "riot" and "shooting." She'd heard the Afrikaners on the vineyard say "that bloody woman shouldn't have been doing what she was" and that "she deserved what happened to her, coming to South Africa with her bloody liberal ideas and thinking that she knew better than they did how to deal with the bloody kaffirs." They used words like "traitor" and "kaffir lover" to describe her mother. And Imogen wished she could understand what was going on. She wished she could understand how her beautiful mother, her father's English Rose, who was loved by everyone, was suddenly gone.

"Immy, Gogo has made supper for us. By the big fire." Amahle tugged her off the stoop and led her toward the huge fire that roared in the pit, where her grandmother sat watching the flames. They sat together, backs resting against a log, plates on their knees as they ate their mealie pap and boerewors. The fire was a huge comfort to Imogen. The snap and crackle of the wood had a hypnotic effect on her, and the jumping embers lit the night sky before dying and leaving her staring at the cold, distant stars.

"At the dawn of time, God the Creator was already old and lonely," Cebisa said quietly from across the flames. "So He created the Earth. He created the land and the great waters. He created the sun and the moon and the stars to help the moon light the night sky. And it was very beautiful. But still He was lonely. He wanted someone to share His creation with. So He created animals, lions, and tigers, and baboons."

Mbali rolled her eyes and stood up. "While you tell your stories, old woman, some of us have work to do. I'm going to the big house and make sure Mr. Alain has everything he needs."

Cebisa clucked her tongue and fixed a pointed stare at her daughter. "How long will you be?"

Mbali stared at her mother. "As long as it takes."

"Are we still talking about work, daughter?"

"What else, Mother?"

"The kind of work no mother wants her daughter involved in."

Mbali didn't answer. She tugged at her top and walked quickly toward the big house Imogen had been unable to get into earlier.

Amahle looked at her, seeming to wonder as much as she did what the conversation was all about. But both of them knew better than to ask while Cebisa stared at Mbali's retreating back, a frown marring her aged, wrinkled face.

"Gogo, will you tell us more of the story please?" Amahle asked.

"Of course, girls, now where was I?"

"He made lions."

"And tigers," Imogen said.

"So he did. He also created the tiger, and the zebra, and every bird in the sky. But they were not enough. They were limited in how they could appreciate the true beauty of the Creator's gift. So He set about creating a creature who would appreciate it."

"Gogo, who did the Creator make?" Amahle asked.

"Why, He created people, little one."

"He made us?"

"He made everything."

"He must have been very powerful, Gogo."

"He still is, child." She raised her cup to her lips.

"If He's so powerful, Cebisa, why did He let my mother die?"

"It is not a simple matter, little one. I wish it was. I wish I could tell you why your mama had to leave us. But I don't have those answers."

"No one will tell me anything."

"That's because grownups hate to admit how much they don't know." She smiled sadly. "We don't have the answers to your questions, but I will tell you what I know, if you like?"

Imogen nodded and waited for Cebisa to impart her wisdom to them.

"When the Creator had finished creating the world and everything in it, He began to notice that the people were getting old. Their skin was scarred from work and damaged from long hours under the hot sun. They began to feel discomfort from their aging skins and the Creator did not like this. They were his favourites and He did not want to see them in pain. So He created for them a new and wonderful gift."

"Gogo, what was it?"

"Don't interrupt, Amahle."

"Sorry."

"You must wait and see. The Creator called to Him His most loyal servant, the chameleon, and asked him to take His gift to the people. He told the chameleon that it was a very special gift, and the Creator would forever be in the chameleon's debt if he would deliver it for Him. The chameleon was so proud to have been sent on such a mission for the Creator. He puffed out his chest and let his skin reflect all the colours of the rainbow to show his pride. God gave him one further instruction. 'Chameleon,' He said, 'do not tell a soul about your errand for me. Not all are so keen on the people.' The chameleon promised not to breathe a word to a living soul, picked up the package, and set out immediately."

"Did he steal the gift, Gogo?"

"What have I told you about interrupting?" She smiled at Amahle and tapped her nose.

"Sorry."

"Sit still. The chameleon hurried quickly from the Kingdom of God and sought out the people. He passed through jungle and stepped onto the hot sand of the desert. He kept moving so as to not burn his feet until he was safely across and began to climb the mountains that separated his home from that of the people. He stopped for a moment to drink from a pool, and his cousin, the snake, approached him."

"I hate snakes."

"One day you will have to learn to keep your mouth shut or it will get you into big trouble, young lady."

"Yes, Gogo."

"Cebisa, will you finish the story? Please?" Imogen asked.

"Of course." She sipped from her cup again and rested back against her own log, the fire slowly dying. "The snake asked his cousin to join him for a meal. It had been long since they had spent time together, and snake felt more than a little neglected by the rest of his family. Now this put the chameleon in a difficult position. He did not want to hurt snake's feelings, but he did not want to take the time to stop either. He decided that he should tell his cousin of his errand so that he would understand why he could not stop. He told snake that he was delivering a gift to the people from the Creator." She leaned forward and stirred the embers of the fire, casting a glittering shower of orange into the dark. "Snake hated people. He hated that they were favoured by the Creator. He hated that the people feared him so and tried to trample him whenever he came near them. He hated everything about people."

"What did he do?" Amahle clapped her hand over her mouth. "Sorry."

"The snake pretended that he did not hate the people to his cousin and invited him to tea. He knew that the chameleon felt guilty that he had not stopped by for so long and decided to use this to his advantage. He wanted the gift from the Creator. He did not care what the gift was. He only cared that he would get it, instead of the people. He told chameleon that he understood how important his errand was, but surely the Creator would understand that chameleon needed food and rest to carry out such an important task. The chameleon was trapped. He could not say no without offending snake, so he agreed to a quick meal before continuing his journey."

"Snakes are bad."

"In this case, yes, the snake was bad. He snuck a sleeping potion into chameleon's food and waited until he fell asleep. When he did, snake opened the package and pulled out the people's gift and draped it about his body like a cloak."

"What was the gift, Gogo?"

"God made new skins for us, child."

"And the snake stole them."

Cebisa nodded.

"I told you snakes were bad."

"When the chameleon woke up, he saw immediately what had happened. Snake had donned his new skin and was so pleased with himself and the results of his trickery. When the people found out what had happened to their new skins they hated snake and his children from that day forward for his deceit and theft. The chameleon was so ashamed of himself for allowing snake the chance to trick him that he cannot face us. He hides. He hides forever from people so that we cannot see his shame. To make up for the loss of the new skins, God gave us His ultimate gift. When our bodies are too old, or damaged, or broken to give us a good life any longer, He gave us the gift of death."

"Why didn't He make people more new skins so we don't have to die?" Imogen whispered.

"Because in death we can live for the rest of eternity with the Creator. That is His greatest gift, little one. Heaven."

"What's Heaven like, Cebisa?"

She scratched her chin, seemingly thoughtful for a moment. "Heaven is the most perfect thing you can ever think of, Miss Immy."

Imogen closed her eyes and remembered her mother tucking her and Amahle into bed the night before she went away, kissing them both on the forehead, and telling them to sleep tight. That was the most perfect thing she could imagine. And it had gone. It wouldn't come back.

"Then Heaven doesn't exist, Cebisa."

"Of course it does—"

"No, it doesn't. We buried it this afternoon." She stumbled to her feet and ran from the fire, ignoring the shouts and pounding feet at her back. She ran as hard as she could through the rows of grapes until she reached the orchard at the far end of the property. She swung herself up into the branches and let the tears fall. The rustling below alerted her to Amahle trying to climb up behind her. But her shorter arms and legs stopped her from being able to reach the first branch. Imogen could have just ignored her plight and hoped that eventually she'd go away. She didn't. In her loneliness, she reached out her hand and helped pull Amahle up beside her. For as long as Imogen could remember, they had been best friends. She needed Amahle, and she knew Amahle needed to help her just as much. She wrapped her arms around Imogen's shoulders, whispered promises to look after her, and held her till the tears stopped falling, and they both dozed.

It was the sound of men crashing through the shrubs, yelling Imogen's name that woke them both as dawn coloured the sky. Imogen's father sounded both terrified and terrifying as he screamed for her. They looked at each other before they quickly dropped out of the tree and waited for Alain Frost to reach them.

"Imogen, get in the car. You're leaving." He grabbed her hand roughly and began tugging her back toward the house.

"Leaving? Father, where am I going?"

"You, man," he said, pointing at the man closest to him, "get the car round the front. Her suitcase is in the hallway. We're leaving in ten minutes."

"Where are we going, Papa?" Imogen looked at Amahle, but she was running to keep up with her father's long stride.

"Mr. Frost, where you going to, boss?" Amahle called after them.

The car was waiting when Imogen was pushed into the backseat. The boot slammed shut loudly and her father dropped quickly into the driver's seat while barking orders to the foreman. "Do not let any of those bastards slack off while I'm gone. I'll be back by the end of the day, and I expect those vats to be so clean I could eat off of them, man."

"Yah, boss."

"And get that kid off my car before it ends up under the fucking wheels." Amahle was leaning through the window, hugging Imogen as he threw the engine into gear and punched the accelerator. The man grabbed Amahle around the waist and hoisted her away.

"Amahle!"

"Immy!" She kicked at the man holding her and set off running as soon as he dropped her, swearing under his breath. "Immy!"

"Stop that bloody snivelling, girl." Her father turned to her. "It's time to move on from childish things, Imogen. Time to grow up."

Imogen didn't say anything as she battled to hold the tears in check, desperate to please her father so that he'd let her return home.

"I know that little black girl was your friend, but that's not how the world works. Do you understand me?"

She wanted to say, no, but thought better of it. "Where are you taking me, Father?"

"To the airport."

"But why?"

"You're going to England, girl. It's all arranged. You'll start school there on Monday. Your mother's sister will meet you at the airport in London."

"But I don't want to go to London."

"It's all arranged."

"I don't know Mother's sister."

"You'll get to know her."

"I want to stay here, Papa, with you."

"We don't always get what we want, young lady."

"Please, Papa. Please don't send me away. I'll be good. Please."

"Enough, Imogen." He slammed his hand against the steering wheel. "That is enough." He pulled over on the side of the road. "It is all arranged. You will adapt. You are strong. And most importantly, you will be safe over there."

"I don't want to go."

"I don't care what you want. I am your father and you will do as you're told. Do you hear me?" He stormed out of the car and walked twenty feet onto the dirt verge. He kicked at stones and clumps of sod, shook his fists, and screamed at the sky.

It looked different. The sky. When she'd fallen asleep under it last night, she'd still believed that everything would be okay. Yes, her mother was dead, and it was hard times, but they'd get through it, and everything would be okay. Now the sky was still blue, it still had clouds, the sun still shone down on them all. But it wasn't the same. It never would be again.

CHAPTER ONE

A mahle looked out from the podium. The auditorium was dark. It was difficult to make out anything more than a few indistinct faces in the crowd of hundreds, but that made it easier for her. Instead of having to look at each woman as they watched her, listened to her, she could focus on the message she was trying to get across rather than worrying whether it was pity she could see on their faces when she got to the part about Grace. She couldn't deal with pity, the biggest waste of time she could ever contemplate. She glanced into the wings and caught the eye of her seemingly ever-present bodyguard and friend, Thambo Umpala. A quick smile and a nod reassured her that everything was fine, and she set about delivering the speech she'd prepared.

"My friends, the constitution of the Republic of South Africa is set on the foundation of human dignity and equality for all. Everyone is equal before the law and has equal right to its benefits and protections as well as its punishments, regardless of their race, gender, marital status, sex, pregnancy status, ethnic or social origin, colour, age, disability, conscience, belief, culture, language, birth, or their sexual orientation. I believe in this. I believe we all deserve these rights. We, as a people, fought for them, generation after generation.

"Our laws say we cannot be denied our freedoms or privileges as South Africans because we are women, or black, or twenty, or fifty. Then why are so many women denied the right to have their rapes taken seriously because we are lesbians?

"Corrective rape. A despicable term for a despicable act. Where the very idea that forcing a lesbian woman to have sex with a man will make her 'normal.' Will make her fit into society's box for her. Will make her—us—what they expect us to be.

"Eight years ago, my partner was raped by three men. They beat her and they raped her. It was reported to the police immediately. Police came into our home and listened to what she had to say. Then they wrote in their little notebooks three words. Lesbian. Corrective. Rape."

Boos echoed around the hall. Amahle held up her hands to quiet the crowd.

"Grace's rapists were never found."

"Bastard Boers," a voice from the crowd jeered at the ineffectual police.

"Grace is not alone. More than five hundred women every year report an incident of corrective rape to the police. In recent years, more than thirty such assaults have resulted in murder. In a country with more than nine thousand reported rapes every year, that seems like a pretty small figure, doesn't it?

"As far as I'm concerned, both numbers are far too high. There should be no incidence of rape. Ever. The police force's ineffective action against any aspect of the rape culture that has gripped South Africa belittles its effort as a whole and makes a mockery of it."

Shouts of "hear, hear" and "yes" chorused through the room.

"I call for all women, lesbian and straight, to stand up and say enough is enough. There is no justifiable reason for rape. Her skirt is never too short, nor is she so butch she deserves it. She can never be so drunk that it just happens, or offensive to his manhood because she doesn't want to sleep with him. There is nothing that makes it acceptable for one man, two, three, four, five, or however many, to beat, hold at gunpoint, or force a woman in any way to have sexual intercourse with him. Nothing."

Applause filled the air. She let it go on for a moment before holding her hands up for quiet again. "In the past eight years, I have seen many changes in South Africa. We all have. Some good, and some not. But I think we can all agree that in some areas there is still a long way to go. This, my friends, is one such area."

Cheers emanated from the darkened seating bank. "As a nation, we know that we cannot win the battle alone. We know the rewards, and the risks, in standing up against those who try to keep us where they *think* we belong. No more, my friends, no more. We fought that battle and won. We will fight this one too. We will achieve our goals. We will realize the rights we are entitled to.

"We cannot turn the other cheek and let these hate crimes go unreported. We cannot hide because we fear what they will do to us.

We cannot turn our backs and let those who are meant to protect us all write off these crimes as deserved or understandable. As though they don't matter.

"They matter, my friends. *We* matter."

Applause and cheers echoed around the room. Stomping feet added a staccato beat against the seating bank, and the auditorium filled with the resounding chorus of approval as Amahle exited the stage to a standing ovation. The wall of sound followed her into the wings and out the door as Thambo escorted her out of the building and straight into the waiting car.

"You don't worry about upsetting the police?" he asked.

"Why should I worry about that? All I do is tell the truth. If they're upset about it perhaps they should do their jobs better and not give me such an easy target."

"I worry more about you becoming a target, Minister."

"That's your job, Thambo." She fastened her seat belt. "Mine, unfortunately, is to make myself one."

He shook his head and turned back to the front seat as they made their way from the University of South Africa to the Houses of Parliament. Her driver pulled up at the members' entrance around the back. The white marble columns and bright red bricks were not quite as grand as the front entrance, but in many ways, Amahle preferred the more understated entrance. It gave her the feeling that she was coming to work rather than attending the theatrical event that seemed to surround much of what went on inside the building.

A second car pulled up at the same time, and her boss climbed out of his car under a much heavier guard than she employed. James Wilson, Minister for Health, former lawyer and judge who made his name and reputation presiding over many of the amnesty hearings of the Truth and Reconciliation Commission, smiled and pulled open the door for her.

"Ah, Amahle, how's it, my dear?"

"Very well, James. You?" She smiled at the elderly statesman. His hair had silvered over the years she had known him, his skin showing a few liver spots here and there, but his mind was as sharp as ever, and he was a giant in the political arena. She'd been grateful for his patronage over the years and grateful for the position he had afforded her in his parliamentary department.

"Not bad, not bad. The old bones are still doing what I tell them to do."

"Long may it continue, James."

"A little bird tells me you were giving a speech this morning."

"And which little bird would that be?"

He tapped the side of his nose. "A gentleman never kisses and tells, my dear."

She laughed as he winked at her. "Is that right?"

"So how did it go?"

"I think it went very well."

"Is this that thing the *Cape Chameleon* rag organized?"

"It's not a rag, James." She narrowed her eyes at him. "They have some very detailed and informative investigative stories."

"Hmm. Not exactly the *Mail & Guardian* though, are they?"

"Not everyone can be your precious *M & G*."

"Still. Be careful."

"Of what? Besides, you didn't hire me to be careful, James. I'm the cannon in your back pocket."

"Yah. And one of these days, young lady, you're gonna blow off my backside." He wagged his finger at her, and she was reminded of her grandmother scolding her as a child.

She laughed. "Only you can get away with calling me that, James."

"I know. No one else would have the balls to try it. Be good, Amahle."

"See you." She tugged on the jacket of her deep purple skirt suit and walked into her office. "Good morning, Claudia," she said to her secretary. As the undersecretary for health, Amahle's offices were substantial, yet seemingly always overcrowded with both people and work.

"Good morning, Minister. How are you today?"

"I'm good. You? Haircut?"

"Very well, thank you. And yes. Do you like it?" Claudia ran her fingers through her red hair. Yesterday, it had fallen to her waist; today, it brushed the tops of her shoulders in bouncing loose curls.

"It really suits you. Brings out your eyes. I'll bet it's cooler too, right?"

"Oh my God, you have no idea. Well, of course you do. It's the same length as yours now, but I mean, after having so much, it was such a relief last night." She chuckled. "I'm babbling now. Back to work. Your first appointment is already waiting."

Amahle cocked her head to one side. She and Claudia had worked together so long now that the younger woman understood the shorthand.

"Mr. Julius Steele. Investigative journalist with the *Mail & Guardian Online*."

She chuckled at the irony given her recent conversation with James, but she could remember nothing of the appointment.

"He arranged an interview when it was announced in the *Cape Chameleon Online* magazine that you'd be giving the speech today."

She still didn't recall the meeting but nodded anyway. "Can you arrange tea for us please?"

"Certainly." She indicated the scruffy looking guy sitting on one of the small chairs in the corridor. His dirty blond hair looked like it had needed cutting several weeks ago and hung in his eyes, causing him to constantly flick it out of his sight line. His jeans dragged on the floor, the backs dirty and ripped having been walked on for far too many months. He wore a buff coloured photographer's style waistcoat with more pockets than Amahle could ever imagine knowing what to do with, and his sunglasses tucked in the front of a T-shirt bearing the slogan "Lies, Damned Lies, and Politics." He stood when he saw her approach and held out his hand.

"Minister Nkosi, how are you this morning?"

"I'm very well, thank you. And you, Mr. Steele?" She shook his hand as she entered the office.

"Very good. Please call me Julius."

"Only if you'll call me Amahle."

He nodded his assent.

"Nice shirt, by the way. Where can I get one?"

He chuckled. "I'll send you one in the post." He sat when Amahle winked and pointed to one of the sofas. "Thank you for agreeing to this interview. It will be on the front page of *M & G Online* by the end of the week." He held up a small digital recorder. "Do you mind? I'm not very good at making notes quickly. I can't read my own writing afterward."

Amahle smiled. "I don't mind at all." She leaned back in her chair, relaxed, confident, and enjoying the small respite in her otherwise hectic day.

"That was a very passionate speech, Amahle."

"Thank you. You were there?"

He nodded and put the recorder on the table between them.

"You did well to get back here before me."

"I'd say I have as little interest in making friends with the police as you do." He winked. "Given your personal history and your sexuality, it's very easy to understand your viewpoint on the subject of corrective rape and indeed on LGBT rights, but I think we'll come to that later if that's okay?"

"Of course."

"What made you decide to follow a career in politics?"

"A combination of things, but there are two standout moments in my life that made me certain this was my path." She ran her fingers over her hair, making sure every strand was in place. "When I was very young, I lost a very close friend. We were more like sisters than friends. I had never felt so helpless. I was devastated."

"How did she die?"

"She didn't. She was taken away by her father and never returned to South Africa. I vowed to never feel so helpless again. I knew Imogen's father was wrong to send her away. For many more reasons than I was able to articulate at the time. I was just a child. I wasn't listened to, and I vowed then that I would always fight for what I believed to be right."

He nodded. "What was the other event?"

Amahle smiled. "I was in school in Stellenbosch and we got a visit from Nelson Mandela." She paused to let the words sink in. "It was before he was elected to the presidency, and he was visiting as many schools as he could. You're probably too young to remember those days, Mr. Steele, but Mr. Mandela was trying to inspire the nation toward reconciliation and peace. He gave a speech about the South Africa he saw. The one he was trying to create, a South Africa where we were all free and equal, no matter the colour of our skin, our gender, our religion, or our sexual orientation. I listened to his words, and my drive gained its focus. I had to help with the creation of our democratic nation."

"There has been much written about the attack upon you and your partner before you ran for office the first time."

Amahle felt a chill run up her spine, but nodded slowly, wondering where the next question would lead them.

"Did you ever consider giving up politics in the wake of that?"

Her palms were instantly slick with sweat and her shoulders ached. Just as they had that night when they had been pulled behind her back and tied there. Grace's beautiful face was even paler than normal, her blue eyes wide with pain and shock; tears ran into her blond hair as she lay on her back, bloodied, beaten, and abused. The man had twisted his fingers into Grace's blood and wiped them over the walls of their home, hitting her again if he needed more than her body was producing. Over and over until his message was clear. *"Back off, kaffir bitch."*

"No."

"Not even for a second?"

"Never." She shook her head to clear the fog that threatened to settle in the wake of the memory. "To do so was to let them win. To give up would have made everything Grace and I survived that night worthless. I had to continue. I had to show them and whoever it was that sent them, that no matter what they threw at me—at what was right—we would continue to fight for what we believed in."

"And what was that?"

"It was the right of all South Africans to receive treatment for HIV and AIDS. The ANC leadership at that time believed that lifestyle choices and nutrition were the key to fighting the battle with HIV."

"Why?"

She knew he knew the answer to his own question, and that he was only asking to get her response on tape. It didn't matter. She'd made her opinion public many times over the years and saw no reason not to give him what he wanted here. "Money. It costs the government now more than a billion rand every year."

"You fought for that?"

"Yes."

"Why?"

"Because it was the right thing to do."

"You don't know anyone with HIV, do you?"

"I know lots of people with it, but I'm very lucky. None of my family has contracted the virus."

"Then you are lucky indeed. As I mentioned earlier, it has been well documented by the media about your sexual orientation and your, shall we call it, slightly hostile relationship with the South African Police Services."

She chuckled. "You could put it that way."

"How would you put it?"

"I'd say that I have a healthy respect for anyone who does their job to the best of their ability, and a substantial derision for those who disregard those who need them and work only to further their own agendas or line their own pockets."

"How do you feel about politicians?"

"The same."

"How do you think you managed to get elected following the assault and the media coverage of it in a country where eighty percent of the population regularly express homophobic attitudes in unbiased polls?"

"Are there such a thing as unbiased polls?"

"Touché, Minister. But the question is still valid."

"I agree." She threaded her fingers together and rested her chin on the bridge she formed. "I'm fairly certain that my first election was based upon my campaign for the HIV treatment programme. I feel with that I gained people's trust and respect, regardless of my sexuality."

"Do you think you gained the sympathy vote?"

"As a result of the attack?"

"Yes."

"No. I don't think so."

"Mind if I disagree with you on that?"

She laughed. "Would it matter if I did?"

"Probably not."

"If it was the sympathy vote that got me elected, Julius, then how did I retain my election for the second term?"

"That's easy."

She waited.

"You're the last honest politician. Didn't you know?"

She laughed again. "Sometimes I worry that you're not wrong. How about a tour while we continue talking?"

"That would be wonderful."

Amahle continued to answer his questions as she led Julius down each corridor, pointing out notable rooms as they passed. Already well into her second elected term as a member of the National Assembly, Amahle still found her heart swelled with pride as the aroma of democracy filled her lungs. She worked hard to ignore the acrid odour of corruption that tainted politics in South Africa, but it was always there. Always ready to wrap its fingers around your throat and squeeze. *It* was ready, even if you weren't.

CHAPTER TWO

Imogen reached for the small green hold and wrapped two fingers around it to steady herself as she used her left leg to propel her up the wall. She slapped at the bell and grinned down at her opponent, still a good six feet off the top of the speed climbing wall they'd just raced up.

"You're getting slower, Ian."

"Yeah, yeah," he said, panting as he gripped the last hold. "I think your man down there's pulling you up." He pointed to the floor where their climbing partners waited on the end of the belay ropes.

"Dan, he thinks you're cheating."

"Come down here and say that," the tall man on the ground grumbled. "I can't keep up with the rope. She goes that bloody fast."

"You're all comedians." She leaned back on her rope, ready to abseil down the thirty-foot wall as her phone rang. She fished it out of the zip pocket on her thigh. "Frost."

"Imogen, I've just had a call."

"Nice to talk to you too, Marcus. How are you this fine evening?"

"Clarke's been rushed into hospital. Heart attack."

"Shit."

"Yeah."

"Will he be okay?"

"Don't know yet. Trouble is, he's due in court tomorrow on the Crown versus Russel case. Do you know it?"

"No."

"Rape case. Tony Russel confessed, buckets full of forensics. Pleading not guilty on grounds of diminished responsibility. Counsel is trying to get his confession thrown out."

"On what grounds?"

"No responsible adult with him at the time of the confession."

"Age?"

"Twenty-five."

She landed back on the ground and quickly disengaged herself from the rope. "Was he under caution?"

"Yes."

"Then what aren't you telling me?"

"He has an IQ of eighty and a mental age of thirteen."

"Shit."

"Been living in a group home since he turned eighteen. Parents are deceased. They were all in an accident that resulted in his brain injury and their deaths. Been on his own since then."

"Who's the victim?"

"One of the care workers."

"Bloody hell, Marcus."

"I know. It's a bit of a messy one." He sighed. "At least they'll give you a continuance on account of old Clarkey's dodgy ticker."

"Courier the files over to my place. I'll be there in twenty."

"You're going to try and run with it?"

"If I can. The victim deserves that much at least."

"She also deserves proper representation, not a half arsed job put together in an hour."

"Have I ever done that, Marcus?"

"I don't see how you can do anything else at this point."

"Arthur Clarke might be cracking on for retirement, but he's a solid barrister. If his strategy is clear and I can execute it, then I'll proceed. If not, I'll request the continuance and work it from the beginning."

"Fine. It's your night to waste."

"Let me know if you hear anything on Arthur." She hung up and turned back to her friends as they changed their shoes.

"Pub?" Dan asked.

"Sorry, no. Arthur Clarke's in hospital and I've just picked up his case for tomorrow."

"Damn, I thought that old bastard was never going to leave chambers." Ian shook his head.

"He's not dead, Ian," Simon said.

"We don't actually know that."

"Well, aren't you all a cheery group." Imogen quickly changed her shoes and grabbed her coat. "I'll see you all in chambers tomorrow. Simon, I may need a second chair."

"My pleasure, Imogen. Want me to come with you now? Two heads and all that."

She smiled. It was no secret that Simon had a huge crush on her, but it didn't detract from the fact that he was a promising young barrister with a great work ethic. It didn't hurt that he was prepared to go above and beyond the call to impress her either. "Thanks, but if I can't get a handle on this tonight, I'll be filing for a continuance. I'll let you know tomorrow. Early."

"I'll be in the office by six. Just email me any instructions."

She said her good-byes and flipped the collar of her coat up as high as it would go as she ran out of the climbing centre and into the rain, fishing her car keys from her pocket as she went.

"It's June, for fuck's sake. Surely even England's supposed to get a dry season." The dark green BMW Z4 purred to life as she gunned the engine and set off across Cambridge. Streetlights twinkled off the rain slicked spires and façades as the windscreen wipers worked hard to keep the window clear. She passed through the industrial estate on the outskirts of the city. The corrugated sheet metal always made her think of the shantytowns she'd been teased about as a child. The townships she'd never even seen as a child but was told to get back to by almost every girl in her boarding school at one time or another. She turned right and sped through the narrowing streets, over several cobbled lanes, and alongside the river for a couple of miles. The rain had driven people inside, but there were a few hardy souls on the riverbank. People who were walking dogs, lovers holding hands, kissing and smiling despite their wet hair and clinging clothes.

As she drove she stopped seeing them all and began running through case law in her head, trying to remember any cases that were similar for her to refer to. She pulled up outside her town house at the same time as the courier arrived and quickly divested him of his burden.

The house was dark. She'd forgotten to turn the outside light on before she left for work that morning, and she flipped light switches as she went, the small halogen spotlights illuminating her way through the darkness. Well, supposedly. She grabbed a glass and a bottle of wine from the kitchen and sat at the table. She poured a generous amount of the ruby red liquid into her glass and allowed the aroma to fill the air. It surrounded her like a warm cocoon, and to this day, she marvelled at how that smell took her back to Africa. To her family's vineyard. To feeling the sun on her face, the earth beneath her feet, and her mother's hand in hers, teaching her the proper way to appreciate the wine. *I was four. I'm amazed I didn't have a drinking problem by the time I was six!*

She took a mouthful and unfastened the ribbon holding the file together. It'd been more than thirty years since she'd stepped foot on African soil, and she had no intention of ever doing so again, despite knowing her father fully expected her to take over the vineyard when he could no longer run it. *Never going to happen.*

She swallowed the wine and pulled her notepad toward her as she shut the memories away. There was work to do, and she wasn't about to lose a case by being underprepared.

CHAPTER THREE

H ello?"
Derek Marais looked up from his computer and waved the blonde in the steel gray power suit toward him. "Mrs. De Fries, welcome to Tygerberg Hospital. Thank you for coming to see me."

"A pleasure, Dr. Marais. You look hard at work there." She smiled and sat across the desk from him.

"If there's a thing I'm never short of, it's more work. It never seems to stop."

"Isn't that the truth?" She smiled sadly. "But we're doing all we can to help, no?"

"Indeed. My associate over at the Polokwane Mankweng Hospital in Limpopo said you have some very favourable rates on some medications."

"And who was that?"

"Dr. Stephen Malan. Why?"

She waved her hand to dismiss his question. "Just curious who recommended my services."

"Your services have come very highly recommended from several sources, Mrs. De Fries. The prices offered by PharmaChem Limited are considerably cheaper than what we are currently paying."

"Not to mention that there would be no import tax, and substantially lower delivery costs."

"Absolutely."

"What medications are you looking at us supplying for you, Doctor?"

"Combivirine."

"Ah. Of course, our new wonder drug."

"I've heard some good things about it."

"We're especially proud of it. It was my mother's brain child, you know?"

"I didn't. She must be very pleased with how well it's doing for your company."

"I'm afraid we wouldn't know. She died a couple of years ago."

"I'm very sorry to hear that, Mrs. De Fries. My condolences to you all."

"Thank you."

He cleared his throat. "Perhaps you could fill me in a little more on the details of Combivirine?"

"Of course, Doctor. It is a multiclass anti-retroviral with a booster included. There are two reverse transcriptase inhibitors, Zidovudine and Tenofivir, and an integrase inhibitor, Dolutegravir, combined with Cobicistat." She handed him a brochure filled with glossy pictures of little white pills and statistical data in small writing at the back.

He flicked through the pages. "Hell of a combination."

"Yes. It allows the usual HIV cocktail to be reduced to one pill in many patients, and as you know, importing the combination pills from America is too expensive to use on the budgets the government has set. The figures on this drug will save you almost a third of your current budget."

"How can you be sure of that figure?"

"Quite easily. I know how much it currently costs to supply every patient with the standard cocktail. Mine is thirty percent cheaper than that."

He scanned through the brochure, supposedly perusing the figures in the tiny boxes at the back. "I run a very large hospital here, Mrs. De Fries. The largest in Cape Town. If I can reduce the costs per patient with HIV, I can treat more people. Funds are finite, and I have board members to account to at the end of the year. You can help me show a significant saving, support to a home-grown developing industry, and an increase in successful patient treatment."

"Doctor, I wish everyone was as easy to convince. You're making my job as a saleswoman very, very easy."

"For me it is merely a question of common sense and helping those who are sick."

"As I said, Doctor, I wish everyone was as easy to convince."

Derek smiled. "I take it you have samples with you?"

"Of course." She opened her briefcase and placed it on the desk facing him. "I brought samples of all our leading sellers, including the Combivirine." She pointed to the various containers.

"Good. How long from ordering a sizable quantity to delivery?"

"How sizable a quantity are we talking about?"

"Start with a million units."

She whistled. "That number would take around two weeks for manufacture, unless we have a stockpile available. I'd have to confirm that with our warehouse on order."

He nodded. "Of course." He picked up the blister pack and popped one of the little white pills into his hand. "They look very different from the capsules I've seen of combined drugs during my research."

She shrugged. "This form is cheaper and easier to manufacture than capsules. One of the reasons we're saving you money. That's all. The chemical ingredients are the same; the way they work is the same. Everything about them is the same, except for the way they look. Have the samples tested. Your people will be able to tell you the same thing."

He held up his hands to placate the suddenly defensive woman. "I meant nothing by it. Merely a statement. In this industry, we're well used to the appearance of medications changing as different, cheaper manufacturing techniques are developed."

She nodded curtly. "I'm sure you're very busy, Doctor, what with running the biggest hospital in Cape Town." She gathered her bag, leaving the case on his desk. "I'll see myself out."

"I'll be in touch about that order, Mrs. De Fries." He saw her shoulders visibly relax, and she smiled as she reached the door.

"I look forward to hearing from you."

He held the small pill between his finger and thumb, trying to decipher all it could tell him, as though he could look through the solid matter and into the molecules inside. He knew this sample wouldn't be what he was looking for. He knew that it would return positive results on every test he could possibly throw at it. But he had to make a start and find out more. The nationwide results for people on Combivirine developing full-blown AIDS was too high to be a naturally occurring phenomenon.

"And you, my little friend, are the start of me finding out what's going on."

CHAPTER FOUR

I will have the money; you must bring the drugs, Tsotsi." Sipho Nkosi spoke as quietly as he could. The last thing he wanted was to be overheard.

"Nah, nah, man. You must come get them. It makes people ask too many questions when I come round by you, up in your fancy white palace."

My fancy white prison, more like. "Fine." *It's not like I have a choice.* "When will you have them?"

"Friday, man. Come then."

"That's too late. She—I need them today, tomorrow at the latest."

The man sucked his breath through his teeth. "That's a rush job, Sipho man, that's gonna cost more."

Doesn't it always? "How much more?"

"One month's supply at a rush," he said. "Plus my discretion. I think a thousand rand should cover it."

"One thousand rand! Are you mad, man?"

"That's the price."

"I can't afford that kind of money."

Tsotsi laughed. "Sure you can, up there in the big house. You can get that kind of money easily."

"I can't afford—"

"The price just went up to fifteen hundred rand, Sipho man. If you're not here today with it, by tomorrow it will be two thousand. Do you understand me?"

Sipho bit back the biting insult that sat on his tongue and ground his teeth. "I understand." He ended the call, walked into the office, and opened the safe. He counted out the fifteen hundred rand, tucked it into his waistband, and left the room.

He climbed into the buckie and drove to Groendal, a township about forty miles from the vineyard as his anger simmered with every mile he covered. Tsotsi's grinning face as he handed over the medicine made him want to smash his fist into the smug expression. Again and again. Only the knowledge that it would be his mother who suffered if he did prevented him from venting the rage that burned. He'd gone over it in his mind so many times, but he still couldn't figure out how he'd gotten here. How he'd resorted to stealing from a man he loved like a father to treat the illness of the mother he despised, and who despised him. Who told him constantly what a disappointment he was to her. How he was a failure as a son for letting his sister best him time after time after time. It didn't matter that he didn't want the life Amahle had, or the job that had cost her so much, or anything else that she had. He was proud of everything she had achieved, but he loved working the land. He loved being a part of the vineyard, feeling the earth beneath his hands, and the wine upon his lips. He loved how Alain Frost had nurtured him from boyhood and allowed him to prove himself. Given him responsibility, pride, and respect.

And I repaid it all with lies. He hung his head in shame and slapped his hands against the steering wheel. *God damn you, Mama. God damn you to hell.*

When he returned to the vineyard there were buckies and tractors pulled up to the main house.

"Sipho, come quick," George called.

"What is it?"

"Boss has doctor with him. Your mother said he very bad. Very sick."

"Where is she?"

"She is with boss and the doctor." George pointed into the house. "In there."

Sipho ran into the house and up the stairs. His heart pounded in his chest and sweat ran down his back. "Mama?"

"In here, my boy."

Sipho burst into Alain's bedroom in time to see the doctor folding his stethoscope away and shaking his head. He put a hand over Alain's face and closed his eyes.

"You should inform his family," the doctor said.

"What? What happened?" Sipho knew Alain had been sick. He had been for a while, but he wasn't dying.

"I won't know for sure until I do an autopsy, but it looks like liver failure." He pointed to Alain's face. "See the yellow colour?"

Sipho and Mbali nodded.

"Jaundice." He put his instruments into his bag.

"How does a man like him get jaundice?" Sipho asked.

The doctor laughed. "There are many ways one can get jaundice or liver problems. For a man like Mr. Frost, in the business of making wine, it's not hard to imagine that the drink would be the issue. Where's the telephone? I'll arrange for transportation to the morgue."

Mbali showed him out of the room and Sipho stared. Alain had been his mentor, his employer, the closest thing he'd had to a father for as long as Sipho could remember. He'd taught him everything he knew about winemaking and the vines. He'd nurtured him, helped him along far more than any of the other boys whose families had worked on the vineyard. Sipho had always been so proud of that. That Mr. Frost had liked him so much and seen such potential in him. And now he was gone. He looked down at the bag he held in his hand. The paper rustled as the small boxes inside filled with pills moved in his trembling hand.

"What is it, Sipho? Could you not get my pills?"

He handed her the bag and nodded at the bed. "We're in big trouble now, Mama."

"What are you talking about?"

"The money, for your medication, I've been taking it from the vineyard."

"But why?"

"Because I don't have enough to pay for it."

"Why didn't you tell me?"

"Because you don't have enough to pay for it either, and you need it or you'll get sick."

"I have HIV, Sipho. I will get sick eventually."

"Not while you take medication."

"How much money do you owe?"

"A lot."

"Don't be obtuse, Sipho. How much do you owe?"

"About a hundred and fifty thousand rand."

"Oh my God. How did you think you were going to pay that back?"

He shook his head. "I never came up with an answer to that question."

Mbali patted him on the shoulder. "We'll think of something."

He laughed sadly and shook his head. "Sure, Mama."

What the hell am I going to do now?

CHAPTER FIVE

Amahle closed the door and dropped her bag on to the chair in the corner. It had been a long day. She snorted. They were all long days. She made herself a sandwich and grabbed a bottle of water before sitting down. She knew if she didn't eat now, she'd get caught up in something and forget. She kicked off her shoes and tucked her feet under her bottom as she got comfortable on the cream leather sofa facing the windows and the Atlantic Ocean toward the spit of land that provided the entrance to Cape Town's harbour. A soft ping alerted her to the article from Julius being posted, and she took a moment to read through it. He'd done a good job. His background research was exemplary, his handling of the more delicate parts of her history were respectful without being overly sentimental, and his portrayal of her work within the ministry was both fair and forthright. All in all, she was exceptionally pleased with his writing.

I'll have to look out for more of his work. She closed the browser down and clicked the remote to set her iPod to shuffle, letting the gentle sound of Beethoven's "Moonlight Sonata" fill the room. The minor chords fit her mood and the darkness she felt inside her.

She put the plate on the table, forgotten already as she retrieved a report that was troubling her. There was a growing trend showing itself that South Africa's HIV treatment programme was failing. There were more than six million people living with HIV, and despite the government now funding a billion rand per year treatment programme, the rate of those developing AIDS while in treatment was significantly higher than the global norm. *It's like the drugs don't work.* She glanced over another report and highlighted several passages. *We need to look into the management of the programmes. Perhaps people are not being instructed effectively on proper use of the medications.* She sipped her drink as she made a note in the margin and glanced up as the wind rattled the windowpanes. The ringing telephone made her jump.

"Hello."

"Amahle. Sipho."

"Hello, brother. How are you?"

"Not good. You should come home."

Amahle laughed. "I have too much work to come for a holiday."

"How about a funeral?"

"Oh God. What happened?" She sank back as she listened to him and mentally went through her diary, checking what she would have to change to go back to the vineyard.

"Will she be there?"

"Who?"

"Immy."

"Why do you still care?"

A question she'd asked herself many times over the years. Was it simply nostalgia? That memories of Imogen were all entangled in a time when life was as simple as what game they would play and what time dinner would be ready for them? Was it her inability to simply let go? "I don't know. She was my best friend, Sipho. I never expected her to just vanish like that. You didn't know her. I just thought she'd write or something. At least let me know she was okay."

"She'd been gone months before I was born, but have you ever considered that maybe she wasn't the girl you thought she was?"

"You're right. You didn't know her. So is she coming or not?"

Sipho sighed. "I don't know. Mama is going to call her in a little while."

"Okay. Let me know when the funeral will be as soon as you can so that I can arrange things here."

"Sure."

They said their good-byes and hung up. The track changed, and a Chopin nocturne filled the room. Thirty-two years had passed since she'd last seen Imogen Frost, and the child inside still missed her while the woman had so many questions that had never been answered. She wanted to know why Imogen had never responded to the letters she'd sent. She wanted to know why she had never once returned. Her father had been sick for the better part of three years, and she hadn't visited him once.

She got a bottle of wine and a glass from the kitchen. A Frost Shiraz, a good vintage. She poured herself a glass and held it up, swirling the liquid in the glass, before inhaling the aroma and letting it waken her senses.

"Rest in peace, Alain. You cantankerous old bastard." She took a hearty gulp and let it sit on her tongue a moment. She enjoyed the warmth of the alcohol and the fruity bite of the berries before swallowing and smacking her lips. She glanced at the label. "One of your best, Alain." She chuckled to herself. "Let's see if Miss Immy can do as well when she gets here, hey?"

CHAPTER SIX

Imogen straightened her shoulders as Judge Booker began her sentencing speech. The case had been simple enough in the end. While Tony Russel wasn't fit to be imprisoned with the general population, he clearly understood right and wrong. The confession had been allowed to stand but with the understanding that it must be seen as evidence of his diminished mental state as well as his guilt of the crime he had never denied committing.

"Mr. Russel, I hereby sentence you to a custodial sentence in a secure mental facility for a length of time yet to be determined. This will be evaluated and decided upon by doctors far more qualified than I am to determine your capabilities and your place within a larger society. Until such time as they see fit, you will remain in their custody."

"Where am I going?" Tony turned to the guard who stood beside him in the dock.

"Mr. Russel, do you understand?" the judge asked, though Imogen was certain she wasn't expecting an affirmative response. Imogen wasn't.

"Where are you sending me?"

"Mr. Longman, will you please explain to your client what will happen next?"

"Of course, Your Honour." Counsel for the defence quickly approached the glass and his increasingly agitated client.

"Ladies and gentlemen of the jury, thank you for your time. Take him down." The guards on either side of him started to edge him out of the dock.

"I don't want to go down!"

"Court dismissed."

"Mr. Russel, we talked about the likely outcome of this," the barrister for the defence said to his client.

Imogen packed her briefcase as they continued to struggle with the new convict. She took no pleasure in seeing him fight his corner. Her job was done. The battle fought and won. She left the courtroom, her dress robes flowing around her, wig upon her head, and a smile upon her face. *Justice.*

"So how did it go?" Simon asked, jogging to catch up with her down the stairs inside the round building of Cambridge's Crown Court.

"The Crown won."

"But of course, Ms. Frost. One would expect nothing else of you."

"Why thank you, Mr. Murphy."

"Celebratory drink later?" He smiled.

"Sorry, I can't. I'm busy. I think Marcus has given me almost all of Arthur's caseload. Plus my own. I'm swamped."

"Another time maybe?"

"Maybe." *And maybe one day you'll figure out that I'm not interested.* "See you later." She turned and left the building before he could respond. Her phone buzzed against her leg. "Hey, Maria," she said to her secretary. "We scored a win on the Russel case. I'm heading back to chambers now."

"Great work, Imogen. I've had a call from a lady called, I hope I'm saying this right, Embala Inkosi."

Imogen laughed gently. "That's pretty good, Maria. What did Mbali want?"

"She said she needed you to call her straight away."

"Why?"

"She didn't say. Do you want the number?"

"It's okay. I know the number."

"Oh." Maria chuckled. "It took me five minutes to get that out of her. Who is she? Is this one of the cases you're taking over from Arthur?"

"No, it's nothing to do with work." She checked her watch. "I'll take care of it."

"Okay. Listen, why don't you call it a day? I know you were up all night preparing for today's trial. Go home. Relax."

She was exhausted, but she hated giving in to it. She stifled a yawn and smiled to herself. *Who's gonna know?* "Yeah, I'll think about it. Look, I better go and make this call. See you soon."

Why was she calling? What did she want? Imogen tapped her

phone against her head, trying to figure out what was going on before getting any information. It was a habit she'd formed long ago when it came to her father and everything in South Africa. Since her father gave her no information, she had to try to guess what was going on. For Mbali to call rather than her father meant something, right? But what? Had her father had an accident? That would explain it. He couldn't get to the phone to talk to her. Not that he did anyway. She hadn't heard from him in almost four years. In fairness, she hadn't tried to call him either. Wasn't that the way they both preferred it? Then she couldn't remind him of the wife he'd lost, and he couldn't remind her of the entire life he'd ripped away from her.

"Fuck it."

She scrolled through her contacts. When she came to one simply titled "Old Bastard," she punched the screen and waited for someone to answer.

"Hello." The thickly accented voice was made more difficult to understand by the tears that choked it and the noisy long distance line.

"Mbali?"

"Yes."

"It's Imogen Frost. You wanted me to call."

"Oh, Miss Immy. You must come home."

"Mbali, what's going on?"

"It's your father. He's passed."

"Passed what?" There was so much background noise it was difficult to make out what she was being told.

"Passed away, Miss Immy. You should come home. You have a funeral to arrange."

"What? But he's...I don't understand." Her knees weakened and threatened to give out on her. She put her hand against a wall then leaned back against it, still not sure it would hold her up.

"Mr. Frost been sick for long time. He was in a lot of pain. It was a good time for him to go. Now he no longer suffers."

"I didn't know he was sick."

"He didn't tell you?"

Imogen shook her head then remembered she was on the phone. "No." Her voice was high and squeaky. She cleared her throat and tried again. "No, he didn't. What was he sick with?"

"Doctor said it was illness of liver. I forget the name. I'm sorry."

"It's okay. Why didn't he tell me?"

"I don't know, Miss Immy. You know your father. He was a

stubborn man. He thought he knew what was best for everyone and no one could tell him any different. You know that better than anyone."

"Very true, Mbali." She ran her hand over her face and blew out. "When did he die?"

"A few hours ago now."

"Can you make the arrangements for his funeral?"

"Well, of course. If you tell me what you want I can speak to the necessary people until you get here."

Imogen closed her eyes and pictured her father the last time she'd seen him. She'd been seven years old and sitting on a plane staring out the window. He stood at the gate watching the plane as they'd taxied away from the terminal. He didn't wave. He didn't even wipe at the tears that had rolled down his cheeks. He'd just stood there and let her go. No, he'd made her go. He'd pushed her away when she'd needed him the most. He'd taken everything she'd known, loved, and needed away from her, and never even explained why.

As an adult, she'd acknowledged that he was trying to keep her safe when the country was going through violent, dangerous times. She'd allowed herself to see that he was grief stricken and hurting, and not making good decisions. Day by day, she'd seen her own face grow more like her mother's than she could handle sometimes, and she was sure her father had been unable to abide the constant reminder of what he'd lost. It didn't make it hurt any less, and it didn't mean she could forgive him. Neither of them could undo the hurt he'd caused them both. Now they'd never have the chance.

"I won't be coming back, Mbali."

"But, Miss Immy, he's your father. You must bury him."

"He's a stranger to me."

"It's a shock, I know. Perhaps you should think about it."

"There's nothing to think about, Mbali. Do what you must to bury him, and I wish you well."

"But what about the vineyard? Your home?"

"It isn't my home. I'll sell it, I suppose. I don't want anything to do with it. Thank you for letting me know, Mbali."

"Don't make a choice you will regret, child."

"I have many things I regret. This won't be one of them. Good-bye, Mbali."

She disconnected the call and looked up at the sky. She wondered when the rain had started to fall and then realized she didn't care. She stepped away from the wall, turned toward her office, and stopped. She couldn't face it. It was a new feeling, and not one she was comfortable with, but the thought of walking into her office and carrying on as though nothing had happened made her pause. No, it made her stop. Maria was right; she had nothing to deal with that couldn't wait for the morning, and the thought of being cooped up in her office—lovely as it was—made her skin itch.

Rain and sweat mingled on her brow, and her heart pounded resignedly in her chest. It wasn't beating fast. It was more like it was beating out of time and forcing itself to the slow cadence of the funeral dirge. She needed to feel alive. She needed to feel her blood move, and her heart rate pick up.

She sent a quick text to Maria, telling her she wasn't going back to the office, and followed the path her feet seemed to be setting of their own accord. Despite knowing that she was in charge of her body, right then it didn't feel like it. *It* needed something, and her brain was more than willing to let it have its way. After all, the slow burning fire that settled in the pit of her stomach promised her brain much needed relief would be achieved if it did.

The Bird in Hand pub was close by. Less than a ten minute walk from the Crown Court. She stuffed her wig in her briefcase and pulled her robe from her shoulders, slinging it over her arm as she pushed open the door and walked in. It was quiet. Maybe half a dozen people littered the handful of tables and carpet covered stools.

"What can I get you, darlin'?" The woman behind the bar wore a black wife-beater brandishing the slogan, "Dip me in chocolate and throw me to the lesbians." She had bleach blond spikes, and a ring through her nose, a studded bar through her eyebrow, and a cocky smile upon her lips.

"Brandy."

"With…? Coke? Lemonade?"

"Neat."

The bartender raised her adorned eyebrow and reached for a glass.

"Make it a double."

"Bad day?" She asked as she put the glass down before Imogen. "Want me to start you a tab?"

"Thanks. That'd be good." She slid her credit card over the bar with one hand and grabbed the drink with the other. "I'm celebrating." She knocked the double back in one. "Another."

"Celebrating what?"

She reached for the second glass and smelled it before putting it to her lips. Her father had drunk brandy the night her mother died. She chuckled and knocked it back. "The end of an era." She could feel the warmth of the strong alcohol begin to thaw out the chill that had settled previously unnoticed in her bones.

"Another one?" She reached for the glass.

"No. Do you have any red wine?"

"We do." She picked up a bottled from the back counter. "Never drink the stuff myself, so I can't vouch for how good it is."

Imogen shook her head. "Doesn't matter. I'm half pissed anyway."

"I'm Nat, by the way."

"Imogen." She accepted the glass and smiled. "Thanks." She perched on one of the tall barstools and sipped the slightly sour wine slowly. "Slow night?"

"It's early yet. Give it an hour and it'll be a bit livelier."

Imogen glanced at her watch. It wasn't yet four in the afternoon. No wonder it was quiet. Only serious alcoholics and students would be Nat's usual patron at this time of the day.

"So why are you really here, Imogen?"

She wasn't sure how to answer. She wasn't sure how much she wanted to say. While her brain was still deciding, her mouth and brandy-loosened tongue made the decision for her. "I'm celebrating and drowning my sorrows at the same time."

"What are you celebrating?"

"I won my case this afternoon."

"Case?"

She nodded and sipped some more, feeling the alcohol on her empty stomach. "Do you do food here?"

"Not till six." She reached under the counter and tossed a bag of crisps at her.

"Thanks." She tore open the packet. "A rapist is off the streets."

"You're a lawyer?"

Imogen shook her head. English people knew more about the American legal system than they did their own. Unless they were part of it. "I'm a barrister. For the CPS."

"What?"

"The Crown Prosecution Service."

"How's that different from being a lawyer?"

"I guess it isn't. Different terminology, different traditions." She shrugged. "That's all. I try to send bad people to prison."

"Do you wear one of those old-fashioned wigs?"

"Yes." Imogen smiled. "Every day."

"That's cool."

"Yeah." She rested her head in her hands.

"And the sorrows you're drowning?"

"What about them?"

"Wanna talk about it?"

"Here, you serving or what?" a bloke shouted from down the bar.

Nat smiled. "Be right back."

Imogen thought about Nat's question while she was pulling pints. Did she want to talk about it? About her dad? Did she want to think about the pain, the loss, the loneliness?

"Top up?" Nat held the bottle over her glass, ready to pour.

"Not yet. What time does your shift end?"

Nat glanced at the clock. "At five."

"How old are you?"

Nat's eyebrow rose again. "Twenty-five. You?"

"Thirty-nine. Fancy coming to dinner with me?"

Nat stared at her, appraised her, and seemed to like what she saw as a slow smile spread across her lips. "I'd love to." She leaned across the bar and whispered close to Imogen's ear. "Then you can tell me all about it."

Imogen put her fingers on Nat's lips. "Oh no. That's my one rule for tonight. No more talking." She smiled and watched Nat gulp. "I have much better plans for those lips."

CHAPTER SEVEN

A mahle smoothed her hands down the front of her black dress and pushed her feet into mid-heeled black pumps. She checked her watch. The last thing she wanted was to be late for the funeral. Her mother was already unhappy about her not going to the vineyard to travel to the church with Sipho and herself, but as she wasn't staying with them, it made no sense to travel fifteen minutes away from the church, only to turn around and come back. Besides, the small room at the Stellenbosch Hotel was comfortable, and staying in the small house on the vineyard with her mother was not an option. Mostly because her mother never asked her to stay there, and if Amahle asked, there always seemed to be some excuse as to why she couldn't.

A knock on the door stopped her wondering how they'd fallen into that particular trap over the past decade. She checked her watch and smiled as she pulled open the door to see her bodyguard, Thambo, waiting patiently.

"Time to go?"

"Indeed, Minister." He drove them carefully through the streets of Stellenbosch to the church and held the door open as she climbed out and scoured the crowd for her mother and brother.

Amahle hated funerals. She had since she was a small child and Elaine Frost's funeral had been the catalyst for the biggest change in her young life. This one was no different. More than a hundred people crowded into the church in Stellenbosch, a veritable who's who of the Stellenbosch elite welcomed each other like it was a brunch meeting at the golf club rather than a funeral. Mbali took a seat on the front pew; Amahle sat beside her, Sipho to her left.

"I still can't believe she won't come, Mama." She kept looking over her shoulder at the slightest noise, expecting her to come bustling in at the very last moment.

"I left the arrangements as long as I could. I left messages with her secretary so she had all the details. I don't know what else I could have done."

"Nothing. I didn't mean that. I just don't understand how a daughter wouldn't make it to the funeral of her own father. She didn't even visit him when he was sick."

"I told you about that, Amahle. He hadn't told her. How could she come if she didn't know?"

"I suppose. But even that's hard to believe. Why wouldn't he tell her?"

Mbali stared at the casket at the front of the church. "We all have our reasons for the secrets we keep, Amahle. I'm sure he had his."

"So you believe her? That he didn't tell her."

"Yes. I don't doubt it. Mr. Frost was a proud man, and he never liked to admit weakness. Nor could he admit when he was wrong."

"If Imogen's as stubborn a woman as she was a child, their relationship could have only gotten more difficult over the years."

"I don't think they had a relationship at all."

The music started and they all rose. It was a lovely service. The eulogy given by one of Alain's old friends, Jim Davitson, was moving; the reading by the priest was beautiful; but the atmosphere was tense. It was almost as though everyone expected Imogen to arrive at the last minute and make some kind of scene. By the time they were all back at the vineyard for the wake, Amahle felt smothered by the expectation, the feeling that something was going to happen.

She stepped out of the drawing room and wandered along the stoop. Leaning against the brick column, she stared out at the fields that had been her childhood playground. The strong twisting vines that had borne the wealth of the Frost family for five generations spread out before her, and the mountains beyond cast their shadows down the valley as the sun began to dip. Orange hues found their way into the blue sky, pink and purple chasing them all the way. She'd forgotten how beautiful it was. How varied the terrain, the colours, and the feeling of peace that accompanied the scent of grapes in the air, and the earth beneath her feet.

"Amahle, they are going to read the will," Sipho said from the doorway. "Mama asked if you'd come inside."

"How can they read the will without Imogen here?"

"They have her on the phone. She has given her consent to read it in her absence. The lawyer gave it some legal mumbo jumbo name and said that they were okay to do it this way."

Amahle shrugged and followed him inside. She sat beside her mother again and took hold of her hand. "Mama, are you all right?"

"Yes, why?"

"Your hand is clammy." She slipped her fingers around her mother's wrist and swallowed her surprise at how frail age had made her vibrant and strong mother. "Your heart is racing."

"I'm fine. Just a little warm." She waved away Amahle's concern. Sipho looked on with a worried frown etched deeply into the lines of his face. She tried to get his attention to ask what was wrong, but he was avoiding her gaze. She was sure of it. She tried to ignore the feeling. It wasn't the first time she had felt her mother was keeping secrets from her, and over the years she had learned that it was usually best to leave them with her. It did little for Amahle's equilibrium to find out too much about her mother's affairs.

She looked around the room, noting some of the little cliques that had inevitably formed. She still found it amusing that of all the people in the room, politically, she had the most power and influence, yet every one of the wealthy, white, older men of Stellenbosch avoided contact with her. An attractive blond woman spoke to Jim Davitson and Fred Pugh, Stellenbosch's most preeminent lawyer and the major general of the Western Cape police force, who looked deeply engrossed in the conversation. From her vantage point, the two men looked deeply annoyed while the young woman appeared to find their concerns boring. Until a tall, slightly rotund younger man with a shock of floppy red hair clapped a hand on Fred's shoulder. She didn't recognize the newcomer, but they all seemed to know him well, and the rolling of Fred's eyes told her he wished he didn't. Jim broke away from the little group and took a position behind the desk and rapped on the surface to gain everyone's attention.

"Ladies and gentlemen, thank you all for attending the service today. I'm sure Alain would have been heartily glad at the wonderful turnout. This"—he lifted some papers from the surface of the desk—"is the last will and testament of Alain Frost, and reads as follows." He cleared his throat in preparation. "I, Alain Peter John Frost, of the Frost Vineyard, Stellenbosch, South Africa, hereby revoke all former testimony dispositions and declare this to be my last will and testament on the fourteenth day of February, in the year of our Lord two thousand and fifteen. I hereby charge Mr. James Davitson as executor of my estate. In the event that he is unable to execute this duty, I trust he will have left in charge of his firm a person of sufficient merit to perform the task in his stead.

"I have much wealth to endow but little of much worth as I lie here, waiting for my final day, alone. There is much I wish I could undo, much I wish I could atone for, but even I must know when to admit defeat. And this battle has long been lost. Please forgive the sentimentality, but I beg a little indulgence here. This is one correspondence I can be certain you will hear, Imogen. Therefore, it is my last chance to explain why I hurt you as I did, and to beg your forgiveness for my immortal soul.

"Fear will make a man do crazy things. Things he could not otherwise contemplate. Grief and pain will make him a fool. When we lost your mother, I was suffering with all of those afflictions, and rather than hold you tighter to me, I pushed you away. I think we can both understand at this point what happened then, but I think perhaps what is harder for you to understand is why I continued to keep you away, my darling daughter. Why I refused every request to come home for holidays, why I kept letters from your friends here in South Africa, from you. Why I did not pass on to them your missives. All of this will be more ammunition for your hatred toward me, of that I have no doubt. But I pray that once you get through the anger you have every right to feel, you will remember that I did everything I did with your best interest at heart.

"I wanted you to build a new life away from the uncertain future South Africa faced. I needed to know that you would never fall victim to your mother's fate, and in your friendship with Amahle, I could see your mother growing in you day by day. I saw her compassion, her kindness, and most importantly, and fatally in this bloody country, I saw her colour-blindness in you. I couldn't stand the thought of losing you too.

"I lost you anyway to my own stupidity, overbearing control, and dishonesty. I beg you to forgive me. I truly thought you would be better off in England. I truly believed you would have a wonderful life at school. I thought making your own way in life, rather than falling into the same patterns, the same expectations, that I was already creating for you would be best for you. I hope you can agree with me, Imogen. You did a far better job than I could have ever imagined. I am so proud of all you have achieved. So proud. I just wish I'd had the courage to tell you this before it was too late. I am a coward. You deserved a better father than you got. Please remember that I loved you with all my heart, Imogen. Despite how it looks from the outside. I did the best I could.

"Now to the matter at hand. I leave a pension of thirty thousand rand per annum to my housekeeper and long time employee, Mbali Nkosi. Enjoy your retirement, my friend. You have earned it. To Sipho Nkosi, I have written references for whoever takes over the vineyard, in the hope that they will continue to keep you on as the manager of the vineyard. But I also bequeath to you two acres of vines, the field backing onto the orchard at the edge of the property. Should they not have the foresight to maintain your employment, Sipho, I hope you can see your way to building your own vineyard from this modest beginning.

"Amahle Nkosi, it has been an honour to watch you grow in the absence of my own daughter, and your father. I was more than happy to help you wherever I could in all matters but one. To you, I return something I should have given to you thirty years ago. The letters Imogen wrote to you when she was first sent to England. She wrote to you for five years before finally giving up hope that you would respond. Perhaps you can find the friend you lost amongst the pages. I am sorry."

The large bundle of envelopes were tied neatly with a green ribbon, and tears slipped from her eyes onto the ink as she ran a hand over the topmost one. She didn't hear the rest of the minor gifts that were awarded; she wanted to walk out the door and spend the afternoon in the orchard. Sitting in the tree where she and Imogen had hidden, reading about the life of her friend in the scary, exciting new world she had been thrust into.

"The rest of my worldly goods, possessions, and wealth I leave to my only child, Imogen Annabelle Frost, to do with as you see fit. Manage it, sell it, return home and live in it. It doesn't matter, Immy. Just find your happiness. Do not die like I did, alone, bitter, and full of regret. There is too much joy in the world for that."

"That's not right," Mbali said.

"I'm sorry, what isn't right?" James asked.

"She wasn't his only child."

"What other child, Mrs. Nkosi?" James Davitson asked. "I knew Alain Frost all my life. He had only one child."

"He had another. A son. He should get half of everything."

Amahle stared at her mother. "Mama, Mr. Frost only had Imogen. There was no son. You must be confused."

"Woman's talking bloody rubbish, Jim," Fred Pugh said from the back of the room. "Ignore her crazy talk."

"I'm not crazy, and I'm not confused. He had a son all right. One he never spoke about."

Jim cleared his throat. "What are you saying, Mrs. Nkosi?"

Silence stretched taut across the room, once again heavy with expectation, and the slightest movement would tip the world on its axis and cast them all off into oblivion.

"Alain Frost was the father of my boy, Sipho."

CHAPTER EIGHT

Sipho grabbed hold of Mbali's arm and pulled her out of the room. "What are you doing?"

"What are you talking about?"

"Don't play dumb with me, Mama. We've got seconds before they come in here and want answers from you."

"And I'll give them answers."

"Why are you lying like this, Mother?"

She stared at him but sullenly refused to answer.

"Mama, we'll have to prove I'm his son."

"Who says you aren't?"

Sipho stared at her. It would certainly make life easier if it were true. "If this is true why have you never mentioned this to me before?"

"I didn't want to admit that I cheated on your father with him. Your father would have gone crazy. At the time, there was still apartheid. I had no choice."

"Are you saying Alain raped you?"

"No, no, no. He just made it clear that it was in all our best interests to do as he wanted. Amahle was very young; my husband had just been promoted and was still learning. If he'd lost his job we wouldn't have been able to find somewhere else."

"But there were never any rumours. No whispered secrets about Mr. Frost using women like that. People used to talk about the fact he didn't marry again after his wife died."

"A man doesn't need to remarry if he has everything he needs without it."

"You're saying he didn't remarry because he was sleeping with you?"

"Because he was in love with me."

Sipho stared hard. The more she spoke, the more unbelievable it sounded. But there was something that nagged at the back of his brain. Like a ghost of a memory, one he couldn't picture but seemed like it was just something he knew. Something about his mother and Alain, but he couldn't recall it. *Or is that just wishful thinking?* Did he want it to be true? He couldn't deny that it would make his life easier if it was. It would make the issue of the missing money something he could deal with at least. He looked at his mother. Her hands trembled, and her breasts heaved. He could see her pulse throb at her temple and knew her heart was racing. Perspiration spotted her forehead, and the dank odour of it filled his nostrils. What he couldn't ascertain was whether it was excitement or fear that made her blood pound in her veins.

Was this the real reason why Mr. Frost liked me so much better than the other boys? Is this why he really took an interest in me? Not because he saw potential, but because he saw the son he wouldn't recognize any other way?

Sipho's head began to pound as he tried to think through a lifetime of questions in a new light.

"They will test my blood."

"You have the same blood group as he did. Besides, he's been cremated. What can they test?"

The door opened and Jim Davitson walked in, the crowd at his back. "Mrs. Nkosi, we need to have a full and frank discussion about your claim. Ms. Frost disputes your son's claim against the estate. She is adamant that her father was faithful to her mother, and that your claim is scurrilous." He cleared his throat. "I would warn you that she will accept a full withdrawal of your accusation, but should you persist, she has threatened to sue you for slander."

"Mama." Amahle stood beside her mother. "Is it true?"

Mbali didn't look at either of her children. "It is true."

Sipho squared his shoulders. Truth or lie, it was out of his hands. The die was cast.

CHAPTER NINE

Imogen grabbed her briefcase from the overhead locker and cursed the heat that was already making her sweat. The sun blinded her as she stepped off the plane and shielded her eyes quickly to prevent her tripping down the steps. Her journey through customs was uneventful, and her luggage was already waiting for her at the carousel when she arrived. Slinging the strap over her shoulder, she headed for the exit.

"Ms. Frost. Ms. Frost." A tall man with a shock of red hair and ruddy cheeks ran to keep pace with her. "Mr. Davitson sent me to give you a lift."

"Did he now? And you are?"

"Roland De Fries." He held out his hand. "I'm a forensic accountant at Davitson, Johnson, and McRae. It's a pleasure to meet you."

"Likewise." She shook his hand and sighed as he wrestled with her case for her. It felt strange to hear the accent in real life again. She wanted to laugh at herself. In England, she still had the faint traces of her Afrikaans accent. Those who worked with her still teased her about it from time to time. They called her springbok if they were feeling brave, the symbol of the national rugby team, reminding her over and over very subtly that she didn't belong to them. Now back on South African soil all she could hear were the clipped English syllables that she'd worked so hard to adopt as a child trying to fit in. And yet again, she was reminded that she didn't belong.

"Mr. Davitson said you're a barrister in England."

"That's correct."

"That sounds very impressive, Ms. Frost. Would you mind if I asked you some questions while we travel?"

She wanted to tell him, hell yes, she minded. But she didn't have the energy. It was only a forty-five minute drive to Stellenbosch from the airport. She was confident she could keep going that long. After all, the flight had only been eleven and a half hours. She'd splashed out and opted for business class seats and spent the whole time reading about South African probate law.

"Where are we up to with Mrs. Nkosi's claim on my father's estate?"

"To the best of my knowledge, where we were when you boarded the flight. I'm not a lawyer, just an accountant really. They don't tell me too much. I do know that she's adamant that Sipho is your brother and thereby entitled to half of your father's estate. Especially as he has been working on the estate and you've enjoyed the benefits of his labour in the form of your education and so on."

"Does she have any proof?"

"She says she does."

"But you haven't seen it yet?"

"No. She says she will produce it when you arrive."

"Of course."

"May I ask a personal question?"

"You can ask." She rested her head on her hand, elbow perched against the car door. "I might not answer."

"Fair enough." He changed gear and pulled out onto the N2 heading east. "Why have you come back now to fight this claim, but you didn't come back for the funeral?"

It was a question she'd been asking herself. She'd sworn she would never set foot back in South Africa; she'd been sure that she didn't care and didn't want anything to do with her legacy. She'd planned to sell the vineyard and be shot of it all. Maybe go on a nice holiday. Climbing in Europe or America, maybe South America. There were plenty of choices. Maybe she'd buy a new house, or set up her own legal practice. She could have left Jim Davitson to fight this claim from the comfort of her life back in England. Yet here she was. Heading back to the last place on earth she ever wanted to see again. Did she regret not coming for the funeral? She still wasn't sure. But hearing her father's words in his will had shifted something in her. She knew in her heart that the man who loved his wife so much that he couldn't stand to look upon his daughter again would never cheat on her. The idea that anything else was true somehow diminished the sacrifice they'd both made. It made a mockery of his justification, and her loss that much more acute. She couldn't stand the thought of everyone her father had cared about thinking him capable of siring a son he never acknowledged.

"In his will he confessed his most shameful secrets. The things he couldn't have said to me while he was still alive. If Sipho was his son, why didn't he say that then too? I think she's lying, and I won't have my family name dragged through the mud like that. I won't stand for my mother's memory being insulted like this. Hell, I don't even remember her having a son."

"I understand." He dropped the sun visor and caught the sunglasses that slipped out. "You have to do this for your mother."

"Yes." *And maybe, just a little bit for myself too.*

"Listening to Mr. Davitson, it would seem that Mrs. Nkosi fell pregnant with Sipho after you left the country. Perhaps you are right. Your father never cheated on your mother. But perhaps she's telling the truth also."

She felt sick. The burn of bile rose up her gullet, acrid and hate-filled. She hadn't considered that for a moment. In her head it was like Africa had somehow ceased to exist from the moment she left. As though time had stood still in her absence. *How fucking arrogant, Frost? The whole world does not revolve around you. Try to remember that when you stand face-to-face with your baby brother.* A whole new set of scenarios formed in her head, and she had to acknowledge that Roland had a point. Was Mbali's claim real? Did she really have family left? Someone on the planet who shared a fraction of her DNA? Who could maybe ease this feeling that was growing inside her? A feeling she didn't want to name, didn't want to own, and wished it would leave her the fuck alone. Funny that. Wanting loneliness to leave her alone.

The journey went by quickly, Roland asking questions about practicing law in England, answering her questions as best he could in return. Everything was different about the country, yet everything looked much the same. Democracy ruled, but black women still walked barefoot along dirt roads with infants strapped to their backs and loads carried on their heads. They were all free of racial divide, but the townships were as overcrowded and poverty-stricken as they had ever been. They were free of tyranny, but brutality still turned the soil red with blood. Would it ever change?

The white lime washed walls reflected the sunlight as they entered Stellenbosch, and for her it was like stepping back in time. Part of her expected to see her mother step out of the chemist, or the butchers, and walk home with her, pointing out flowers and animals as they went.

"Do you need anything while we're here? I have no idea what will be available at the house."

"No, thank you. If I need anything I can always grab one of the cars from the vineyard."

He laughed. "I can't see you driving a buckie."

"In that case I guess I'll have to grab the keys to one of the tractors instead of the pickup." She smiled. It felt alien on her face, the muscles unused to that particular expression.

"Now that, I would pay to see, Ms. Frost." He looked over at her and grinned.

"Who is in charge of the vineyard now?"

"I'm afraid I don't know. Mr. Davitson said he would discuss those matters with you tomorrow, when you've had a chance to recover from the flight."

"Of course."

"He said he'll be here at eight a.m. He'll bring coffee." He pulled to a stop outside her old home.

"Good deal." She peered out the window and gripped the door handle. She didn't want to get out of the car. She didn't want to put her foot back on the property. She'd vowed she never would, and she hated breaking promises.

"It's been a long time, yah?"

"Yes, it has." She nodded. "Thirty-two years."

"Not been back at all?"

"No. I was in exile." She laughed bitterly. *Enough.* She took a deep breath and pushed open the door, not stopping until she was on the stoop and pulling open the screen door to the house where she'd been born.

Memories assailed her left and right. Her mother walking down the stairs, wiping dirt from her face, and telling her to put her shoes on before going out to play. She could see her father with his arms wrapped around her mother's waist while she stirred something on the stove. It felt like a knife twisting through her chest, and she did something she hadn't done since she'd left this house. She cried. Thirty years of grief and anger streamed down her cheeks, her hands shook as she moved from room to room, and she let them all come. She was glad Roland had left her bags on the stoop and disappeared. She didn't want anyone to see her like this.

Footsteps behind her made her hold her breath as she spun around.

"Who is it?" She squinted into the darkened doorway and then shook her head as she recognized the aged face in the shadows. "How dare you? What are you doing here? Get out! Get out of my house!"

"Miss Immy, I didn't mean to startle you. I saw lights and came to make sure everything was okay. I will leave you now."

"Don't you dare come the Miss Immy with me, you lying old witch. Get out of my house."

Mbali bristled and straightened her shoulders. "I was already going."

"In fact, get off my property. I want you and your son—your son—off Frost Vineyard immediately."

"This is our home, Miss Imm—Ms. Frost. You can't make us leave."

"Yes, I can. My father's will left this to me. It is mine. I have every right to say who stays here and who doesn't. My father bequeathed you a generous pension in his will. I won't contest his wishes. Now use it and get off my land."

"Mama, go."

Imogen saw a young man behind her. "Ah, my supposed brother." He was tall, easily six foot one or two, with broad, muscular shoulders, a lean physique, and a confidence in his bearing that Imogen recognized. Authority. He was used to giving orders and having them followed. He was used to being in charge. He was in control—of himself, his mother, and the situation. Sweat trickled down her back, and for the first time, she truly allowed herself to consider that this man might actually be her brother.

He nodded to his mother and waited until she had left the room. He looked at her and their eyes meet.

They were dark as night, unwavering, and as familiar as they were strange. There was nothing of her or her family in the face of this young man. Only the familiar set of features she'd seen on the face of her childhood friend. Her doubts about his lineage faded for her in that instant. That's when she saw it. The shadows lurking behind the confident façade. The questions that he too was asking. He had no more idea about the claim than she did, and the confidence he was trying to project blew away like dust on the wind.

"I can assure you it came as quite a shock to me too."

Imogen bit back the sarcastic retort that settled on the tip of her tongue.

"My mother is old, sick, and grieving. I ask you respectfully to let her be while you and I sort out this mess she has dumped on our laps. I will make sure she stays out of your way."

"And you?"

"Excuse me?"

"Will you also stay out of my way? Or will I run into you as I look around my vineyard?"

"I have been managing the vineyard for the last six years or so. I have continued to do so since your father passed away."

She felt the thrill of victory when he continued to refer to Alain as "her father" and not "theirs" or "his."

"And if I don't want you here?"

"Then you can sack me, of course. But I know this vineyard like the back of my hand. Whatever else is between us, Ms. Frost, do not let the vineyard suffer. There are too many people who need their jobs here."

She nodded. As much as she didn't want to admit it, right now she needed the stability he brought to the business, as she knew nothing. She shook her head. What did that matter anyway? She was going to sell it and go back to her life in England as soon as this business was sorted out. Her research had shown that selling the vineyard as a going concern would be much more profitable than selling it piecemeal would. Besides, she was confident now that the matter would be resolved quickly, and in her favour. What did she need to worry about?

"Fine. But keep her away from me."

❖

"I mean it, Mother. Stay away from her or I will have no chance of getting the money back before anyone notices it's gone."

"You still haven't told me your grand plan to get that much money."

"I'm going to try to get a loan against the two acres Alain left me."

"That scrap of land isn't worth that much money."

"Maybe not, but it's a start."

"And then where will you find the rest?"

"I know a guy."

"A loan shark?"

"Just a guy." A guy he wished he didn't know, but one he had no choice but to call on. "Just stay away from her and don't make anything worse."

CHAPTER TEN

D r. Marais looked at the readout on his screen and shook his head. He picked up the phone and dialled home.

"Hello?"

"Honey, it's me."

"Don't tell me. You won't be home for dinner."

"I am sorry, my love. There's just something here that I have to take care of."

"And what about things here, Derek? Will you ever have time to take care of them?"

He frowned. "What do you mean?"

"You missed parents' evening tonight. Isabella's very upset."

"Shit." He rubbed his hand over his face and tried not to think about how upset his nine-year-old daughter would be. "You said you were going to remind me."

"I did. I called and left three messages with your secretary today."

"I didn't get them." He shuffled pages on his desk and found the sticky notes—all three of them—stuck to the bottom of the file he'd been looking at. "Shit. I'm sorry."

"I'm not the one you need to make this up to, Derek."

"I'll make it up to her."

"So you keep telling us."

"Please don't be like this. I will make it up to you both. There's just something here I have to take care of."

"You have a whole hospital staff at your disposal, Derek. Delegate."

The dial tone rang in his ear as she hung up. "Some things I can't delegate, honey. No matter how much I wish I could." He put the receiver down and tried to let go of the heaviness that settled in his heart. Another fuckup he'd pay for. But what was more important? A parent teacher evening for a daughter he knew was very bright, well-adjusted, and excelling, or the thousands, perhaps millions, who were at risk if his hunch was right? As cold as he felt making the decision, he knew it was the right one. The needs of the many and all that.

He leaned back in his chair and waited for the next round of tests to confirm his suspicion. The delivery of Combivirine from PharmaChem had arrived earlier that day, and he'd painstakingly selected fifteen random packets to test alongside another fifteen he'd had delivered from his friend in Limpopo. Aesthetically, the pills looked the same. Small, white caplets. Little oblongs of antiretrovirals that had the power to hold HIV at bay. To prolong health and maintain the viral load at a level where the person could carry on a relatively normal life. People could work, parents could take care of their kids, and the state was not continually paying out for the palliative care and eventually, the burial of those who couldn't afford to help themselves.

The first load of pills he'd received for his hospital passed all his tests. Genuine Combivirine. Quality medication that he would have no qualms about prescribing to his patients. The first five tests on the Limpopo pills had all come back as nothing more than aspirin. Great for a headache, a fever, and thinning the blood. In fighting HIV?

"About as useful as a chocolate bloody teapot."

All he had to do now was confirm that the rest of the pills from Limpopo were fake. Then he'd place a second order with PharmaChem. The operation was slick. He'd give them that. But he was sure the genuine pills wouldn't keep coming for long. They couldn't. Not at the prices they were charging. They'd be bankrupt within a month.

CHAPTER ELEVEN

A mahle sat in her room at the Stellenbosch Hotel, staring out the window across field upon field of grapevines and off to the mountains behind. The craggy summits and gray rocks were a familiar backdrop to her dreams. She plucked at the green ribbon. She was still unable to unwrap the bundle and read through what she was sure were heartbreaking letters from a child who no longer existed.

She knew a part of her was still in shock. She could see that clearly in her shaking hands and the way she was unable to let go of her mother's revelation over the past two days. She tried to play back all those years, but she was far too young to remember anything of value in the interaction between her mother and Alain Frost. Was there an affair that had led to the conception of her brother? She didn't know. Would she put it past her mother to do that? She wished she could answer no, but she couldn't. Since her father had died, her mother had proven herself to have a considerable urge for the desires of the flesh. Something young Amahle had been forced to deal with on more than one occasion. Returning home from school to find her mother passed out drunk on the sofa with a half-naked man on top of her.

Unfortunately, she had no problem imagining her mother committing adultery. Mr. Frost? That one was more of a struggle, but in real terms, how well did she really know the man? The dates were the thing that really troubled her. Based on when Sipho was born, her mother got pregnant right around the time Elaine was buried. She'd grown up in Alain's household; she'd loved his wife and daughter as though they were extensions of herself. She'd seen the way he'd acted around Elaine when they thought no one was watching. They had always seemed so in love. He'd worshipped her, not just loved her. She

had watched him grieve and fade away in the shadow of that love. It
didn't feel right. It didn't feel like something he would do. She glanced
down at the letters. But then again neither did this.

Grief had done strange things to the man. Was it beyond the
realms that in his pain he had reached out to her mother for comfort?
Was it possible? Certainly. Did it happen? She tried to dredge up every
memory she could of that time, but her memories seemed to be entirely
focused on her own pain and loss. Both of Elaine and Imogen. She
barely remembered her mother being around at all. Suspicious?

One way or another, the question of her brother's paternity would
be resolved and they would have to deal with the fallout. Her mother
had sworn she was telling the truth. Amahle had little choice at this
point but to believe her and carry on from there.

She opened the door to her room. "Thambo? Would you help me
please?"

"Of course, Minister."

"I need to find a lawyer for my brother and mother so that they can
further this claim correctly. Also to fight the slander suit that Ms. Frost
has threatened."

"Of course."

"I think someone local would be best."

"That would make sense."

"Will you ask around and find someone reputable for me?"

"Minister—"

"Amahle. We've worked together far too long for you to still be
referring to me as *Minister* all the time."

He sighed heavily. "Fine. Amahle, I can't leave you. We don't
have enough people to give you adequate protection out here."

"Who do you expect is going to attack me?" She pointed around
the room. "The pillows?"

"That's not the issue, and you know it."

"You have my word; I won't leave the room without you. I'm just
going to sit here and read my letters." She indicated the bundle.

He shook his head in defeat. "Fine. But not one little toe outside
this room."

"Scout's honour."

"Yeah," he said as he opened the door, "like I believe that."

She smiled at his back and tucked her feet under her. The top
most envelope was dated only a couple of days after Imogen had

been sent away. The handwriting was neat, cursive, and exactly as she remembered Imogen's to be.

Amahle,

I don't know why he's doing this, but I'm in England. I'm at Bruton School for Girls. It's like a prison. I'm not allowed to go out unless they say it's okay. I can't go to the kitchen if I get hungry. I can't do anything. I miss you and it's so cold, Amahle. So very cold. I want to come home. Please, will you talk to him? Ask him what I need to do to make him let me come home. Whatever it is, I'll do it. I swear. I just don't know what I did wrong.

Please tell Cebisa that I'm sorry I got mad at her. I wasn't really, and tell her thank you for the story. I'm sorry I got so upset. Will you tell her that, please? I don't want her to be upset with me too. I don't think I could stand it if she hated me too.

Thank you for keeping me safe in our tree. It's the last time I remember feeling warm. I wish you were with me. It's always easier when you're with me, no matter where we are.

Your best friend,

Immy.

xxx

Amahle shook her head and read through letter after letter. Each one telling her a little about life in boarding school, while continuing the same hunt for answers as to why her father had sent her away, why Amahle never wrote to her, and why she was never allowed to return home. Eventually, anger was the only discernible emotion in Imogen's letters. She shook her head. She needed to get out of the hotel. She shoved her feet into her shoes, grabbed her jacket, and picked up the keys to the car. She wiped the tears from her eyes as she crossed the town and made her way to the vineyard. She didn't stop at the main house. That wasn't what she needed to see. She drove on to the orchard. The forty twisted little apple trees that had been their shelter, their protection, their playground, and the graveyard of their friendship.

"I wasn't sure I'd be able to find it again. It's been so long."

Amahle whirled around and stared into the chestnut brown eyes she remembered so well. But that was the only shred of the little girl that remained. In place of the scrawny, dirty little blond girl was a beautiful blond woman. Her hair was short, just a few inches all over, framing her head and highlighting her high cheekbones. The soft pixie cut, highlighting her femininity, and her luscious full lips pouted naturally in a sexy invitation. Long, willowy limbs and gentle curves filled out the rest of the package, and Amahle's heart rate increased. Nerves played an equal part to her newly aroused libido. *Nothing for eight years, then bam. Well, thanks a lot, libido, your timing sucks.*

"Immy?"

Imogen nodded, a shy smile on her lips and tears forming in her eyes. "Minister."

Amahle laughed and decided humour was the best way to ease her discomfort. "I feel like I'm seven years old again, not the damn minister."

"Want to climb the tree?" She pointed to the branches above their heads.

"I take it back. I feel like I'm nearly forty and work behind a desk."

Imogen laughed. "Every damn day."

"I don't know whether to hug you or wrestle you."

"Do I get to pick?"

"Didn't you always?"

"Ha. I wish." Imogen wrapped her arms around Amahle's shoulders and held tight.

Amahle breathed in deeply and wrapped her arms around Imogen's waist. "You've grown."

"Yeah." She chuckled. "You didn't though."

"Hey." She poked Imogen in the ribs. "Be nice."

"How did you know I was here?"

Amahle shrugged. "I didn't. I was reading the letters your dad kept and I just needed to be here." She eased out of Imogen's arms and touched the tree trunk nearest to her. "I used to come here all the time. Mostly when I missed you."

"So you weren't looking for me?"

"Not yet. I wasn't sure I was ready yet. Wasn't sure if it was a good idea even. I don't know what to say."

Imogen frowned. "About what?"

"About your dad—"

"And your mum."

Amahle nodded.

"Nothing to talk about."

"You know what she's saying."

"Doesn't matter. I'm sorry, Amahle, but she's talking shit. My dad was a bastard, but he loved my mum. He wouldn't have cheated on her." Imogen's eyes darkened and her cheeks flushed.

As much as Amahle had questioned the same information herself, it grated to hear someone else doing the same thing. What gave her the right, this damned stranger, to waltz back in and judge them?

"You should talk to her and tell her to drop it, or I will sue her for slander. I'm not having my father's name tarnished by the likes of her."

"Excuse me?" She stepped back further. "What exactly do you mean by that?" She balled her fists and planted them on her hips.

"You know exactly what I mean, and don't pretend you don't." Imogen mirrored her stance, leaning forward until they were eye to eye.

"No, I don't. You'd better explain." She licked her lips. "And you might want to be careful or I'll be suing you for slander, Ms. Frost."

A cold smile slid onto Imogen's lips. Her eyes narrowed, and Amahle fought not to swallow and back away from her. A chill settled around them.

"I meant simply that your mother has never made any mention of Sipho being his son while my father was alive. Your father's name is on his birth certificate. And seemingly, she waits until my father's dead and unable to defend himself to come up with this 'truth.' She's obviously just after the money." She curled her fingers into quote marks.

"My mother gives a very…telling…account of what happened between them. And we both know that your dad had plenty of secrets and regrets that he's taken to his grave. It's not so difficult to believe that this is one of them."

"Yes, it is," Imogen ground out through clenched teeth.

"Why?" Amahle asked sweetly, sensing that this would annoy Imogen more than shouting would.

"Because it is." Her voice dropped, and Amahle knew she was right.

She smiled sensing victory. "Not a very good reason."

"Maybe not, but it's better than the crap your mother's spouting."

Amahle narrowed her eyes. She'd known that her childhood friend was long gone, but the child in her had kept up the hope that Imogen had missed her as much as she had, and somehow they'd just pick up where they left off. She wanted to laugh at her own foolishness, but she just couldn't see the funny side of it. It hurt too much. Imogen wasn't the only one who had grown up in the last thirty years. If she wanted to make this adversarial, fine. She walked to the exit of the orchard. Before she left she turned her head over her shoulder and shouted, "I guess we'll see about that."

CHAPTER TWELVE

Imogen stormed into the house and grabbed the phone intent on calling her would-be lawyer, Mr. Davitson. Ronald had told her eight a.m. Now it was approaching eleven, and she still hadn't seen hide nor hair of him.

"Excuse me, Ms. Frost?"

She whirled around and stared at the man. He was in his early sixties, his hair greying at the temples, his hairline receding around his head, but his smile was kindly and confident. He seemed entirely sure of himself.

"Jim Davitson." He held out his hand.

"I was expecting you this morning."

"My apologies, Ms. Frost. I was detained, looking into something for you."

She took his hand and shook it firmly. It was a point she always made in her first interactions with anyone new. There would be no polite handshake, no pandering to the male ego. Not for her. She was the equal to or better than any man she had met; she would not display anything less with a weak handshake. She smiled as she noted his eyes widen slightly in a silent acknowledgement. "Shall we get to work?"

"Of course. We certainly have a lot to get through." He pointed out of the door. "Shall we go into the office? I daresay we may need to look through some of the paperwork."

"Of course." She rolled her head from side to side and tried to ease some of the tension from her shoulders. She hated how she'd let Amahle get to her. Control was something she prided herself on, and Amahle had made her lose it in a matter of seconds.

"You okay?"

She forced a smile onto her lips. "I'm good, thanks. Would you like something to drink before we settle in?"

"No need. Mbali will bring something shortly, I'm sure."

"No. She won't."

"Excuse me?"

"She is not welcome in my house, Mr. Davitson."

He looked at her for a moment before nodding his head. "Jim, please. Mr. Davitson makes me feel rather old in your company, young lady. Perhaps some iced tea would be nice."

"Perfect, Jim." Imogen busied herself with the tea while he unpacked his briefcase and booted up the computer in her father's office. "Sugar?"

"Yes, please."

She spooned in a generous amount and passed him the glass.

"How much do you know about your father's financial affairs?" He took a sip. "Lovely. Thank you."

"You're welcome. And I have to admit, very little." She pulled the visitor's chair around the back of the desk so that she could easily see the screen and sat beside him.

"Well, I've had one of our accountants and one of our business managers take a look over the past couple of weeks. That's standard practice for our company with an estate of this size."

"An excellent policy, I'm sure."

"Yes. The business manager assures me that the vineyard, the processing plants, and sales are all in tip-top shape. If you wish to take over the running of the vineyard, you've inherited a well-oiled machine, as he put it." He pointed to a file he copied onto the computer from his flash drive. "The report's there. Take a look when you've got a moment and make sure you're happy. If you're planning to sell, this will help speed up the process as the new owners won't have to have this generated for themselves."

"That's very good news."

"Yes, yes. But I'm afraid the young fellow looking into the accounts, young Roland De Fries. I believe you've met him."

"Yes. He picked me up from the airport."

"Quite. Well, he has alerted me to a number of irregularities in the company finances that have us a little concerned." He copied another file. "This is some spreadsheet information and the report from him."

"Such as?" She frowned.

"The accounting practices are shoddy, to say the least. I was amazed your father's accountants have let him get away with it. So much so, that I went to ask them about it this morning. That's why I was late."

"What did they say?"

"They said that they haven't been servicing the accounts for the Frost Estate for almost six years now. Apparently, it was taken in-house at that time."

"So who has been responsible for the bookkeeping?" Alarm bells rang in Imogen's head.

"I'm not sure at this point."

"I don't like the sound of that. What are the irregularities?"

"I'm not much of an accountant, Ms. Frost. When the young chap was explaining it all, I'm afraid a lot of it went over my head. I can set up a meeting for you with him if you like?"

"I'd appreciate that. In the meantime can you freeze the bank accounts, or better yet, have me assigned as sole signatory?"

"Certainly. Better safe than sorry, hey?"

"Yes."

"Best to get all the information before we jump to conclusions and start to throw around accusations that can damage someone's reputation. As you're aware."

"Yes, I am, Jim. I guess that brings us to the main reason for being here."

"Of course. Now, I've done some checking, and the way these things stand is that while he can contest that he is your brother and deserves half of the estate, your father did make provision for him in the will. As such, we can contest that this was what your father decided he wanted Sipho to have, regardless of the paternity issue."

"And through the South African court, how long will that take?"

"Anywhere from six months to two years."

"Bit of a difference there, Jim."

"Well, you know how these things go. It depends on how good his lawyer is, how stubborn you both are."

"Two years might not be long enough," she said.

Jim chuckled. "Is that right?"

"Hmmm. And while this is ongoing I can't sell?"

"No. Not while the will is being contested."

"Fine." *There's no way I'm getting stuck with this shit for two years. I want this done and finished. And I want it done yesterday.*

Rearranging her life in Cambridge had taken a colossal effort, and it wasn't something she was planning to keep on hold forever. Certainly not for two years. There were a limited number of options for resolving the situation and a limited number of ways she could entice her opponents into ending this situation quickly. She had no doubt that Amahle would be offering her brother advice, and Amahle was most definitely a worthy adversary. "Here's what I want you to do. I want you to tell them that I'll agree to split the estate with Sipho—"

"What? Why? That's a terrible—"

"If you'd let me finish. I was going to say on the condition that he takes a DNA test. If that proves he is my brother, then I'll split the estate."

"Ms. Frost, as I said, even if he is your brother, your father made provision for him in the will. We can contest that it is valid as it stands, and you need never have to give up any of the estate."

"Mr. Davitson, that man is not my brother." She knew it in her bones. "I know this sounds like I'm taking a terrible risk. Gambling with this place. But I'm not."

"That's what all gamblers say. That it's a dead cert."

"I know. But I want this claim settled and over with as soon as possible. I want to get back to my life. I have a job, a very important one, waiting for me. You're a lawyer; you understand that. A DNA test is the quickest way to end this. If we drag our heels and try to negotiate with him, he will continue with this charade. I will dig my heels in more, and this will only get messy. I won't have it. I can't have my mother's name dragged through the mud."

"You're prepared to risk losing hundreds of thousands of rand for the sake of the reputation of a dead woman?"

"I don't believe it to be a risk."

"Ms. Frost, I have to advise against this. Yes, we need to get the DNA test, but agreeing in advance to giving away half of the estate in the event of a positive result is ludicrous."

Imogen closed her eyes for a moment and took a deep breath, controlling the temper she could feel rising inside her. She knew she was still riled up from her encounter with Amahle, and taking it out on Jim wasn't going to help. No matter how much she felt like lashing out or how unwelcome his assessment of her decision. All she needed from him was to do as she instructed. "Are you or are you not my lawyer?"

"Yes, of course."

"Then do as I am instructing." She stared at him. "As your client."

"I have to advise against this."

"I know."

"The risk is too great."

"Not for me." She held up a hand to stop him carrying on. "Look, I get it. If I were in your place, I'd advise my client to do anything but what I'm suggesting now. You're right. It's ludicrous, and risky, and insane. But it's also the right thing to do. For me. Right now I need to do something to resolve this. I can't stand hanging around, waiting. It's not something I've ever been very good at." She grinned. "Sometimes you've gotta take a chance, Jim."

"Go big or go home. Isn't that what they say?" He sighed. "Well, you're my client, and I will do as you ask." He clicked his tongue and grinned. "Man, you got some rock solid balls to even suggest this."

"Ovaries, Jim. I don't have any balls."

CHAPTER THIRTEEN

G oddamn it." Derek Marais grabbed the stress ball off his desk and launched it at the door. "Fuck."

"What's going on?" His secretary, Melissa, opened the door and stared at him.

"Sometimes I hate being right."

She smiled and picked up the stress ball. "No, you don't." She put it back on his desk. "Didn't Isabella give you that?"

"And?"

"Don't abuse your daughter's gift."

"It was meant to relieve stress. Squeezing the bloody thing wasn't working."

"And throwing it against the door did?"

"No. But arguing with you has." He slumped back in his chair.

"So what are you right about now?"

He shook his head. "You don't want to know."

She put one hand on her hip. "Are we getting sued?"

"I wish."

"Christ, it must be bad."

He waved her off. "Just a mix-up, I'm sure. I'll get it sorted just now."

"Need me to do anything?"

"Nah. Thanks."

She closed the door behind her. He waited until he could hear her tapping away at her computer before bringing up the test results again. "You bastards. You're fucking killing people."

He entered the data into a spreadsheet under a new heading. "Steve Biko, Pretoria." A third hospital supplied by PharmaChem, Ltd. Another batch of fake pills confirmed. And the results of his new batch of Combivirine just minutes away. If they came back as fake, he knew he'd have to approach someone about it. He couldn't sit on it any longer. He knew he needed more evidence, but he couldn't let it continue while people's lives were at stake. The question was who? There were few people he would—could—trust with the information. And fewer still who would be able to do anything about it. Maybe there was one. He tapped his fingertips on the desk. Maybe.

The computer pinged and his heart sputtered in his chest as his fears were confirmed. PharmaChem were supplying him and as many hospitals as they could contract with aspirin instead of the antiretroviral drugs they ordered. There was no mistake in his results. He'd run the tests far too many times for that to be possible. There could be no misunderstanding in what they were doing either. The first batch he'd received had been genuine. Sent to deceive him and any test he wanted to put them through in order to gain his confidence.

It hadn't worked, and now he needed to figure out what to do with the information he had. He'd worked alongside many politicians over the years. His position in the hospital had necessitated it, especially when they had been trying to convince the powers that be that nutrition and lifestyle choices were all it took to fight HIV. He shook his head. Bloody fools.

"So why do I feel like we're back at square fucking one, man?"

He put his head in his hands and tried to come up with a name, a face, someone he could trust with this. Someone who would fight for what was right, rather than what was right for their coffers. Was there someone in PharmaChem he could take it to? He remembered Mrs. De Fries and her defensive attitude. It didn't fill him with confidence that taking it to anyone there would be a good idea. The hospital board had already congratulated him on the savings he was making with the new drug regimen. Half of them had gone straight out and bought shares in PharmaChem.

That left him with three options. The police, the press, or the politicians. Otherwise known as the rock, the devil, and the deep blue sea. *What I need is a life vest.*

CHAPTER FOURTEEN

S ipho cradled the phone to his ear. "She wants what?"
"It's a non-invasive procedure, Mr. Nkosi. All they do is take a few skin cells from the inside of your cheek and they make a DNA profile from it. They can compare your DNA profile to that of Ms. Frost and determine if you and she are siblings."

"And if I don't want to do that?"

"Well, she's been very accommodating, in all honesty. She has agreed that when the DNA test comes back positive she will agree to share the estate with you. To refuse the DNA test in the light of that doesn't look good, sir. In fact, it looks very incriminating."

"Incriminating?"

"Like an admission of guilt, or in this case, an acknowledgement that he's not your father."

"I haven't done anything." He barely recognized the squeaky voice that escaped his mouth.

"Neither has Ms. Frost. But she must also have the procedure to give the doctors a comparison."

Sipho felt trapped. He knew his lawyer was right. He couldn't refuse the test. But at the same time, he didn't want to know. Either his mother was lying to them all now, or his mother and father had lied to him all his life. He wasn't sure which version of that he wanted to be true anymore.

"Is there a problem, Sipho?"

"I hate doctors."

"Don't we all. But seriously, is there something you want to tell me?"

"You mean, am I lying?"

"It can be easy to get caught up in something that is very difficult to get out of sometimes."

Sipho wanted to laugh at the truth in the man's words. "I was as shocked as everyone else at my mother's claim. I have no more idea than you do what the truth of the matter is."

"Very well. I'll call you with the appointment for the test."

"Thank you." He hung up the phone and rubbed his hand over his face and shaven head as he contemplated what it would mean to them all if it turned out he was Alain Frost's son. He wouldn't have to worry about the money for his mother's care again. He'd be able to get her into one of the private clinics for treatment and make sure she was taken care of in comfort. As well as discreetly. It wouldn't have to impact Amahle's career.

He'd always been so proud of his big sister, forging a career in the crucible against all the odds. He loved how she had always fought to do what was right, no matter the personal cost. It was something he couldn't stand to see ever taken away from her. She did too much good. Achieved so much, helped so many people. If all he could do with his life was whatever it took to keep her in office, then he considered his life well spent. The ramifications of their mother's condition on Amahle's political career were unpredictable, but he was pretty sure that given her vehement campaigning for the HIV programme, people would immediately suspect that she did it all for her mother's good. The fact that she didn't know wouldn't be believed against a backdrop of corrupt politicians doing nothing more than feathering their own nests. The thousands of lives she had helped to save, the millions that she had given hope and care to would not make the slightest bit of difference. He was certain it would mean the end of her career. He wouldn't allow that to happen.

He chuckled to himself. *Maybe I can use some of the money to help her too. Fund her next campaign. Maybe even toward helping her further her career.* He smiled. *President Amahle Nkosi has a nice ring to it. Maybe it will all be okay, after all.*

"Sipho?"

He sighed. *Or maybe not.* "Yes, Mama?"

"Where are you?"

"In the kitchen."

She stumbled through the door and dropped heavily into the chair beside him.

"Mama, what's wrong?" He looked up and clocked the dishevelled appearance, the drooping shoulders, and the uneven, cruel looking smile upon her lips. She looked drunk.

She sucked air through her teeth and pointed at him. "You didn't get me all my medicine."

"The pills were all there, Mama, I checked before I left."

"The medicine, the liquid, that wasn't in there."

"What liquid?"

"The morphine liquid."

"It was at the bottom."

"Shit, that one little bottle?"

He nodded.

"That's gone already."

"Mama, that's for emergency use. Only when the pain gets too bad."

"It has been very bad, boy. Very, very bad."

So not drunk then. High. "It shouldn't be so bad, Mama. Are you taking your pills?"

"Do you think I'm stupid, boy?"

"No."

"I need more medicine."

He closed his eyes. "I'll see what I can do." He walked out of the room and climbed the short flight of stairs. He dragged his laptop from under his bed and booted it up, quickly logging on to the Internet. He tried his password for the vineyards bank; he needed to know how much was in there. He knew the morphine was going to cost him. He stared at the screen. "Incorrect Username and/or Password." The message directed him to try again. He did. And again, and again, and again. He checked the notebook with the codes all written down and tried again. Still he couldn't log on. There was only one thing that made sense. They'd been changed.

And if they'd been changed, that meant they at least suspected about the missing money. He couldn't get any more. He wouldn't be able to take the cash he'd need to get the morphine.

He checked his watch, picked up the phone and dialled the bank. If he could mortgage the land that Alain had left him, it would be a start. It took them less than twenty minutes to turn him down. He couldn't mortgage land, as the will was being contested. All assets of the estate were frozen until the claim was settled.

Sipho tried to pull air into his lungs but it felt as though they too were frozen.

He could hear his mother singing downstairs, a lazy, languid song. Her words slurred, and there was the occasional bang on the table, her attempt at a drum beat. It was only a matter of time before she needed her next dose. She was in pain, she was suffering, and he couldn't deny that. Did she make matters worse—for both of them? Every step of the fucking way.

He picked up the phone again and dialled a number he wished he didn't know.

"Yeah, man?"

"It's Sipho."

"Well, well, well, my friend. Long time no see." He sniggered down the phone. "Not." He laughed at his own joke. "What can I do for you today?"

"I need more morphine."

"Sure, sure. That's not too hard to get hold of. How much you want?"

"As much as you can get."

"You looking to start selling this shit, man?"

"No. It's for someone who's sick."

"Right."

"I'm serious."

"Well, serious or not, it's not cheap. Morphine's the good shit, man. Fifty rand a bottle."

"I haven't got any money."

"Don't bullshit me, man."

"I'm not. The old man died. I can't get any more money."

"Well, well, well. Looks like you're walking back on earth with the rest of us kaffirs now. Hey, boy?"

"I need the medicine."

"You ain't got no cash, you ain't getting nothing from me."

"Wait, Tsotsi." Sipho cringed as he spoke the next words. "I'll earn it."

Laughter rang in his ears. "How you gonna do that, boy? Peel me grapes until I get sick of you and send you away with your precious morphine?"

"I know you know people who need help. Put me in touch with them. You know I boxed at school."

"You wanna play the little heavy, man?"

"I'll do what needs to be done."

"All right. I got a job for you."

"What is it?"

"Not over the phone, fuck wit. I'll tell you when you get here."

"Right."

"Boss."

"Excuse me?"

"You want to work for me, you call me boss."

Sipho swallowed down the bile that rose in his throat. "Yes, boss."

CHAPTER FIFTEEN

A mahle had returned to Cape Town and spent the night tossing and turning, trying to get Immy's stunningly smug face out of her mind. She drifted from the thought of it being stunning to smug, to stunningly smug, and back again. Until she'd tried to recall any other face to take its place. She'd even been willing to risk a nightmare and tried to picture Grace's face. It hadn't worked. In the end, she'd stumbled from bed more tired than when she'd crawled between the sheets. She poured her third cup of coffee and crossed her fingers that this time the caffeine would kick in. She placed it on the table a little too hard and cursed as the hot liquid sloshed over the rim, drenching the papers on the wooden surface.

"Christ. What next?" She mopped up the spillage and tried to save the papers. The phone rang, startling her and causing her to knock over the cup. "For fuck's sake. Me and my big mouth. Claudia, I need some help in here."

"Coming."

She picked up the phone. "Yes?" She mouthed her apology to Claudia as she left the room to gather supplies.

"Minister?"

"Yes, who's this?"

"It's Dr. Marais."

"Doctor, what I can do for you today?" She covered the mouthpiece while she thanked Claudia for cleaning up the mess she'd made and asked her to make another copy of the report she'd ruined.

"You may remember me. We worked together briefly some years ago on the HIV treatment programme."

Amahle tried to place the name, but couldn't. "I'm very sorry, Doctor. I'm afraid I don't recall."

"No matter. I'm the CEO of the Tygerberg Hospital in Cape Town."

"Of course. An excellent facility, Doctor. I've worked with your people on many occasions then."

"You have and thank you. Your charitable work over the years has been invaluable."

"You're most welcome. So how can I help you today?"

"I wondered if you had time to meet me. I have something I wish to discuss with you that is both urgent and sensitive."

"And that would be?"

"Something I'm unwilling to discuss over the phone."

Amahle shook her head. "I'm sorry, Doctor. I don't have time to play games."

"This isn't a game, Minister. I assure you this is deadly serious."

Something about the tone of his voice made her pause.

"I've been running some tests over the past three or four weeks, Minister. Tests that you need to see the results of."

"Very well. Do you wish to come here?"

"No. There are too many politicians there." He laughed, but she caught his meaning. Whatever he needed to share was sensitive enough to be of interest to some who may not want his results shared.

"Do you want me to come to the hospital?"

"No, I thought we could meet at your house."

The thought of any stranger in her home sent a chill down her spine. It was not something she tolerated easily. And not if she had any other choice. "Why not yours?"

"I have a wife and daughter. I do not want them to know anything of this."

Her curiosity was roused, but not enough to override her anxiety. Yes, she could be reckless in the political arena. Yes, she was headstrong. But she had also been burned. Her home was her sanctuary, and not one she wanted invaded. Not if she had a choice in the matter. "I'm sorry. That doesn't work for me."

"Minister, I promise you, this will be worth your time. People's lives are at stake here."

No choice it is then. "Very well, Doctor. Do you know where I live?"

"No."

She gave him the address. "When should I expect you?"

"Eight o'clock."

"See you then." She hung up and smiled as Claudia placed the replacement report on her desk.

"Are you okay?"

"Yes, of course. Why?"

"The phone call. I don't remember us having any dealings with any doctors at the moment, and given your unusual state this morning...I was concerned."

"Oh, no, no, no. Thank you for your concern. I'm fine." She took a deep breath. "He wants to talk to me. At my house. Tonight."

"Do you trust him?"

She shrugged. "I don't know him. Why?"

"Just worried about you." She shook her head. "Never mind."

"No, Claudia, what's on your mind?"

"You're not acting like yourself lately. You haven't been since you went to that funeral. You seem distracted. I know I'm your secretary, but I'd like to think we're friends too. And as your friend, I'm worried about you."

The sentiment caught her by surprise. Pleasantly so. She smiled and rested her head on her hand. "I'm fine. Just a little tired. That's all. I was hoping for an early night tonight so I hope the doctor's visit is quick. I'm sure there's nothing to worry about with him."

Claudia sighed. "I hope you are right."

"So do I. Can I ask you a question?"

"Sure."

"Would you mind joining me for this meeting tonight? I'd feel more comfortable with someone else there."

Claudia smiled. "No problem." She closed the door behind her.

Claudia's question rang in her head. *Do I trust him?* She shook her head. She had no idea. *Well, that's about to change.*

CHAPTER SIXTEEN

Imogen couldn't stand the silence any longer. Nothing but the wind creaking through old windowpanes and the branch of the old oak tree clattering against the glass every time it blew. It was driving her mad. She grabbed her iPod and set it to shuffle. She shook her head and cranked the volume up to max as the electric tones of Muse set her soul alight with their "Supermassive Black Hole." Drumming her hands on the kitchen worktop, she let her body sway to the music before breaking into a rousing air guitar performance.

"Now that's more like it." She opened the cupboard under the sink looking for black bags. There was nothing in the house but memories— bad memories—and she wanted rid of them all. If she had to be here till this was resolved there was no way she was going to be reminded every second of the life that had gone on so smoothly without her.

She set a cap backward on her head, stuffed bags in the back pocket of her cut off denim shorts, and headed for her father's room, dancing every step of the way. She sorted clothes into different bags— shirts in one, trousers in another, and another for clothes that would see the inside of a bin rather than one of the charity drives in the townships. She emptied drawers straight into bags. Her father's underwear and socks weren't something she wanted to touch.

She pulled open the second wardrobe and stopped as she took in what she saw. Her mother's clothes hung on the rail, protective plastic bags covering each garment. Her hand trembled as she reached out and stroked the fur coat she remembered from her childhood. The one her mother had worn when they'd gone out to a fancy dinner or one of the mayor's balls her father was always invited to. She remembered asking her mother why it was so soft and warm as she'd snuggled with her before she went out one evening. Her mother had told her it was God's way of keeping the animals warm and comfortable. She hadn't realized then what her mother meant. She lifted the plastic cover and ran her hand over it. It was even softer than she remembered, but the idea of the fur made her feel nauseous. She pulled it out of the wardrobe and dumped it into a bag. She reached for another item and stopped again.

Thirty-two years. These clothes had sat in the wardrobe for thirty-two years. She could smell the dust and the musty odour of mothballs, and she knew that they'd never been taken out of there in all that time. How could people think, for even a moment, that he'd cheated on her mother? It wasn't possible. Surely?

It didn't feel right to leave them hanging there any longer, but it didn't feel right to throw them out, or give them away either. She wondered at the fact that she had no qualms whatsoever about throwing away anything and everything that had been her father's, but anything he'd kept of her mother's felt like a museum piece. Like it had to be put in a glass case and preserved. Cherished. As her father had seemed to.

It took her an hour to empty the rail, painstakingly folding each item and boxing them into a trunk to go into the attic. She didn't want to leave them lying around, and until she could figure out what to do with them all, it would have to do. Amongst the shoeboxes at the bottom she found a photo album with thick card pages covered with sticky plastic to keep the pictures in place. The first picture was an image of her mother and father on their wedding day. They looked so young, so in love, and so happy. She remembered the days when her father had smiled at her mother and then hoisted Imogen onto his shoulders and set off down the rows of vines, holding her mother's hand and talking to them both about the grapes, his plans for the business, and what she'd done at school.

The next image showed her mother, heavily pregnant and grinning into the camera. One hand rested on her swollen abdomen, the other shaded her eyes from the sun. She looked radiant. Tears dropped onto the plastic cover before Imogen even realized she was crying. She wiped hurriedly at the moisture. The last thing she wanted was to damage the pictures of her mum. She didn't ever remember seeing these before, and she intended to spend many hours looking at them after this.

She turned page after page, smiling through her tears at pictures of her mother holding her as a newborn, holding her up in the bath, chubby little arms suspended mid-splash. Until she got to one that shouldn't have been there. The picture of her dressed in leather pants, aged twelve, when she'd played Sandy in the school's production of

Grease. She remembered being glad at the time that she'd been given a girl's part, rather than having to play one of the T-Birds. But what was that picture doing in her father's album? He wasn't there.

The next was her dressed for her school leavers' ball. Then her university graduation ball. There was a picture of her in her lawyer's robes and wig. She recognized it from one of her first cases. It didn't make sense. Why did he have all this when he couldn't even pick up the phone and talk to her? Why did he keep these moments of her life captured, preserved, but not want to know her? It wasn't like he was displaying her achievements to show off to his friends. They were just there. Mementos of his child's life. Like any other father would have. But he wasn't any other father. He was her father, and he was the one who had stolen that relationship from them both.

She tossed the album on the bed and slammed the door closed behind her. She couldn't stand to see her life immortalized for him. It felt hollow. As though she'd been cheated further of the father she'd always wanted, but could never have.

She started running as soon as she stepped off the stoop. She didn't know where she was going. She didn't care. She just couldn't stand to be there anymore.

CHAPTER SEVENTEEN

Derek approached the six-foot-high gate, the sharp spikes on top a certain deterrent for anyone looking to break into the grounds. The intercom flashed a red light as a distorted voice asked who he was and what he wanted.

"Dr. Derek Marais. The minister is expecting me."

"Look in to the camera please, Doctor."

Derek did as he was asked and accelerated as soon as the gate swung open. The house was large as he made his way down the drive. Three stories of glass and stone that looked like it had been carved out of the rocks of the Lion's Head and looked out over Bantry Bay. In the daylight he was sure the view was stunning. As it was, he could see the last of the sunset seeping into the ocean as his tires crunched over the gravel driveway. Thick shrubs and trees hid most of the building from his view when he stopped outside the large oak door, with a huge stone arch, and a security camera positioned over it. He was impressed and more than a little disconcerted at the level of security, but given what had happened to her, he could certainly understand it.

A thickly muscled black man in his early thirties showed him through the open plan ground floor. The kitchen area to the left and a hanging fire in the centre of the room caught his eye. Both looked spectacular, showstopping pieces. But neither looked like they'd ever been used. The view out the window was as stunning as he'd expected, and he wondered idly how much the place cost.

"Dr. Marais."

"Minister Nkosi. Thank you for agreeing to meet me like this, and please accept my apologies. I realize this is not the way you would normally do things."

"You're right. It isn't. Very few people come into my home."

"It is a beautiful house."

"Thank you. This is my secretary, Claudia. She'll be making notes for us."

"Nice to meet you." Derek shook hands with the young woman and wondered why the minister insisted on her being there. Then the thought occurred to him that she probably felt more comfortable meeting a stranger in her home in the presence of someone she knew. The thought made him smile.

"Shall we sit while we talk?"

She led him to a recessed seating area with a leather sofa that swallowed him as he sat where she indicated.

"So, Doctor, what is it that you couldn't tell me over the phone, in my office, or in your office?"

"Minister, I've been aware of your career since we worked on the campaign and you first ran for office. I remember you being exceptionally passionate about the programme and doing what was right for the people, regardless of how much pressure was put on you from your own party, from your superiors, and by those bastards who came after you. I feel you are the best, no, the only person I can bring my concerns to." Derek pulled a sheaf of papers from his briefcase and handed them to her.

She glanced at them. "Why don't you fill me in?"

"Of course," Derek said. "Over the past year or so I've noticed a worrying trend with the HIV programme. When I look at the statistics, I can see that people on treatment programmes in certain areas are not responding as well as in other areas of the country. At first, I put it down to natural trends in the population. People not being treated as quickly as others, poorer economic areas so higher incidences of secondary infections making the population sicker and so on."

"But this wasn't the case?" Amahle frowned and handed the documents over to Claudia.

"No, it wasn't. At first, Limpopo seemed to be the only affected area. A very poor area, as I'm sure you are aware."

She nodded and waited for him to continue.

"But this is not isolated to one area."

"You are dancing around your thoughts, Doctor. Why don't you tell me what you suspect is going on?"

"The drugs being supplied to some of the hospitals in the country are fakes, Minister."

"You suspect that's the cause?"

"I don't suspect it is. I know it is. I've tested it myself. How much do you know about the cocktail?"

"Enough for you to skip to the important parts."

He chuckled. "Very well." He pulled two bottles of pills out of his pocket and popped the lids of each. "This is a combined pill, made up of two RTIs, a booster, and an integrase inhibitor." He offered the caplet to Amahle and dropped it into her hand. "It's called Combivirine."

Amahle frowned at the little white pill as it sat innocuously in her hand while he slipped one from the other bottle next to it. The solid white pill was smooth and sported the chemical letters that should be on all medications.

"This is being sold by a well-known South African pharmaceutical company at a significant cost saving." He pointed to the real pill. "But this is what's actually being delivered."

"They look identical."

"Yes. But I can assure you, this one is not what the hospitals are paying for, nor what they believe they are prescribing for their patients."

"If this is a fake, then what is it?"

"Aspirin."

"You have the chemical analysis to back this up?"

"I do," he said.

"So why not take this to the police? Why bring this to me?"

"I believe that this operation is nationwide, Ms. Nkosi. I believe that these people are warehousing and distributing nothing more than aspirin to people who are suffering from HIV, and I believe you to be a politician whom I can trust. In this government, there are not many we can say that about. You know as well as I do that the police are as bad, if not worse than your colleagues over in parliament." He could see from the way her jaw worked and her eyes flashed that she hated his reasoning, but she couldn't dispute it either. *Maybe that's what she really hates. The fact that it's true, rather than the fact that I think it.*

"What do you want me to do, Dr. Marais?"

"I need someone to give me official authority to investigate this, and I need funding."

"How much funding?"

"I don't know."

"I'm afraid I don't have access to an open checkbook, Doctor."

"I realize that. But you do have access to funds to get this started on the grounds of investigating health concerns in poor communities. Once I can generate the official reports needed, then we can get things properly investigated and get this out of circulation." He pointed to the bottle of fake tablets on the small coffee table.

"Very well, Doctor." She smiled and nodded. "You're right, of course. This has to be investigated, and it needs to be handled correctly or we'll end up with a huge mess on our hands. We can't afford to ignore the consequences of a health scare that will affect thousands or millions of some of the poorest people in our country." She nodded toward Claudia. "What do you need from me? Be specific, Doctor. We can't afford to get this wrong."

CHAPTER EIGHTEEN

P lease, Amahle, I know you're very busy, but it would mean a lot to
me if you could meet me there."

"Where?"

"Stellenbosch Clinic."

"It'll take me an hour to get there."

"I know. But I'm your little brother, and you're supposed to look
after me."

She laughed. "Since when do you need me to look after you?"

Sipho almost told her the truth. That he always needed her to look
after him, and if she had, he might not be in the mess he was now.
Instead he said, "I just don't like the idea of all this."

"You don't have to do it."

"I do. We'll get no further without it, and it's the only real way to
know if there is any truth to Mama's story or not."

"What do you think?"

He shrugged. "Part of me thinks it would answer a lot of questions,
and part of me wonders if Mama was drunk when she said it."

"Are you worried about this?"

"Not worried, no. Anxious perhaps."

"I understand. I'll leave now and meet you there."

"Thank you."

Sipho hung up and jumped in the shower. If he left in twenty
minutes, he'd be there at the same time as Amahle. He was looking
forward to seeing her again. They spent so little time together these
days. She was always so busy, and he was always trying to keep their
mother under control.

Twenty minutes later, he opened the door, caught sight of the figure standing by his truck, and quickly tried to close it again without being seen.

"Eh, Sipho, man, come on out here. I see you."

Fuck. Sipho pulled the door open. "Just getting my keys, Tsotsi. I've got an appointment I have to get to." He pulled open the door of the buckie, but Tsotsi shoved it closed before he could get in.

"I need to borrow a phone." He held his hand out to Sipho.

"Well, you can use the one in my house, I guess. Just close the door when you finish."

"Nah, man. I want a phone. A mobile one. I need to call people."

"You have one, Tsotsi. I call you on it all the time, man."

"Give me your phone."

"I don't have time for this."

Tsotsi's fist caught him in the eye, and Sipho found himself slammed against the truck while Tsotsi fished through his pockets and divested him of his phone and wallet.

"Get off me." Sipho pushed back and managed to swing his arm enough to connect with Tsotsi's jaw. The next thing he knew he was on the ground with a boot in his stomach and red-flecked spittle landing on his head.

"For that you don't get your phone back." He started to walk away. "Be ready tonight. We have a job to do."

Sipho watched him walk away before dragging himself to his feet and back into his house to clean up. He was already late. What difference did it make if he took a few more minutes to make himself look presentable?

CHAPTER NINETEEN

W here's your client, Mr. Mabena?"
Amahle could hear Imogen's voice from the other side of the door. "He's not here yet?" Amahle asked as she walked into the waiting room and watched Imogen shift in her seat, crossing one leg over the other. "He wanted me to meet him. He only called me an hour ago."

"Let's hope he doesn't take too long about it. I'm sure you're very busy, Minister."

Amahle bristled. "I'm sure we all are, Ms. Frost." She couldn't put her finger on why, but it seemed every time Imogen opened her mouth she managed to annoy her. No small feat given that she had spent her life in the company of politicians whose sole purpose in life seemed to be to annoy her. "Why don't you go in while we wait?"

"The purpose of this open testing arrangement was so that everyone could see the samples being taken, bagged, labelled, and shipped off to the lab." Imogen smiled. "Me going in first would seem to negate the whole idea. Don't you think?"

"I wasn't aware of the arrangement." Amahle ground her teeth and wondered what the hell was keeping Sipho. She took a seat across the waiting room and stared about the room. Unable to settle on anything, she stared out the window for a moment then at the posters on the wall advocating the use of condoms to reduce the spread of chlamydia and unwanted pregnancies. Anything to stop her looking at Imogen with those mocking brown eyes and pouty lips. At her soft, pale skin that she wanted to reach out and touch, to stroke like she had when they were children. But so different from when they were children. She glanced over and saw the cocky smile on her lips. *Forget that. I want to slap that smug smile off her bloody face.* The thought was infinitely satisfying, and she imagined the look on Imogen's visage as she walked out the door, no doubt with her jaw still hanging open.

A commotion at the door drew her attention.

"Sorry I'm late." Sipho almost fell through the door in his rush. His hand was bloody, his knuckles scraped raw, and a cut over his eye wept.

"Sipho, what happened to you?" She pointed to his eye and reached for his hand.

"What?" He touched a hand to his cut and winced. "Oh. I had a flat tyre on the way. I had to change it. I hit my knuckles on the ground trying to get the nuts off the wheel and caught myself with the tyre iron. I'm okay."

"You look a mess."

"Nice to see you too, Ami." He smiled sadly at her.

"Nurse, can we get someone to take a look at him, please?"

"I'm fine. Really. Let's just get this over with. Everyone's been waiting for me long enough."

She smiled. He was the only one who still called her by her childhood nickname. "You need to get that cut looked at."

"I will. As soon as we finish, okay?"

She heard feet shuffling behind her and knew they were about to be hurried along. "Fine. But I want you checked out before we go and sort out a new tyre for your car."

His eyes widened. "We don't need to do that. I can sort it out myself. I know how busy you are."

She narrowed her eyes at him. If that were really true he wouldn't have asked her to accompany him for this test. "What aren't you telling me?"

"Nothing—"

"Are you ready or not, would-be brother of mine?" Imogen had her arms crossed over her chest and tapped her foot impatiently.

Sipho squared his shoulders and met Imogen's gaze. "Yes, I'm ready."

"Wonderful." She indicated the door. "After you."

Amahle managed to hold her tongue and followed Sipho through the door, Imogen and the entourage of lawyers at her back.

"There's still time to back out of this, you know," Imogen said.

"Why would he do that?" Amahle sneered.

"Because this is a load of shit. We've had that conversation already."

"Ms. Frost," Sipho said, "I don't know the truth of those things any more than you do right now."

"I know—"

"No. You suspect. You suspect my mother is lying, but the only other person involved is dead and cannot dispute her claim. We can confirm or refute her claim today, with this test. I assure you, I am as interested in the result as you are."

"Why?"

"Because all of my life I wondered why your father took an interest in me. An interest you weren't there to witness. I wondered why he chose me over all the other boys on the vineyard. I wondered what potential he had seen in me. Why he even looked in the first place. And I never had an answer." He looked her in the eye. "I don't know if this is truth or fiction. But I want an answer as much as you do."

"Of course you do." She pointed at his chest. "You want to get your hands on the money."

He nodded. "I won't lie. It would be nice not to have to worry about money. It would be nice to be able to take care of my mother properly, and perhaps help out in a campaign for the first female president of our country." He smiled at Amahle. "But what I really need is to know who Alain was to me."

"And if he isn't your father?"

"Then he was a most generous benefactor to me and I will be forever grateful. And I wish you all the luck in the future." He held out his hand toward her. "And if he is, I look forward to having another sister in my life."

Amahle watched as Imogen swallowed, Sipho's hand extended between them.

"Whatever the result of this, he was more of a father to you than he ever was to me." She looked at the doctor. "Can we get this over with?"

Amahle shook her head, saddened that her brother's efforts had been rebuked so callously. He was trying to make the situation as easy as possible for them all, and she just couldn't accept that he was as much in the dark as she was. She just wouldn't allow for the possibility. *Stubborn bloody arsehole.*

It took less than two minutes for the doctors to swab the inside of their mouths, seal, label, and have the samples signed by each party for authenticity. The lawyers were the first to leave as a nurse took Sipho down the corridor to check his wounds.

"Are you always so adversarial?" Amahle asked.

"It comes naturally to me," Imogen replied.

"It didn't always."

"Yeah, it did." She looked at Amahle and their eyes met. "Just not with you for some reason."

"Is that why you didn't come to his funeral? Why you never came back home?"

"Personal curiosity or feeding the rumour mill?"

"Excuse me?"

"The reason you want to know."

"You know what? Forget it."

"No, no, Minister, I'm curious now. Why so interested? Trying to work out another angle to get your family what they so desperately want when this idiotic claim falls though?"

"We neither need nor want your money, Ms. Frost. We're doing just fine on our own."

"Really?"

"Yes, really. You know, the Immy I remember—" Her ringing phone interrupted her. "Shit." She fished it from her bag and held it to her ear, still scowling at Imogen and the arrogant look in her eyes. "Hello."

"Is this the Nkosi bitch?"

Amahle pursed her lips and felt the creases on her forehead deepening. "Who is this?"

"I'm asking the questions here. I said, is this the Nkosi bitch?"

"I don't respond to pathetic name calling."

His laughter rang in her ears. "Well, I do, bitch."

"Who is this?" She hated that she could hear the tremor in her own voice and that her hand shook. Angry phone calls she could deal with. Insults were water off a duck's back. But the sinister voice on the line reminded her of the calls she and Grace had received in the lead-up to the attack. Just a few words put her back to that night. She leaned against the wall and closed her eyes, willing herself to regain control.

"None of your business."

"Then I'm hanging up." The muscles in her shoulders tensed and a hand on her arm made her jump. Imogen held her hand out in apology, a look of concern on her face.

"I wouldn't do that if I were you," he said.

"Why not?"

"Because then you won't get the message. And that would be bad."

Amahle felt the flood of adrenaline course through her body as her heart rate picked up speed and her desire to run was almost overwhelming. "What's the message?"

"Back off, kaffir bitch. Or you'll be seeing more of me than you want to." He blew a kiss at her and hung up, laughing.

Her knees gave out under her, and the only thing that stopped her hitting the floor was Imogen's arms as she eased her into a chair. Her chest felt tight, and she couldn't get her breath.

"Put your head between your knees for me." Imogen eased her forward, arms securely holding onto her shoulders. "Breathe now. Nice and steady."

Amahle tried to follow Imogen's instruction, but her brain couldn't make sense of them. Her breath was coming in rapid pants, and all she could see before her was Grace's face. Grace's blood smeared across the wall of their home. Message received. Loud and clear.

"Ami, look at me."

Hands cupped her face and directed it, but her eyes wouldn't focus.

"Ami, focus. Here. Look at me."

She could feel her body being shaken, but she couldn't do anything about it. She knew she wanted to pull back and tell whoever it was touching her to get the fuck off. Her body just wasn't listening to her.

"Oh fuck. I'm sorry about this, but…"

A stinging slap landed on her cheek, and her world snapped into sharp relief. Imogen was kneeling before her, a look of contrition upon her face as she cupped Amahle's aching face.

"You called me Ami."

"I always called you Ami. I do believe I was the one who gave you the nickname." She brushed her hair off her face and tucked it behind her ear. "You finally got your ears pierced then?"

Amahle smiled. "About twenty-five years ago. Gogo did it for my birthday."

"Is she still…"

Amahle shook her head. "No. She died twenty years ago. She talked about you a lot."

"Damn. I wished I'd known. I would have come back for her funeral."

"But not your father's?"

"I didn't respect him."

"But you respected my grandmother?"

"I loved your grandmother." She smiled sadly. "I used to wish she was mine."

"And I used to wish your mother was mine."

Imogen laughed. "No offense, but I can't say the same."

Amahle chuckled. "None taken." She shook her head. "She really went off the rails when Gogo died."

"I'm sorry to hear that."

She waved her hand. "Long time ago." She patted Imogen's hand where it still rested on her cheek. "It was all a long time ago now."

"Yeah." She moved her hand and let it fall into her lap. "Want to tell me about the phone call?"

"Not really."

Imogen chuckled. "Let me rephrase that." She cleared her throat. "Tell me about the phone call."

"Is that your barrister voice?"

"Yes. What do you think?"

"Very authoritative. One could even say bossy."

"Perfect. So give. Who was it?"

"He didn't give a name."

"But he knew yours?"

"Well, he called me Nkosi bitch."

"Imaginative."

"Quite."

"What else?"

"He said he had a message for me."

"And that was?"

"To back off."

Imogen looked at her, clearly waiting for something more. But there was nothing more to give.

"That's it? That's all he said?"

"Yes."

"So what are you supposed to back off?"

Amahle shrugged. She had a pretty good idea, but she had no clue how the information about her investigation into the fake pills had gotten into the wrong hands, and as helpful as Imogen was being, she really didn't know her.

"So why the panic attack?"

She didn't want to talk about it anymore. She wanted to get out of the waiting room, out of Stellenbosch, and back home where she could lock the doors, put on the alarm, and pretend that there wasn't a scary world outside the door.

"Tell me."

"Still as tenacious."

"More so."

She smiled. "His words brought back bad memories."

"How? Of what?"

"Let it go, Immy. I don't want to do this now. I don't want to open up old wounds."

"It looks to me like he already did that."

"Then let me close them again."

Imogen looked like she wanted to argue with her, but instead she sighed. "Did you come alone?"

"No. Thambo is waiting in the car for me."

"Husband?"

Amahle laughed. "Bodyguard."

"Bodyguard?"

Amahle nodded.

"Well, what bloody good is he down at the car? Why isn't he beside the body he's supposed to guard?"

"I prefer to be alone."

"Well, that's just bloody stupid, Ami. How can he do his job if you won't let him?" She stood and pulled Amahle up with her. "Come on then. You can introduce me to Thambo. I'll be bodyguard in his stead till we get you to your car."

"Don't be silly, Immy. I don't need —"

"If you even think about telling me you don't need a bodyguard after what I've just witnessed in the past ten minutes, I might have to slap the other cheek because you're obviously still in shock." She settled her hands on her hips.

"You look like your mum when you do that."

Imogen looked down at herself. "I know. No wonder the old man couldn't stand the sight of me, hey?"

"By the end, he couldn't stand the sight of himself."

"Don't try to make me feel sorry for the old bastard."

"I'm not."

"Right."

"Just telling you the truth. You seem to be someone who would appreciate that."

"I do." She took Amahle's arm and led her toward the lift. "It's a rare beast indeed."

The doors closed as Sipho walked out of the treatment room. It was too late to stop the lift, but not for it to change Imogen's whole demeanour. Her arms tensed under Amahle's hand and the muscles in her jaw clenched visibly. The friendly Imogen of moments ago was, once again, gone.

CHAPTER TWENTY

Imogen pulled open the door and smiled at the grinning face of Roland De Fries holding a large platter of something smelling deliciously sweet.

"My wife made koeksisters for us."

"Oh my. I can't remember the last time I had one of those."

"Well, get the kettle on, Ms. Frost, and we'll feast before we get started on these books. I need rooibos tea with my koeksisters."

Imogen held the door for him as he blustered in and made himself at home in the kitchen. Once the tea was brewed and the pot set on the table, he uncovered the platter. She could feel the saliva pool in her mouth as the scent of sugar, lemon, and ginger assailed her senses. The syrup soaked fluffy dough transported her back in time. She could practically feel her mother's hand on her back as she taught her how to rub the fat into the flour to help make the dough. The acrid odour of the tea was the perfect counterpoint to the sweetness of the syrup. She'd never been able to find them in England. Doughnuts had been as close as she'd managed to find, and the powdered sugar on top of those just wasn't the same.

"Nothing like them, yah?"

She nodded, not trusting her voice.

"Mind if I plug in?" He pointed to his laptop. "Damn thing has about a ten minute battery life."

"Go ahead."

He licked his fingers clean and wiped them dry on his trouser leg. She smiled, not envying his wife her laundry.

"So, Mr. Davitson told you I have a few concerns about the way the books have been kept?"

"He did. He also confirmed that the accounting firm my father used in the past was no longer servicing the account as it had been taken in-house."

"Correct."

"What does that mean, exactly?"

"It means that essentially the vineyard established its own accounting department that would be run by a qualified accountant, preferably a team of them, who operate within the established laws, guidelines, and current good practices."

"Effectively, it becomes its own accounting firm within the main company?"

"It's a little more complicated than that but, effectively, yes."

"Okay. And did that happen?"

"No."

"What did happen?"

"It appears there were a few people who 'did the books.'" He curled his fingers in the air to put the term in inverted commas.

"Who?"

"Your father, Sipho, and for a while there was a third person. From my inquiries, though, she would appear to have been a tutor brought in to help teach Sipho how to run the accounts. She has an impeccable reputation, and I have a hard time believing her capable of this kind of thing."

"What kind of thing are we actually talking about here, Mr. De Fries?"

"Please, call me Roland."

"Very well, Roland."

He smiled and polished off his second pastry. "What we're talking about is fraud and embezzlement."

"That sounds so much more exciting than plain old theft."

"It does, but it amounts to the same thing. Just a different technique to do so." He clicked open a spreadsheet, slid the computer toward her, and pointed to a column. "See these figures along here?"

"Yes."

"That's the profit and loss that has been filed for the vineyard. This is a matter of public record. Anyone can see this." He pointed along the screen. "Each year, there was an increase except for the odd occasion when some external factor influenced the estate."

She noticed the year of her mother's death showed the lowest profit in the vineyard's history. Since then it showed a steady upward climb. Until recently.

"For each of the last six years, as you can see, there has been a steady decrease in profit."

"Are there external factors to explain this?"

"For some, of course. For example, here," he said, pointing to a specific column, "we had a drought, so the crop yield was down." He pointed to the lowest figure on the spreadsheet. "And here, your father purchased some new land. But the turnover figures show a healthy, growing turnover, year upon year, so the rest of these should show an increased profit. Not a shrinking one."

"How much are we talking about here?"

"Somewhere between twenty and twenty-five thousand a year."

"Over the six years?"

"Yes. Around one hundred and fifty thousand rand, total."

"And this money is actually, physically missing. Not just lost in a paper exercise somewhere?" She sipped her tea.

"The bank accounts tally within fifty bucks to the turnover, income, and expenditure spreadsheets."

"Is that a yes or a no?"

"I've never looked in the safe to see if the funds are in there. It is possible that the money is there and the accounting technique used here hasn't properly accounted for it."

"Or…?"

"It's actually, physically missing."

"So, my supposed brother is skimming off the top."

"It looks incriminating, but it's also possible that your dad was using the money and not accounting for it."

"Why would he do that?"

"I don't know. But he was ill, so perhaps he paid medical bills with the money and forgot to put it through the accounts because of his illness."

"Wouldn't his medical insurance cover his bills?"

"Usually. But I don't know the details of his coverage, or what exceptions were put on his cover."

"Can you check that with the hospital?"

"With your permission, of course." He pulled a stack of forms from his briefcase. "I came prepared."

She grabbed the document and, after a brief perusal, signed to give her consent to the disclosure of the information. "So what next, Roland?"

"I keep digging. Now that you are the only signatory on the account, and we can safely rule you out as a suspect due to your absence, I can begin digging down into the specifics of when the funds went missing. From there we try to ascertain where they went."

"Can you do that?"

"If they were electronically transferred, absolutely. If they were withdrawn in cash deposits, then I will be able to prove who withdrew them. Then we can call in the police." His face shone with pride and excitement.

She laughed and clapped a hand on his shoulder. "I love to see a man enjoy his work, Roland."

"That I do, Ms. Frost."

"Imogen. If you insist I call you Roland, then you have to call me Imogen."

"Done deal."

"How long before you'll have confirmation for me?"

"A week." He shrugged. "Maybe two. If I have to get a court order for CCTV footage from the local bank it will drag it out a little."

"Please be discreet. If it is Sipho, I don't want him running before we can have him arrested."

"I'm afraid that horse will have already left the stable."

"What do you mean?"

"As soon as the information on the accounts was changed into your name, his access was cut."

"Yes—so as soon as he tried to access more funds he would have been aware that we were suspicious at the very least."

"Exactly."

"Shit." She remembered the bloody knuckles and the cut over his eye from the previous day. Was there a connection? Her brain was spinning with no destination or focus, just too many unanswered questions.

"Yup, this is one great big pile of it. Oh, before I forget." He fished an envelope out of his pocket. "Jim asked me to give you this."

"What is it?" She turned the envelope over.

"An invitation to the mayor's ball on Saturday."

"Talking of shit, huh?" She laughed.

"Right, yah." He chuckled. "I'll be there with my wife. She'd love to meet you."

"I'll think about it."

"Jim said you were thinking of selling this place."

"Yes, I am."

"Every vineyard owner in the Western Cape will be there. And every moneyed bastard from Cape Town to Pretoria will be showing up too if you want to get the feelers out to sell this place as soon as this business is dealt with." He closed his laptop lid. "Saturday night's the place to start."

She sighed. "I better see if I have a frock in my suitcase then."

"A what?"

"A frock. A dress, fancy gown, all that shit."

He chuckled. "If you're lucky you'll find something in town."

"If not?"

"Cape Town."

Suddenly, the idea of a shopping trip didn't sound quite so unpleasant. "You know something, Roland, I think I might take a trip over there. I only ever remember seeing the airport."

"Better take your platinum cards, Imogen." He closed his briefcase. "And don't be outside alone after dark."

"It can't be that bad."

He snorted. "Is it worth the risk?"

CHAPTER TWENTY-ONE

Amahle wondered at the cryptic message she'd received from Dr. Marais and why he felt it was necessary for her to go to his office after his initial refusal to have her meet him there. His office was situated amongst a maze of buildings, corridors, and wards that took her and Thambo an age to navigate.

"I'm glad you could make it, Ms. Nkosi," Dr. Marais said.

The office was a mess. Papers strewn across the floor. Broken glass littered every surface, and computers and equipment were smashed everywhere she looked.

"I've been cleaning up all morning, but I'm not all that sure I've made much progress."

"What happened?"

"I came in the morning and found it like this."

Thambo picked up a chair and righted a teetering tower of flasks that looked about to fall. "Who else has access to your office?"

"It's a hospital. The cleaning staff comes in and out, my secretary, and the administrators have keys. There's the security service too."

"We need to find you a more secure location," Amahle said.

Dr. Marais frowned. "I'm the hospital CEO. Where do you suggest I go to?"

"I don't know right now, but you staying here doesn't seem like a sensible option to me, Doctor. Does it to you?"

"No, but reasonable solutions are just as difficult."

"Then what about a guard?"

He looked over his shoulder. "I've got to admit this has made me feel more than a little uneasy. I have a wife, you know. And a daughter."

"I know."

"A guard sounds like a reasonable option to me." He waved his hand about the room. "I don't mind admitting that this terrifies me." He wrapped his hand around her arm. "I have even more respect for your courage now, Ms. Nkosi. I don't think I could have gone through all you did and been able to go on fighting afterward."

She nodded but wanted him to drop the subject. "Have you looked into protection, or do you want me to arrange it for you?"

"I'd very much appreciate your assistance with that, Minister."

"I think I can do that." She smiled. "Do you have somewhere I can make some calls?"

"In my secretary's office." He pointed to the door at the far end of the room.

She pulled her phone from her bag as she stepped inside and felt the hairs on the back of her neck stand on end. The room looked untouched.

"They damaged nothing in here, Doctor?"

"Apparently not. The door was unlocked. They came through here to get to my office, but it seems they were intent on making a mess in my office only."

It didn't make sense. Why wouldn't a thug targeting him trash this room too? She sat at the desk and looked around her. She couldn't see anything incriminating. She picked up the phone, but something in her told her that this wasn't right. Since the attack, her instincts had become much sharper and she'd learned to trust them. She didn't feel comfortable here.

She walked out of the room and leaned in close to the doctor's ear. "I don't like it. Do you have any way to test if these rooms have been bugged?"

He stared at her, his eyes wide, and shook his head.

"Thambo."

"Yes?"

She waved him over and whispered the request in his ear.

"It will take me a little while, but yes, I can."

"Do it."

"I'll be in the hallway." He waved his phone to let her know why he was going to the hallway.

"You can go and sort out whatever you need to, Thambo."

"Not going to happen, Minister. Not now." He looked at her pointedly and she could see the resolve in his eyes.

She nodded and turned back to the shaken doctor. "You said you had more to show me. Can you still do that, or is it in this little lot somewhere?" She glanced around the room.

"Can we talk in here?" he whispered.

Amahle thought through his query. Maybe it was her paranoia, maybe it was the fact that there felt to be so many similarities to her previous experience, maybe it was her natural inclination to make decisions and never question them, but it made sense to her that acting in a way that triggered more suspicion from whoever was targeting them was a bad idea. What they needed was time to gather their evidence, to make their plans, and to find the people behind this. It seemed perfectly logical to her that arousing suspicion that they were aware of the increasing vigilance on them would only make their watchers nervous. Probably more dangerous too.

"If you already had it, then they already know about it. I can't see what it changes at this point by you telling me." She spoke quietly. "The only thing we don't want is for anyone who is listening to suspect that we suspect they are listening." She smiled. "Do you follow me, Doctor?"

"Of course. I have reports now from twelve different clinics. Ten of them have been supplied with fake medications by PharmaChem."

"Are they all aspirin like the ones you had before?"

"Yes. Plain old simple aspirin. They cost pennies to produce or buy, and disguising them as Combivirine means they can sell each pill for around ten times the price of a whole packet of aspirin."

"You said ten out of twelve clinics. What's different about the other two?"

"They are private medical clinics."

Shit. "Every one of the clinics you've tested offering free treatment is using fake drugs?"

"So far."

"How large is your sample area?"

"I've got a sample from Jo'burg, Bloemfontein, two from Pretoria, two from Cape Town, two from Polokwane. I have one from Durban, two from Pietermaritzburg, and one from the clinic in Stellenbosch."

"All over the country then."

"Pretty much."

"Does this company supply all the hospitals?"

"No. Not at all. They supply around forty-five percent of the large hospitals in South Africa at the moment. The rest are supplied by other South African companies or more commonly, they're importing the drugs from America or the UK. There will be many places still using the proper medications."

"But the private clinics, the people with money, they're still getting the proper drugs?"

"I've only had two samples, but both were offering genuine treatments, despite being supplied by PharmaChem."

"How many people are we talking about here, Doctor?"

"I don't have a definitive number, but if every hospital PharmaChem supply is getting aspirin instead of their cocktails, then I'd estimate around three million people are currently being given counterfeit medication."

It was almost too big to get her head around. The lack of empathy for all those suffering people boggled her mind. The level of greed required to even contemplate, never mind carry out, something like this was despicable. As much as she wished it wasn't happening at all, she wished she couldn't believe that it was.

"I think I need to start looking into some of my opposition to the HIV health care programme."

"Ms. Nkosi, are you sure that is a wise idea?"

She shook her head. "I'm pretty certain it isn't." She smiled. "But it is the right thing to do. Can you get me a copy of that report? At least three or four copies please."

"It's on my computer, I can—" He pointed to the smashed box.

"Let me take the remains of that and see if we can get an expert to fix it."

He nodded as they both began the task of tidying and reorganizing the office. After an hour or so, the door opened and Thambo walked inside with a small handheld device. He didn't say a word as he scanned the outer office and then moved on to Dr. Marais's office. Amahle watched him intently as he held it discreetly in his hand as he wandered seemingly aimlessly around the room before backing out and waving them to follow him into the hallway.

"There are recording devices all over the place. Video and sound. There's also something going on with the computer that I don't like. It's smashed to pieces, but there are some weird energy readings coming out of it, and considering that it's turned off, and unplugged, I really don't like that. I want to get that out of here and examined by a specialist I know."

"Is he reliable?" Amahle asked.

"He's my brother."

"I guess that's a yes then."

"I'm sorry it has come to this, Doctor," Amahle said.

"I brought this to you. It's my own fault."

"No, it's not either of our faults. That's down to the bastards who are stealing from the sick to line their own pockets." She hoped he hadn't noticed the trembling in her hand, or the quiver she could hear in her own voice. Or if he did he put it down to the understandable anger she was also feeling. She gathered the nervous energy and channelled it into activity that would yield productive results. *No time for feeling sorry for yourself, Ami. No time for fear. Too much to do.* Just one more battle to fight on behalf of her people.

"Oh, and, Minister?" Dr. Marais said.

"Yes?"

"I'd look into those who didn't oppose the programme. Someone very high up knows this programme inside and out. They have to in order to get this rolled out on such a large scale. I'd be more inclined to think it was someone who was part of establishing it from the very beginning."

She closed her eyes and nodded. It made sense. It made her sick to think about it, but it made sense. This was organized, efficient, and he was right; they knew the system inside and out. They had to be a part of it. Whoever this mysterious "they" was, it was likely someone she had considered an ally, if not a friend. She thought about the words the man had said to her on the phone. They'd been exactly the same as those written in Grace's blood. At the time she'd thought it a coincidence. Not anymore.

CHAPTER TWENTY-TWO

Tsotsi, no. I don't want to go back to Cape Town. Smashing up shit is for fools. I don't even understand why we had to go all the way up there. There's hospitals in Stellenbosch, and ones that are easier to get into than that one was."

"You do as you're told, boy. You came to me, remember? You wanted a job to earn your fucking morphine. Well, now you do as you're told. Do you hear me?"

"I hear you."

"Good. Now get your backside over here. We're leaving in half an hour."

"What do you need me to do?"

"Smashing up shit didn't work. Now we need to take more direct action."

"What do you mean?"

"You were a boxer, right?"

Sipho swallowed the bile rising in his throat. "Yes."

"Then think of it as a match."

"Who am I fighting?"

"Does it matter?"

"Why am I to fight him?"

"Because I'm telling you to."

The silence following the disconnection made his ears ring and he cringed. The cut over his eye from the shattered glass stung, and he wanted nothing more than to curl up on his bed and never move again.

"Sipho, where's my medicine?" Mbali shouted down the stairs.

He sighed and grabbed his work coat. "I'll have it for you tomorrow." He looked down at the coat then hung it back on the peg.

He selected an old, dark brown leather jacket instead. Easier to clean blood off, and easier to hide any he might miss.

"I'm in pain, boy. I need it now."

He didn't answer. He just closed the door behind him. He tried to harden his heart with every step he took, knowing that he didn't have a choice. He had responsibilities, his mother had needs, and he had debts to pay.

So why do I feel like I'm walking toward the gallows?

CHAPTER TWENTY-THREE

"A ny chance of getting up there for the sunrise?" Imogen asked the man in the ticketing window and pointed to the top of the mountain.

"Same as everyone else. First car doesn't run till eight thirty."

"No exceptions?"

"I don't run the cars, lady. I just take your money."

Imogen grinned. "Worth a try."

"Yeah, yeah. You want a ticket or not?"

"Return please." She handed over her card and waited for her ticket to be printed. "Thanks." She retrieved her card and made her way through the barricade to the front of the queue as the dusky pink of the early morning touched the deep purple of the sky. She truly wished she could have been at the top of Table Mountain to see the sun rise over the Indian Ocean, and chase away the night, but even she had to accept that she couldn't always get her own way. She didn't have to like it. But she did accept it. Occasionally.

She was the first one in the cable car when it left the station. The temperature dropped significantly as the car neared the plateau, and she wrapped her coat about her shoulders, grateful she'd planned ahead and packed her down jacket. The only people at the top when the car stopped were workers. Those lucky few who got to see the magnificence of this view every day. *And I bet they never see it anymore.*

She stared across at the Helderberg Mountains, Bloubergstrand, or "blue mountain beach" as it was better known, Sunset Beach, Devil's Peak, the 12 Apostles, Camps Bay, Signal Hill with the nipple-like protrusion of Lion's Head standing sentry over Cape Town itself. Way out in the bay sat Robben Island, the notorious prison island, infamously holding its place in history as the holding place of political prisoners during the apartheid regime. Most notably, Nelson Mandela had resided there in a tiny cell for almost twenty years before being transferred to Pollsmoor Prison. It looked like a rock on a pond from where she stood.

She turned to the east and watched as the sun finished its ascent into the sky and the ocean glistened beneath it, so vast and so distinct. The meeting edges of two great oceans was as visible to the naked eye as a child's crayon line down a page from Simon's Town to the end of the world. To the east the turquoise warmth of the Indian Ocean pitched and heaved invitingly, while to the west the deep indigo of the Atlantic rolled and crashed against its counterpart, the soft white foam of the surf punctuating the seemingly endless expanse of water.

She could have sat and watched it all day with its subtle variations, shifts, and the infinite give and take that was the power of the sea. This was the Africa her father had talked to her about when she was a child. The Africa of wonder. Nights when she'd been unable to sleep, he'd told her of his adventures as a boy, climbing mountains, and watching elephants wander the plains. For the first time, she looked at Africa with a sense of pride and awe. And for the first time that she could remember, she looked out with a sense of peace.

She couldn't stop her mind drifting. Sitting on a rock at the top of the mountain, she found she didn't want to. She thought about her mother, her father, the situation with Sipho and Amahle. How quickly her feelings had shifted from anger to the need to protect when Amahle had gotten that phone call. She'd watched the strong woman struggle to maintain her control, her dignity in the face of her obvious fear. What was she so afraid of? Yes, threatening calls weren't nice. Far from it. But she couldn't see it affecting Amahle the way it had. She'd had a panic attack. Panic and the woman she'd gone toe to toe with so far weren't concepts that worked together. So what was behind it? What did that call trigger? More importantly, why hadn't she just been able to leave her to it?

She'd watched those plump lips tremble and her breasts heave as she struggled with her feelings, and Imogen had only wanted to make it easier for her. She'd watched Amahle's beautifully expressive eyes ricochet between fear and fury and back again, and all she'd wanted to do was kiss her and take the fear away.

Wait. Back up there. Kiss her? Where the fuck did that come from? Over exaggeration there, Frost. There was no kissing, and no kissing wishing. She tossed a pebble over the edge of the barrier and into oblivion. *What the fuck's kissing wishing when it's at home?* She leaned forward, resting her elbows on her knees. *Okay, logic works. Walking her to her car, I was practically holding her up, fraternizing with the enemy.* She sniggered. *It sure didn't feel like that. It felt completely natural. To offer her support, friendship, and yeah, maybe something more.* She tossed another pebble off the mountain.

"Sometimes I fucking hate logic."

She glanced at her watch and decided it was time to get on with the rest of the day. Cape Town was laid out before her, and watching it from the top of the mountain wasn't going to help her find a dress for the ball on Saturday.

She tried to recapture the tranquillity of her early experience as she wandered around shops, cafés, and tourist destinations. No particular destination in mind, just walking. It was mid-afternoon when she found herself standing in front of the Houses of Parliament. The impressive white colonnades and the pristine red brick towered up before her, and she felt a small burst of laughter bubble up from within her chest.

"Well, that's Freudian."

She glanced at the tours board and saw she was far too late to book one and wander the halls where Amahle worked on the off chance that she would run into her.

"Do I want to run into her?" She thought about the question seriously. She knew so little of her old friend, of the obviously remarkable woman she had become, and of the woman she'd comforted just a couple of days ago, and yes, she knew she wanted to know more. Amahle had fascinated her as a child. As an adult, it seemed she'd lost none of her appeal. After the phone call and its aftermath, surely checking she was all right was a reasonable thing to do. Wasn't it?

Decision made, she walked into reception and asked for Minister Nkosi's office.

"Is she expecting you?"

"Not exactly, no. But if you could call her office and ask if she'll see me, I'm more than happy to wait."

"Who should I say is calling?"

"Tell her Immy's here."

The receptionist arched an eyebrow at her and seemed reluctant to pick up the phone.

"I'll just wait right here, till she says yes or no." She smiled and rocked on the balls of her feet. As always with her, the more difficult the receptionist made it for her to see Amahle, the more adamant she became that it was going to happen. The only question became how quickly the young woman caved in to her demands.

The young woman scowled as she picked up the phone. "This is reception. I have someone here who wants to see the minister." She snorted. "She said she won't leave until the minister says yes or no to seeing her." She chuckled. "Yah, I know. Her name's Immy."

Two minutes. That's all it had taken.

"I don't mind waiting while you ask her," the receptionist said. She put her hand over the mouthpiece. "Her secretary is going to ask her."

"Thanks. I'd ascertained that."

"Huh?" The woman frowned, clearly listening to the voice on the other end of the line rather than her. "What?" She glowered at Imogen. "Her secretary will be here in a few minutes to show you to her offices."

Boom! And that's how you do it. "Thank you." She fought to keep a smug expression off her face. From the glare she was continuing to get from the receptionist, she doubted she was successful.

"Ms. Frost?" A tall woman with shoulder length red hair held out her hand and smiled at her. "I'm Claudia, Ms. Nkosi's secretary."

Imogen shook her hand. "Pleased to meet you."

"If you'll follow me please, the minister is very busy."

"Of course."

The woman's heels clicked on the parquet floor while Imogen's walking boots squeaked, and a scrape could be heard now and again. *I must have a stone caught in the tread.* Her casual attire was perfectly suited for a day sightseeing, not visiting the ministerial chambers in the Houses of Parliament.

Amahle laughed as Imogen walked through the door. "I bet Rebecca on reception was having a conniption."

Imogen grinned. "I can vouch for that. She doesn't like me. I think I've sullied the place."

"Oh, I think not," Amahle said. "Far worse than you have darkened these hallowed hallways."

"How very Machiavellian, Minister."

"Sad but true. So how can I help you today, Immy?"

"Would you believe I was in the neighbourhood and wanted to see if you were okay?"

"Probably not."

"Ah, all right then. Hang on while I make something up instead."

"What were you doing in the neighbourhood?"

"Shopping." She held up her bags. "A little sightseeing."

"And this brings you to my door?"

"Well, no. It brought me to Cape Town. I've been invited to the mayor's ball in Stellenbosch on Saturday night. And I didn't have a suitable dress."

"Okay. And then you end up here?"

"Well, it wasn't planned. I just seemed to end up here, and when I was I thought I should check on you."

"Why?"

"Because last time I saw you I practically had to carry you to your car, and I was…concerned."

"You did not have to carry me."

"I said practically."

"Is that how you twist things in court?"

"It's not twisting. It's stating the facts as I see them."

"A-huh. It's twisting. And you damn well know it."

"And you damn well haven't answered my question."

"I lost track of it."

"Sure you did." Imogen sat and leaned her elbows on her knees, staring intently at Amahle. "How are you feeling?" She could see the slight tremor in her hands as she pushed her fingers through her hair.

"I'm fine, thanks. Is that all you came here for?"

Imogen could tell she was lying, but decided this was one time when pushing wouldn't get her the answers she seemed to need. Instead she changed the subject. "No. I thought I could try to persuade you to have a drink with me." She wasn't sure where the words had come from, but as soon as they left her mouth, they felt right.

Amahle laughed. "Are you joking?"

"Nope." She leaned back in her chair.

"Why?"

"You ask a lot of questions, don't you?"

"I haven't changed that much, Immy. I always did."

"True."

"So?"

"I don't know anyone in Cape Town. I just don't want to be on my own tonight."

"I don't think it's a good idea."

"Why not?"

"Do you mean besides the situation between you and my brother?"

"Yeah. Besides that."

Amahle laughed. "Well, I guess besides that, it's probably still not a good idea."

"Why not?" Imogen laughed. "You should probably tell me because I'm starting to repeat myself."

"I'm not a babysitter."

"I know."

"I have a lot of work to do."

"I know."

"I'm going to call you Polly."

"I know." She laughed. "One drink, and I'll leave you to your work, I promise."

❖

Amahle could think of so many reasons why spending time with Imogen was a bad idea. Paternity and work issues aside, there was a weight of expectation to pursuing a friendship with Imogen. They'd been so young; there was no reason to believe that they'd have continued to be friends had their friendship been allowed to develop naturally. But it hadn't. It had been cut down at the point when it had been strongest. But they weren't children anymore. And there were more obstacles in the way than just a dispute over Sipho's paternity, and that's if she forgot the whole embarrassing episode at the hospital. But she was curious, and she had to admit it was kind of sweet. Seeing the big bad barrister all playful, and…flirty?

"Please. I promise I'll be nice the whole time."

"The whole time?"

"Every second."

"Fine. But I don't want to go out anywhere."

Imogen looked confused. "Okay. I guess my hotel has a bar or something."

Amahle shook her head. The idea of sitting in a bar surrounded by strangers was too unsettling. She wanted—needed—to be able to see everyone around her and know if there was anything she needed to worry about. She needed to relax, clear her head, not make herself more paranoid. Besides, it was Thambo's night off, and while she could get cover for him if she needed to make an engagement, she much preferred not to. She hated that anyone had to fill this need in her life. She'd gotten used to Thambo over the years. She didn't want to get used to others too.

"I'll make dinner." She scrawled her address on a piece of paper and handed it to Imogen. "Eight o'clock?"

"Perfect." She studied the paper. "Am I supposed to be able to read this?"

"I'll see you later."

"Is that a six or a B?"

"A B. Good-bye."

"Right." Imogen stood up, still staring intently at the paper. She glanced over as she reached the door, and Amahle felt her stomach quiver. Her mouth went dry, and she was glad she was still sitting down as Imogen wet her lips and smiled again. "See you later," she said with a wink and closed the door behind herself.

"Yeah. Later." *Oh, this is such a bad idea.*

CHAPTER TWENTY-FOUR

The view as she climbed the slope of the Lion's Head toward the address Amahle had given her was simply stunning. Looking out over Bantry Bay, it was hard to keep her eyes on the road. She wanted to stare out at the sea and watch the ships round Sea Point before they slid out of view and into port. She wondered briefly if Amahle had a sea view, then shrugged off the query. She'd know soon enough.

She followed the sat nav until it decreed her destination reached, and she looked for the gateway onto the property that did indeed have a view out to sea. She buzzed the gate and smiled up at the camera. She was glad to see that Amahle had a decent looking security system. She just hoped she used it properly. *Unlike the bodyguard who it seemed wasn't allowed in the same building as said body.* She sniggered. *You promised to be nice, remember?*

She whistled as she parked the buckie, covered in signs for the Frost Vineyard, in front of the building and saw what appeared to be a three level building seemingly cut into the edge of the mountain. Floor to ceiling glass walls looked out to sea, the rest seemingly solid rock, with heavy steel beams, and solid oak doors barring entry to any unwanted guest.

"Hi." Amahle smoothed her hands over the flat plane of her stomach as Imogen turned to see her standing in the doorway.

"Hi." She nodded toward the bay. "Nice view." The view of Amahle wasn't bad either. She wore a white skirt that floated around her mid calves, sandals on her feet, and a deep red halter top. Her hair was twisted up on top of her head, captured haphazardly with decorative chopsticks to keep it in place.

"Thanks."

"No bodyguard tonight?"

"It's Thambo's night off. I've got the security system. It calls the police if a door opens and I don't set a code in thirty seconds." She held the door open. "So you best hurry up and come in."

Imogen caught the scent of her perfume as she passed her. Chocolate, caramel, and patchouli. A deeply musky scent that could only be one. "Angel?"

"Excuse me?"

"Your perfume. Angel?"

"Oh, yes. Sorry. I know some people don't like it."

"Smells like chocolate." She winked. "I love it."

"The perfume or the confectionary?"

"Both."

"I'll bear that in mind."

"Do I get the grand tour?"

"Sure. But dinner's almost ready. Afterward?"

"Sounds good. What are we having?"

"How does mealie pap and wors sound to you?"

Imogen threw her head back and laughed. They'd shared the meal of South African sausage and the maize porridge, made to the consistency of mashed potatoes, so often as children it felt almost expected to see them on the table when Amahle showed her into the dining room.

"Do you make pap as well as your grandmother used to?"

"No."

"Then not so good."

"Thank God. That's why I decided on something else instead."

"A-huh. And that would be…?"

"A surprise."

"I'm not great with surprises."

"Why's that?"

"Never had a good one, I suppose."

"Never?"

Imogen shook her head.

"Then tonight will be a first." Amahle wandered through the open plan space into the area clearly defined as a kitchen. Pots and pans hung from a suspended rack over a centre island, and a range of pristine looking equipment littered surfaces that looked barely used.

"Need any help?"

"Here, grab this." Amahle held out a bowl of salad and a bottle of wine.

"Yes, madam."

"I just better check; you're not allergic to anything, are you?"

"Mushrooms."

"Damn." She shrugged. "Oh well, more for me." Amahle chuckled, and Imogen knew her mouth was hanging open. "Just kidding. I can't picture you as a vegetarian so I got us a couple of steaks."

"This looks delicious." The steak was cooked to perfection, a timbale of pilaf rice, tossed salad, coleslaw, and potato salad finished off the meal.

"It's hardly a gourmet meal."

"When you live on ready meals and take-away, trust me, this is."

"You don't cook?"

"Nah. Not really. I didn't take home economics at school, and I never had anyone else to show me how. Never picked up the bug, I guess."

"Hmm, it's a good job my grandmother taught me, or Sipho and I would have starved after she died."

Imogen took a bite of her food and tried to ignore the mention of his name. "I'm sorry you had a rough time after she passed away."

"We both went through rough times after losing someone we loved."

Imogen swallowed another bite and nodded slowly, not sure what to say.

"I read the letters you sent me," Amahle said.

"When?"

"The day we both ended up in the orchard."

"Oh."

"I wish he'd given them to me. I wish he'd sent you the letters I gave him for you."

"You wrote to me?"

"Knowing what we know now, do you really think I wouldn't have written to you then?"

Imogen shook her head. "No, I suppose not. Do you still have them?"

"No. I have no idea where they are. They weren't with the letters I received from you. I thought he might have given them to you."

"No. I wish he had."

Amahle ate for a few moments. "Are you still angry?"

"About which part?"

"In your letters you were angry at being sent away and not allowed to come home."

"I'm still hurt by that, yes. I'm still hurt by it all, but I don't think angry is the right word anymore." She took a sip of wine. "I was thinking about that this morning while I was up Table Mountain. I can't say I'm not angry about it, because if I let myself I can feel it build up inside me again. I think it's more that I chose not to let it, I don't know, infect the rest of my life." She swirled the wine in her glass. "It happened and I can't undo it. I can't bring back the past. All I can do now is move forward and refuse to let myself be victim to someone else's will again."

"Commander of your own ship, as it were?"

"Something like that." She drank the last of her wine and placed the glass back on the table. "Do you remember that night?"

"Your last night?"

"Is that how you think of it?"

"Yes. And yes, I remember it vividly."

"Do you remember your mother going to the main house and your grandmother saying something to her about it?"

Amahle looked down at her plate. "Yes."

"I didn't understand it then. I know you didn't either. Do you think she was sleeping with my father?"

"I've asked myself that same question a thousand times since his funeral. I've gone over a thousand conversations, a million looks, and just don't know, Immy. I honestly don't."

"But it is possible, isn't it?"

"That Sipho's your brother as well as mine?"

"No. He's not."

"Why is it so hard for you to believe that your father sired Sipho but not that he slept with my mother?"

"Honestly?"

"Of course."

"Timing."

"Excuse me?"

"I don't believe my father cheated on my mother." She shook her head. "I can't accept that. I can't believe he'd put us through what he did because he loved her so much, but that he was willing—no, able—

to cheat on her." She tapped her temple. "It just doesn't compute up here, and I think your mother was pregnant before my mother died."

"I've gone over the dates myself, Immy. It's bloody close."

"That's why I don't believe it. He wouldn't cheat on my mother. Her clothes were still hanging in the wardrobe when I got here. Did you know that he never got rid of them? Never even packed them away." She watched Amahle shake her head. "He wouldn't have done that. But once my mother was gone…" She shrugged. "I don't know." She reached for the glass of wine as Amahle refilled it. "Maybe."

"Why does that make a difference to you?"

"The only way I can accept that my father threw me away is that I reminded him too much of her. That he loved her so much he couldn't bear any reminder of what he'd lost. If he could cheat on her, it reduces all that pain to nothing. It means his illegitimate son was worth more to him than I was. It means that I wasn't good enough for him." She wasn't sure where it was all coming from, and she wasn't sure why she needed Amahle to understand. But she did. She needed Amahle to not only understand but accept her reasons. Accept her. "I'm not trying to be difficult, or call your family liars. I'm simply trying to keep my sanity intact." She stabbed at her steak.

"I understand."

"You do?"

"Yes. Stop playing with your food. It's already dead."

"Sorry." She took a large bite. "It's really good."

"Thank you."

"Enough about me and all this shit. Tell me about you."

"What about me?"

"Well, you're gorgeous, successful, live in one fucking awesome house, and you're not married. Pick a place to start and we'll go from there."

"You know, I was interviewed not long ago, and I was talking about how what happened to you inspired me to go into politics."

"How so?"

"I vowed never to be helpless in the wake of someone else's power."

"And that drove you to politics?"

"No, that drove me to excel. Nelson Mandela giving a speech at my school." She smiled. "That drove me to politics."

"Must have been some speech."

"It was. He talked about how we can't expect our lives to be made better by the state simply because we have needs. We need to go out there and work for the changes we need to see in our lives. We need to work for the changes we want to see in our country, and in our people. We need to be leaders who lead by example, people who put the greater good before their own individual needs in order to make a South Africa that we can all be proud of."

"And are you?"

"What?"

"Proud of the South Africa you are a part of?"

A shadow crossed Amahle's face. "Sometimes."

"What aren't you proud of?"

"Many, many things."

"Can you change them?"

"I'm working on it."

"You're very cryptic, Ms. Nkosi."

"I'm a politician, Ms. Frost. It comes with the office."

Imogen laughed. "I'll just bet it does. You know, in so many ways you're exactly as I expected you would be."

"And in others?"

"You couldn't be more different."

"That's the problem with expectations, Immy. They always let you down."

A phone rang and Amahle stood to go and fetch it.

"Never off the clock?"

"Apparently not."

CHAPTER TWENTY-FIVE

A mahle smiled at Imogen as she picked up the phone. "Hello."
"I warned you, bitch."

"How did you get this number?" She gripped hold of the side table and swallowed hard. There was noise in the background, but it sounded muffled and unclear as he breathed heavily into the mouthpiece.

"Not the question you should be asking."

"Then what is?"

"Who's that screaming behind me?"

Suddenly, her focus shifted. She blocked out the laughter that bubbled in her ears and zeroed in on the bloodcurdling, pain-filled scream in the background. "Who...who is that?"

"Someone you know."

She tried to listen behind his voice again. A sharp expulsion of air followed by a gut wrenching, hacking cough filtered through. "Please don't hurt him."

"You don't even know who it is?"

"It doesn't matter." Imogen crossed the room and placed her hands on her waist, her gaze filled with questions and a deep concern. As much as she wished she didn't need it, she sank into the comfort being offered and placed her hand over Imogen's. The only person she could think of it being was Dr. Marais. It made sense that it was him. He was her secret weapon, her informant, and the biggest danger to her enemies. Letting them know she knew would no doubt cause him more suffering so she decided to play along. "Whoever it is doesn't deserve to have you torture him." She closed her eyes and hoped that the doctor wasn't badly hurt. She reached out for a pad and searched for a pen, dragging open a drawer. Imogen seemed to figure out what she was looking for and quickly handed her what she needed.

"Maybe he does."

She scribbled across the pad, "Get Thambo, please." Imogen nodded and held her hands up in a questioning gesture. Amahle pointed to her phone. "No. If it truly was someone who deserved that, you wouldn't be on the phone to me while you did it. You said it's someone I know, and I don't know anyone who deserves to be hurt like that."

"Well, maybe he deserves it by association. Did you think about that, bitch?"

Imogen quickly placed the call and watched Amahle as she waited for him to answer. "Association with whom?" Amahle asked.

"You."

A loud thud sounded in the distance followed by the most harrowing scream yet. Indistinct words flowed into each other so quickly she couldn't make any of them out.

"Now, back off, kaffir bitch, or maybe I'll come visit you next." Then the laughter came again. "Oh, and, Minister, Thambo's just missing you to pieces."

"No!" she screamed down the line as it went dead in her hand.

"Amahle, sweetie, tell me what he said?" Imogen wrapped her in her arms as the tears slid down her cheeks and her knees gave way, dragging them both to the ground.

"Thambo," she cried.

"No answer. I left him a message."

"No, he can't come."

"Ami, he's your bodyguard, and you're being threatened. He needs to be here."

"No, you don't—"

"Amahle? What happened? What did he say?"

"He said Thambo's missing me to pieces."

Imogen put the phone on speaker and dialled Thambo's landline and waited for an answer.

"Hello?"

"Thambo?"

"No, he's not here."

"Who's this?"

"His brother. Sizewe."

"Do you know where he is? Amahle needs him and he's not answering his phone."

"He went to get food. About an hour ago now. He should have been back by now."

She heard banging on the other end of the line.

"Wait a minute. That's probably him now. Must have forgotten his keys."

She heard a soft bang as the handset was put down and a scream as a hinge creaked. Sizewe's cries and shouts for help in the distance turned Amahle's knees weak. She slid to the floor even as she heard Imogen dial an ambulance and search through Amahle's phone for Thambo's address. They could all hear Sizewe shouting that his hand was gone. That he couldn't stop the blood. That Thambo was bleeding to death.

She shook her head and managed to get enough air into her lungs to make her brain work for a few seconds. Just long enough to give them his address and find out which hospital he'd be taken too.

"I'll take you."

"You don't have to do that," Amahle whispered.

"What?"

"Take me to the hospital."

"I know. But I am."

"What if I don't want you to?"

"Tough."

"Imogen, I'm serious. I don't want you near me. I won't put anyone else in danger."

"I can take care of myself."

"That's what everyone says. Then it's three men, with guns to your head, taking turns, beating you, raping you." The hands that had been rubbing her back froze for a moment then the grip around her body tightened.

"Who did that to you?" She felt lips pressed against her hair. "I'll kill the bastards."

She pushed herself out of Imogen's arms. The fierce look of protective determination made her eyes shine. Her chest rose and fell as she saw clearly the effects of the adrenaline that coursed through Imogen's veins, and there was no doubt that she was ready to fight. *If only it were so simple.*

Amahle shook her head. "Not me." She ran her hand down Imogen's arm, feeling the tense muscles beneath the butter soft cotton shirt. She fought the urge to continue touching Imogen, just feeling something rather than living with the thoughts in her head, but there was simply too much she had to do. Too many responsibilities that she needed to deal with, and too many people who needed her. She couldn't give in to the feelings that threatened to spill out. Fear or anything else. It didn't matter when there was work to be done.

"I think you've got some explaining to do, Ami." Imogen rose gracefully to her feet and held her hand out to help her up. "And since I'm taking you to the hospital and then I'm not going anywhere, we've got plenty of time."

"I don't want to."

"And I don't want you to be in danger, but you most definitely are. So that makes us even."

"Your reasoning defies logic. You know that, don't you?"

"Not getting you out of this."

Amahle sighed. She didn't have time for delays to go over old ground. She didn't have time to rake over the past and discuss her feelings. She had a shrink for that shit. She didn't need another one, but the stubborn set to Imogen's jaw told her that she would be in for a long fight to get her own way here, and time was not a luxury she had. "Fine." She walked toward the sliding glass door. "If we're doing this we're doing it while you drive."

"Fine."

"And I don't want any interruptions."

"Grrr. Fine," Imogen agreed, somewhat reluctantly. "Where do you want me to start?"

"Three men with guns at your head."

"Starting off easy?" Amahle climbed into the car and fastened her seat belt.

"I thought I'd break you in gently."

"Gee, thanks."

"Welcome." She waited for the automatic gate to open and eased out of the drive. She waited until it was closed and no one had entered behind them before setting off.

"You already know about my work with the HIV treatment programme."

"Yes."

"Well, when we first started working on it, it wasn't very popular with the ANC leadership. In fact, it was in outright opposition to the leadership of the time, Thambo Mbeki. His cabinet stated and maintained that HIV did not, could not, progress into AIDS. He said that a virus could not cause a syndrome."

"The man was a fool."

"You're not the first to say that, but he was the president at the time, and his policies were what we had to deal with. By standing with a few, and I do mean a very few, of my colleagues in defiance of this policy we were risking our political careers within the ANC party."

"Did you think about switching parties?"

"At one point, yes. The IFB set out its manifesto on the basis of providing HIV and AIDS medication to those infected and antiretroviral drugs to any victim of rape."

"Why didn't you?"

"They have no realistic chance of gaining power and this was something that needed to change. Fast. HIV is at epidemic proportions here. We need this treatment programme."

"So you chose to fight from within to effect the change you needed to see."

"Exactly."

"Just like Mandela said."

She smiled. "I suppose so."

"So what happened?"

"We all began to receive threats."

"All?"

"All of us who were campaigning for the programme. Letters at first. Then phone calls. One of my colleagues was beaten. His back was broken when he tried to crawl away from his attackers."

"Christ."

"It was pretty nasty shit."

"What did they do to you?"

"One night they broke into our home."

"Our?"

She nodded. "Grace and I had been living together for about ten years by that time." Her throat closed up, and she took a long moment before she could continue. "She was a lawyer, one of the ones we consulted with about the campaign, actually. She knew everything that was going on, and she said it would all be fine. That we could handle the threats, and the letters, and the disgusting phone calls." She rested her head back against the chair. "When they broke in they hit me over the head with the butt of a gun. Knocked me out. When I came to they'd tied me up in the living room. My arms were tied behind my back, wrists to ankles. One man kept dragging me around the room like that, until my shoulder dislocated. Then they just made me watch."

Imogen pulled into a parking space but didn't say anything. She didn't move or turn off the engine. She just waited for Amahle to finish.

"They took turns with Grace. One after the other."

"I'm so sorry."

"One man painted the walls with her blood. He left me a message." She laughed. "He left us all a message. 'Back off, kaffir bitch.'"

"What happened to Grace?"

"She left me." She turned to look at Imogen, and her breath caught at the look of compassion in her eyes. "I can't blame her. After that happened, I should have put her first. I should have spent more time with her."

"You didn't?"

She shook her head. "I became so driven that they had to either give me the programme or shut me up. Permanently."

"But you didn't care at that point."

"No, I didn't. I'd lost Grace. I was going to get something out of the whole fucking nightmare even if it did kill me." She chuckled. "At that point I had nothing left to lose."

"What about the rest of your family? Your mother, Sipho. They could have gone after them."

"And make martyrs of them? They couldn't risk it. They would have only given me more ammunition."

"That explains why these calls are affecting you so much, but why are you getting them?"

"Because they want me to back off, again."

"Back off what?"

She released her seat belt. "Not until we know how Thambo is. This is going to take a while."

CHAPTER TWENTY-SIX

Sipho hung his head out of the car door and emptied the contents of his stomach by the side of the road. He accepted that he had only to do as he was told, and that it was none of his business why Tsotsi had wanted that man mutilated. But the fact that he knew him had only added to the nausea. He'd never much liked the man. Thambo Umpala had always been more than a little too serious for his liking, but he was a good man. He'd worked for his sister for a long time. They'd shared many a meal together. Watching Tsotsi shoot Thambo in the back with a Taser when he got out of his car seemed to happen in slow motion. Part of him wished he'd known where they were during the hours they had lain in wait for him. Oscillating between boredom and fear as the three of them had hidden in the bushes beside Thambo's drive, he wished he'd known what was going to happen, that he could have sent him some sort of message to warn him. He might not have liked Thambo, but he didn't deserve what had happened tonight.

The blitz attack was over before he could get over the effects of the Taser. Sipho had dragged him into the bushes while his body still convulsed. Beating on him had felt like a betrayal of Amahle. Holding him, watching everything else that had happened. No. Being accomplice to everything else that happened. He retched again.

"Don't get any of that shit in my car, man." Tsotsi sucked his lip through his teeth and drummed his fingers on the steering wheel. "Fucking pussy."

The third man in the rear seat laughed and rubbed his pangas over the dirty denim on his thigh. The broad, heavy knife was covered in blood. "Pussy."

"You said we were just going to rough him up a bit. That's all," Sipho cried before vomiting again. "What if you killed him?"

"We didn't kill him," Tsotsi said. "Did we, Professor?"

"No, no, he's not dead."

Sipho glanced over his shoulder at the man sitting in the back. Professor was obviously a derogatory nickname that the poor wretch was too stupid to even realize he'd earned. He grinned at Sipho.

"Wanna see it again?"

"No. Fuck no. I don't know why you fucking kept it, you twisted bastard."

The Professor frowned. "My uncle lost his hand in the mines. He's always saying he misses it." He grinned broadly. "It's his birthday tomorrow." He held up the newly acquired appendage and scratched his head with it. Tsotsi laughed, and Sipho threw up again.

"Not in my fucking car, man." He pushed Sipho further out the door. "Fuck."

Sipho wiped his mouth with the face mask Tsotsi had insisted they all wear. He'd done what he could to staunch the flow of blood coming from Thambo's wrist, but he'd continually tried to push him away. Not that Sipho could blame him. The Professor was wandering around holding his hand like it was his fucking girlfriend's. He was just glad that he'd been told to leave him on his own doorstep and that someone was home. He wasn't sure how he'd manage to call help for the man otherwise. But he knew he'd have had to try.

"It's done."

Sipho turned his head just enough to see Tsotsi talking on his phone.

"Not fatal, no. But I think the message was received."

Sipho hung his head between his knees and tried to make the world stop spinning. Message? Who the hell were they supposed to be sending a message to? What was Thambo involved with? Who was he involved with that could warrant this kind of message? Sipho shook his head and tried to dislodge the idea that his sister was the intended recipient of Tsotsi's message. That was just too much for him to contemplate.

"Send me the address and we'll take care of it, man." Tsotsi laughed. "Have I ever let you down? Just send me the address and what you need. We'll get it done. When do I get the next shipment? I have customers waiting on the product, man." He waited, obviously listening to whoever was on the other end, before clicking his tongue and ringing off.

"Well, pussy, looks like you're along for the ride some more. Till this job's done, no more *medicine* for you. No more for anyone." He slapped Sipho on the back. "Get in the car. We've got plans to make, pussy."

Every time he hit what he thought was as low as he could go, Tsotsi opened up a new level of hell for him to sink into.

Where will it end?

CHAPTER TWENTY-SEVEN

Imogen poured coffee into a mug and stared out across the ocean. The deep indigo of the Atlantic breaking against the golden sands and the powdery blue sky broken by soft clouds looked so perfect it was difficult for her to comprehend that everything was far from fine. But it wasn't. She'd slept poorly, tossing and turning once they returned from the hospital. Thambo had been badly beaten, but his body would recover. His hand, however, had not been with his body when his brother had opened the door. The surgeons had nothing to reattach so the wound was closed as a stump to save his life. She stared at her own hand as she held her cup. How would she feel, waking up without her hand? She tried to calculate the innumerable ways her life would be affected. From something as simple as holding her coffee cup, to making coffee in the first place. She didn't want to think about it anymore. It was too horrific for her to get her mind around. Instead she focused on something she could do something about.

All night, she'd kept going over everything Amahle had told her. Every word had made her more determined to protect her. She couldn't put her finger on why, so she decided not to even think about it. It was simply what she had to do. In the light of everything Amahle had told her, it was the right thing to do. Amahle was trying to help save lives. She should and must, as a decent human being, do all she could to help her for no other reason than it was the right thing to do. Was it really as simple as that? Could she really keep it all separate in her head? The paternity issues, the question of the missing money, her father's relationship with Amahle's mother. Could she just ignore it all in the face of Amahle's need? Keep it professional. After all, it wasn't just Amahle's need. It was the plight of a lot of fucking people. *What did she say, about three million of 'em?*

So that's it. Ignore all the personal shit and focus on the parts that are important. Anyway, I don't do personal. Hell, I don't usually do breakfast. She stared at the coffee cup in her hand. *Yet here I am, sipping coffee and trying to decide on the best way to keep her safe no matter how difficult I know she's going to make it.*

The coffee had gone cold, but she drank the bitter brew trying to decide what to do next. She had few contacts here, but the ones she had, she trusted. She wasn't sure she could say the same of the countless contacts she was certain Amahle could call upon. She pulled her phone from her pocket and dialled.

"Good morning, how's the shopping going?"

She smiled. "Not bad, Roland. I have an appropriate frock."

He laughed a deep belly laugh that helped her focus on something beyond the darkness that was gaining a hold of her current situation. "I look forward to the unveiling. Now, I'm sure you didn't call to chitchat about frocks and the like, and I don't have the results of the investigation for you yet, so how can I help you today, Imogen?"

"I need some advice, and I need your utmost discretion."

"Advice about what? And I'll pretend I didn't hear you insult me."

"Thank you. I need a private security firm."

"Why? Is someone threatening you? I told you not to go out alone after dark."

"Not me. I need it for a friend."

"A friend? I thought I was your only friend."

"Almost." She heard the rattle of keys as he tapped away at his keyboard.

"Okay, I've got you something. I think you'll like it. Want me to email this to you?"

"Please."

"Done. Anything else?"

"Yeah. Actually, there is. I need two things." She quickly outlined what she wanted from him and thanked him for his help before hanging up.

She smiled. If he could find what she'd asked for, they'd have options. Perhaps not great ones, but choices nonetheless. She scrolled through her emails and sent one to the company Roland had recommended.

She wandered back inside and began pulling open cupboards looking for food. She managed to find some croissants in the larder and put them in the oven to warm while she carried butter, jam, and honey back outside.

"Ransacking the kitchen?" Amahle said.

"Shit." She put her hand to her chest. "Don't sneak up on me like that. My heart can't take it anymore."

Amahle laughed. "It never could. And I wasn't sneaking."

"No, just approaching silently."

"Exactly."

Imogen led them back outside with the plate of warm croissants in one hand and a carton of orange juice in the other.

"Making yourself at home, I see."

"Well, my host decided to spend the morning in bed."

"It's only just eight o'clock."

"And some of us have been awake for hours already."

"Well, some of us should learn to stay in bed."

"I haven't changed that much." She winked as she repeated Amahle's words back at her.

Amahle rolled her eyes and poured coffee into their cups. "I need to get going soon. I need to get in touch with the hospital."

"I called them already." She glanced at her watch. "About thirty minutes ago."

"And?"

"No change."

Amahle's face lost what little was left of its vibrancy, and the dark tone of her skin looked flat, almost lifeless, as the blood rushed away from her face. Perspiration beaded on her forehead, giving it an unnatural waxy pallor that Imogen had seen on Amahle's face once before. She knelt at her side and turned her face toward her.

"Look at me, Ami. This wasn't your fault. Stay with me." She patted her cheek gently and decided to tap into one of the traits that had often gotten them into trouble as kids. The competitive streak they both had. "Come on, don't let it beat you."

The effect was instantaneous. Amahle's eyes focused on her face with laser sharp intensity, and some of the gray undertone that had tinged her skin began to recede.

"That's more like it. Now, we need to talk about what we do next."

"We? There is no we."

"Don't be stubborn, Amahle. This isn't the time."

"I'm not being stubborn." She shook her head. "Okay, maybe I am, but this is for your protection."

"I don't need protection."

"Anyone in my life needs protection."

"I don't believe that. Thambo's attack wasn't random."

"No. They targeted him because he knows about the investigation. So do you. I shouldn't have told you about it last night. You need to forget—"

"You're wrong. He was targeted for several reasons, and all of them very, very smart. Firstly, because he knows what's going on. Secondly, because you know him and his torture was bound to have an effect on you. Thirdly, because he's an inconsequential player in the larger game, unlike you or Dr. Marais. His attack would not really draw the attention of anyone outside of those in the know. You and the doctor are much higher profile targets. But most importantly, he was attacked to eliminate your protection and make you vulnerable. Do I need to spell out what that could mean?"

"You think this was a precursor to an attack on me?"

"I'm not willing to take the chance that it isn't."

"All the more reason for you to stay away from me."

"I really can take care of myself. And you."

Amahle shook her head. "We talked about this last night."

"I'm not Grace."

Amahle's eyes instantly blazed with fury. "Get the fuck away from me." She shucked her arms away from Imogen's touch and pushed herself away from the table. "Don't you dare."

"I'm sorry. I shouldn't have said that."

"No, you shouldn't. She didn't deserve what happened to her."

"No one does."

"I couldn't protect her."

"And I'm not asking you to protect me. I'm asking you to let me help you. There's a difference, Ami." She sat back on her heels. "I have an idea, if you'll let me explain."

Amahle crossed arms over her chest, her mouth set in a tight line, her eyes bored holes through Imogen, and Imogen had never felt such a strong desire to kiss anyone as she did right then.

"Well, what's this plan of yours?"

"I…" She shook her head trying to dislodge the image, but it was still there. She started to reach for Amahle, and her hands were half way to Amahle's shoulders before she realized what she was doing. She tried to hide her true intentions by gripping the arms of Amahle's chair and pulling herself up. She felt disoriented and unsteady on her feet as she reclaimed her own seat. "I've got a friend of mine looking into a couple of things for me." She ran her hand through her hair. "I've also contacted a private security firm and set up an appointment. They should be here in about an hour."

"What? I don't want other people protecting me."

"You need to be protected."

"I have protection."

"No, Ami, you *had* protection." She could see Amahle fighting it. She could understand the desire to deny the danger she was in. Hell, she wouldn't want to admit it in Amahle's place. She wouldn't want to accept strangers into her life and literally ask them to stand in harm's way for her. She actually couldn't think of much she'd hate more. And everything she saw of Amahle, everything she'd learned so far, told her that Amahle probably hated it far more than she could comprehend. Imogen hoped she never would, because she had a feeling that she'd have to have witnessed everything Amahle had to fully appreciate it. But she could also see something else flitter across Amahle's face. Resignation.

"Fine."

"If you don't like these people, we'll find something else, but I figured that people on the payroll will be more likely to be out of the government's control than the police or security services at this point."

"Which company?"

"Castle. British company set up by a former SAS guy by the name of Chris Castle."

"British company?"

"Yes. Operating internationally, obviously, but I felt comfortable that they weren't...I mean that they were from..."

"That they wouldn't have any ties to South Africa that could influence the protection they would offer?"

Imogen nodded, hoping she hadn't offended Amahle and undone some of the headway she felt they'd made.

"They may still be working with locals."

"It was part of my brief that only non-nationals would be part of your protection team."

"They agreed to that?"

"They did."

Amahle chuckled. "So much for equal opportunities."

Imogen laughed, relieved that Amahle didn't seem upset by her insinuations. "I think they have more than enough work that this request hasn't cost anyone a job."

"Hmm. Anything else?"

"Well, erm, yes, actually."

She glanced at her watch. "We don't have all day, Imogen."

"I've got my friend trying to locate two names for me."

"Who's the friend and what names?"

"Roland De Fries. He's a forensic accountant with Jim Davitson's company."

"How do you know him?"

"That's another story. Let's stick with this one, shall we?"

"Fine. What's he looking for?"

"I've asked him to find me the name of a police officer who has an untarnished record and reputation. Discreetly."

Amahle shook her head. "No. No police."

"You need to find somewhere that you can take this information, or all these people have to do is pick you off and carry on doing what they're doing."

"The police are corrupt."

"Not all of them surely."

"We wouldn't know. They had the anti-corruption unit shut down in 2001 and have had enough power and influence to keep it closed ever since. Despite growing demands from the public to reinstate it, and a colossal number of corruption complaints. The ones who aren't probably won't be able to do enough with the information before it gets buried from the top by those who are."

"Okay, you know more about it than I do. So that brings me to point number two. Getting the information out there so fast and on such a broad scale that they can't pull it back in."

"How?"

"I have Roland looking for a journalist for me."

"Go to the press?" Amahle drummed her fingers on her coffee cup, her irritation showing in the set of her jaw, and the way her shoulders inched closer to her ears.

"Yes."

"You really are trying to get me killed, aren't you?"

"No."

"You waltz back in here after thirty-odd years and you think you can save the day. You were always like that. Grow up." She put her cup back on the table with enough force to slosh the contents over the side. "This is Africa, not some little courtroom drama you play at with your lawyer friends and then go back home to your nice comfortable life. You don't know how things work here. You don't know—"

"Christ, I'm trying to save your life without compromising everything I believe you stand for. I'm trying to help you do the right thing here. Don't I get a little credit for that?"

"Sure. We can get it engraved on our headstones. Here lies Amahle Nkosi, died of Imogen trying to do the right thing." She smiled sourly. "Catchy, don't you think?"

Imogen took a deep breath and managed to bite back the retort that settled on her tongue. She knew Amahle wasn't going to make it easy. She wouldn't have if their places had been reversed. "Then what's your master plan, huh? How do you propose we sort out this fucking mess?"

Amahle laughed. It was a sound that rang bitterly in Imogen's ears. "I haven't got a fucking clue. And all the while I'm trying to figure out this mess they're at least twenty steps ahead of me. I don't know who I can trust. My political friends may be the ones running this racket. My political foes have everything to gain by leaking the scandal in a way that would destroy the programme and what little trust the people still have in the government."

"Surely that's a bit strong."

"No, it really isn't. This could shake the foundations of the democracy we have been building for the past twenty years."

"Then isn't it worth a try?" She reached across the table and gripped Amahle's hand. "If, as you say, the democracy of South Africa is at stake here, what the hell have we got to lose?"

The buzz of the gate broke the tension.

"It doesn't look like I have much choice." Amahle picked up the handset and released the gate when she heard the security company had arrived. Three men and a woman climbed out of the 4x4, sunglasses covering their eyes as they scanned the perimeter. Laura, Josh, Nick, and Greg introduced themselves before taking seats around the deck.

"Stunning view, ma'am," Laura said, an American accent firmly placing her in the non-nationals category, exactly as requested.

"Thank you," Amahle said. "I like it."

"We've been sent here to assess threat levels and ascertain your needs. Then work out the best way for us to meet those needs. Not for me, thanks." Laura held her hand up to ward off the coffee pot as

Imogen poured cups for them all. "Why don't you fill us in on what's going on?"

"I've been receiving threatening phone calls."

They exchanged looks between them, clearly waiting for her to continue. Imogen sighed when Amahle clammed up.

"Last night she received a call and they were torturing someone in the background," Imogen said. "As he hung up he said that Thambo was missing her to pieces. At the time we didn't know what that meant."

"You do now?" Josh asked, his clipped British tones marking his public schoolboy roots, and Imogen was reminded of her friend Simon. She immediately felt comfortable in his presence. He felt familiar and safe, even if he did remind her of her lonely life back in Cambridge.

"Unfortunately. Thambo is Amahle's usual bodyguard. The man they were torturing and who is now in hospital missing his hand."

"Do you know who is threatening you?" Laura asked.

"Not specifically, no," Amahle said. "There are a number of possibilities."

"Are the police investigating the phone calls?" Greg asked.

"No. I haven't reported them."

"Why not?"

"In my experience, it is neither productive nor pleasurable. I refuse to waste my time in such a manner."

Greg frowned. "I'm sorry. I don't understand."

"The last time I had cause to report something to them, they wrote off the brutal gang rape of my partner while I was forced to watch as corrective rape. They refused to believe that it was a political warning aimed at me, despite them having written it on the wall. In her blood." Amahle pushed herself away from the table and slammed the patio door closed behind herself.

The tension around the table was thick, and Imogen wasn't sure if she should follow her or stay where she was.

Laura cleared her throat. "I'm very sorry to hear what happened to you."

Imogen turned to look at her. "I'm sorry, what?"

"I said, I'm very sorry that happened to you." She looked uncomfortable and clearly wanted to move on from the subject.

"It wasn't me. I'm not her girlfriend."

"Oh. My apologies. I assumed..." She shook her head. "I made a rookie error, Ms. Frost. I made the assumption that you being here at this hour in the morning meant something it clearly doesn't. Please accept my apology."

"Not necessary." She waved her hand. "I'm not offended." Far from it. Something inside her was smiling at the thought. "The police are investigating Thambo's attack, but she didn't tell them about the earlier call."

"Just the one?"

"To my knowledge. There may have been more that she hasn't told me about."

"Why didn't she mention the other call or calls to the police?"

"It really is as simple as trust. She has none in them, so she refused to take the time."

"Very well. Perhaps you can give us more details while we wait for Ms. Nkosi."

"Sure. I'll tell you what I can." They spent the next twenty minutes going over every detail that Imogen could remember of the phone calls, which phones they had rung, what specific words they used, and what they were attempting to get Amahle to back off from. Imogen kept the details of the fake pills particularly vague, but told them clearly that Amahle was working on a politically sensitive issue that would have far-reaching repercussions. The glances that passed between them told her that she had been as obtuse as possible.

"I'm sorry about that. Where are we up to?" Amahle stepped back through the glass and smiled as she sat down.

"I need to tap your phone lines, Ms. Nkosi," Josh said. "So that we can try to trace the calls that you're receiving."

"I don't want my calls recorded."

"We won't record anything unless you indicate it's him. Without the tap and trace, we won't be able to locate this man, or eliminate him as a threat."

"Eliminate him? What does that mean?"

"Hand him over to the authorities with sufficient evidence that they have no choice but to imprison him."

Amahle pressed her thumb and forefinger into the bridge of her nose. "Fine."

"I'll also need to take a look at your current security system."

"Fine. The controls are in the safe room."

His eyes lit up. "You have a safe room?"

"Yes. In the basement." Josh was up and headed indoors with Greg and Nick in tow.

"Boys." Laura scoffed. "Do I take this to mean we have the contract?"

"Yes. On one condition."

"Which is?"

"Confidentiality. The work I do is sensitive, official, and I will not have people around me who do not respect that."

"You have my personal guarantee."

"Fine. Have your office send the contract over for me to sign. I just want to feel safe again. I want to be able to do my work and not have to worry what I'll hear every time I pick up the damn phone."

"We'll take care of that. I'll need a copy of your schedule to begin coordinating your protection."

"My secretary, Claudia, can get you a copy." She gave her the number and looked at Imogen. "Do you make everything happen this quickly?"

"When I have to."

CHAPTER TWENTY-EIGHT

Derek Marais opened document after document and read each one quickly before discarding it and moving on to the next. He still wasn't sure what he was looking for specifically, but he knew there had to be something, somewhere, that would give him a clue as to who was in charge of this deception. He had electronic copies of every file and document related to the HIV programme from Amahle's office. There had to be something in there.

His computer pinged when the latest set of test results completed. Yet another hospital with fake drugs. He entered the data into his spreadsheets. Twenty hospitals, so far. Twenty of the largest hospitals in South Africa prescribing and supplying medication that simply wasn't fit for purpose. He knew of six more major hospitals that PharmaChem supplied, but he had yet to get any samples from them to test. He was sure he knew the outcome already, but empirical data was all that would convince the authorities to do anything about it.

He clicked on the webcam in his laptop and pressed record.

"This is Dr. Derek Marais. This is the fourth week of my investigation into the Combivirine being supplied by PharmaChem. My research so far has been illuminating as in how widespread the supply has become, and how unscrupulous these people are in their distribution. No public funded hospital is receiving genuine medication, while every private hospital and clinic I've had the opportunity to test has shown genuine product. The medications look identical, but the chemical analysis is clear. I've taken steps to safeguard my evidentiary samples and test results. Following the attack on Minister Nkosi's bodyguard and the break-in to my office, I have reason to believe I will be targeted. And probably sooner rather than later.

"At the hospital we frequently have cause to carry out forensic medical examinations, then record, safeguard, and store the evidence until it is collected by the authorities. I have followed the same procedures to record and preserve the evidence of my investigation too. I have entered the evidence into the safe storage area we have at the hospital also. The information to access it all is in file PCEV0615.doc stored in a Dropbox account. In the event that anything happens to me, the relevant people will be informed of this account and granted access to all the evidence I have collected so far. I am wary of putting too much into cyberspace, as I do not know enough to protect it very well from hackers.

"Minister Nkosi has been immensely helpful and steadfast in her assistance in this matter. The documentation she has provided will help me isolate who is in charge of this operation. Of that I have no doubt. My only concern is the amount of time it will take to go through the mountains of paperwork. Times like this I wish I had a research team to help me search, but that isn't possible. Firstly, I wouldn't know who to trust with the information, and secondly, I am loath to expose anyone else to the risks involved. The minister's bodyguard was a trained professional and they managed to hack off his hand. There will be increased guards with my family from now on. Every time they leave the house, there will be someone with them.

"The house is pretty well protected, I think. Besides the razor wire and the dogs, there's also an alarm that will call the police if the circuit is broken without the code being inputted within twenty seconds. My wife doesn't want strangers in the house upsetting our daughter, so at this point I've decided not to authorise the security personnel that Minister Nkosi had contact me. I'm uneasy about the decision, but have agreed to abide by it for now. If anything else happens though, I'm sure we'll reassess that decision. I considered asking the police to increase their patrols past the house, but I don't have any way to justify the request without explaining what's going on, and I wouldn't even know who to trust with the information. For now, it looks like I must load my gun and sleep with it under my pillow.

"In the meantime, I've been looking at the records of who authorizes the suppliers' contracts from each of the hospitals who have the fake tablets to see if I can find any common thread there. So far I don't see one. The people in the hospitals who are signing and countersigning the contracts are all different, and there are no obvious connections. No universities or schools in common, that sort of thing. There may be deeper connections that I'm not able to uncover, but I don't think so. My feeling is that the hospitals are acting in good faith. I think this goes higher than that. I'm going to start looking at PharmaChem now. As much as I can anyway. There seem to be a limited number of documents for me to go through on this, which surprised me given the nature of their business and their connection with the Department of Health. Minster Nkosi's secretary, Claudia, is looking around for anything else for me. Upcoming drug trials, medications awaiting approval, and so on. I have a few of those documents, as I said. But given the number of samples I was offered by Mrs. De Fries, there should be considerably more.

"Each one should have been granted approval for use by the South African FDA after the conclusion of clinical trials. I would expect some evidence of those to be with the Department of Health. Somewhere." He ran his hand over his head and combed his fingers through his hair. "They have to be there. The company simply couldn't legally operate without them." He chuckled. "Not that what they're doing is legal anyway." He shook his head. "I'll report any significant finding straight away, as per usual, if not, same time tomorrow."

He stopped the recording and stretched his arms over his head, smiling at the satisfying crack when his spine slipped back into alignment. He opened another file and settled down to another night in front of the screen.

CHAPTER TWENTY-NINE

I can't believe I let her talk me into this. It's a ridiculous idea." Amahle adjusted the neckline of the deep green dress, the plunging bodice exposing more of her cleavage than she was used to. "Why do I keep letting her talk me into things?" She smoothed her hand over her stomach and eased a wrinkle down to the flare over her hips, where the fabric draped to the ground. "Never mind. I don't want to think about it."

They'd agreed to go to the ball from Amahle's place and then stay at the vineyard afterward rather than drive the hour back to Bantry Bay. They'd agreed it made sense, and as Josh, Laura, Nick, and Greg were with them, Amahle would be safe. What she didn't understand was why Imogen had insisted upon staying with her for the past two days, and that Amahle attend the ball with her. But what was even harder for her to get her head around was why she'd let her. She hated people in her home. She hated people in her personal space, her personal life. She hated people putting themselves in harm's way for her. Imogen walked in and instantly she was surrounded by people constantly. Every moment of her life, whether awake or asleep, someone was watching out for her safety. In her house and her life. So why hadn't she stopped it? Why hadn't she told them all to leave? Why hadn't she felt like she was crawling out of her skin when they were all in her house?

That's what she'd expected. That's what she'd gotten used to over the past eight years. Feeling like she'd been invaded when one person had entered her space. But not right now. Was it because the threat was real now that their presence easier to bear? Or was it just because it was Immy? She sighed. She didn't know, and the questions were driving her insane. Whatever it was that made her comfortable enough to keep moving forward, given everything that was going on, surely that was a good thing. Right?

She checked her makeup in the mirror before switching off the light and making her way downstairs.

"Where's Imogen?" she asked Laura.

"In the guest room. Want me to go and hurry her up?"

"I'm ready," Imogen said from the top of the stairs. She grasped the royal blue fabric in one hand and lifted the hem to avoid tripping on the long length as she walked—no, floated—down the stairs. Her hair was a crown of glistening golden curls. Thin spaghetti straps crisscrossed her shoulders and held the heart-shaped bodice in place. "Are you okay?" She placed a hand on Amahle's upper arm. "You look a little shaky."

She blinked. "I'm fine. Just a little warm." She took a step back from Imogen, desperately in need of a little space. "Shall we get going?"

Imogen extended her arm toward the door. "After you. You look lovely, by the way. That colour really suits you."

"Thanks. You too."

Greg pulled open the door for her.

"So why are we really going to this ball tonight?"

"What do you mean?"

"You always seem to have a reason, Immy, or should I say a list of reasons. So, why are we really going tonight?"

Imogen wagged her finger at her. "Can't it just be to get you out of the house and let you forget for the evening?"

"That may be one reason. But I'm sure you have more. You're a strategist. Mapping out the moves. I'm sure it makes you very successful in court."

"Sometimes."

Amahle arched her eyebrow suspiciously.

"Okay, a lot of times it does."

"So, tell me your strategy for tonight." As much as she hated to admit it, she loved learning how Imogen's mind worked. She was so different from anyone she'd known before.

"I hate that you can read me so easily."

"Yeah, yeah. You're an open book. Now read me a story before I get bored."

"I want to connect with Roland and see if he has the information I requested."

"And?"

"And I want to check in with Jim Davitson. He's been leaving messages for me, but we keep missing each other."

"And?"

"And I think it's a good idea that you're seen doing everything you normally do."

"Why?"

"So they know they aren't winning. Keeping these people scared will stop them from going to ground. They have to keep putting pressure on you or they run the risk of you outmanoeuvring them."

"Upping the pressure on them means they will up the ante with me. That means more people getting hurt."

"We have protection in place now on all the major players. It's a calculated risk."

Amahle wasn't sure they could ever be secure in the protections they had established, especially as Thambo was a highly trained professional and still fell foul to these people, but at this stage she couldn't fault the logic either. She was almost certain that it was her fear that made her question their security rather than an actual weakness in their defences so she chose to ignore the niggling feeling in her gut.

"What else?"

"There may be contacts there for me to make in regard to the vineyard."

"Buyers?"

"Maybe."

Amahle exhaled and tried not to let it get to her. She didn't want to think about Imogen returning to England. To life after Immy. Again.

"Anything else?"

"I want the people moving against you to see you're far from being unprotected. That to get to you they are going to have to go through walls."

"Damn straight," Laura said. "Sorry. Didn't mean to butt in."

Imogen smiled. "No problem. See? Big, burly walls of protection."

"Big, burly walls of people who can get hurt too."

"Ma'am, with the greatest respect, three tours in Afghanistan and one in Iraq couldn't hurt me. Some dude with a machete isn't going to get close." Laura grinned and touched her finger to her forehead. "We fight smart, and we don't take prisoners."

Amahle wasn't sure if that made her feel better or not, but it certainly did make her feel sure that someone, somewhere down the line was going to get hurt. She looked at Imogen. *Please don't let it be someone in this car.*

The rest of the journey passed by quickly. Small talk and banter filled the cab, and it was easy to see how close a team they were. They knew each other and their jobs, and they fitted together like a well-oiled machine. She was glad Imogen had insisted upon bringing them in. She just wished Imogen would take herself out of the equation rather than continually throwing herself into the middle of it all.

The town hall in Stellenbosch had been adorned in all its finery as every prominent official in the Western Cape walked up the steps and into the ballroom. Tuxedos abounded and every colour of ball gown caught Amahle's eye as she walked toward the security checkpoint with Imogen at her side. It wasn't until she was waved through the x-ray machine and she had to let go of Imogen's arm that she realized she had taken hold of her elbow as they walked. The need to touch her was unconscious but overwhelming.

"How did you manage to score these tickets again?" Amahle asked.

"Jim Davitson invited me."

"A-huh. Why?" She remembered him from the funeral where he'd been direct, professional, and courteous toward her. Even after her mother's revelations.

"I presume he has a buyer lined up for Frost Vineyard and wants to introduce me."

"Do you trust him?"

"Who? Jim?"

"Yes."

"As much as I trust any lawyer."

Amahle laughed. "And that means?"

"Lawyers are all out for what they can get." She swiped two glasses of champagne from a passing waiter and handed one to Amahle. "Didn't you know that?"

"Must have missed that news bulletin. I know some very ethical lawyers."

"Do you?"

Amahle looked her straight in the eye. "Yes, I do."

Imogen inclined her glass in acknowledgement of the compliment then took a sip.

"Do you see your friend yet?"

She grinned. "He's over at the buffet."

Amahle turned and watched the tall man wave at them, hitch up his pants, and start toward them.

"Imogen, how's it?"

"Good, Roland, good. You?"

"Can't complain, you know."

"This is my friend, Amahle. Amahle, Roland De Fries."

"A pleasure." He wiped his hand on his pants before offering it to her.

She shook his damp palm gingerly. "It's a pleasure to meet you too, Roland."

"Listen, Imogen, I'm glad you could make it. There're a couple of people I'd like to introduce you to. Let me go get my wife, and see if I can find 'em. She's been so excited to meet you. Wait here, okay?"

"Okay." Imogen smiled at him as he walked away.

"How do you know him again?"

"He's a forensic accountant with Jim's firm."

"Did that answer the question?"

"Yes."

"Then why am I still confused?"

Imogen shrugged. "Slowing down in your old age, Minister?"

Amahle slapped her arm. "You're three months older than I am."

She rubbed her arm. "Yeah, but I'm not confused or slowing down."

"How do you know him?"

"Jim said it was standard practice to complete a financial report when an estate of this size was passed on to a new owner. Roland was the guy who compiled the report. He was also the guy who picked me up from the airport. He's nice. He's harmless."

She could see Imogen was hiding something from her. Her eyes darted to the left as she looked around, probably for some way to distract her. "You're lying."

"What?"

The look of shock on her face clearly told Amahle she wasn't. She might not be telling everything, but she wasn't lying.

"I am not. I wouldn't do that."

"Then what aren't you telling me?"

"Things that I don't have the answers to, and don't want to cause problems between us if there's no need for them to."

Amahle tried to make sense of what she'd said, but she couldn't.

There were too many missing parts for her. "Could you be any more cryptic?"

"Probably not." She ran her hand over the back of her head. "I promise as soon as I know anything for sure, I will tell you all about it. But until then, can you give me the benefit of the doubt, please? That's what I'm trying to do for someone else at this point."

"When will you know?"

"I'll ask Roland when he comes back. While you're here. How's that?"

Amahle narrowed her eyes and replayed Imogen's words in her mind. Several things stood out, mostly the giving the benefit of the doubt to someone, not wanting it to cause problems between them if it didn't have to, and the only things that could do that were her mother or her brother. She sighed. "More generous than I'd probably be."

Imogen laughed. "I doubt that."

"This is my wife, Beth," Roland said from over Amahle's shoulder. "Beth, this is Imogen Frost and Amahle. I'm sorry I didn't get your family name."

"Nkosi. A pleasure to meet you, Beth." She shook Beth's hand and noted the worried look on Roland's face. "What's that about?" She pointed at his frown. "Why so serious all of a sudden?"

"Erm, I…nothing. No reason."

"Roland, I was telling Amahle that you'd have completed your investigation into the financial situation of the vineyard pretty soon. Do you have a closer approximation for me yet?"

His eyes widened further. "I'm afraid I had to apply for that court order that we'd discussed so it will be several more days before I can complete my findings and show you the evidence. Tuesday or Wednesday probably."

"Can you share anything with me so far that is indisputable?"

"Nothing more than I have already shared with you. That there is evidence to prove that money is missing."

The realization of what Imogen suspected hit her. She knew with absolute certainty who Imogen and Roland suspected of stealing from the company. *She's trying to give him the benefit of the doubt.* Given what her mother and brother were claiming against Imogen, she doubted she would be so diligent in her pursuit of the truth. *And still she's here with me. Helping me. Protecting me.*

Imogen leaned close to her ear and whispered, "You aren't your family, Ami."

"How did you know what I was thinking?"

"You're an open book." She winked and took the empty glass from Amahle's hand and deposited it on the tray of a passing waiter. "Beth, I've got to thank you for those delicious koeksisters the other day. They were amazing."

"I'm glad you liked them. They're Roland's favourites," Beth said.

"I can understand why that is. Are you a chef or something?"

Beth laughed. "No, not at all."

"Beth works as a sales representative for a pharmaceutical company." Roland smiled proudly at her. "She's their top seller. May as well be the only one they have on staff. Isn't that right, darling?"

Beth smiled tightly. "Might as well be."

Amahle noticed the tense set to Beth's shoulders and wondered what Roland had said wrong; her demeanour was so different from the last time Amahle had seen her. The bored young woman at Alain's funeral was most definitely missing tonight. "We're in the same industry then, Mrs. De Fries. Do you have to travel or are you based in Cape Town?"

"Oh, call me Beth, please. I get to go all over the place really. Anywhere the company thinks I can make a deal for them."

"They must value you a great deal then."

She shrugged. "Oh, I'm sure it's all about the sales figures. In my industry you're only as good as your last deal."

"Cutthroat."

"You have no idea." Beth sipped from her glass.

"Oh, there he is. Fred," Roland called over their heads. "Over here." He motioned the older man toward them. "Fred Pugh, this is my friend Imogen Frost. Imogen, Fred here is the major general of the Stellenbosch Police Department. He is a man with a sterling reputation, and someone I can vouch for personally." He clapped his big hand on the general's shoulder. "After all, he's my father-in-law."

Fred shook Imogen's hand and kissed Beth's cheek before holding out his hand to Amahle. "Minister." He inclined his head. "An honour."

Amahle remembered him from the funeral too. He was the man who had been arguing with Jim and Beth and then broke off the argument when Roland had appeared. She wondered what they'd been arguing about. It certainly hadn't seemed like the appropriate time or place for a disagreement, hence it had stuck in her memory. As he pulled his business card from his pocket and gave it to Imogen, Amahle felt a shiver run up her spine and glanced around to see where the draught was coming from, but she could see nothing. She looked back at the general and noticed that his hand shook slightly as he held the card. She could smell the sweat coming off him and saw it bead on his upper lip. While he looked calm, collected, and confident, she realized that underneath it he was anything but. What she didn't understand was why.

"Roland said you have something you need to speak about. Call me." He pointed to the card now in her hand. "I'm free all day tomorrow."

"Thank you," Imogen said. "I really appreciate it."

"No worries. Now I best get back to my wife, or she'll have my guts for garters. Roland." He clapped him on the shoulder and kissed Beth's cheek. "See you both for brunch?"

"I'll come with you, Papa." She turned to Imogen and Amahle. "It was lovely to meet you both. Perhaps you'll join us for brunch tomorrow? Roland could pick you up."

"Oh, thanks. We'll see. If we can make it I'll call Roland and get the address," Imogen said before Beth disappeared into the crowd. "She's lovely."

"Yes. Fred really is a good guy. I'm not just saying that because he's her dad. He's fair and doesn't stand for any kind of shit in his department."

"That's good to know."

"Can you tell me what kind of trouble you're in?"

"It's best if you don't know, Roland."

He whistled. "That kind of trouble, man." He tapped the card still in Imogen's hand. "Call him first thing. He'll help."

"Thanks."

Jim Davitson walked over to them, a broad smile on his face and his arms spread open wide. "Imogen, you look ravishing, my dear. Simply ravishing." He wrapped his arms around her and kissed her cheeks. Amahle stared at him as his hands slipped lower and lower down Imogen's back.

"Jim, thank you for the invite." She reached around her back and gripped his hands, pulling them around playfully. "You've met Minister Nkosi?"

"I do believe I've had that pleasure." He bowed over her hand, placing a theatrical kiss on it that made her skin crawl. "At your service, Minister."

"Thank you, Mr. Davitson."

"Have you met up with your boss?"

"James is here?"

"Yes, yes. I invited him myself. He's around here somewhere." He waved his hand in a circle to encompass the whole room. "Now, Imogen," he said as he slung an arm around her shoulders, "I have someone I'd like you to meet." He steered her away from the small group, leaving Amahle alone with Roland.

"He's not normally such an old letch."

"I'm sorry?"

"The wandering hands. He's a decent guy. He lost his wife last year, and I think he's a bit lonely. Too much punch."

She frowned at him.

"You looked like you were going to flatten him when he put his arm around her. I didn't realize you were seeing each other."

"Why do you assume we are?"

"I'm sorry. Everyone around here knows your story, Minister. Whether we've met you or not, we all know what happened to you and your girlfriend. You and Imogen seem very close." He shrugged. "I'm sorry if I offended you."

"You didn't. But you're not the first to assume we're seeing each other either." She stuck a thumb over her shoulder at her protection detail. "They did too." She remembered laughing when Imogen had told her about the assumption Laura and her colleagues had made. Suddenly, it didn't feel so funny. It felt dangerous.

Across the room, she could see Imogen practically fighting with Jim's increasingly daring hands.

"Maybe it's because of the way you're looking at her now."

"How's that?"

"Like you want to rip his head off and ride off into the sunset with her."

Amahle laughed. "You have a sappy romantic heart, Roland."

He shrugged. "It works on my wife."

She shuddered. "That's more information than I needed to know."

He placed his hand on her back. "You go rescue your not girlfriend, and I'll go find my other friend to introduce to you both. He's always late, but he should be here by now."

❖

"Mr. Pienaar, It's lovely to meet you." Imogen shook hands.

"And you, Ms. Frost. Jimbo here tells me you might be looking to off-load some of your land."

"Oh, no. I'm not looking to split the land and holdings. If I sell, I sell it as a going concern, Mr. Pienaar."

"That's some sale you're looking for there, missy."

"It's a large one, for sure, but it's a good business with a lot of export trade. It's a good investment for anyone."

"Sure, sure. But in the current economic market, you'll get a much quicker sale if you parcel it off."

"I'm not in need of a quick sale."

"Imogen?"

She turned at Amahle's voice, immensely grateful that she'd stepped in between her and Mr. Snake Hands himself. "Hi."

"Roland needs you for a second, if you can spare the time?"

"Certainly." She wrapped her fingers around Amahle's hand. "Gentlemen," she said as she let Amahle lead her away. "Thank you," she whispered into the back of her hair.

"You're welcome."

"I feel like I've been slimed."

"Huh?"

"Don't you remember watching *Ghostbusters* when we were kids?"

"Oh God, yeah. The little green snot thing."

"Exactly."

"Ew."

"So who's he got lined up for me now?"

"I've no idea. He said he was going to find his friend, but he wasn't sure if he was here yet."

"Ah, so you came to rescue me."

"I'd say you looked like you needed a hand, but I think you really had too many."

"Very funny."

"You can't blame him, I suppose."

"What's that supposed to mean?"

"Well, look at you."

Imogen looked down her body. "What?"

"Don't give me that. You're bloody gorgeous, and you know it."

She grinned at Amahle. "You think so?"

Amahle stared at her, looking like she wanted to say something but wasn't sure if she should.

"I don't see Roland. Would you do me the honour?" Imogen held out her hand and inclined her head toward the dance floor as the band struck up a gentle fox-trot.

"You want me to dance with you?"

"Yes."

"Here?"

"Yes"

"At the mayor's ball? In Stellenbosch? In South Africa?"

"Where else?"

"The moon. Do you have any idea how that will be received?"

"It's just a dance, Amahle."

"No, it isn't. Not here, it isn't. Do you have any idea of the level of homophobia that is entrenched in this country?"

"You're an out lesbian who's been elected, twice, to the Houses of Parliament. How bad can it be?"

"Trust me, it's bad. I might be an out lesbian, but people haven't had to face my sexuality as I haven't had a partner to confront them with."

"Why would that make a difference?"

"They can ignore the fact if it isn't presented to the public every day. Dancing with you on that dance floor is asking for trouble. And that's without even thinking about the current mess we're in."

"If you were in a relationship you think you wouldn't have been voted in?"

"I know I wouldn't."

"But South Africa was one of the first countries to give equal employment rights to the LGBTQ community."

"I know. It was one of the first campaigns I worked on."

"So, how can you say there's homophobia?"

"Because it's true."

The contradiction had her head reeling. Was it really as divided as Amahle said, or was she worrying for no reason? Was it really so difficult?

"Every year at least five hundred lesbians are subjected to corrective rape. They're raped so they'll 'get a taste of a real man and straighten themselves out.' Five hundred plus. Simply because they're lesbians. A hate crime, and do you know how many of those five hundred per year reported crimes have ever gone to trial?"

"No."

"Thirty."

"What? Thirty per year is a ridiculous—"

"No, thirty total. Since 2000, when the phrase was coined by a lawyer from Amnesty International. Since then, thirty corrective rapes have gone to trial."

"That's fifteen years. What happened to the rest?"

"No one was ever charged because the rapists weren't found, despite some of the victims naming their attackers. Naming them, giving the police officers addresses, and getting all the evidence collected in a timely fashion. The police don't investigate corrective rape."

"Why the fuck not?"

"Because they don't disagree with it. They don't see it as a crime that needs to be investigated and so won't 'waste' police resources on it. I've even heard some people refer to it as a public service."

"That's fucking sick."

"Yes, it is. So, no."

"Huh? What?"

"No, I won't dance with you."

Imogen shook her head at the quick change of subject, but a fire in Amahle's eye made her think there was more to her answer. "If we were somewhere other than the mayor's ball in Stellenbosch, would you dance with me?"

Amahle bit her lower lip and dropped her eyes for a fraction of a second before meeting her gaze with a smouldering look that caused Imogen's belly to flood with desire. "Maybe."

"Amahle, what an unexpected pleasure." An elderly white man with a well-established comb-over and a rotund physique clasped Amahle's shoulder with his puffy, wrinkled hand. "You usually avoid these things like the plague, my dear." He leaned in and kissed her cheek.

"James, it's lovely to see a friendly face here."

"Another friendly face, surely." He indicated his head toward Imogen. "You always did have exquisite taste." He held his hand out to Imogen. "If she won't introduce me, I'll just have to do it myself. James Wilson. Minister for Health."

"Forgive me. I don't know where my manners are." Amahle shook her head. "James, this is Imogen Frost."

"Ah, the lady who inherited that beautiful vineyard down the road."

"That would be me, Minister. It's an honour to meet you."

"And it's a pleasure to meet you. Amahle, could I have a moment?"

She nodded. "I'll just be a minute."

"No problem," Imogen said. She watched Amahle follow him and what looked like a teacher giving a student a stern talking to. She chuckled to herself at the image it conjured in her brain.

"Imogen, this is Julius Steele," Roland said as he approached her, startling her from her reverie. "He's an investigative journalist with the *Mail & Guardian Online*."

Imogen tore her gaze from Amahle and James and greeted him. "It's nice to meet you."

"And you, Ms. Frost. Roland here tells me you have a story for me."

"Not me." She pointed to Amahle. "She does. She'll be back in a moment, I'm sure."

"Not a problem. May I ask how you fit into the story?"

Imogen smiled as Amahle gestured emphatically at James and walked away from him, clearly pissed at whatever he had said to her. "Call me an interested bystander." When Amahle returned her smile looked forced, stilted. "You okay?"

Amahle just nodded. "Julius, are you Roland's friend?"

"I am. It's a pleasure to see you again so soon. You have a story for me?"

"Yes. But this isn't the right place."

"I have to head back to Jo'burg on the five a.m. flight, Minister. Where would you like to talk?"

"We can head to the vineyard now." Imogen looked at Amahle. She looked shaken. "This was the best plan we could come up with, remember? This way, whatever happens, it's all out there. Genies don't go back into bottles once they're out."

Amahle closed her eyes, and Imogen watched her gather her strength. "Let's go then."

Once they were in the car, Amahle began to talk. She told him everything, starting with her own suspicions and ending with Dr. Marais's initial findings.

"Can I get a copy of that report?" Julius asked.

"Yes. I'll call the doctor and have him email it through to you now," Amahle said.

"I can do that." She took the phone from Amahle and spoke quietly so that they could continue the interview. "Dr. Marais, you don't know me, but I'm working with Amahle Nkosi."

"Is she there? Can I speak to her?"

"Sure." Imogen handed the phone over and listened as Amahle confirmed that she was okay and not acting under duress.

"What do you need?" he asked when she took over the call again.

"Can you send copies of your reports to the following emails please?" She read off the address that Julius had given her, Amahle's, and her own. "Can you send a copy of all your data to the last two addresses too?"

"There's too much."

"Zip files?"

"Still too big to send. I have video files, as well as all the data that Claudia sent me from the Department of Health. I even managed to find some information on PharmaChem that I haven't had a chance to look through yet."

"Like what?"

"Shareholder profiles. FDA reports, pending drug trials, pending lawsuits. You name it, I have it."

"How did you get it all?"

"Most of it's in the public record. You just have to know where to look. The rest of it I managed to get hold of as the CEO of the hospital. If I say I'm interested in various drugs trials, the people over there tend to let me access what I like."

"You've been busy, Doctor."

"I have."

"Is there any way you can get a copy of your data out?"

"You're worried?"

"Cautious."

"Semantics. I can post a copy on a large capacity pen drive. Do you have an address?"

She gave him the address at the vineyard and listened while he sent his daughter to the mailbox at the end of their drive with it. "Thank you."

"Have you heard anything about Thambo?"

"Sizewe called earlier today. He'll recover. I'm told he's trying to decide on what prosthetic he wants. A hand or a hook."

"At least he's keeping his sense of humour. I don't understand these people."

"Life's cheap."

"But people aren't, Ms. Frost." He sighed. "Good night."

"Good night, Doctor. And thank you." She handed the phone back to Amahle.

"So what happens now, Julius?" Amahle asked.

"I go over the reports your doctor has. Try to verify some of this independently, and then I'll be in touch."

"You need to be careful."

He nodded. "Always am. Now take me back to these threatening calls, Amahle."

CHAPTER THIRTY

Sipho sat in the back of the car this time, the Professor had been promoted to the front after their last "mission." He hated Cape Town, he hated Tsotsi, and the Professor, but most of all he hated himself. The stench of guilt and fear clung to his skin and hung in his nostrils. It made his stomach constantly queasy, and every time he passed something reflective he saw disgust etched on his face.

The farmhouse was a simple one. Single story, wraparound stoop, and a pair of dogs asleep in the yard. The chain-link fence was six feet high and topped with razor wire. Typical. What he knew would also be typical was the alarm that would notify the police or a private security firm in the event of intrusion, the affluent neighbourhood which would have periodic drive-bys from the police.

The Professor tossed a pair of steaks under the gate as Tsotsi instructed him to. The hungry dogs seemed unable to resist the scent of the fresh bloody meat and wolfed them down.

"Twenty minutes, boys. Then we cut the chain and give this guy his message."

"What about the police patrol?" Sipho asked.

"What about it?"

"If they drive past before we go in, or when we go in, it's over."

"It's all taken care of."

"What do you mean?"

Tsotsi grinned. "Patrol has been taken care of."

"I don't understand." Sipho frowned at him. "How has it been taken care of?"

"Let's just say I have friends in high places." Tsotsi spat on the ground. "You don't need to know anymore than that, boy."

Friends in high places meant only one thing to Sipho. Someone in the police was on the payroll. A chill ran down his spine. If it was big enough to pay off officials then it was much bigger than Sipho had realized. Who else was in on this? And more importantly, what exactly was this?

Tsotsi checked his watch and rubbed his hands together gleefully. "Fifteen minutes, boys."

Sipho swallowed hard. "Tsotsi, no knives this time."

"Afraid of a little blood, Sipho?"

"No. Afraid of jail."

The Professor laughed. "Fucking pussy."

It had become his new mantra, and Sipho was sick of being the butt of the joke. He turned his head and stared out the window, watching as a young girl came out the door, illuminated only by the weak porch light. She stroked the dogs' heads and skipped down the garden path to the mailbox. She stuffed her envelope inside and raised the flag to let the postman know it was full then she skipped back to the stoop, stroking the dogs' heads again.

Sipho hoped that neither Tsotsi nor the Professor had seen her. He didn't like the possibilities of where that scenario ended.

Half an hour later, Tsotsi clicked his fingers and they pulled their masks over their heads. The chain gave way easily under the bolt cutters he wielded, and the sleeping dogs never stirred as they passed them and smashed their way into the house. Screams emanated from two directions. Tsotsi and the Professor headed for the loudest. Sipho turned a corner and ran toward the room of the softest scream. He prayed he'd picked the right room and quickly located the girl trying to crawl under her bed. He gripped her ankle and pulled her out, wrapping his hand around her mouth and whispering into her ear.

"If they don't know you are here, they will not hurt you. I can only protect you if you stay silent and hidden. Nod if you understand me."

She did.

Sipho quickly opened the window and looked out, the child still in his arms. There was no drop to speak of, but the path to the road was too exposed and he didn't know the layout of the house. If Tsotsi or the Professor could see to the road from where they were, they were both dead before the girl could reach the gate.

"Hide in the bushes just there." He pointed along the house. "Whatever you hear, do not come out until that car leaves. Do you understand me?"

She nodded again.

"Good." He lowered her out the window and let go of her mouth, holding a finger to his lips. "Go." She nodded and disappeared.

"Where you gone, man?" Tsotsi opened the door.

"I thought I heard something in here."

"Well? Did you?"

"Can't find anything."

He sucked his lips though his teeth. "Pussy. Get in here. We've got work to do."

The woman cowered on the bed, her hands bound with tape. Her mouth was covered, and a thin cut down the length of her cheek seeped blood down her chin until it dripped onto her nightie. She looked toward the door, terror written on her face. He looked toward the girl's room and mouthed a single word to her. "Safe." Her shoulders relaxed a little and a sob wracked her body.

"Eh, man, looks like missus there's just dying to meet you." Tsotsi pushed him toward the bed.

"I don't want no white bitch round my Johnson. Fuck that shit." He hoped she could see the apology in his eyes as he said the only thing he could think of. Tsotsi and the Professor laughed.

"You ain't got no worries about your little dick dropping off if it touches white pussy, have you, Prof?"

"Nah." He shoved his filthy jeans down his legs and dragged her down the bed as Tsotsi held the man up by his hair to face her.

"You getting the message now, boss?"

The man was crying, his bound hands held up before him, begging in the only way he could for them to stop. The woman screamed as the Professor tore off her underwear, and Sipho couldn't do it anymore. He couldn't stand by and let this happen. He grabbed the gun from Tsotsi's hand and squeezed off a round into the ceiling.

"Fuck, man, you'll have the bloody boers here. What the fuck you doing?"

"Get off her." He pushed the barrel of the gun against the bare skin of the Professor's leg. "Now."

He jumped up and fell over as he tried to pull up his pants. "What? Fucking pussy, man."

"Shut up. Shut up. Shut up. Enough. They've got the message. Right, man?" He looked at the man on his knees in front of Tsotsi, his hair still held tight in his hand, but he nodded for all he was worth. "Right. So we've done what we came here to do. We gave him the message, now we can leave, Tsotsi. We can just go, man."

Tsotsi roared and wrapped one arm around the man's neck, let go of his hair, and gripped his chin. In one swift motion, he ripped his arms open and twisted the man's neck to an unnatural angle.

"Don't ever say my fucking name." Tsotsi moved so quickly that Sipho couldn't react. He was still staring at the body of the man on the ground when Tsotsi yanked the gun from his limp grip, fired three shots into the woman on the bed, and smashed his fist into Sipho's face.

Sipho felt like he couldn't move his feet as he was dragged from the house and tossed into the trunk of the car.

"Light up the house, Prof. Here, use this shit." Tsotsi grabbed a can from behind Sipho's back. The unmistakable odour of petrol wafted over him. He slammed the boot closed and the Professor's sick laughter faded.

He wanted to go home and try to forget what he'd done. He wanted to go home and forget why he'd done it, but he knew that would never happen. She'd be there, demanding her drugs and telling him how worthless he was until he gave in and went to fetch them for her. She didn't care how he got them. Only that he did. He cursed his own weakness and stupidity at how easily he'd let her manipulate him. He'd tried so hard to be a good son. A good brother. But what had it gotten him? More nightmares than he could count, and a prison cell in his near future. Or a coffin. Probably the coffin.

He didn't care anymore. He just wanted it to end.

CHAPTER THIRTY-ONE

"Are you always up early?" Amahle asked, yawning from the doorway.

"Pretty much." Imogen smiled. "Boarding school habit."

"What was it like?"

"You read the letters."

"I did. Sounded like you hated it."

"I did." She shrugged. "Don't get me wrong, I did very well, and I'm not sure I'd have forged the career I have without it. I made a lot of connections while I was there, and it got me through the door to Cambridge, but would I have ever chosen to go there? No. Would I ever send a child there myself?" She shook her head. "Never."

"Why?"

"A couple of thousand young girls all under one roof. It was a breeding ground for over-competitive bitches. I was seven, I had a weird accent, and I cried for you in my sleep. What do you think happened?"

"I hate it for you."

She smiled. "Thanks. Coffee?"

"A bucket should do."

"Coming right up."

"Did Julius make his flight?"

"Yes. Greg drove him to the airport and waited till the plane took off."

"Can I ask you a question?"

"Sure."

"How come you aren't married?"

"Excuse me?" Imogen's voice was more like a squeak.

"You heard me."

"Yes, I just wasn't expecting that." She put the coffee mug down.

"Well?"

"Never found a woman I wanted to wake up next to."

Amahle took a mouthful and swallowed quickly. "Shit, that's hot."

So I'm not imagining the attraction between us.

"Just brewed."

"What do you mean by that anyway?"

"You're not exactly the blushing virgin, Ami. Work it out."

Amahle chuckled at Imogen's theatrically wiggling eyebrows and her meaning became abundantly clear. "But why?"

"What do you mean, why? I like to have sex, but I don't want a relationship. Why do you think?"

"I mean, why don't you want to wake up with them?"

The smile slid from Imogen's lips. "Because I don't want to care about them."

Amahle stared at her. It didn't make any sense. Imogen was one of the most caring women she'd ever spent time with. How could she not care about them? Why would she withhold that part of herself?

"I've lost everyone I ever cared about. They were all taken from me."

"So you purposefully keep yourself lonely so that you don't get hurt?"

She shrugged. "Is it any different from you keeping yourself lonely so that they don't get hurt?"

"I don't do one-night stands."

"Maybe you should." She winked. "Let loose a little, Minister."

"No, thanks. Not my style."

"You don't know what you're missing."

"Amahle?" Laura said from the doorway.

"Yes?"

"There's something I think you need to see on the news." She followed Laura into the living room and stared at the TV. The picture of Dr. Marais and his wife, and a second of a burned down house filled the screen as the newscaster gave his monotoned report.

"That news again, ladies and gentlemen, last night Dr. Derek Marais and his wife Sylvie were murdered in their home before it was set alight. Police say they are looking for three armed men. The couple's only child, nine-year-old Isabelle, managed to escape out the window and hide until the attackers had fled."

"But I spoke to him last night." Imogen wrapped her arms around Amahle's shoulders and held on. Her voice shaky and her gaze fixed on the screen.

"I need to call Thambo," Amahle said and wrapped her arms about Imogen's waist. She needed to feel something solid and real. "I need to make sure he's okay."

"I've just spoken to his brother, Minister," Greg said. "No change at that end."

"That's good at least." She leaned in against Imogen, glad to feel the warmth of her body against her own.

"Call Julius—"

"Already on it," Josh said and waved the phone toward her.

"Seems like I'm surplus to requirement."

"Never, Minister. But when you surround yourself with good people," Laura said, "things get done."

"So it would seem."

"Perhaps it's time to call Fred?" Imogen whispered against her hair.

"It would seem like it." The niggling in her gut increased at the mere mention of his name. *Is it just because he's a police officer? I have no other reason to distrust him. So why does he make me feel so uncomfortable?*

"What if we can't trust him?"

"We have Julius."

"And if he is bad, we'll be tipping off our enemies to exactly what we know."

"Then don't tell him everything. If you don't trust him while he's here, just outline the suspicions that Dr. Marais brought to you as a lead to his murder. Don't tell him what evidence you have until you're comfortable with him. How does that sound?"

It made sense. It didn't explain why she'd approached the general prior to the doctor's murder, but she could just say she was going to ask him for advice on how to deal with the suspicions should the doctor find the evidence required. Would he buy that? Would she? Probably not, but what option did she have at this point? She couldn't continue to sit on information that would help in the doctor's murder investigation and bringing his killers to justice. Whether she liked it or not she had to go to the police.

"Laura, can you look into this guy for me?"

"Sure."

"In the meantime, let's give the general a call and fill him in on what the doctor was looking into and how we think it links to his murder," she said to Imogen.

"Are you going to tell him about Thambo and the calls?"

"I'll play that by ear."

"Good plan."

Thirty minutes later, Fred sat opposite them and listened to everything Amahle said, scribbling in his notebook from time to time, asking the occasional question, but mostly just listening.

"Well, Minister, this is a bloody awful mess."

"You have a knack for understatement, General."

He chuckled. "I've been told that before. Now, I need your full cooperation from here out. Agreed?"

"Any information I have, I'll gladly hand over."

"Do you have the raw data that the doctor had?"

Amahle shook her head. "Just the initial report he brought to me in my office."

"And he didn't send you a copy of anything else?"

"No."

"That's a damn shame. So all you have is the report to back up your story?"

The hairs on the back of her neck stood on end. He was being far too careful to clarify the point. "Yes, that's all the evidence we have."

"Right. Well, that's a bloody shame. A real bloody shame. And have you spoken to anyone else about this?"

Something about his questions and his over-the-top, repetitive reactions just didn't sit right. "Just the people on my security detail."

She saw Imogen reach for her phone. "Sorry. Buzzing." She pretended to silence it, but Amahle saw her send a quick message to Roland asking him to call her ASAP, and she was hugely grateful that Imogen had caught on to her wavelength so quickly. When her phone rang, she picked it up and looked apologetically at him. "I'm sorry, for them to keep trying like this it must be really important."

"Of course."

She stepped outside to take the call.

"Is there anything else that you can think of that might help us track down the people behind this?"

"I wish there was, sir. But I can't think of anything." She watched as Imogen shut off her phone and spoke briefly to Josh before stepping back in and nodding to Amahle.

"Sorry about that."

"No need to apologize, Ms. Frost. We're all very busy people. It's a bloody shame you have no evidence, Minister. You're making it very hard for me to do anything with this. I'll fill in the detectives investigating his murder, but I wouldn't get my hopes up that it will crack open the case. Sorry. I'll see myself out, since you've just made me even busier."

They stood side by side on the stoop until the car was out of sight. "Roland said he hadn't mentioned Julius to our friend there." Imogen pointed down the road. "He said he wouldn't as it would just make the family angry. Apparently, Julius was a friend from university, and he's not well liked by them. He asked me not to mention Julius to Fred."

"Why not?"

"He said they don't like his kind of journalism."

"Ah. So he's not aware that I'm unsure about the general?"

"Correct. So what happened in there? What made your mind up not to trust him?"

"Too much of a bloody shame."

"I'm sorry?"

"He was too fixated on the fact that we have no evidence about the counterfeit pills. Made me uncomfortable."

"That's it?"

"Something just felt wrong." She shrugged. "I can't explain it. I'm sorry. Maybe it's an overactive imagination, I don't know, but sometimes I get this…feeling…like someone's watching me but there's nobody there. Or a chill that goes up my spine when it's a hundred degrees. Something just feels wrong."

"Are you ever wrong with this feeling?"

"Probably. But I've also been kept safe with it. So I tend to trust it."

"A protective instinct."

"I guess so."

"So what about Roland? Do you think we can still trust him?"

"Not sure. I hope so." She ran her fingers through her hair and pointed down the lane. "He may or may not be what Roland thinks he is, but if not, I hope that's just family loyalty rather than anything sinister. I'm inclined to think that if it was anything else, he wouldn't have introduced us to Julius."

"How can you be sure that he's not on the take or something?"

"Who? Julius?"

"Yes."

Amahle shook her head. "No, he's genuine. I've been interviewed by him before. I know his stories, and I know him. When you first mentioned talking to the press, he was the first name I thought of. His stories have been hard hitting and anti-corruption all the way. Roland hit the jackpot with him. So what do we do about Fred?"

"Well, you've got Laura looking into him already, and I asked Josh to stick a tracker on his car before he departed. I wasn't sure what was going on in there, but I felt it was better to be safe than sorry. Did you get it?" she asked Josh.

"Yup. Even managed to get one in his coat pocket when he was getting back in the car."

"Well done," Imogen said.

"No sweat."

"Laura, do you think we can find out what's happening to the doctor's little girl?" Amahle asked. "I hate to think of her out there alone and scared."

"I'll make some inquiries."

"Thank you."

"Are you okay?" Imogen asked.

She shook her head. "I don't think so. I'd like to go for a walk, but I don't really want the entourage with me."

"What if we go to the orchard and sit in a tree for a while? We can make them stay out of the orchard. By the time we get there, they'll know there's no one around, and we can pretend to be by ourselves." She smiled. "How does that sound?"

"Sounds pretty good."

"Let me go and fix it with Nick and Greg. I think Josh and Laura have other things they need to do right now."

"Okay." She watched Imogen walk away and wondered how everything could feel so wrong and yet so right at the same time. She hadn't felt at home on the vineyard since she was a girl, but right now, she felt like she belonged. She felt whole again in a way she hadn't imagined she ever could. And as Imogen stepped back into her view, she realized why. It wasn't the vineyard that made her feel like she belonged. It was Imogen. It had always been Imogen. She'd looked everywhere for her, all her life. The blond hair, the tall, willowy frame—barring the brown eyes, Grace was a dead ringer for Imogen.

Physically, at least. Even down to the high cheekbones and long, long eyelashes. But the steel core of Imogen was hers and hers alone. And something that was magnetic to Amahle.

Imogen held out her hand. "You ready?"

Am I? She looked up into Imogen's eyes shining with trust and hope and she knew Imogen was thinking the same things she was. Everything she'd ever wanted was there for her if she was just willing to let go of the fear that held her frozen.

She placed her hand in Imogen's and smiled as she was tugged to her feet and shuffled out the door, Imogen never letting go of her hand.

"I've no idea."

CHAPTER THIRTY-TWO

Nick and Greg trailed behind them as they stepped off the stoop and headed for the vine field that led to the orchard. Stealing shy looks from one another, they entwined their fingers and walked silently between the gently rustling leaves.

"Is it wrong that I feel happy right now, given everything that's going on?" Imogen asked.

"Depends."

"On what?"

"Are you happy because of what's going on, or despite it?"

"Definitely the second one." She squeezed again. "Definitely despite it all." She felt something impact her back and put herself between Amahle and whoever was aiming at them as a high-pitched scream cut through the air.

"You traitor."

"Mama." Amahle turned to look at her mother, jostling Imogen behind her.

Greg and Nick took closer order of their protectee, and Imogen was pleased to see how quickly they closed the gap between them at the first sign of trouble. She just wished that trouble wasn't in the shape of a dishevelled looking Mbali Nkosi. She glanced over her shoulder at the spot where something had hit her and saw a handful of red dust. The remnants of a mud ball, no doubt.

"Haven't you shamed us enough with your other white whore? You have to do it again? With this…this…bitch."

Oh hell, no. I'm not taking that from you, you lying old witch. "Excuse me?"

"Mama, I won't have you talk to Imogen that way."

"You never would. Stubborn as a mule. Always was, always will be. Except when it came to her. All she had to do was click her fingers and her little nigger came running. Didn't ya, girl?" She clicked her fingers, but her coordination was off, and the motion made her stumble and the sound inaudible. "Just like a little puppy dog."

"Stop it, Mama. You've no idea what you're talking about."

"Don't I?"

"No." Amahle took hold of her arm and turned her back toward her house. "Go to bed and sleep it off."

"It's you who doesn't have any idea, daughter." She spat on the ground. "You don't know anything." She threw her head back and cackled. "It was my idea, you know?" She pointed at Imogen. "To send you away. I told him you wouldn't be safe here. That the men who killed your mother were so angry with her that they were looking for you too." She chortled to herself. "He believed me. Stupid fool that he was."

"Mama, why? Why would you do that? She was just a little girl."

"She was making you believe you could be something you couldn't. She was making you think like you were a white child."

"You had her sent away to keep me in my place?"

"That's right."

"To stop me dreaming of better things?"

"You had to learn. And so did she."

"I graduated top of my class, Mama. I worked my way up from intern to being the first open lesbian to be elected to the Houses of Parliament. I am the highest ranked woman in the House. I did all that on my own. I did all that and more without help from you or her. What could she make me want that I haven't achieved?"

"It was a different South Africa then. You couldn't have had it then."

"You're wrong. It was already changing. Because of people like Imogen's mother, and the ANC, and all the other people who fought for our freedom. It makes no sense, Mama. Why did you make him so afraid for her?"

"Because he didn't want me," she screamed. "Because I wasn't good enough for his bed."

Imogen wanted to feel angry at her. This pathetic, bitter old woman who had been so insecure she'd had to vent her rage at the world on the only victim she could find. A seven-year-old child. She wanted to look at her and be able to hate her, for everything she'd stolen, but in those few words she'd told Imogen that it was never the child she was that Mbali had been angry at. It was everything she had represented then. A white child. A child of privilege. A child of opportunity. A child who had a prosperous future all mapped out before her. A child with choices and a voice that would be heard in their world. And those were options Mbali had never had. But worse, they were options that she could never see appearing for her, or her children. Mbali was a child of oppression, a child of fear, a child subjugated to the vile will of a regime that not only treated her as less than human, but labelled her as such. She had every right to be angry at the world she'd been born into. Imogen couldn't deny it. She couldn't blame Mbali for the way she felt. For her actions, yes. For the hurt she'd caused her, yes. But if she were honest with herself, she couldn't say with any certainty that she wouldn't have done something just as spiteful. She looked over Amahle's shoulder and saw not an old woman who had caused her so many problems. Instead she saw the legacy of apartheid. Or at least of those who were unable to let go of it.

Imogen refocused on Amahle's back, and her pride in Amahle grew with every word she spoke. If Mbali was the rotten legacy of apartheid, then Amahle was a true child of the rainbow nation. Inspired by greatness to let go of the hatred and fear that threatened to destroy every possibility of peace, Amahle followed a noble path. The path lit by wisdom and compassion, and she would take every step. Even if she had to do it alone.

"Does Sipho know?" Imogen asked. She had no desire left to fight with Mbali. None at all. All she felt for her was pity, and in the pit of her stomach, shame. Shame that she had in any way been a part of that. Shame that any part of her represented it to someone else, and it made her feel more uncomfortable than she could have ever imagined.

"Know what? The stupid boy knows nothing. Nothing at all." She tipped a bottle to her lips. "Besides, he's gone." She wiggled her fingers. "Poof, just disappeared."

"Give me that." Amahle snatched the small bottle from her hand and passed it to the person closest to her, Nick. "What is it?" She tried to hold her mother up as she struggled to regain possession of the bottle.

"It's Oramorph," he said, reading the label. "It was prescribed for your father, Imogen."

"You stole it from my house?" Imogen shook her head. Nothing really surprised her about this woman any more.

"What?" Amahle asked her mother.

"A solution of oral morphine. It's prescribed as a painkiller," Nick said, misunderstanding who her question was aimed at.

"I know what it is. I meant—never mind."

"What's wrong with her?"

"Nothing that I know of."

He shook his head. "You can't get this stuff over the counter, and it isn't the usual stuff for a junkie looking for a high. People tend to get addicted to this shit after they've been prescribed it for something."

"Where is he?" Mbali threw herself at Imogen, her dirty fingernails curled like talons aimed at Imogen's eyes.

"Mama, no."

Greg caught her around the waist and hoisted her off the ground. "Which way is her home?"

Amahle pointed. "It's easier if I show you."

"My boy. My boy's gone. What did you do to him? Where is he?"

"I haven't done anything to him. Why would you even think that?"

"Because he went out for my medicine and he never came back."

"What medicine, Mama?"

"That medicine." She pointed to the Oramorph. "He didn't get enough when he got the rest of the pills."

"What pills?"

"Many, many, pills." She stopped struggling in Greg's arms and tried to snuggle into his chest as the Oramorph took hold of her.

"Is she okay?" Imogen asked.

"Passed out, I think," Greg said. "Thank God," he whispered, not quite low enough to prevent him being heard.

Amahle led them into the small house that Imogen had spent so much time in when they were children. The rooms were small and squalid. The once clean and tidy surfaces were littered with beer cans, uneaten food, and a half empty packet of condoms. Amahle looked around, and Imogen could see the look of shame settling on her features. But that wasn't right. She wouldn't allow Amahle to feel ashamed of where she had come from. No, not where she had come from, but where her mother had sunk to. They weren't the same place.

She grasped Amahle's hand and whispered into her ear. "That look on your face, right now, I've seen it before. I see it every time I look in the mirror and I think I wasn't good enough to help my father through his grief. I see it every time I look in the mirror and think I wasn't good enough to keep my mother from going that day. Neither was anything I could affect in any way. Was it?"

"No, of course not. They made their own choices."

"Your mother has made hers. Feel sorry for her, try to help her. But don't take on responsibility for her choices. Don't feel her shame."

Amahle turned her head to look at her. "Is that what you feel?"

"For far too long." She blinked. "It gets inside you and poisons everything."

Amahle covered her hand. "I know." She squeezed gently. "Thank you."

She showed Greg to the bedroom and watched as he gently deposited her mother on the bed, pulling a blanket over her.

"For what it's worth, she looks sick, ma'am."

"Don't all junkies look sick?"

He dipped his head and left the room without saying a word.

Imogen touched her arm. "Maybe we should have a look around. See if we can figure out what's going on?"

"I'm not sure I want to know."

"She's your mum." Imogen smiled. "It's the law."

Amahle offered a tiny smile. "Damn you lawyers."

"Please, I'm a barrister."

"Yeah, yeah. Tell it to someone who's impressed."

"You're not?"

She looked up at her and answered honestly. "Terribly." She pushed a lock of hair behind Imogen's ear. "I wish you could be too."

"I'm impressed by you. All this," she said, indicating the room with a twist of her finger, "only makes you more remarkable. Now, enough with the mutual appreciation society. We need to know what's going on here and why your mother thinks I've had your brother kidnapped or whatever. Do you want to take the bathroom or the kitchen?"

She looked back through to the kitchen and realized there weren't many more secrets it would be able to give up. "Bathroom."

Imogen nodded and gave her a gentle push toward the door. "Have at it."

The tiny room was quick to give up its bounty. The cabinet over the sink was a veritable treasure trove of pillboxes and medicine bottles. One name stood out amongst all the others. Combivirine. Her hands shook as she pulled open one of the bottles and tipped a few of the solid white pills into her palm.

She almost missed the sink in front of her as she vomited. She felt hands on her arms, then circles being rubbed over her back and knew it was Imogen.

"Are they—"

"Fake." She held out the pills, then tossed them in the sink and turned on the tap. "As useful as water against HIV."

"You didn't know?"

Amahle shook her head. "Seems I'm the last to know anything in my family. It would appear they don't trust me."

"I'm not sure I agree with that. If he didn't trust you, why would Sipho have wanted you at the hospital with him the other day?"

"Then why didn't they tell me about this? Why keep it a secret from me? She said he's been going out to get her medicine. Why didn't they tell me?"

"If she went through official channels to get treatment, it would end up in the papers, wouldn't it? Your mum, HIV."

"Yes. No doubt."

"Would it affect your career?"

"Probably."

"Is it possible she's getting treatment under a different name to avoid that?"

"You think she was trying to protect me?" Amahle shook her head. "You saw her out there. Do you really think she cares about protecting me or my career?"

"Maybe not. But I think Sipho does."

Amahle shrugged. "Maybe." She turned the bottle so Imogen could clearly see it all. "There's no prescription label on any of these bottles."

"Meaning?"

"They aren't official."

"Black market?"

"Looks like it."

"She's been buying her medication."

"Looks that way."

"Christ. I'm sorry."

"What for?"

"About your mum."

"I'm sorry about her too. Everything she said outside. All the lies. To you, to your father. She deliberately sabotaged your relationship with him."

"And with you."

"Yes, and ours, because of petty jealousy. If she hadn't lied about

Sipho being your father's child you wouldn't even be here now. You'd still be in England. You'd be safe."

"And I wouldn't be here with you." She rubbed her hands down Amahle's back.

Amahle looked up at her, and she could see clearly that there was more she wanted to say. Imogen did too. She wanted to tell her that none of it mattered and that they'd get through it all, and move on. She wanted to make promises she never had before and say something rash like "we'll be fine," or "we can work this all out," or better yet, "I'll always be here for you." But Imogen bit her tongue. She wasn't naive. She wasn't foolish enough to think that a few words could put everything right. No matter how much she wished. It appeared Amahle felt the same.

Amahle sighed. "I need to find a doctor. One I can trust to get her proper treatment." She tossed the package on the bed. "Not this shit."

"We also need to figure out where Sipho is. For her to confront us like that she must be concerned. Does he still live here, with her?"

"No. Your dad gave him his own place years ago."

"Show me?"

Amahle tucked the blanket under Mbali's chin and kissed her forehead, whispering words too quiet for Imogen to hear before she led her out of the house and across the small dirt yard. Sipho's home was the complete opposite of his mother's. Walls had been freshly lime washed, there was a single cup and bowl on the sink drainer, the curtains were clean and open, and the fridge was well stocked. But there was no sign of Sipho. The bed was made, clothes hung in his wardrobe and lay neatly folded in his drawers, and his shoes were lined in a long neat line along the wall under the window.

"Do you notice anything out of place or missing?"

"I haven't been in here in years," Amahle said." I couldn't tell you. It looks like he always kept things when he was a kid though. He was always neat and tidy."

"Just like you."

Amahle shrugged.

"Can you try calling him? I'll find one of the guys and try to figure out when he was last here."

Amahle pulled her phone from her bag. Imogen went back outside, instructing Greg to stay with Amahle. It took her a good five minutes to find someone, but she was quickly able to ascertain that Sipho hadn't been seen for three days. She wished she knew if that was as unusual as the man told her it was. Amahle was sitting on the sofa looking through a small address book when she arrived back to the house.

"No answer on his phone. But I found this."

She perched on the arm and looked over Amahle's shoulder. "Anything interesting?"

"I wish I knew. There's nothing under 'if I go missing try this number' though."

"Funny. Want to take this to our friendly police general?"

"Not sure that's a good idea."

"Does he ever go off on his own for a while?"

"Never. He's always stayed close to Mama. Only ever going beyond Cape Town if it was on business for the vineyard."

"And that's not happening now or I'd know about it."

"Or the guys on the yard."

"True. No one's seen him for three days." She bit on her thumbnail. "Does he have a girlfriend? Someone he might have wanted to hole up with?"

"Not that I know of."

"Maybe we should ask—"

Josh walked in. "I've been talking to a few of the hands around here. It seems Sipho has no girlfriend at the moment, no real friends off the yard that anyone seems to know about either. One of the younger boys said that he hated going into town because he was looked down on. He got into fights with the locals about the way they spoke of his mother and sister, and it was rather fractious between them." He indicated his head out the window. "They all said that this place was his life."

"What do you mean fights over his mum and Amahle?" Imogen asked him.

"They mocked him because I'm gay and our mother slept around," Amahle said.

"I don't understand."

"His mother's the village whore and I'm a dyke. They question his masculinity. The boys did it at school after Gogo died. She went wild for a while. Sipho took the brunt of their teasing and bullying. Your father taught him to box. He got to be pretty good at it too. It gave him confidence and helped him look after himself when the other boys decided that name calling wasn't enough anymore." She dropped her head. "I never meant to make his life more difficult."

"That's not your fault," Imogen said.

"No? I haven't exactly gone out of my way to make Sipho's life easier in any way. And now he may have been kidnapped because of me."

"Ami, that's something you really don't know. And besides, if that was the case they'd have been in touch before now." She shook Amahle's hand and tried to make her look at her. When she stubbornly refused, she gripped her chin and turned Amahle's face to hers. "Three days is a long time. If the man who's been calling you had him, he'd have contacted you by now to taunt you if nothing else." It was the only thing that made sense to her. The bastard had called with Thambo in the room, and the Maraises hadn't been hidden. They had established a pattern of leaving their destruction plainly visible to increase the threat against Amahle. Taking her brother only made sense if they intended to use him to further increase that fear. Some form of display, a call, a ransom, anything but silence.

"Then where is he?"

"I don't know. I think we have to report him missing to the police and see if our team here can turn anything up."

"They have enough to do, and I wouldn't trust our Major General Pugh to find ice in Antarctica for me."

"Then we go and report him missing the normal way. By walking into a police station."

"And we bring in more people, ma'am," Josh said. "Whatever it takes to get the job done. We don't let people down. Wherever he is, we'll find him."

Imogen smiled. The confidence in his voice was reassuring, comforting even. She chose to ignore the fact that he made no promise as to what condition Sipho would be in when they located him. After three days missing, she didn't want to think about the possibilities.

CHAPTER THIRTY-THREE

A mahle plucked the photograph out of the frame and stared at it. *Why didn't you tell me, Sipho? I could've helped.*

There was nothing but questions running through Amahle's head. Questions she had no answers to, and likely never would in some cases. Every time she thought she knew the worst thing about the whole situation, something else happened to drag her down to another level of hell. And this time it had become more personal than she could have ever imagined. If she were totally honest with herself, she wasn't entirely surprised that her mother had contracted HIV. She'd been sleeping around, unprotected, Amahle was sure, at a time when HIV was spreading through communities like wildfire. No, that wasn't so much of a shock. What was a shock was them not telling her. And why would Sipho get her drugs off the black market? Why not go to a clinic? This was their mother's life they were talking about. So what if it had an impact on her career? So what if it made her life more difficult and made people question her motives? So what if people thought she'd only campaigned for the programme because of her mother? She knew the truth, and whatever her motivation it was still the right thing to do. It was still what was needed. And her mother's condition would not have stopped her from continuing her work. Even if it might have impacted upon her success.

Was Imogen right? Were they trying to protect her? She snorted a bitter laugh. Her mother hadn't protected her from anything. Ever. Why the hell would she start now? No, she wasn't trying to protect her. But Sipho? Amahle ran her finger down the photograph as though caressing his cheek. That she could actually believe. But surely he could see that this wasn't going to work. His resources were finite. One day, probably far too soon, his money would run out and he'd—

"Shit."

"What are you doing?" Mbali snarled from behind her.

"I need this." She held up the picture and slipped it into her bag. Ignoring her mother's tone.

"Why?"

"The police will want one when I report Sipho missing."

"You don't need the police. Ask that white bitch you were holding hands with."

"I refuse to go into that with you, Mama. Imogen hasn't done anything wrong. If I were you I'd apologize to her and hope she doesn't throw you out on your ear."

Mbali spat on the ground, showing exactly what she thought of that idea.

"Fine." She slung the strap of her bag over her shoulder. "Where are you getting your medication from?"

"What are you talking about?"

Amahle stared at her mother. "Your medication? The pills? You told us you'd run out, that you were sick?"

Her mother scowled at her. "You're lying."

"Mama, we put you to bed a couple of hours ago. You drank yourself unconscious on morphine and told us that Sipho hadn't come back with your meds. When was that? Where did he get them from? Who did he meet?"

"I don't know what—"

"Stop. Just stop. No more lies. You've told enough. You've hurt enough people. Sipho is missing. Do you understand? He went out for your drugs, and no one has seen him since. Now where did he say he was going?"

Mbali shook her head. "You're the one who is lying."

"For Christ's sake." Amahle stormed passed her, grabbed pill bottles and boxes out of the bathroom, and dumped them onto the kitchen table. "Now enough. When did you last see him?"

"Thursday. He went out on Thursday morning. He said he'd be back with medicine."

"Thank you. What was he wearing?"

"I don't know."

"You saw him. What was he wearing?"

"I don't know. Jeans, maybe." She wrung her hands in front of her. "Maybe a T-shirt."

Amahle stared at her. "That's it? That's all you can give me?"

"What more do you want?"

"What colour T-shirt would be a start. What kind of shoes. Maybe a coat, or jacket? Did he have a hat on?"

"I don't remember."

"This is important, Mother."

"I was high." She dropped down into the nearest chair, seemingly unmindful of the junk she had sat on. "I was in pain so I had taken my morphine. It wasn't helping enough, so I kept taking more." She rubbed at the seam on her skirt. The same spot over and over again. "Before I knew it, it was all gone and I needed more."

"So that's why you stole it from the house."

She sucked her lip through her teeth. "He's already dead. He doesn't need it." She slapped her chest. "I do. I'm in pain."

"Aren't we all?" Amahle ran her hand over her face. "Do you know who Sipho got your medication from?"

"No."

"Really? This could be important. That person could know where Sipho is."

"I have no idea. All I know is that Sipho promised to take care of it all. He promised to take care of me."

"Why didn't you go to the clinic?"

"Do you know what they say about people like me?"

Amahle sighed. Unfortunately, she knew all too well the spurious insults that were levelled at many sufferers of HIV. The sad fact of the matter was that it was women like her mother who earned them those insults. "I'm aware."

"Then why would I go there?"

"To get treatment."

"I got everything I needed without having to step foot inside those doors. As soon as that doctor told me." She waved her hands as she spoke. "I haven't stepped foot back in there since."

"And when was that?"

"Six years ago."

"Why didn't Sipho make you go to the clinic?"

"I told him I didn't want to go there. He said okay. He would take care of me."

She realized that she would get nothing more from her mother. She didn't know her own son, she didn't know his reasons, only what she chose to believe of his actions. But Amahle knew him better. She knew he'd have a reason, a real one, to justify abiding by her mother's wishes. She just hoped he hadn't done all this for her. This wasn't something she wanted to be responsible for. She had enough guilt to shoulder.

A knock on the doorframe jolted her from her musings.

"You ready to go to the police station?" Imogen asked. "I know it's been three days, but the sooner we get this done, the better."

"Yeah, I know. I just seem to be having a little trouble making myself believe he's really missing." She shrugged. "I don't want to believe it."

"Get out of my house."

Amahle watched as Imogen's jaw worked as she seemingly fought down whatever it was she wanted to say. Amahle was pleased to avoid another confrontation between the two of them, but she wasn't sure she'd have been able to bite her tongue if their situations had been reversed. Mbali had earned Imogen's rancour, and it told Amahle a great deal of Imogen's character that she refused to be baited.

"Greg's got the car so we can go straight from here. Everyone's waiting."

"Thank you. I'll be there in just a minute."

Imogen nodded and closed the door behind her.

"And good riddance."

"Mother, enough. I don't know how much you remember of earlier, but you told us both everything. We both know what you did, and why. We know about all the lies. So drop the attitude and hope she lets you stay."

"That girl is nothing but trouble. Always was."

"You have no room to talk." Amahle let the door slam behind her and climbed into the car. Imogen took her hand and squeezed gently as she sat down, offering her silent support. Amahle was grateful she hadn't had to ask for it, as she wasn't sure she'd have been able to. The last time she'd been inside a police station had been to make her statement after the attack on Grace and herself.

Unable to find a parking spot on the street nearby, Josh decided he would drop the rest of them outside the gate and wait with the car until they called for him to return to get them. Laura was the first one out when he stopped, and she pulled the door open for Amahle even as she looked to be scanning the vicinity and looking everywhere but at the car. Imogen followed her, with Greg and Nick taking up positions on either side of her. *One great big protective cuddle. Not.*

The police officer behind the reception desk eyed them warily as they approached. He was a big guy, maybe six-three, with hugely muscled shoulders and hands the size of shovels.

"How's it? What can I do for you all this fine Sunday evening?" He clasped his hand on the desk and leaned on his elbows.

"I have to report a missing person, Officer."

"I'm sorry to hear that, Minister. How long has the person been missing?"

Amahle didn't like the way he stated her title. She could hear the sneer behind the smile. It wasn't new, and it was something that she'd learned to deal with over the years. She plastered on her face a smile she knew was as sweetly disingenuous as his was and said, "Since Thursday."

"That's not good." He scratched his chin. "Wait here please. I'll get the paperwork." He returned in just a couple of minutes and held a clipboard out for her. "Fill this in."

"What is it?" she asked as he handed it to her.

"Form 55A. It's your declaration that the person is genuinely missing and gives us permission to distribute a picture of the missing person."

"You don't want any details of the missing person?" Imogen asked.

"There will be an officer down in a few minutes to go through all of that with you. While you wait," he said, pointing to the clipboard, "this will save time." He pointed to a bank of plastic chairs. "You can wait over there."

An hour and two cups of coffee each later, a black man walked toward them. "I'm sorry you've been kept waiting, Minister. I was only just given the message that you were here and needed to speak to someone." He shook her hand and inclined his head to the rest of the group. "I also apologize for the coffee. If you'll come with me, I hope we can get this resolved quickly for you. I'm Sergeant Solongo. How can I help you today?"

"They didn't tell you why I'm here, did they?"

"I'm afraid not." He took the clipboard from her. "But this does. Who's missing?"

"My brother." She sat in the seat he indicated. "How long have you been a sergeant?"

He cleared his throat. "This is my first case, Minister. But please do not worry. I will find your brother."

His new appointment and his seeming unpopularity with his colleagues actually served to put Amahle's mind at ease. The chances of him having been corrupted seemed more remote. "We all have to start somewhere, Sergeant."

"Thank you. Now please tell me, what's going on?"

Amahle quickly went over what they knew of Sipho's disappearance as he took copious amounts of notes. When she got to the part about him leaving to buy medicine, he froze over his page.

"You think, or you *know* he was going to buy drugs?"

"We know. But not recreational drugs. Prescription drugs."

"For?"

"My mother has HIV. He was buying her medicine rather than taking her to a clinic."

"Why?"

"I'll be sure to ask him as soon as you find him."

"Buying medicine like that is not cheap. How could he afford it?"

"I don't know."

"You weren't supplying him with funds?"

"No."

"I think I know how he was funding it," Imogen said.

"How?" He looked at her.

"There's money missing from the vineyard. Lots of money."

"How much?"

"More than one hundred and fifty thousand rand."

"And Sipho had access?"

"Yes."

"When did you find out about this?"

Imogen quickly explained about her father's death, the financial investigation, the paternity claim, and Mbali's revelation of the night before.

Solongo whistled. "Does he know about the investigation?"

"I don't see how he couldn't at this point."

"I don't understand."

"His access to the account was revoked. His well dried up and he went to try to get more drugs."

"I see. Are you sure he hasn't run away of his own free will?" He tapped his pen on the page. "I mean if the investigation proves he has committed fraud, he's looking at prison. If I were him, I'd be putting distance between myself and the vineyard too."

Amahle shook her head. "I could maybe believe that if he hadn't promised to return with my mother's medicine. Sipho always keeps his promises, Sergeant. Always."

"I understand that it is difficult to think of one's family in this way, Minister, but perhaps he went to get the drugs, found out the well was dry, as Ms. Frost said, and simply decided that he was out of choices. The only thing he could do was run."

"No."

He stared at her. She could see in his eyes that he didn't believe her. She could see that he thought Sipho was nothing more than a thief on the run trying to save his own skin. She couldn't blame him. If she didn't know Sipho, hadn't known him her whole life, she'd believe the same thing.

"I'll make some inquiries and get in touch, Minister Nkosi."

"Thank you, Sergeant." As he showed them out, she shook his hand. She shook her head. "Well, that'll be the last time we hear from him."

Imogen tugged at her collar, readjusting it with the strap of her bag. "I wouldn't be so sure about that. I think Sergeant Solongo wants to prove himself, and finding Sipho will help him. Whether he's finding a missing person or a criminal on the run, he gets to make something of a name for himself because of your involvement."

"I'm starting to hate being 'The Minister.'"

Imogen chuckled. "You expect me to believe that?"

"Humour me."

CHAPTER THIRTY-FOUR

"Hello?" Imogen answered her phone without opening her eyes.
"I pulled some strings and I've got some news for you, Imogen."
"Who is it?"

Laughter echoed down the line. "Roland. I thought for sure you'd recognize my voice by now."

"Sorry, Roland. I was still asleep."

"Right. Well, some of us have been up working for hours now."

"And the rest of us thank you for it. Now spit it out so I can go back to sleep."

"You might not want to when you hear what I have to say. I've got the CCTV footage from the bank and some DNA results sitting on my desk."

"I'm one hundred percent certain you're going to tell me that he's no relation and he was stealing from the company."

"Well, you certainly know how to burst a guy's bubble."

She yawned. "Sorry."

"I've got some other good news though."

"What's that?"

"After the ball, Pienaar has started asking some pointed questions about buying Frost Vineyard. As a going concern."

"That is good news." Wasn't it? It meant she could go home. Get on with her life back in Cambridge putting criminals behind bars. *And crawling out of young women's beds in the middle of the night.* Walking into her cold, empty town house, and for the first time she could remember, that didn't appeal to her in the slightest. She frowned as the thought of it bounced around her head, making her feel out of balance. *What the hell's wrong with me?*

"I thought so. I'll let you go. Let me know if you need anything else, Imogen."

"I will, Roland. Thanks."

She turned over and tried to find a comfortable position, but the scent of frying bacon and coffee wafted under the door and had her down the stairs as she finished tying her robe.

"That smells amazing." She walked into the kitchen and smiled as Amahle drained the bacon on paper towels.

"Good morning, lazy bones. What happened to the early riser? I've got a lot to do today, and since you seem so determined to tag along everywhere I go, I've decided to make use of you."

Imogen shrugged. "I was tired." She stole a piece of bacon and dodged the swat to her backside. "So what's on the agenda?"

"I need to find a doctor for my mother, find my brother, return to Cape Town and give a speech this afternoon, and figure out who's behind the fake drugs racket without my secret weapon."

"Secret weapon?"

"Dr. Marais."

"Ah. You're right. Busy day." She frowned. "I was thinking about that, the doctor, I mean. I think we need a new secret weapon."

"I agree. We definitely need a new doctor, but we need to be sure he hasn't been bought off and can't be bought off. And preferably one who doesn't have a family to be threatened with."

"Heck of a wish list."

"Yeah. That's your task."

"Me? How come?"

"Greg is looking into the local black market. He's going to try to pick up some leads on Sipho. He's also going to keep an eye on my mother. I don't want any more of my family disappearing."

"So he won't be returning to Cape Town with us?"

Amahle shook her head. "Josh's organizing some more people, for both locations."

"I thought that was Laura's department."

"Laura is tracking down information on Major General Pugh and your friend Roland. Just to be safe."

"Right. Speaking of Roland, it was actually him calling that woke me."

"And what did he have to say?"

"Confirmed what we already surmised after your mother's disclosures. Sipho's not my brother and he has been stealing from the vineyard. He also said that there's someone interested in buying the vineyard."

Amahle seemed to pause for a split second as she deposited bacon onto plates.

"That's what you wanted, right? To sell up and go back to England."

"That was the plan, yeah." But now that it was a possibility, it didn't feel as right as she'd expected it to. *England must be losing its appeal.* She glanced over at Amahle. *Nope. More like South Africa's appeal's growing.* "Any doctors on your list for me to start with?"

Amahle shrugged and started eating her breakfast. "I've got enough other things to worry about right now."

Imogen frowned, but Amahle kept her eyes fixed on her plate. Imogen sighed. "Right. Okay then. I'll get on it. Just as soon as I finish my breakfast."

CHAPTER THIRTY-FIVE

Amahle rubbed her tired eyes and tried to focus on the screen as the words swam away from each other. She fought the feeling of nausea she always felt when she tried to work while travelling. Now wasn't the time for comfort; there was far too much to do. By the time Nick stopped the car on the drive back in Bantry Bay, her head throbbed, and it was clear that the reports she had from Dr. Marais weren't enough to get them any closer to the source of the issue.

Laura closed her phone. "I'm sorry. The police said that the house fire was devastating. All electronic equipment was destroyed."

She looked over at Imogen as she sat steadily tapping away on her own laptop. "Looks like whoever you find will have to start from scratch."

"Well, not exactly," Imogen said while she scratched her head, which left her hair adorably stuck out. "We've got the report and we know where to direct the new team I'm lining up."

"Team?" Amahle said. She felt queasy enough at dragging one more person into this situation. A team sounded like a disaster waiting to happen.

"Yes. One thing this has made abundantly clear is that we need a bigger system and a bigger group of people to get this done, and get it done fast. We need everything to be accessible and not reliant upon a single person. That's where this falls down. It makes one person a target and too easy to silence."

She couldn't deny the logic, but likewise it didn't make her feel any easier about the additional people who were going to be at risk. "No. There's already too many people involved. The bigger the team, the more likely we'll have a leak. We don't know who we can trust."

"At this point a leak doesn't exactly matter, Amahle." Imogen frowned. "The people behind this already know we know. They're already coming for us. What difference does that make at this point? And you've already involved the media, so a leak on that front wouldn't cause any more issues than we've already got."

"It leaves too many people open to being hurt."

"I think you're wrong. I think it reduces the possibilities. It means there are too many targets for them to effectively control the knowledge. Ultimately, we want this information to be out in the media. Yes, we want to control the flow, but at the end of the day, in real terms, the sooner this is out there, the better. The more people who know now, the better."

"You can't just throw people at this situation and hope it will stop."

"That's not what I'm doing."

"Isn't it?"

"No. I want everyone safe. I want this situation resolved. I want your family safe. I want you safe." Imogen scrubbed her hand over her face. "Isn't that what you want too?"

"Yes."

"Do you have a better idea?"

It was the fact that Amahle didn't have a better resolution that rankled her. Imogen was right; there was no real reason to worry about the information being leaked at this point. In fact, it might well work in their favour. She was right about that too. It made sense that more targets would make it too complicated, too difficult for the people behind this to eliminate them all and therefore ensure the investigation was completed.

"If the information gets out before we're ready and the perpetrators go to ground, they'll get away with it."

"If that's the worst-case scenario, I think we can live with that. Don't you?"

"Not if that means the abolishment of the treatment programme."

"If the public know what's happened, I don't see how the government could make that happen."

"She's right," Laura said. "They'd never get reelected if they did. The public outcry would be too great."

"Thank you," Imogen said. "So do we go ahead with this or not?"

"I don't have an unlimited amount of money to spend on this, you know?"

"I get it. And don't worry. I won't break the bank." She grinned.

"That smile isn't very reassuring. Don't use it on your clients."

"I don't. I use it on my opposition."

Amahle chuckled. "So who's on this team?"

"You'll meet them in a few hours. They're going to be meeting at your house."

"My house? Why there? Why not my office?"

Imogen frowned, clearly thinking the reason was obvious. "Because you don't know who you can trust over there."

Amahle felt like slapping her own head, but the thought of so many strangers in her home made her skin crawl. It had been difficult enough for her to adjust to having Laura and her team in the house with them. Funny that she'd never thought twice about Imogen being there though. Instead her presence had been comforting. But more strangers. More people she didn't know inside her private space, her sanctuary. She wasn't sure she could deal with it.

"We can try to find an alternative if you're not comfortable with that," Laura suggested, and Amahle hated that her discomfort was so obvious that a stranger was able to pick up on it.

"At such short notice we'd have a job," Imogen said. "Without breaking the bank anyway." She smiled sweetly and winked to take the sting out of the comment.

Under other circumstances Amahle would probably have laughed. Instead she took a deep breath and calmed her nerves. It was for the greater good. Other people had suffered far worse than having some strangers in their homes. *Suck it up, Minister. Time to earn that trust they've all placed in you.* "No, it's fine. I wasn't thinking. Do you have a list of the people coming?"

Imogen handed her the list. "If you're really uncomfortable with it, we can figure something else out."

"No, you're right. It's fine."

"Someone once told me that when a woman says fine it stands for fucked off, insecure, nervous, and exhausted," Josh said from the front seat.

Laura slapped the back of his head. "And when a guy says that it means fucked up, idle, nonsensical, and exasperating."

He rubbed his head. "Didn't know you cared, Lor."

"I actually have a problem with it. How many names are on your list, Imogen?" Nick asked.

"Six."

"And they're arriving when?"

"In three hours."

"We don't have time to vet all six between now and then. Inviting them into the house isn't the best security move we could make."

"Well, we can't exactly keep them outside," Laura said. "I'll ring around a few hotels, see if I can find a room."

"No," Amahle said. "Let's keep it outside. There're no neighbours to overhear what we discuss. There's no one overlooking the property."

"Not very friendly though, Ami."

"It will be if we get the braai going?"

"Braai?" Laura asked.

"Barbeque," Imogen supplied. "We'll need supplies. If we're going to make it feel like a party—"

"I'll take care of it," Nick said, smiling. "One poolside braai coming up."

❖

Imogen stretched her arms over her head and let the cramps ease before diving into the pool and letting the cool water wash away the remaining tension. The braai had been a success. A collection of half a dozen virologists, pharmacologists, and clinical doctors had sat around the patio eating steak, boerewors, and drinking cans of beer while Amahle had outlined everything she knew, the few things she could prove, and the plethora of things she suspected. More than one of the group had admitted to noticing the high rate of AIDS development of those supposedly in treatment, but not given it a second thought. They hadn't realized their own problem was a part of a larger trend.

They'd all decided where their skills lay best in collecting, testing, analyzing, and reporting the findings. All of them were doubling or tripling up their research, and they planned to test samples from each source in at least three different laboratories. They knew that a single source would be brushed under the carpet as faulty equipment, or flawed technique. Something that none of the group wanted to happen.

Amahle was explicit. She told them in minute detail everything she had suffered since the beginning of her investigation. She told them everything that had happened to Thambo, and to Derek Marais. She told them that her brother was missing under suspicious circumstances. Not a single one of them balked. Imogen smiled as she remembered how the group had become more resolute with every detail Amahle told them. They came together as comrades with a common purpose, intent on taking their portion of the responsibility. Imogen had researched each of them as much as possible. Each man and woman at the table was married to their jobs rather than another person. They were imminent specialists in their fields, with sterling reputations for their work. In other words, she'd found exactly what Amahle ordered. People who were ambitious and wanted to leave their mark on the world. Each one of them could see this was a chance to do that, and then move on to even greater things.

But for now all they had to do was repeat Derek Marais's work and get them the evidence they needed.

She broke the surface and pulled herself through the water with long, powerful strokes. Each one helping to loosen her muscles and let her relax. Just a bit. Her head began to clear, and her thoughts drifted from little white pills and threatening phone calls to the woman behind it all. Amahle. She confused her. Yesterday, it had felt like they were getting closer. As though the attraction she knew was between them was pulling them together. Today, it felt as though Amahle was pushing her away again. She executed a perfect tumble turn and kicked off the wall before settling back into her rhythm. One, two, three, breathe. The shy smiles they'd exchanged on the way to the vineyard had felt so natural. She'd felt so happy. Now she felt like she couldn't get a smile out of Amahle.

She knew the strain Amahle was under was immense, but in reality was it that much different from when they'd set off on that walk? Before they'd run into Mbali and discovered her secrets and lies. Before they'd discovered that Sipho was missing. If it was, she couldn't see it. They still needed the evidence to put this drugs racket out of operation and get the real medication back into circulation. They still needed some sort of lead as to who was behind it all in the first place. And they still needed to find Sipho because he was facing jail.

She tucked her legs under her and turned again. That was another thing. What would she do about the stolen money? Should she press charges given that she was certain he was stealing the money to pay for medication for his sick mother? If she didn't, she couldn't claim for the lost funds on the insurance, and how would she explain the discrepancies to her new buyer? One, two, three, breathe. If she did press charges, where would that leave her and Amahle? Would Amahle accept that she had to and let it go? Or would she turn her back on Imogen and whatever it was between them before they even had a chance to figure out what it was? Given how reluctant she'd seemed to even talk to her today, was that something Imogen needed to worry about?

One, two, three, breathe. She flipped her turn and came up on her back, gliding through the water, her arms brushing her ears with each stroke. Why did it matter anyway? What did she want from Amahle? Yes, she was gorgeous. Yes, she was smart and funny, and yes, she could feel the spark between them, but she already knew that Amahle wasn't the one-night stand kind of girl. *And I don't stick around for breakfast. So why even bother worrying about it?*

Her arm hit the side of the pool. She cursed herself for missing her turning mark and rubbed at the sore spot on her forearm.

Why was she even thinking about it? Because she was already sticking around for breakfast, and the thought of being anywhere else made her skin itch. Because the thought of anyone hurting Amahle made her want to hunt the bastards down and tear them limb from limb. Because the idea of anyone else touching Amahle, kissing her, made Imogen's brain implode in a fog of jealousy.

"Hey," Amahle said as she squatted beside the pool. "I'm going to bed now. Let Josh know when you're done. He's going to lock up."

Imogen looked up and noticed how dark it had gotten. Ship lights far out to sea twinkled red and green on the inky black ocean beneath a blanket of twinkling white stars in the vast night sky.

"I didn't realize it had gotten so late."

"You seemed like you were lost in your own little world for a while there."

"Is everyone gone?"

"Yes. The last one left about half an hour ago." She reached out toward Imogen's face, but stopped before she touched her, seemingly catching herself in the act of doing something unconsciously that her conscious mind didn't want her to do. "Well, good night, Imogen. Thanks for all your help today."

"Can you stay a minute? I'll get out now."

"You don't have to. Just tell Josh when you're done."

She reached out and caught hold of Amahle's hand, stopping her from standing. "Please."

"Why?"

"Because I'd like you to."

Amahle smiled. "That's not a very good reason."

"Isn't it?"

The smile slipped from her lips. "It's not a good idea, Immy."

"What isn't?"

"This. Us. You and me."

"Why isn't it?"

"Because you don't do breakfast and I can't go down that route again."

"What if I've changed my mind? About breakfast."

"I still can't do this." She pulled away from Imogen's hand as she stood up and almost ran from the pool.

Imogen pulled herself out of the water and ran after her, doing her best not to slip on the tiles and concrete. She grabbed hold of Amahle's upper arm as she reached the door and spun her, pinning her back against the glass.

"How do you know if you don't try?"

"Please don't do this." Amahle brought her hands up to Imogen's chest, seemingly intent on pushing her away. The moment her hands touched the bare, wet skin, Imogen felt the electricity between them. She didn't move any closer. She wouldn't. Not until Amahle said she wanted her to, but she wasn't going to back away while Amahle's hands were on her flesh. She couldn't. She felt as though those hands were branding themselves onto her very soul. But it was Amahle's eyes that held her transfixed. In them she could see everything she needed to know about Amahle. She could see her vulnerability and her strength. She could see every fear and the courage she had to overcome every one, and the longing that cast a shadow over her heart. A shadow she hid within to prevent the world from seeing her pain. All Imogen wanted to do was be the light for her. To show her how to step out of those shadows and shine.

"You make me want something I've never had." She stroked her fingers up Amahle's arm. "You make me long for something I was always afraid of."

"What?"

"Tomorrow. With you." She slid her fingers around the back of Amahle's neck. "When I look at you I see you." She pushed her fingers into her hair. "I see you today, and tomorrow, and every day after that."

"Immy, this isn't the right time."

"No, you're probably right. But this is the time we've got, and I refuse to have a second of it taken from us again."

Tears shone in Amahle's eyes and her lip trembled. Imogen had never seen her look more beautiful. Amahle closed her eyes as she slid her hands over Imogen's chest and around the back of her neck, attempting to pull her head down for the kiss they both craved. Imogen let her pull her closer until their mouths were within a hair's breadth, their foreheads touching.

"Is this what you want?" Imogen asked.

Amahle whimpered and tried to close the final distance.

"No. You told me you didn't want this." She braced her arms on the glass on either side of Amahle's body. "Do you want me?"

"Oh God, yes."

Imogen sighed and captured the lips so close to her own. Amahle moaned against her lips, goose bumps erupted all over her body, and she couldn't help thinking that it was the most erotic sound she'd ever heard. She ran her tongue along the plump flesh of Amahle's lower lip and gently sucked it before claiming Amahle's beautiful mouth. She stopped thinking and just allowed herself to feel. She felt every inch, every plane and curve, she tasted every second of that sweet kiss. The kiss she knew in her heart should have been her first kiss. She brought her hands to Amahle's cheeks. She wanted to feel her. She felt the dampness of tears against her palms even as Amahle continued to kiss her.

She pulled away enough to whisper against Amahle's lips. "Am I hurting you?"

Amahle shook her head and stretched to kiss her again. Hungry and raw. Amahle's teeth tugged gently on her lip, her tongue sought and gained entrance, and still the tears rolled down her cheeks.

"Please tell me what's wrong." She wrapped her arms around Amahle's shoulders and held her tight. She moaned as Amahle's lips settled against her neck, and a shiver ran up the length of her spine.

"Nothing." She kissed her neck. "Don't stop." Amahle pressed her hips into Imogen's and grasped her backside, pulling their bodies tighter together.

Imogen groaned. "Not here."

Amahle growled and nipped at the skin on Imogen's shoulder. "Don't you dare get me started then leave me."

"No chance." She kissed her again. She poured every ounce of passion she felt into that kiss. Promising with every fibre of her being that the fire she started she intended to douse. "But you deserve better than a quick fuck against a wall."

"What if that's what I want?"

Imogen's head spun at the husky, desired filled tones of Amahle's voice. "Then we can arrange that for next time." She trailed her hand down Amahle's back. "You never did give me the full tour. How about showing me your bedroom?"

Amahle didn't say a word as she took Imogen's hand and led her through the door. Imogen needed to feel more of her, and she couldn't wait until they made it through the house. She tugged gently and pressed herself up against Amahle's back, inhaling the scent of her. The mouthwatering mix of Angel perfume and the slightly spicy musk of Amahle's skin was intoxicating. Her head swam, and it was all she could do to make her feet work.

Amahle didn't even turn on the light when they entered the room and Imogen hurriedly began opening buttons. From the dip between Amahle's breasts to her waist, she tugged at the tiny discs of plastic until the front of Amahle's dress hung open. The royal blue cotton gaped to expose the white lace encased breasts with stone hard nipples straining against the fabric.

"Christ, you're beautiful." Imogen licked her neck and palmed her breasts, squeezing, teasing, and tugging on her nipples. Amahle reached between them, fumbling with Imogen's belt.

"Off. Take it all off."

"As you wish." Imogen stripped quickly, watching Amahle do the same by the light of the moon filtering through the windows.

"Lie down."

Imogen lay back against the pillows loving the way Amahle's hips swung from side to side and her full breasts bounced a little as she walked toward her. She wanted to pay her another compliment, but she couldn't form the words. If she were honest, she couldn't even think of the words. She'd had sex more times than she cared to remember, but watching Amahle draw nearer, she realized that this was different. Tonight she cared more than she ever had before. Tonight she wanted to please and be pleased in a way that hadn't even occurred to her before. It wasn't just Amahle's body she wanted to touch. It was her heart. The only thing that scared Imogen more was the fact that she wanted Amahle to do the same for her.

The first touch of Amahle's body covering hers was almost enough to make her come. Amahle's fingertips trailing over her skin caused her to shiver even as her flesh felt like it burned. Everything felt new, but at the same time she'd never felt so comfortable. Every kiss turned her on more, flooding her body with desire, coating her sex with arousal, and filling her heart with something that she'd told herself she'd never find. Something she'd told herself she didn't deserve. Every touch of Amahle's hand, her lips, her body filled her with love.

"Ami, look at me." She needed to see that she wasn't alone in the way she felt. She wished she was brave enough to voice her feelings, to ask if Amahle felt the same, but she knew she wasn't. She knew that right now the best she could hope for was to see her heart reflected in Amahle's gaze.

Amahle opened her eyes and slipped two fingers inside her. A sexy smile tugged at her lips, but her eyes told Imogen everything she needed to know. She rolled her hips, enjoying the sensation of Amahle's fingers sliding deeper inside her, and the powerful orgasm coursed through her veins. Every nerve in her body burned, her muscles tensed and strained, and every breath merely fanned the flames of the inferno her pleasure made her.

Imogen couldn't be sure how long it took for her to return to her body. It could have been minutes or hours, but when she did there were tears flowing down Amahle's cheeks.

"Did I hurt you?"

Amahle shook her head. "It's just been a long time."

A tiny alarm bell rang in Imogen's head. "How long?"

"Since Grace."

Imogen cursed her own thoughtlessness. "I'm sorry."

"What for?"

"For upsetting you. Reminding you." She shrugged. "Whatever I did wrong."

"You didn't do anything wrong. And you didn't upset me."

"Then why are you crying?"

"Because I kept thinking that kissing you felt like the most natural thing I've ever done."

Imogen smiled, inordinately pleased that Amahle's thoughts echoed her own. "I felt the same."

"And that made me feel guilty."

"I don't understand."

"It felt like I'd dishonoured everything that Grace and I went through, all she suffered being with me, because for that moment I regretted that I'd ever touched another woman."

Imogen tried to hold on to her as she pulled out of her arms and rolled onto her back.

"Please don't say that."

"I'm sorry." Amahle put her arm over her head. "I think you should go."

"What? You can't be serious?"

"Please, Imogen. This is awkward enough."

"It doesn't have to be." She leaned over her, desperate to see her eyes again. To see Amahle's heart. "You don't have to send me away."

"Imogen, I'm sorry. I shouldn't have made love to you, but please. Don't make this more difficult than it has to be."

Imogen knew she needed to fight her corner, to make Amahle see that it was a mistake to evict her from her bed, but she couldn't think. Her precious logic deserted her in the wake of her burgeoning feelings and the sting of yet another rejection. "You wanted me too."

"Yes." She sat up and wrapped her arms around her knees. "But you're the one who doesn't do breakfast. Remember?"

"Shouldn't we at least talk about this?" *You're a fucking barrister! Think, woman!*

"What else is there to say?"

"I don't know. But a lot I'd imagine."

"Good night, Immy." Amahle climbed out of the bed and walked into the bathroom, closing and locking the door behind her.

Imogen stared at the locked door. Goose bumps covered her from head to toe, but she couldn't decide if it was from the chill that had settled on her skin, or the chill that had settled in her soul.

CHAPTER THIRTY-SIX

S ipho squinted into the daylight. He wasn't sure how long he'd been in the boot of Tsotsi's car, but his legs were cramped and refused to work when they dragged him out and dumped him in the dirt.

"See, I told you I still got him. He's a fucking pussy, man. Let me waste him. That'll send her a fucking message."

A thick glob of spit landed on his face. He tried to wipe it off, but his hands were tied together and his effort was uncoordinated.

"That's not how we're gonna play this. She isn't getting the message."

Sipho zeroed in on the new voice. It sounded familiar, but he couldn't place it.

"Then we take her on directly."

"And just how do you plan to do that? Use him?"

"Nah, man, I thought I'd go see her. He's fucking worthless."

A boot touched his chin and pushed his head upward. Not painfully, just so that his face could be seen clearly. He wanted to see who this new person was, but as he opened his eyes, all he could see was a silhouette against the bright sun.

"Always thought so myself. But I think he has information we could use."

"Like what?"

"Like how we can discredit his sister. If she won't back off, my friend in the ministry tells me that killing her will raise too many questions now, so all we can do is dig up so much dirt on her that the people want to kill her themselves. Then it doesn't matter what she finds out. They wouldn't believe her if she told them the sky was fucking blue."

Sipho closed his eyes and wondered how they planned to make him tell them information he didn't know. Then he remembered their mother and hoped that whatever they decided to do to him wasn't enough to make him talk.

"I still don't see why we can't kill her."

"If she's dead there has to be an investigation into who killed her and why. That trail doesn't end well for any of us, Tsotsi, my friend. If we discredit her, then it's her they investigate, and our friend at the ministry can direct them to a trail of breadcrumbs that will cast enough doubt on her part in this so she won't know which way to run."

"I still don't get it," Tsotsi said.

But Sipho was beginning to. At least his part in it all. Whatever was going on behind all this, they were determined to bring down his sister. And he'd played straight into their hands. He remembered how Tsotsi had stolen his phone on the day of the DNA testing. The phone with Amahle's number in. The phone with Thambo's address stored in his contacts list. The phone where he'd stored the passwords to his bank account, emails. Everything. And Tsotsi and his mysterious friend had access to it all. He didn't know how many "friends in high places" the bastard had. It didn't matter. They'd gotten more than enough from him to do God knows what to his sister. *I'm sorry, Ami. I'm so sorry. I was only trying to do the right thing. For Mama. For you. I'm such a fool.*

"That's 'cause you're a fucking genius, man." He laughed. "Just get me dirt on his sister and leave the rest to me, brain box. He's been buying HIV meds from you for years, but you still don't know who he's buying them for, do you? You see, that. That tells me something." He patted Sipho on the cheek. "Take him to this address. And break him."

Tsotsi laughed. "I can do that."

Sipho heard a piece of paper being scrunched up and land on the ground before he was dragged to his knees and a thick piece of rope tied around his bound wrists. "You ready to run, boy?"

"Just make sure he can still talk when he gets there."

"Yes, boss."

Sipho heard a car door slam, an engine rev, and flinched as a shower of dirt and stones were kicked in his face.

"On your feet." Tsotsi and the Professor hauled him to his feet and untied his ankles.

"Tsotsi, did we do wrong?"

"Shut the fuck up."

"But he said not to go see her."

"I said shut the fuck up, Professor. I'm in charge here. Besides, we didn't go see her."

"No, but—"

"Shut up. We didn't do nothing wrong by going there, okay? Nothing."

Sipho felt slow, disoriented, and confused. He wasn't sure he was piecing the conversation together correctly. Why did they want to discredit Amahle? What messages was she not getting? Had they been in contact with her? If so, why? How was his sister connected to a piece of shit like Tsotsi? He started to see that there was something much bigger going on than him working off a debt for medications. But his brain wasn't keeping up with it all.

Tsotsi climbed in behind the wheel of the car, passed the rope about his hands through the window, and gunned the engine. The Professor laughed as he sat on the passenger window and banged on the roof of the car.

"Run, pussy, run."

Sipho tried to keep his feet beneath him as the car gained speed across the rocky, dusty ground. He didn't know where they were taking him. Their choice of transportation indicated they weren't going far, or along any public roads. And he knew the chances of help finding him were slim to none. He didn't see the stone he tripped over, but as soon as he felt it beneath his foot, he braced himself for impact. His shoulder slammed into the side of the car and he tried to angle his body away from it as he fell. The last thing he wanted was to be dragged under the tyres.

His knees hit the dirt. His hands were still on a level with the window when his right foot got wedged under the back tyre. He couldn't release his body to let the tyre pass over it. It was stuck in front of it as Tsotsi continued to drive. He screamed. And the last thing he saw was the gold tooth in Tsotsi's mouth as he grinned evilly at him.

CHAPTER THIRTY-SEVEN

A mahle pulled the blanket over her head and tried to block out the sun. She slapped at her alarm. She didn't want to get up. She didn't want to walk out of her bedroom and have to see Imogen again. She knew she'd hurt her last night, and she didn't want to deal with that. They were both grownups; they could deal with a little one-night stand. Imogen had said that was her usual fare anyway, so what was the difference? *She said "next time" before the first had really begun. That's the difference. I knew she wasn't just looking for a quick fuck and then gone.* She groaned and took a deep breath. Big mistake. Her sheets smelled of Imogen and the passion they'd shared.

She threw the covers off and stared up at the ceiling fan, spinning around and around. She had so many other problems to deal with. Sipho. Her mother. The counterfeit drugs. Too many important things to keep worrying about Imogen Frost.

"So why can't I keep her out of my head?"

Every time she had closed her eyes throughout the night, all she'd seen was Imogen touching her, those milk white hands roaming her skin with abandon. She felt her kisses again and again, and the exquisite moment when her sex had tightened around her fingers and she'd come apart before her eyes. It had been enough to make Amahle come. Something that had never happened to her before, and guilt had washed over her in the wake of her orgasm. It didn't seem to matter that Grace had left of her own accord. It didn't seem to matter that she'd been alone ever since that door had closed. All that mattered was that Grace was broken because of her. Why should she be able to move on with her life when Grace couldn't? Why should she be able to not only touch and be touched again, but for it to feel better, when Grace was still haunted by those memories? What gave her the right to move on? No matter how much time had passed.

She rolled out of bed and stumbled into the bathroom. There was too much to do to stay in bed. She was determined to focus on the tasks that needed to be completed rather than the one subject that her brain was fixated with. By the time she made her way to the kitchen, she'd prepared her most professional demeanour, and no one was going to shake it today. Not even Imogen Frost. Laura was pouring coffee and held the pot up in invitation.

"Definitely. Thanks," she said as she accepted the mug.

"So what's on the agenda today?" Laura asked.

"I'm heading in to my office. I've got work I need to do and then I'm opening a new children's ward at Tygerberg Hospital."

"I saw that on your schedule." She put her mug on the kitchen counter. "It leaves you very exposed. I don't like it. Especially as it was the hospital that Dr. Marais was in charge of."

"And that's especially why I have to do this. I can't be seen to be afraid, Laura. Do what you need to do, but Imogen was right when she said I need to carry on doing what I normally would. I can't let this situation or these threats dictate my life. I simply can't let them win." *I've fought too many battles to let that happen.*

"I understand that. But the opening has been well publicized and the majority of it is set in the hospital's memorial garden, correct?"

"I believe so."

"You understand that if anyone wanted to, they could already have a sniper in position to shoot you and we'd have no chance of being able to stop that?"

"I understand, Laura, and I won't hold you responsible if that happens."

"If that happens, Minister, you won't be around to absolve any of us of the failure."

"Then take my word for it beforehand."

Laura sighed loudly. "You have to follow every instruction we give you, exactly when we give it."

Amahle crossed her finger over her heart. "You have my word."

"Somehow, Minister, I'm not sure I believe you."

Amahle laughed. "Damn, you haven't even known me a week."

"And why would that make a difference? Surely you know the first law of politics by now?"

"And that would be?"

"If a politician is speaking, assume they're lying." Laura's smile softened the words and told Amahle that Laura didn't truly hold that opinion of her. Even if she did of other politicians.

Not that I blame her. Amahle shook her head. "I should've stayed in bed. I shouldn't be getting insulted like this in my own home."

"Who's insulting you?" Imogen asked as she crossed the kitchen and poured coffee into her cup, never once looking at Amahle. The temperature in the room suddenly became frigid.

"I was just explaining the first law of politics to the minister," Laura said.

"Oh, the one where they're lying if their mouths are moving?"

"That's the one."

"And as I was saying, I shouldn't have to put up with this in my own home," Amahle said. She wrapped her fingers around her cup and tried not to look at Imogen. She was still in her pajamas, a pair of lightweight cotton shorts and a soft looking lilac tank top with thin spaghetti straps bisecting her shoulders. The left strap had slipped down, and she quickly swept it back into place. Amahle licked her lips and swallowed. She tried to forget what it had felt like to kiss that shoulder. God, it had felt so good to feel. To feel Imogen's body against hers. She couldn't remember ever feeling so incredibly alive as she had when Imogen's lips had first touched hers.

"How does that sound to you, Amahle?" Imogen asked.

"I'm sorry. What did you say?"

"Laura offered to make breakfast before we have to go. Would you like some eggs and toast?"

"Oh, right, sorry. I must have spaced out there for a second."

Imogen smiled. "So do you?"

Laura's gaze bobbed from one to the other, suspicion written in the frown that marred her forehead. Amahle sighed, annoyed with herself that she seemingly couldn't keep up with a simple conversation.

"Want some eggs?"

"Oh, yes, thanks. Eggs would be great." She hitched her thumb over her shoulder. "I think I'll go and get ready."

Imogen looked at her for the first time since she'd walked in, and the distance between them opened up like an icy crevasse that threatened to swallow her whole should she get too close to the edge. Even in the beginning when Imogen had been so angry about her mother's claim, Amahle had always seen the warmth, the passion, in Imogen's

eyes. Now it looked like there was no emotion at all in Imogen's eyes. Intelligence, focus, determination. But no emotion.
Fuck. What have I done?

❖

Amahle led the way through the maze of corridors and pushed open the door to her outer office. The plant that Claudia watered so diligently was on the floor, soil strewn in its wake and trampled into the carpet. Books had been knocked off shelves and littered the floor. Papers were torn and scattered about the room like confetti. Claudia sat at her desk, phone to her ear and tears in her eyes. She hung up as Amahle walked in.

"I was just calling you. I opened the door seconds ago and found it like this. I haven't even opened the door to your office yet."

"How the hell can someone break in here?" Imogen asked. "This is the Houses of bloody Parliament, for Christ's sake. Don't you have security?"

"Of course we do." *The only way someone gets in here past security is if there's someone inside letting them in,* Amahle thought. It was the only thing that made sense, and one of many things she couldn't say in here. It wasn't safe. She had no idea who she could trust in this building anymore. "Call security. I want copies of the security footage from the weekend, and I want to see the sign in logbook," Amahle said.

"Yes, ma'am."

"Once you've done that call the police. You want to speak to Major General Pugh," Amahle said.

"You trust him with this?" Imogen asked. She perused the scene, seemingly taking it all in her stride.

Business as usual, Ms. Frost? "Doesn't matter. I have to report it somewhere, and somewhere high up as this is a major security breach. The security people here are going to have a nightmare on their hands."

"But if he can't be trusted—"

"Why do you think I want the logbook and the CCTV footage before they get here?"

"Will they give it to you?"

"Yes." She shrugged. "If not, I'll threaten to have the man terminated and get Nick or Josh to steal it for me."

Josh sniggered. "Just say the word, ma'am."

She leaned toward Laura and whispered, "I need this place scanned for listening and video devices. I also want those computers checked for anything that's been accessed since Claudia left. Find out when that was. Discreetly. And then determine if anything has been stolen from the hard drives in here. Your people can do that, can't they?"

"Yes, ma'am, anything else?"

"I don't know. Anything you think we should be checking for on there?"

"I'll have the guys check to see if any Trojan horses or viruses have been deposited. See if they plan on keeping an eye on you from here on out."

"Good thinking. Remember, I want this done discreetly. I don't want them to know we are looking at that if we can help it."

Laura nodded and walked over to Claudia as Imogen approached her. She ignored the pulse of electricity that surged through her as Imogen whispered close to her ear.

"What was that all about?"

"Dr. Marais's office was trashed like this. They planted listening devices and video recording equipment."

"Shit."

"Yup." She turned as she heard the door open. The captain of the security team and two of his men stopped just inside the threshold.

"Minister, the police are on the way, and I have the logbook as requested." He handed it to her.

"Thank you, Captain. And the copy of the footage I asked for?"

"The man who knows the system is not yet in the office. I don't know how to do it, and do not want to risk damaging any of the evidence of what happened here."

"I know security systems," Josh said. "Let me take a look. I'll have it all ready for the police to take their copies when they get here too."

The captain's eyes widened a little, but he nodded curtly and instructed one of his men to show Josh where the security monitors and recorders were all kept.

"Thank you for your help, Captain."

"Minister, I think you and your people need to leave here. The police will need to take fingerprints and photographs. You mustn't contaminate the crime scene."

"I agree. We haven't touched anything but the phone on the desk there." She pointed to the one Claudia had tried to ring her from. "Claudia, did you touch anything else before we got here?"

"Just the keyboard to check the number I was dialling from the contacts list on the computer."

"So the computer was already on?"

"Yes."

Amahle frowned. "Did you leave it on when you left on Friday?"

"No. But I had to come back in on Saturday. I was trying to find that information you needed."

Amahle didn't remember asking for information over the weekend but played along. "Of course, thank you."

"I may have forgotten to turn it off then. I can't remember."

It wasn't like Claudia. She remembered everything, and always turned her computer off when she left. She was fastidious about security, and an open computer was a hackable computer as far as she was concerned. "Okay, thank you." She made a mental note to ask her about that as soon as they were alone again.

"Would you like me to find you an alternative office, Minister?" the captain asked.

"Thank you, that's very kind."

He smiled. "I shall be right back."

When he left Amahle opened the door to her office and slipped inside. The carnage was just as bad in here, but amidst the mess and destruction a box sat on her desk. Neatly placed atop everything else. The hairs on the back of Amahle's neck stood on end and her heart rate accelerated. Curiosity and trepidation warred within her. But the need to know was stronger than her fear.

Imogen stood beside her as she approached, and she was grateful she wasn't alone, despite the emotional distance between them. Her heartbeat thundered in her chest so loud that she could hear it in her ears. The blood rushed through her veins in between beats and drowned out all the other sounds in the room. The box was battered, well used, and covered in stains. Grease, dirt, and something else that she couldn't place, but it smelled. It smelled like a rusty can and roadkill.

Imogen grabbed her arm. "I don't think you should open that."

"I have to."

"Maybe we should get Nick to open it. Make sure it's nothing dangerous."

"What do you think it is?"

Imogen shrugged. "I don't know. But I'm scared it might be a bomb."

"A bomb!" Amahle stared at the box, suddenly terrified to move.

"What the hell makes you think that? They haven't said anything that would lead me to that conclusion."

"Then what do you think it is?"

"Haven't a fucking clue, and I won't until I open it."

"Nick," Imogen called.

"Stop it," Amahle said. "You're making a bigger deal out of this than it needs to be. It's a box. There'll be something in it that's meant to scare me, to further warn me off. That's all."

"Like what?"

"I told you. I don't know until I open it, do I?"

"Please let Nick open it."

"You're being ridiculous." Amahle sliced open the tape with a sharp knife and carefully pulled open the flaps. The scent of something rotten hit her nose and made her stomach roll. She fought to keep hold of her breakfast as she lifted one of the inner flaps and a swarm of black flies buzzed and flew out of the box. Imogen covered her mouth with her hand, her face pale, perhaps even a little green tinge to her pallor.

"If you're going to throw up, don't do it in here," Amahle said.

"I won't."

"Right." Amahle lifted the final flap on the box and found a sheet of paper laid on the top.

"I can't read it upside down. What does it say?" Imogen asked.

"It says, 'You're running out of chances, kaffir bitch.'"

"Imaginative."

"Aren't they just."

"What's underneath it?"

Amahle used a bull clip on her desk to lift the page out without touching it, before wishing she hadn't. She wished she could put the paper back and unsee what lay beneath it. But closing her eyes didn't banish the image. It was already burned on the back of her eyelids, branded in her brain.

"Holy fucking shit. Is that—"

"Thambo's hand?"

Imogen nodded.

"I can't imagine it being anything else." Maggots wriggled and squirmed around the severed end of the appendage, and Amahle felt sick as she thought about how those disgusting little creatures were feasting on the decaying flesh that sat inside the box. Spots of blood had dripped into the box, but nowhere near enough for it to have been in the box since it had been cut from Thambo's arm. The once vibrant, warm, living flesh was now grey-brown in colour and stone-cold worm food. What next? What would they do next to draw her off her investigation? Who was their next target? Who else would get hurt for her?

She swallowed down her revulsion and focused instead on what needed to be done, not how she felt about it. There would be time for that later. Right now she had to do something. Anything. Fuck, everything. "Nick, get pictures. Scan the note. Do whatever you have to do to make sure we have everything we need to investigate this too."

"Ideally, I need to dust it all for fingerprints. You won't be able to explain that away to the police."

"We can't do that. You'll have to make do with photographing the box and contents."

"Yes, ma'am." It took him less than two minutes to photograph and lift Thambo's hand to make sure there was nothing underneath it. He wore latex gloves and worked hard to ensure he didn't destroy any evidence for the police to find too. It took the captain twenty minutes to return. By the time he did they had everything they needed.

"Captain, thank you for your efforts, but in light of my discovery on my desk, I think I'll work from home until we can return to the office. I've already informed my staff of this, so we'll get out of your hair. I'll leave a contact number and a number to divert calls to with reception."

"The police will need to talk to you."

"Major General Pugh has my number."

"He's coming here?" He pointed to the floor. "To look into a simple break-in?"

"Captain, you and I both know that a break-in here is a huge risk to national security and there will be many difficult questions for you and your team to answer. I can assure you they will have as many questions for you as they do for me, if not more. You are in charge of the security of the Houses of Parliament. Do you think a breach like this will be tolerated?"

"We have never had an issue before."

"Not true anymore, is it?"

"But yours is the only office they've been into?"

"Yes. But your people are meant to stop them from being in here. No matter who or why they might want my office, or anyone else's for that matter. You've failed in your job, Captain. If I were you, I'd start thinking about another one."

"You can't fire me."

"I'm not doing. Call it a warning." She watched to see if the phrase had any other significance to him. Wondered if he'd steal a glance at the box with her warning note inside it. There wasn't even a flicker.

"It sounds more like a threat to me, Minister."

She shook her head. "Not at all. A friendly warning. You might want to watch your back. Because other people will be covering theirs already." She looked at the rest of her team. "Are we ready to get out of here, everyone?"

Amahle pulled open the door, and everyone rushed to keep up with her as she went back to the car. She needed to get out of there. She needed to breathe the scent of clean air instead of rotting flesh and corruption. She needed to feel the sun warm her body as fear chilled her to the bone.

As soon as they were in the car, Claudia wedged in with them, Nick following behind in her car. As soon as he checked it for GPS devices, Amahle turned to Claudia. "Why did you come in on Saturday? What did you need?"

"It was for Dr. Marais. He wanted files from the Department of Health. Files about PharmaChem, the HIV programme. That kind of thing."

"Why?"

"He said he was trying to figure out who was behind PharmaChem."

"He thought it was someone in the ministry?"

Claudia shrugged. "He didn't say. Just that he needed the files."

"Do you have a list of what you sent him?"

"No, I'm sorry. I thought the smaller the paper trail, the better."

"That makes sense."

"I think I can remember most of it though."

"Try to re-create what you sent him."

"Sure."

"Where are we going, Minister?"

"Back home." It was fast becoming the only place she felt safe, secure. "I need to wash the smell of that off me."

CHAPTER THIRTY-EIGHT

I said break him. Not try to fucking kill him." The man wrapped a belt around Sipho's lower leg, and a burning agony shot through him.

"Well, he won't try to run now, will he, boss?" Tsotsi said.

Sipho opened one eye a crack. The other was too swollen to move. He saw Tsotsi's head turn with a blow that made spit fly out of his mouth, and Sipho wanted to applaud the man. But his hands wouldn't work when he tried to lift them. He wasn't sure why. He couldn't feel any pain in them, but he couldn't feel any pain from anywhere specifically anymore. Everything hurt.

"Now, boy, you listen to me, and you listen good. I want to know everything about your bloody sister, and I want to know it now. Do you hear me?"

"'Es."

"Good. Now we know about Dr. Marais, and we know your sister has approached a member of the constabulary." Everyone sniggered when the man said that. "Shut up." The titters died down and Sipho wondered what the joke was. "Who else is she talking to?"

Sipho frowned. At least he thought he did, because he had no clue what the man was talking about.

"Come on, boy. I don't have all fucking day."

Sipho stared at the man who stood again in the silhouette of the window. His voice sounded familiar, but he couldn't place it.

"Come on. Who's she talking to?"

Sipho shook his head. He didn't understand the question.

"You know, boy, I used to like you." He clicked his fingers. "Strip him."

A cool breeze flittered over his skin as his clothes were cut away.

"Plug it in, Tsotsi."

Sipho managed to turn his head toward the big man; his gold teeth glinted evilly against the sparks he made striking a set of jump leads against each other.

"Last time, boy, or he's gonna light you up like a fucking Christmas tree."

Sipho bucked against the chair with his one good leg, but he couldn't even shuffle it backward in the dirt. Another click of the fingers and the shock of cold water hit his body like a thousand icy needles. He gasped and tried to gather all his strength. He hadn't expected to make it out of the car boot, but here he was. If he was going out like this, then he was going out fighting in every way he could.

"Fuck you."

The man laughed. "Very good, Sipho." He tossed something to the Professor. "Wrap it around his testicles and put the clippers on that."

Sipho tried again to make the chair move. He needed to get away.

"That's right, boy. Now you get it." The man laughed and looked at Tsotsi again. "When his dick drops off, call me again."

Tsotsi's cackling laughter followed the man out the door. Sipho opened his mouth as they wrapped copper wire around his genitals, and he screamed with everything he had in him.

CHAPTER THIRTY-NINE

B etter?" Imogen asked.
      Amahle turned around, startled, and pulled the towel tighter
around her body. Imogen was sitting on her bed, staring out the window.
      "What're you doing in here?"
      "Waiting to talk to you."
      "Well, I'm fine, thanks." She sat at her dressing table, one hand
still clutching the towel about her body. "You can leave me alone again
now." *What happened to distant Imogen? The one who was around all
morning?*
      "You're not fine and we both know it." She ran her fingers through
her short hair. "Christ, I feel bloody shaky and I barely know the guy."
      "I'm sorry?"
      "Thambo? I barely know him and seeing that shook me up. I can
only imagine what you must be feeling."
      Right. Hand in a box. That's what she's talking about. "I'm fine,
Imogen. I don't want to talk about it." She couldn't do this. She couldn't
make the jump from the cold and distant Imogen she'd been faced with
all morning to the friendlier, more supportive Imogen she'd known
before. The one she'd made love to. The switch was disconcerting, and
right now she couldn't deal with the Jekyll and Hyde routine.
      "I get that. I'd want to forget about it too. I'm beginning to see
your pattern, Minister."
      "What's that supposed to mean?"
      "You forget and ignore everything that bothers you."
      "I don't know what you're talking about."
      Imogen laughed. "Yes, you do. You just want to forget about
it." She pushed herself off the bed. "Go ahead then. Forget last night
happened. Forget you wanted me to make love with you. Forget you

wanted me." She leaned down behind her so that Amahle could see her face in the mirror over her shoulder. Her lips mere inches from her ear. The smouldering heat in Imogen's eyes burned through her, leaving only ashes in its wake. Amahle heard herself moan as she let go of the towel. She desperately needed to touch Imogen. She needed to feel her, to know she was real, and alive, and safe here with her. She needed to take herself away from the mess in her office, the evil that she'd been dragged into, and let herself go from everything around her.

It wasn't until she felt Imogen tucking the loose end of the towel into the cleft between her breasts that she realized what she was doing. She quickly grasped the fabric to hold it in place and protect whatever modesty and dignity she still had.

"Even if you can forget, Ami..." She inhaled deeply, and Amahle could see she was holding back tears. "I won't."

Amahle closed her eyes and heard the door click shut. Why now? Why was this happening now? For eight years, her body had been dormant. Not once had she craved the touch of another. Not once had she reacted to anyone. Now when she most needed her focus all she could see was Imogen's face. She craved her touch as much as her company, and she was fast becoming her drug of choice. *I think I've made the biggest mistake of my life with you, Immy. I just don't know if the mistake was inviting you to my bed, or banishing you from it.*

Everyone was working at their respective stations on a myriad of tasks when she returned from her room. Their heads were hunched over their screens, and they were tapping away on keyboards, scribbling notes, or speaking quietly into cell phones.

"I think we need to rethink this event this afternoon," Laura said as she disengaged herself from her call. "I know we talked about it this morning and you said no, but given what's happened this morning, I think the risk of exposing you is too great."

"Laura, I'm going, and that's final."

Laura threw her hands in the air and stared at Imogen. "Will you talk some sense into her?"

Imogen looked up at her, obviously startled. "What makes you think she'd listen to me?" She looked at Amahle. "I'm no one."

That one sentence made everything about Imogen make sense. Her hyper-competitiveness, her need to be the best, first, to be seen, to be noticed. It all stemmed from an insecurity she hadn't seen in her before. An insecurity that stemmed from the rejection she'd suffered as a child. She wanted to pull Imogen into her arms and tell her she was wrong. That she had never been and never could be no one. She had been everything to her back then. She wanted to tell her how special she was, how caring, how important she'd become to her in such a short space of time. She wanted to tell her all that and more. But she couldn't. *What right do I have to say something like that and then disappear back into the shadows? How would it be fair to Imogen to do that? She deserves so much better.*

"Please, Minister." Laura touched her arm. "It's too big a risk."

"I've never let big risks stop me from doing my work, Laura. I won't let it stop me now." *Shame I can't say the same about my personal life, hey?*

Laura sighed. "Then I would like your authorization to get extra bodies on this."

"Do whatever you feel you need to do. I trust your judgement. I just can't bow to it. I'm sorry."

"Then we need to leave in an hour," Laura said, already dialling the phone before she finished the sentence.

"I'll be ready." She glanced over Claudia's shoulder and pointed to her screen. "What's that?"

"Some of the documents I sent to the doctor on Saturday."

"Yes, but what is that?"

"A list of all the drug trials that PharmaChem has pending approval."

"When was their version of Combivirine approved?"

"Almost three years ago."

"And we haven't heard a dickie bird about it."

"I don't know what you mean."

"Big, home-grown company saving the health services billions of rand with their own development. Why hasn't there been anything in the news about it? It's a great story."

"Because no one knows about it."

"Exactly. Because PharmaChem doesn't want attention drawn to it." Amahle drummed her fingers on her thigh.

Claudia held out a sheaf of papers.

"What's this?" Amahle asked as she took them from her.

"Information about the hospital you're going to and your speech for this afternoon. I wasn't sure you'd had time to write one so I put one together based upon your last couple of opening speeches."

She leaned over and kissed Claudia's cheek. "You're a star. I thought I was going to have to wing it."

"Not a good idea. Now go. I'm busy."

Amahle leaned away from her and tucked her feet under her bottom as she settled in to go through the information. She caught Imogen watching her before quickly turning her attention back to her computer screen and ignoring her again. Amahle sighed and started reading.

CHAPTER FORTY

Concentrate, Frost. Pull your shit together. It's not that big a shock. Imogen stared back at her computer screen but couldn't focus enough to make the pixels form words. It was just a jumble of colours that didn't make sense. The slightest noise or movement from Amahle drew her attention, and she wanted to know word for word what she was reading. She wanted to hear Amahle's voice, even if it was only her speech preparation. She wanted to help. No, she wanted Amahle to want her help. Instead Amahle didn't even want her in the same room.

She sighed. That wasn't true either. Amahle's reaction to her in her bedroom just a few minutes ago proved that. She did want her. She just didn't want to want her.

And that hurts more. She can't help the attraction to me, but she doesn't want me. And that's never happened before, or mattered to me before. She knew that it was about more than a bruised ego, but she didn't want to face that particular image.

Enough. I can't be doing with this wallowing in self-pity shit. Pull yourself together and get the fucking work done. She closed the lid of her laptop and went to the dining room table. *Get done, and then get gone.* She opened another document, clicked through another website, and started trying to piece together more bits of the puzzle. There was something that kept niggling at her. And that was how the bad guys knew that Dr. Marais was investigating them from the start? From Dr. Marais approaching Amahle to receiving the first threat was less than twenty-four hours. Either the doctor told someone else what he was working on and who he was going to talk to about it, or Amahle had. Amahle had told her everything the night Thambo had been assaulted. She had no reason to believe she was holding anything back. That left the doctor. But why? His investigation was dangerous, he knew that, and he took precautions when he approached Amahle. She'd been very clear on that. So it didn't make sense that he would let the information slip.

There was something she was missing. And it was pissing her off almost as much as Amahle's reaction to last night.

She shook her head to clear the intrusive thoughts and opened up the website for PharmaChem. She was determined to read everything on every page. The answer was in here somewhere. It had to be. She just had to figure out what she was looking for. *Or hope I recognize it when I see it.*

❖

"Are you ready to go, Minister?" Josh asked.

"What?"

"It's time to go. Are you ready?"

"Already?" she said as he nodded. "Bloody hell."

"Interesting stuff?"

"Not really. Just trying to learn my speech." She climbed to her feet, slipped on her shoes, and followed them out to the cars. Claudia waved from the door and closed it tight behind them.

Her phone rang as she fastened her seat belt. "Hello?"

"Minister, it's Sergeant Solongo. Do you have a moment or two to talk?"

"Certainly, Sergeant. You have some news for me?"

"More questions, I'm afraid. I still have very little for you in the way of answers."

"Very well. How can I help you then?"

"Does the name Tsotsi mean anything to you?"

"Name of a gangster film I believe."

He chuckled. "Quite. Nothing else?"

"Should it?"

"It seems the film has spawned a thousand Tsotsis in its wake, and one of them is the local drug dealer. Apparently, he can get anything for anyone. As long as you can pay."

"You think he's hurt my brother?"

"Until I find him and talk to him, I have no idea. I don't know if your brother knew this man."

"But you can't find him, can you?"

"That's why I asked if you had heard of him."

"No. Have you asked my mother?"

"She says she knows nothing."

"You're lucky. At least she spoke to you, Sergeant."

"I'll bear that in mind."

"Anything else I can help you with?"

"Yes, another name that has come up in my enquiries is the Professor. Does that mean anything to you?"

"Do you have anything but nicknames to go on?"

"I'm afraid not."

"I'm sorry. I don't know either of those monikers."

He sighed. "It was a long shot, but I had to try."

"I appreciate it. Please keep me informed of your progress, Sergeant."

"I will."

She put her phone back in her pocket and stared out the window.

"No news?" Imogen asked quietly.

"No."

Imogen raised her hand and then let it drop back to the upholstery. Obviously thinking her touch wouldn't be welcome. That her comfort wasn't wanted. Amahle only wished that were the truth.

The rest of the journey was uneventful. The thirty kilometres passed by quickly and quietly. Everyone in the car seemed focused on what they were going to do at the hospital. Except for Imogen. She stared out the window seemingly lost in thought. Amahle imagined asking her what was on her mind, but in a car full of other people she was afraid to hear the answer.

The hospital was massive. Almost two thousand beds at full capacity, and the new children's ward today was another step closer to them attaining that figure. Her connection with this particular hospital was long and well known. It was the teaching hospital for Stellenbosch's medical school, and she had long ago become their patron. She'd thought it one of the reasons that Derek Marais had approached her in the first place.

A marquee and tables had been set up on a grass field outside the children's unit. There was a man with donkeys already giving rides to some of the children. Others were in wheelchairs, only able to clap on their friends and stroke the nose of one particularly timid mule when he was brought close enough.

Amahle decided to ditch her suit jacket and laughed when a clown squirted water in an orderly's face as he smelled his flower. Laura, Josh, and Nick were constantly scanning not only the crowd but also the high buildings all around them. She didn't want to think about what they were looking for. Instead Amahle greeted the doctor who approached her with a warm smile.

"Good afternoon, Minister. I'm so glad you could make it."

"I wouldn't miss something like this, Doctor. Is everything ready for the opening?"

"Absolutely. The ribbon's ready for you to cut, the champagne's chilling, and the kids are ready for a party. We decided to make it a more child oriented event. After all, that's why we're here, right?"

"Of course. I think it's a marvellous idea."

The young doctor showed her around, introducing her to one child after another. She spotted Imogen talking to a couple of kids with their parents over at a hotdog stand and smiled as she watched her apply lashings of ketchup on one before handing it to a small girl looking up at her. Half an hour later, she was standing on a small stage that had been erected, addressing the crowd. Laura and her guys looked confident if a little edgy as they continued to scan the crowd for threats. Imogen stood at the edge of the crowd, close to the steps where Amahle would exit the stage, a plate full of goodies still in her hand as she munched her way through Amahle's speech. Amahle pointed west, to the view of Table Mountain.

"Could you think of anywhere better to be on a day like this? I mean look at that view, kids. Isn't that great?" Murmurs of agreement rippled through the crowd. "I like it way better than my office view anyway. So you can all go back to school. I'm staying here."

Giggles erupted from the children, who all declared she was allowed to stay with them if she wanted.

"Well, thank you, kids. I'll remember that. Now, I believe we're opening up a new ward for you all. Is that right?" She waited for them to nod. "And I'm told it's got a great view of that mountain over there. Is that right?"

"We don't know. We haven't seen it yet," one brave boy shouted.

"You haven't?" A chorus of noes from the crowd had her rubbing her hands with glee. "Well, maybe we should do that in a minute then." The children all cried yes and clapped. "First, we've got to do some of the boring grown-up bits, okay?"

"Grown-ups suck," the brave boy shouted again.

"Thanks. Now, in a minute the waiters will be bringing some drinks round, so I'd like to raise a toast—"

A loud pop rang through the clearing and echoed off the walls, ricocheting around until Amahle couldn't figure out where it had come from.

"Down, down, down." Laura slammed into her, taking her to the ground, and covering her body with her own. Screams from the children bounced around the enclosed area as fear spread like a ripple on a pond. She heard chairs clattering to the ground, and children's crying fading fast as they were obviously carried away from the marquee. Amahle tried to locate where she'd been hit, but the only part of her that hurt was her ribs, where Laura's holster dug in and her elbow, which she'd banged on the side of the makeshift podium when Laura had flown at her.

She felt herself being dragged up and off the stage, Laura's strength hurling her toward Josh and the prone figure he was protecting.

"Stay with him while Nick and I secure the area."

She didn't have time to question the order or why they were staying under a flimsy canvas marquee and not seeking the safety of the brick building twenty meters away. Laura was gone in a flash.

Josh lifted himself up, and Amahle caught sight of what, or rather whom, he had been protecting. Imogen lay in the grass. Blond hair like a halo, eyes closed, a faint blue tinge colouring one prominent cheekbone, and a vivid slash of red stood out vibrantly against the white blouse she was wearing.

"No. No. Imogen, no." She twisted her hands in the fabric and lifted Imogen's torso off the ground. "Wake up." She shook her and gathered her in her arms, holding her against her chest. "Don't you dare die on me. Not you too." She smoothed her hair down and ran her hand over Imogen's face.

"Ma'am, put her down, please. Let me check her."

"Imogen, Immy, wake up."

"Ma'am, please." Josh's big hands tugged gently at Imogen's arm and eased her away from Amahle's chest. "Please let me help her."

She let go and watched him ease her to the ground and run his hands over her body. He cursed under his breath, leaned back on his haunches, and looked around angrily.

"Don't stop. Help her then. What the hell is wrong with you? We need a doctor. She's been shot."

"No, ma'am, no, she hasn't. See?" He swiped his finger through the bright red stain on Imogen's blouse then stuck it in his mouth. "It's just ketchup."

"What?"

Josh pointed to the plate dropped nearby, the food crushed. "I must have crushed it against her when I dove to cover her."

"Then why isn't she moving?"

He ran his hand over her head. "She must have bumped her head. There's a pretty big lump back here. She'll be okay in a few minutes, and then we can get out of here."

"She's not shot?"

He smiled. "No. She's not shot."

"False alarm. Repeat, false alarm." She heard Nick shout. "The waiter uncorked the champagne for the toast."

Josh shook his head and whispered, "Someone needs to take a fucking chill pill."

"She's not shot."

Amahle felt like she was floating, watching her body from above as it crumpled over Imogen and sobbed. Wrapping her arms around Imogen's still unconscious body and clinging to her like a life raft as she floated out to sea. It didn't feel like a false alarm. It felt like a wake-up one.

CHAPTER FORTY-ONE

Imogen opened her eyes and squinted into the light. She felt warm arms around her, contrasting strangely with the cold ground below her. She tried to sit up, but her head was spinning and the movement made her feel dizzier. She lifted her hand to her head. Confident it was still attached, she let go and let her hands explore who was holding her. She smiled when she felt Amahle's skin and smelled the now familiar scent of Angel and Amahle all rolled into one. *My idea of heaven.*

Amahle's shoulders shook, and Imogen could feel that the front of her blouse and neck were damp.

"Hey, what's wrong?"

"You're not shot."

"That's usually a good thing, not cause for tears. Unless you hired the sniper?"

"Funny."

"I try." She coughed and the movement made her head hurt worse. "Christ, I feel like I've gone ten rounds with Mike Tyson."

"No, Josh."

"Why did Josh beat me up?"

Amahle chuckled. "He was protecting you."

"Next time I'll take my chances with the other guy."

"Probably a good idea. The other guy this time was an eighteen-year-old student trying to earn some extra cash as a waiter. He uncorked the champagne a little too vigorously and the team protected us." She eased Imogen away from her. "Vigorously."

"Did you get hurt?"

"Not too bad. Laura's a bit lighter."

"Damn, I got the brick shithouse straw."

"Do you want the doctor to take a look at you? You've been out for a good minute." She wiped the tears from her face, and Imogen was glad to see her regaining her control. Just as glad as she was to see that she'd lost it when she thought Imogen was hurt.

"Nah, I'll be fine. Why'd you think I was shot?"

"I saw red."

"Huh?"

Amahle waved at her blouse. "You're covered in ketchup like a two-year-old or something."

"Great." She looked down at the huge dirty stain right above her heart.

"Come on. Let's get out of here." Amahle clambered to her feet and held her hand out to help Imogen up. "Take it easy. Laura's gone for the car."

"Who was it that overreacted to the cork?"

"Laura," Amahle said, her mouth stretched to a tight, thin line.

"Well, at least you know she's got great reaction times."

"And overreacts."

"You knew she was concerned about the risk here. You can't blame her for doing her job."

"There was no job to be done."

"This time. But wouldn't you rather she react to every possibility than to miss the one that does end up with someone shot?"

"Stop talking sense. You were unconscious. You should be a jibbering wreck."

"I'm sorry. I'll try harder next time."

Amahle paused mid-step and dropped Imogen's hand. "There won't be a next time."

Imogen frowned and followed her to the car. She closed her eyes and rested her head back against the cool leather. It felt great on the warm skin of her neck. "Sorry. I didn't mean to say anything wrong. I'm sure you're right. There won't be a next time. Laura won't overreact, and this mess will all be sorted before we know it."

They sat in silence until they were almost back to her house. Imogen closed her eyes and dozed, trying to ease some of the headache that had settled inside her skull.

"There won't be a next time because I want you to leave."

"What do you mean?"

"Leave, Imogen. Leave me alone."

"And do what? Go where?"

"I don't know. Go back to the vineyard. Live there. Sell it. I don't care. Go back to England. It doesn't matter. Just leave me alone."

"But I don't understand. I'm helping you."

"No, you're not. I want you as far away from all this as possible."

"Don't do this, Ami. Don't send me away. I know you're scared. I know it. But we can work through that."

They were getting closer to the answers; she knew it. The answers to the medication situation, and the answers to what was between them. She was sure of it. Amahle may have thrown her out of her bed after they made love, but her reaction to the non-shot this afternoon was evidence enough for Imogen that she felt something. She was sure of it, and she was just as sure that it terrified Amahle. She was scared of what it would mean for her career, she was no doubt scared of how she could reconcile herself to a new life emotionally, and Imogen understood all that, but she also knew they could do it. It was meant to be. The two of them taking on the world. Together. They were both smart, motivated, driven women. Together, she was sure they could find a solution to any problem they put their minds to. Anything.

"There's nothing to work through, Ms. Frost."

CHAPTER FORTY-TWO

Amahle jumped out of the car as soon as it stopped, ran through the house, and closed her bedroom door behind her. She didn't want to argue with Imogen. She didn't want her to talk her into letting her stay. She wouldn't take that chance. She wished she could send them all away. She wished she could eradicate everyone from her life so there was no one for those bastards to target. No one they could hold over her head. But she knew that wasn't possible. Too many of them were already known parts of her life. Expelling them from her life at this point wouldn't remove the bullseye from their backs. And even she had to admit that the security team were a necessary evil. She felt better knowing that Greg was still in Stellenbosch keeping an eye on her mother, but she needed to organize something for Claudia before she left the house today. She wasn't taking any more chances.

"Amahle?" Imogen knocked and spoke through the door. "May I come in?"

"No. I already told you to leave. Just get your things and go."

"Please don't do this."

"It's already done."

Imogen pushed open the door and strode into the room. "No. I'm not going. I know you're scared, and what happened today, all of it, has scared you more. I get that. But I don't understand how sending me away will help. It just means you'll have to deal with it all on your own. Let me help, Amahle. Let me be with you." She grasped Amahle's hand. "I know you feel it too." She bent her head and captured Amahle's lips in a fierce, hungry kiss.

Amahle couldn't stop herself from responding. She wrapped her arms around Imogen's neck and buried her fingers in her hair. She opened her mouth and moaned when she felt Imogen's tongue stroke hers. She knew she had to push her away and tell her to leave. She knew she had to stop her and turn away. But the warmth of Imogen's body against hers was too much. The desire in Imogen's kiss mirrored what she felt in her heart, and she wanted to feel again.

She realized that for the past eight years she had been sleepwalking through her life. Achieving everything she could have ever wanted, but none of it meant anything with no one to share it with. She'd closed herself off to life in order to survive day to day.

With Imogen's arms around her, she had no choice but to feel. Physically, emotionally, she felt herself ripped apart and healed in the same instant. It was too much. Tears ran down her cheeks as Imogen's kiss gentled and she cradled her head against her chest.

"You have to go, Immy. I don't want you to stay."

"You do. I can feel it."

Amahle rallied her strength and pushed away from the comforting cocoon of Imogen's embrace. "I'm attracted to you, I admit it. But that's all. There will never be anything between us, Imogen. Never. We're from different worlds."

"It's more than just attraction and you know it."

She steeled herself for what she had to do. "No, it isn't. I'm emotional right now. I feel vulnerable because of what's happened to Thambo, and Sipho being missing. You're taking advantage of that."

"Taking advantage? Are you serious? I'm trying to help you. I've done nothing but try to help you since I saw you in the orchard."

"If you really wanted to help me, you'd do as I asked and leave. Staying here, with me, doesn't help me. You're just another thing I have to worry about."

"Another thing?"

Amahle knew she'd hurt Imogen with her words, dehumanizing her, belittling her, but if that's what it took to keep her away and safe, so be it. "I have enough things going on right now. I can't deal with any more. You coming in here like this, pushing me, I have neither the time nor the inclination to deal with your lust. So if you really want to help me, you'll pack your bags and go."

Imogen stared at her. The muscles in her jaw clenched and unclenched over and over; her fingers flexed into fists and relaxed as she worked admirably to control her feelings. Amahle was impressed that the voice and the words that came out of Imogen's mouth were quiet, with no waver or crack anywhere to be heard.

"I'm sorry my presence in your life has been so difficult, Minister.

Please accept my apologies. I thought I was doing..." She shook her head. "It doesn't matter." She closed the door quietly behind her.

Amahle had to force herself not to follow Imogen. She kept telling herself it was for the best. That it was the outcome she wanted—needed. She kept telling herself that the only way to keep Imogen safe was to keep her out of her life. In her head, it made sense. Every time she closed her eyes she saw the bright red stain on Imogen's chest, but it wasn't ketchup. It was blood. And it was spreading. Just as Grace's had. Seeping from her body across the floor tiles, smeared on the walls, and seared into her brain. It was the right thing to do. This investigation was a juggernaut gaining speed, and she wasn't the one in control of it. Well, that had to change.

CHAPTER FORTY-THREE

Imogen pulled up in front of the white house she'd once called home. The vineyard to her left looked as she'd always remembered, with the twisted little vines all growing in long, uniform rows off toward the mountains. The leaves rustled in the breeze, and the sun beat down on the grapes as they ripened. The scent of the sun warmed earth and the fruit was a combination she had once tried to reimagine over and over. Today she wished she smelled Angel again.

She dropped her bag on the floor of the hallway. "Honey, I'm home," she said to the empty house. She still couldn't decide if she'd done the right thing or not abiding by Amahle's wishes and leaving Cape Town. She still wasn't comfortable being so far away if she was needed. She snorted a quick laugh. Who was she kidding? Amahle didn't need her. She'd made that abundantly clear. She didn't want her; she was a momentary distraction. Nothing more. Nothing.

The rejection stung. She was old enough and knew herself well enough to acknowledge that Amahle's rejection tapped into every feeling of insecurity she'd ever felt. It was rooted in her isolation as a child and her fierce independence as a grown woman. She was also self-aware enough to acknowledge that her dismissal was the cause of the itch at the back of her skull that made her need to solve this puzzle. She wouldn't be written off so easily. She was not the powerless child she had been thirty-odd years ago. Now she was a force to be reckoned with and she would show them all. Amahle wanted her out of her way. No problem. She'd do this on her own. Just as she'd done everything else in her life.

Attraction, emotion, feelings were no longer relevant in this equation. Her dismissal gnawed at her sense of pride. She could've helped Amahle crack this open, and she wouldn't be written off as an ally. That was a rejection her ego simply couldn't take.

You don't want to fuck me, that's just fine. But I'm not someone you can fuck with, Ami. I deserve more respect than that. And I will bloody well show you that.

She grabbed her laptop and let it boot up while she dumped her bag in her bedroom and grabbed a notepad and pen. The first thing she wanted to know was as much about PharmaChem as she could find. She put a pot of coffee on to brew as she pulled up the company's website and started reading. It was going to be a long night.

CHAPTER FORTY-FOUR

S top it." Claudia slapped a sheaf of papers over Amahle's head and dropped them on the desk in front of her. "It's been three days already."

"What?"

"Stop moping."

"What are you talking about?"

"You sent her away. If you want her back, do something about it. If not, wipe that miserable bloody look off your face and get on with it."

Amahle bristled. "You don't know what you're talking about."

"No?"

Amahle picked up the papers and ignored her.

"How long have we known each other?"

"What is it now? Two years? Three?"

"A-huh. Long enough that we should know each other pretty well, wouldn't you say?"

"I'd like to think so."

"Good. Now, I get why you sent her away. I get why you think it was your only choice. I disagree with you. But I get it. But I refuse to have to sit here and watch you revel in your loneliness anymore. It was your choice. So, as my Grandpops Johan used to say, shit or get off the pot."

"What's that supposed to mean?"

"Get on with it and do what you need to, or move on."

"I have."

"Bullshit. You can't concentrate. You don't eat. You don't sleep. You're driving me insane. I've got too much work to do to be pandering to your lovesick backside."

"I'm not lovesick."

"No? Have you looked in the mirror lately?"

"What's this?" She pointed at the report Claudia had just given her, hoping the change of subject would work.

"The report you asked for."

"Which one? I asked for many reports."

"Smart arse. The list of information I sent to Dr. Marais."

"It's been three days. Why have you only just finished it now?"

"I've had some trouble getting access to my files."

"What kind of trouble?"

"There's something wrong with the computers in the office, so I'm having problems getting a secure remote link to the server."

"Was that in English?"

Claudia laughed. "Yes. Basically, your server system over at Parliament is compromised."

"How compromised?"

"Ask Laura or Josh. They can tell you more."

Amahle walked into the kitchen and spotted Laura. "Compromised how?"

"Huh?" Laura looked at her blankly.

"The computers."

"Oh. Right. I was just going to come and see you about that."

"Well, you can see me now." The air between them was still strained, and had been since Monday afternoon, but she had neither the time nor the inclination to pander to the woman's bruised ego. She'd overreacted and caused a fuckup. What more needed to be said now?

"As far as we can detect, someone has been accessing the information on your server since sometime on Sunday."

"Whoever broke in?"

Laura shook her head. "From what we can see on the CCTV, the two men who deposited the box on your desk smashed the place up, but didn't do anything to the computers besides smashing a monitor or two. They seem like thugs, with no more expertise than their fists."

"Then who is?"

"We don't know yet. Whoever it is has considerable skill covering their tracks, and they were already in the system before the thugs broke in."

"What? How?"

"Claudia left a connection open between her computer and Dr. Marias's when he contacted her on Saturday for more files. Not something she would normally do, but something that has left a door open for whoever stole the doctor's computer before the house was torched."

"So they have his work?"

"Undoubtedly."

"Shit. They know more about what he was up to than we do." The odds were stacking higher and higher against them. "Why can't we trace the connection back to the source?"

"We're working on it, but the signal is being bounced all over the place, and they're planting viruses as they go. We're basically having to clear a minefield as we go to try to avoid tipping off the fact that we're looking for them."

"Because they'll disappear as soon as they know we're on to them."

"Exactly."

"Keep me informed. Anything else?"

"Not right now. Julius called earlier though. Wants you to call him back."

"Thanks." She picked up the phone.

"Hello?"

"Julius, you left a message for me."

"Amahle, thanks for calling back."

"No problem. How's it going?"

"Slowly. Too slowly. I don't like it."

"Are you not able to verify the doctor's results?"

"Not without his physical samples. I have no idea where they are."

"Can't you get more?"

"I'm a journalist. As soon as I ask for the samples people will get suspicious."

"I thought you had a scientist you were going to work with?"

"So did I. But right now, my guy says he's too busy to help me now."

"Has he seen the research?"

"Some of it. I'm looking into him. Don't worry."

"Just out of curiosity, where did your guy work?"

"In the Stellenbosch University Hospital."

"Tygerberg?"

"Yes."

"Too many connections to be coincidence. Dr. Marais was the CEO at Tygerberg."

"I know. My feeling too. I want to start running a couple of opinion pieces, start asking questions of the Department of Health based upon the published statistics that originally aroused your suspicions. See if we can't make the powers that be a little nervous."

"We don't have the answers yet to the questions that will be asked."

"Maybe a little pressure will start to loosen tongues."

"You know that isn't how it works, Julius. Pressure makes evidence disappear and people turn up dead."

"Then what do you suggest, Minister, because we can't keep going backward and forward like this?"

"Do you know any computer hackers?"

"Excuse me?"

"Someone's hacked my server at the ministry, and we need to figure out who it is and where they are. Do you know a good hacker? My security team don't seem to be able to make a great deal of headway with this guy."

"I'm sorry, no, not really. The only person I know who used to fiddle with computers was Roland. While we were at university, he was always messing around with that shit. Said his girlfriend's sister was a real genius at that shit though. She taught him tons of stuff."

"Roland? Roland De Fries?"

"The one and only. One time he hacked the administrator's computer, and no matter what grade we got on our papers we got a hundred percent added to our scores. Upped our grades like you wouldn't believe. He said it was the girl who showed him how to do that."

"Is he good enough to help here?"

"I have no idea. If he was I wouldn't imagine he'd be an accountant though. Would you?"

"No, I suppose not. What about the girl? Do you know who she is?"

"Sure, he was with Beth back in uni. They're married now. You just need to find her sister and see if she can help."

"Do you have a name?"

"Not sure, it was a long time ago, my friend. Claire or maybe Chloe. Something like that anyway."

"Thanks, I'll look into it."

"We have to do something, Amahle. We can't sit on this."

"I'm not suggesting we do. I just want to make sure the bastards behind this are caught. That they can't pull something else like this in the future."

"Makes sense. But it doesn't stop the threat right now. The longer we wait, the worse the outcry is going to be."

"I know that." She ran her hand over her face. "Okay, write the first piece, but let me see it before you publish it, please. Give me a chance to prepare a response."

"No problem. I know you're doing all you can."

"Thanks. I just wish it felt like it was enough."

"It will be. I'll get that piece over to you this afternoon."

"Thanks." She hung up and started going over the list of information that Claudia had given her. "Hey, Claudia, did you ever finish that shareholders list for me?"

"I put it on your desk."

"Thanks."

CHAPTER FORTY-FIVE

Imogen scribbled on a sticky note and plastered it on the wall. She stood back to look at the tapestry of little coloured squares, the connecting lines she'd drawn across the white wall, and the pattern that was emerging. She didn't like the path it was leading her down. Too many things were tentative and circumstantial. But too many of them set off alarm bells in her head.

The door opening startled her, and she grabbed the carving knife she'd taken to keeping beside her when she was alone.

"Whoa." Greg held his hands out to appease her. "Sorry I startled you. I did knock." He held up a package. "Postman left this on the stoop for you."

"I'm sorry." She put her hand on her chest and the knife down on the table. "Sorry. You startled me." She could hear her heart pounding in her ears.

"No worries." He pointed to the knife. "Glad to see you taking precautions."

Imogen laughed. "Yeah."

He pointed to the wall. "I didn't realize you were into mosaics."

"I'm not. Just trying to piece together a puzzle."

"Mind if I take a look?"

"Help yourself. Maybe you can tell me if I'm crazy."

"Oh, you're far too smart to be crazy, Ms. Frost."

"I thought we agreed. It's Imogen. Tea?" She held up the teapot. "I was just going to make a cup."

"It's not that red crap, is it?"

"Rooibos?"

He nodded.

"I can always change it."

"I'll have coffee if that's all right."

"Wuss. This stuff'll put hairs on your chest, man."

"My girlfriend prefers me smooth-chested."

"I'll just bet the lovely Laura does."

"How did you know?"

"Eyes. I have two of them."

"Hmm. So do I. So what happened between you and the minister?" he said as he followed one of her tracks along the wall, his eyebrow hiking as he reached the next sticky note. "Seriously?" He pointed. "James Wilson sat on the TRC?"

She nodded. It had been a shock to her too. It seemed like an odd path for someone to take. But the more she learned of James Wilson's history, the more his career made sense. A judge of the appeals court for fifteen years before he was brought into the Truth and Reconciliation Commission, Wilson presided over some of the most horrific amnesty trials brought before them.

The commission had sought to bring about a lasting peace in the wake of the crimes committed by both sides of the apartheid fight. Murder, rape, torture, mutilation, the horrific deaths brought about by necklacing—the act of putting a tyre over the victim's head, filling the well with petrol, and setting his "necklace" alight. Every repulsive transgression was to be brought before them, admitted to, missing people or bodies returned to their families, and honesty was to be rewarded with amnesty. Only a full and frank disclosure of your deeds would absolve you of facing prison for the crimes. Everything had to be admitted to in front of those you had wronged—if they were still alive, or their families if not. More than seven thousand petitions were made. Eight hundred and forty-nine people were granted amnesty.

"It's the only link I can find."

"How did you know where to look?"

She shrugged. "I didn't. Not till I looked closer into PharmaChem. But I looked at the transcript of the De Villiers hearing. Given his confession, his amnesty should never have been approved. There were several comparable cases, and all of those were refused amnesty under the terms of the commission." She pointed to the picture she'd managed to find. "His wasn't."

"Why not?"

"At a guess, the panel or the chairman of the hearing was bought off."

Greg whistled. "That's going to be a tough pill to swallow. Peace, as it is in South Africa, is built on these hearings. Finding out there was corruption in them…You're lighting a fuse, Imogen."

"I know. But it fits. Look at it all."

"I see it. But just because this fits doesn't mean there isn't another equally likely and more plausible scenario out there."

"Don't play devil's advocate. I know that. I need to know if this theory is crazy. Not whether or not it's worth the fallout." She sat down again, tore open the package, and tipped the contents onto the table. "Oh fuck."

"What? What is it?" Greg looked over her shoulder.

"A pen drive." She flipped it over and whistled. "A big one too."

"Who'd send you a pen drive?"

"Someone I asked to send me one and then forgot all about it," she said as she plugged it into her laptop and opened the directory.

"Can you stop talking in riddles?"

"It's from the doctor."

"Doctor who?"

"Marais."

"Imogen, he's dead."

"I know. He sent it on Saturday night when I spoke to him on the phone. When we found out he was dead the next day, I forgot all about this." She scanned the files in the directory and noted something she hadn't expected. "Video files? No wonder he said it was too big to send electronically." Her phone rang. She reached for it without taking her eyes off the screen. "Yeah?"

"Imogen. Roland."

"Oh, hi." She leaned back from the screen. "What can I do for you, Roland?"

"Jim asked me to call. He wants to know if you want him to pursue the sale with Pienaar for you?"

"Sale?"

"Yes, we talked about it on Sunday, I think it was. Or was it Monday?"

"Monday."

"That's right. He's interested in buying the vineyard as a going concern just like you wanted. Jim wants to know if you want him to follow that up."

"It's only Thursday, Roland. What's the rush?"

"Pienaar's an impatient guy."

"Mr. Pienaar asked my father to sell the land to him at least once a year for the past fifteen years. I've been talking to my staff here. He'll wait until I'm ready to talk about this deal."

"Imogen, alienating a man like Pienaar, or Jim for that matter, won't make your life any easier. You wanted to sell from the beginning. Hell, you didn't even want to be in Africa at all. Why are you dragging your heels now? Jim says he's offering a very fair price."

Imogen felt her ire rising. She didn't know if she could trust Roland or not at this point. There was pretty damning circumstantial evidence pointing toward not, but even if he was trustworthy, he was in far too deep with all the wrong people for her to be playing bosom buddies with him anymore. "Well, I tell you what, Roland. You can tell Mr. Pienaar that I'll meet with him on Friday, next week, to discuss it. Have him call my secretary in England to set up a time. Bye." She hung up.

"In England?"

"He was pissing me off. And if that's right, I don't know that I can trust him as far as I could throw him."

Greg nodded. "That wouldn't be very far at all."

"Exactly. Now let's see what the doctor has on these video files." She clicked on the one dated earliest and crossed her arms on the table.

"My name is Dr. Derek Marais. I have decided to keep a video log of this investigation to corroborate and record my findings. If you are watching this now, it means one of two things. My suspicions have been corroborated and this record is being used in evidentiary hearings, or I'm no longer around to corroborate my results myself. If that is the case, it is my sincerest hope that my death has not been in vain and that the perpetrators of this vile act of sabotage against the South African people have been brought to justice."

❖

"Now tell me I'm crazy?" Imogen said to Greg. "He came to the same conclusion with different facts."

"I didn't say you were crazy before. Just that this was fucking dangerous. He's a cabinet minister, for Christ's sake, and she knows everything."

"I wouldn't care less if it was President Zuma himself, right now. As for her," she shook her head, "I'm not sure how Amahle's going to take that."

"You still don't have the evidence, Imogen."

"No, but I know where it is now." She pointed at the small pen drive sticking in her computer. "We need to make copies of this."

"I've got a flash drive with my gear."

"Good. I think I've got a spare one around here too." She plugged in the drive and dragged the files across to copy before picking up her phone and punching in a number.

"Hello?"

"Julius, it's Imogen."

"Oh, hey. Listen I haven't finished the article for Amahle to read through yet. Probably going to take me another couple of hours."

"I don't know what you're talking about. I'm not at Amahle's. Not yet anyway. I've got information you need to see. Meet me at her place in two hours."

"I'm in Jo'burg at the moment. It's going to take me at least three or four hours to get to the airport and get a plane over there."

"You won't regret it."

"Give me a clue?"

"I know who's behind PharmaChem, and I know who's pushing the buttons for them in the ministry. I also know why he's doing it."

"I'm on my way to the airport. How did you get all this?"

"It was all in public records."

"You're joking?"

"No. It's amazing what you can find on the Internet these days."

"Isn't it just. Later."

She grabbed her phone and took a picture of the wall then collected the piles of reports, copies of transcripts from the Truth and Reconciliation Commission, and bundled them into her laptop case. She needed to take it to Amahle. She needed to show her what she'd found and she needed to explain it all in person. The threads were a little tenuous, and she needed to show her the research to back it up. But now that she had Marais's research detailed, it was rock solid.

"Want me to come with you?" Greg asked.

"No, you should stay here and keep an eye on Mbali."

"You sure? I don't like that you're leaving here alone, with the keys to cracking this wide open."

"I'll be fine. You're the only one who knows."

He gripped her arm and pulled her close enough to whisper in her ear. "Are we sure about that? Amahle's office was bugged, Marais's office was bugged, maybe his home too. How do we know here isn't? That bitch has been here, after all."

She'd never even considered it. She'd never thought it a possibility that they would consider her place as somewhere that needed to be monitored. *How fucking stupid can you get, Frost? For fuck's sake, that's a rookie mistake.*

"Can you sweep and see?"

He nodded. "Don't leave before we know the results. I can have someone come over here and pick you up if don't want me to take you."

She sat on the stoop while she waited. Ten minutes later, he sat beside her and wrapped an arm about her shoulders. To anyone looking, it would look as though he were offering her comfort. He whispered against her hair to mask the movement of his lips.

"Audio bugs only. No video."

"Shit. They know we have the recordings of Dr. Marais."

"I don't want to wait around for someone to turn up, Imogen. I'm taking you to Cape Town. Laura's got another body en route to take over and watch Mbali."

"Does she know I'm coming?"

"Laura said she wouldn't tell her. We decided that we'd just deal with it when you get there rather than risk Amahle refusing to let you in. Right now, you're in more danger than she is."

"So are you."

"No. I can't tie this up like you can. All I've got is a vague idea that some old white dude's not as squeaky clean as we'd hope he was, and that cops are fucking dirty bastards. Nothing new. You've got all the pieces to the puzzle."

"I want to put this in the post on the way. That way—"

"I get it. If anything happens it'll get to someone else. Don't tell me whose name's on that thing, okay? No one gets to know that from me."

"Deal."

"Okay, let's get out of here."

There was a flutter in her chest as she thought about seeing Amahle again, a movement that she hadn't felt since she'd walked back in to the house on Monday evening. For the first time in days, she felt as though her heart were beating normally again.

CHAPTER FORTY-SIX

A mahle sat on the patio and stared out to sea. She wished she was out there. Anywhere but where she was. The sun beat down on her skin, but she'd never felt so cold. She felt cold inside. Frozen to the core. She closed her eyes and tried to remember the last time she'd felt warm, but all she could see were Imogen's eyes. Claudia was right. She couldn't concentrate. All she could do was worry. She tried to focus on page after page, but every time she found herself distracted.

"Please don't have them shoot me before you give me the chance to explain why I'm here."

Amahle whirled around in her chair. She couldn't believe her eyes. Imogen stood with her hands held up in surrender, a thin cotton shirt wrapped around her body, but the buttons were mismatched, her hair was dishevelled, and her shorts were crumpled. She looked like she hadn't been to bed in days; the dark smudges under her beautiful eyes were testament to that. And the ice began to thaw.

"You're so stubborn."

"So are you."

"Why are you here?"

"Who are you and what have you done with Amahle?"

Amahle simply waited. She didn't want to even try to explain that this was what she made her. She didn't even want to contemplate who or what she was anymore.

"I expected to be hung, drawn, and quartered."

"Might still happen if you don't start talking. You said you wanted to explain something to me."

"We need to take a walk, away from the house."

"Don't be ridiculous."

"I swear, Ami, I'm not being." She lifted the bunch of papers. "But

I need to make sure we can't be overheard until Greg has something under control."

Amahle narrowed her eyes but stood and followed her through the gardens. "Is this good enough for you?" She waved her hands indicating the abundance of foliage and the rocks at their backs.

"Yeah, this'll do." She positioned herself so that she was facing outward and continually scanned around her.

"Have you been taking lessons from Greg or something?"

"Huh, what?"

"Never mind. What have you got to tell me?"

"I've figured it out."

"Figured out what?"

"Who's behind it all. I called Julius. He'll be here in a few hours. If you want me to wait and go through it all when he gets here, we can do that."

"Do I hell. Start talking."

"Have you seen who the shareholders of PharmaChem are?"

"Yeah, it's another company. Well, three of them actually. Davit Imports, SecPlus International, and a company called Platinum Products."

"Got any further into those?"

"No."

"Well, that's where it starts to get interesting. Davit Imports holds twenty-five percent of PharmaChem and is a shell company owned solely by one James Davitson."

"Your lawyer?"

"Hmm. I'm only claiming him by default."

"Whatever. How does he get involved with a pharmaceuticals company?"

"Through his best friend who owns the other twenty-five percent company, SecPlus International."

"His best friend?"

"Yes. Fred Pugh."

"I knew I couldn't trust that slimy bastard."

"It gets worse."

"Couldn't possibly."

"It does. The company that holds fifty percent, Platinum Products."

"Another shell company?"

"Yes. Owned by Elizabeth De Fries and Claudia De Villiers."

"Excuse me? What?"

Imogen didn't say anything. She simply took hold of Amahle's hands and waited.

"Did you just say De Villiers? Claudia De Villiers?"

"Yes. I'm sorry, Ami."

Amahle pulled her hands away. "But she would have told me."

"Ami, you know that's not—"

"She'd been a friend to me. She's been here through every single—" Every moment of the investigation flashed through her brain. Her first meeting with Dr. Marais, she remembered how Claudia had made her question her safety with him. A feeling that had led to her asking Claudia to be there, taking notes, the whole time they had talked. Every bit of news she'd received she'd had Claudia document. Every report she'd read, barring the one from Dr. Marais, had been gathered or written by Claudia. Every move they made, Claudia was informed or with them. Every discovery they made, Claudia knew too. The words that they'd said on the phone came from her.

"How do they get to be the shareholders in a billion rand company? That doesn't make sense."

"It does, but you're going to have to follow this back a bit with me. Fred Pugh was married to a woman called Nicole. Did you know that?"

Amahle shook her head. "Why would I?"

"Old Stellenbosch family, I thought you may have heard of them. Nicole Pugh was born Nicole De Villiers."

"As in Colonel Johan De Villiers?"

"Yes."

"Everyone in Stellenbosch knows of that old bastard. Most of us watched his amnesty hearing."

"You were there?"

"Yes. One of the atrocities he sought amnesty for was killing Mandla Nkosi."

"He was the bastard who killed your dad?"

She nodded. "My father was part of the resistance. The police arrested him one night. Dragged him out of the house and just took him. We didn't know where they took him. The police wouldn't tell us. They didn't have to. We were just another black family looking for another political prisoner."

"How old were you then?"

"Nine, almost ten."

"What happened?"

"My father never came back. When the TRC began the hearings, Gogo went to them. She wanted to know what had happened to her son. There was enough evidence to bring Johan De Villiers to trial, so he did what everyone did back then. He petitioned for amnesty." She stared ahead of her, no longer seeing Imogen or the gardens where they stood. Instead she saw the town hall in Stellenbosch. Three tables set upon the stage, the dance floor covered with benches and chairs. As many as they could cram in.

"I was supposed to be in school, so I sat at the back of the hall. Mama and Gogo sat at the front. Mama was crying, like she always could for an audience. And this man sat there and told everyone what he did to my father. He told them how he beat him. He whipped him until the skin fell off his back. He told them how my father refused to give them the information he had, so they had to escalate his interrogation." She snorted a bitter laugh. "Interrogation, that's what the bastard called it. He had his body doused with water and cooper wire wrapped around his testicles. They electrocuted him. Over and over again."

"Jesus."

"No, he wasn't there that night. But my father wasn't the only wretched soul they subjected to that particular technique. Every police officer had their own signature move. De Villiers and his particular little gang loved the copper wire trick. He said most men talked very quickly when this technique was used. If they didn't, it would eventually just drop off."

"That's a mental image I could've lived without."

"Me too."

"I'm sorry. I didn't have time to read all of the transcript. Just enough to know that he never should have been granted amnesty."

"Very true. But how does that explain those four being the shareholders in PharmaChem?"

"Nicole Pugh was a doctor. A pharmacologist. And Daddy funded her to start a small pharmaceuticals company with ill-gotten gains from his days as a corrupt policeman before the end of apartheid. Johan De Villiers owned the company until his death in 2000, when ownership passed to Fred and Nicole Pugh. From the looks of things, in 2004, the company ran into trouble and a third partner was taken on to help them out. Jim Davitson. Fred and Jim were at school together, university; Jim even tried out for the police before he went to law school and then sat the bar."

"Okay, so that's the history of the company."

"Not quite. Nicole Pugh was a brilliant pharmacologist by all accounts. She was the one who developed the genuine Combivirine. She reduced the production cost and produced the required evidence to get it to the FDA, but she died six months before it was due to come to the review board. She never had the chance to get it out there."

"Right, so who did?"

"When Nicole died her daughters inherited her share of the company."

"Beth De Fries and Claudia De Villiers."

"Correct. Neither of them are the scientist their mother was, but seemingly they have other skills. Beth, by all accounts, is an exceptional saleswoman and has a knack for talking people into doing what she wants. From buying drugs from her, to approving incomplete drug trials. Claudia apparently has more talent with computers. Anything from hacking to creating a software programme in the company's ordering system that allows them to input the correct code for the Combivirine, and the computer produces replica pills made of aspirin, all the while no one knows any different on the packing floor, the delivery drivers, no one."

"So how does a company like this manage to get a drug approved when their developer was already dead?"

"The drug was complete. The reports for the final trial just hadn't been completed and signed off. I believe a little blackmail may have been utilized in this instance."

"Blackmailed who?"

"Your boss, James Wilson."

"With what?"

"You knew that before he went into politics he was a judge, didn't you?"

"Yes."

"He was the advocate who granted Johan De Villiers amnesty."

"You think he was bought off."

"Yes."

"Can you prove that?"

"No."

"But?"

"Don't you think it's a little odd that he never mentioned it to you?"

"Perhaps he didn't want to rake up the past. I mean, I was there and I didn't even recognize him. All I saw that day was De Villiers."

"Maybe that is the reason he didn't say anything. Maybe it isn't. But Johan De Villiers was found dead, supposedly hung himself six months after he literally gets away with murder. I saw a news article where 'friends' said he couldn't live with his deeds on his conscience. Even if the commission saw fit to forgive him, he couldn't forgive himself. Does that sound likely to you?"

"I'm not aware of many people who were granted amnesty taking their own lives. No."

"The day after, James Wilson declared his intentions to run for office."

"Coincidence?"

"Maybe. But there was a query about where certain aspects of his campaign funding came from."

"James Wilson is a sixty-five-year-old man."

"Who's about to retire and collect a very healthy pension for the rest of his life."

"Who isn't going to be going around chopping people's hands off and burning down houses. Besides, have you forgotten that Isabelle's account says it was a black man who put her out the window? James Wilson's as white as you are."

"Do you think it's possible that people have been hired to do the dirty work? Do you not think that these men are more than capable and in supreme positions to find thugs to take care of things like that? A police major general and a lawyer?"

"You're clutching to make your theory fit."

"I'm not the only one to come to the same conclusion."

"Who else?"

"Dr. Marais. He came to it a different way, but he got there too. He found all the PharmaChem FDA approval filings, and found that only one had been signed off by James Wilson. When he followed that he discovered that this was the only approval Wilson ever signed."

"Not very clever if you want to keep your identity secret."

"Without this, what reason would anyone have to question it even if they did find it?"

"How do you know he found that information?"

"He sent me his files. I got them earlier today."

"But he only would have gotten those because Claudia gave him access. How do we know they aren't corrupted?"

"Think about it. Claudia gave him what he was after, yes. On Saturday afternoon. Saturday night, he was murdered and his house…

all the files…were destroyed. Everything gone. I spoke to him on the phone on the way back from the ball while you were talking to Julius. Claudia wasn't there. That was the only time she wasn't privy to the information that we got from the doctor. She left his link open so that she could distract from what was really going on. The link wasn't to spy on you; it was to spy on him."

"Then why leave it open?"

"Because closing it would look suspicious after the break-in."

"Did Derek name them all too?"

"No. He had the shell company names and he found Fred and Jim. He got James Wilson from the FDA stuff."

"But not the girls?"

"He was suspicious of Beth De Fries. She was the woman he met with from PharmaChem. He didn't know anything about Claudia. He gives sworn accounts in video logs of his investigation and all his findings."

"Are they admissible?"

"Given his death, the fact that we know now where his evidence is hidden, I don't see why it wouldn't be admissible in court. Despite what the defence will try to argue."

"So, it's over? We have all we need to break this and get it taken care of?"

"As soon as we secure your secretary and find a cop we can trust to arrest people."

"Is that what Greg was supposed to be taking care of?"

"Yes."

"Which leaves us with finding a police officer. I'd suggest Sergeant Solongo, but I don't think that would work. He's too low in the food chain."

"We can ask Julius who he suggests when he gets here. He knows who's trustworthy and who isn't."

"How did you manage to work all this out when we've been working on it for weeks and couldn't?"

"It wasn't that difficult in the end. As soon as I started doing my own research it was all there in publicly accessible files. I just had to do the looking myself, rather than take it as gospel from Claudia."

"Of course."

"She's sabotaged your investigation from the outset. You know that, don't you?"

"It does make sense."

"You need to be careful. If she's as good with computers as it would seem, we need to ensure that she hasn't been burying a trail that leads away from her and straight to your door. After all, your connection with her is a lot stronger than James Wilson's."

"You think she's trying to set me up?"

"I think she's a very manipulative, clever, and deceitful woman. And I think she's very capable of doing that. Whether or not she has remains to be seen."

"I'll get Laura's people to start digging. Now that we know what to start looking for, that should be easier."

They stood in silence for a few moments as she tried to absorb everything Imogen had said. It wasn't happening. There was simply too much for her to process. One betrayal after another, peeling back the layers of her soul and leaving her exposed. James had mentored her through her early days in office. Now she knew why. Guilt was a powerful motivator for some people. But not as powerful as money, it would seem. Claudia. She couldn't reconcile the woman who had sat by her side, her supporter, her sounding board, her friend. She'd trusted her implicitly. Her duplicity shook Amahle to the core.

How could she be so wrong about someone? How could she trust so soundly and be betrayed so thoroughly? But it went even deeper, didn't it? It went to her mother and her brother. The lies they'd told, the secrets they'd kept from her, all added to the disloyalty that surrounded her. Was there no one she could trust? Was there no one she could say, hand on heart, she was sure of?

From time to time over the years, she'd watched the clouds settle over Table Mountain, cover the flat top, and float down the side like a white linen cloth wrapping it up. She often wondered what it would be like to be up there at that moment. The second the fog came down and removed one's sight, muffled the sound, and enveloped one in a cocoon of sensory deprivation. She wished she was inside that now. The idea of not feeling anything was so very appealing.

Right then there was only one thing that she was sure of any more. Imogen. She'd sent her away and still she'd worked to help her. Not just help but done everything in her power, on her own, to fix Amahle's problems. She'd proven herself loyal and true, and she'd done so after being rejected. Amahle was disgusted with herself. That she could have treated her in such a way made her feel nauseous.

"I'm sorry," Amahle said.

"What for?"

"For telling you to leave."

She heard Imogen swallow. "Which time?"

"Every time."

"Thank you. That means a lot to me." Imogen turned around. "I'll leave you to your thoughts."

"Please don't go."

"I thought you wanted me gone?"

"So did I."

"What changed?"

"Nothing. Everything. You."

Imogen looked at her for a long time, and Amahle felt like an insect under a microscope. "I'm sorry, but I don't think it's a good idea. I'm going to go and find a hotel I can check into later."

"A hotel? Why?"

"The house at the vineyard is bugged. I don't want to go back there."

"They've bugged it? And you're seriously thinking of leaving here? Are you crazy?"

"Look, Amahle, I won't stay where I'm not wanted. Never have, never will. You made it clear you didn't want me here. I needed to let you know what I learned so I ignored your wishes. I'm sorry for that. Truly, I am. But I've done what I needed to do now. I won't impose. I'll wait till Julius gets here and then once I've told him, I'll leave you alone."

It may have been what she wanted a few days ago, it may well have been what was in both of their best interests, but the idea of Imogen walking out the door again was more than Amahle wanted to contemplate. It wrapped around her brain like the fog over Table Mountain, enveloping her in a suffocating blanket of dread and confusion. Despite every act of perfidy she faced, despite the fact her whole world now stood in ruins, she knew she could handle it all. She couldn't face Imogen saying good-bye. Not now. Not ever.

"Imogen, listen to me, please. I only wanted you to leave so that you weren't in danger. That time has passed now. You are in danger. Leaving here will increase that. Don't leave. You're safer here with the team than in a hotel."

"I've told you. I won't stay where I'm not wanted."

Amahle reached out. "You're very wanted here."

❖

"I don't think so."

"Immy, you are. Everything I said was my attempt at keeping you safe. That's all I wanted. For you to be as far from danger as possible. When I saw you on the ground on Monday, I truly thought you'd been shot. I thought you were dead. I flipped. Half the time I looked at you on the way home and I saw Grace, the other half, I saw your face on her wounded body." She wiped the tears off her cheeks. "I couldn't do it. I couldn't risk that happening to you."

"That was my risk to take, Amahle. Not yours."

"I know, and sending you away didn't stop you from taking it. I know. Without you we wouldn't have the pieces we have and this thing wouldn't be almost over." She reached out and took hold of Imogen's hand. "You were right in what you said. I do want you, and it is more than just a casual attraction." She bit her lip. "So much more already. I know we haven't been in each other's lives for very long, but a part of me feels like you've always been with me. And that scares the shit out of me. You scare the shit out of me."

Imogen laughed at the honesty. "Me too."

"But you're braver than I am. You always were." She ran her thumb over the back of Imogen's hand, and Imogen couldn't suppress the shiver that ran up her spine. "Since the minute I found out your father died I haven't been able to stop thinking about you. Wondering if you were coming back. Wondering if you would even still remember me."

"I never forgot you."

Amahle smiled. "I know, and I never forgot you."

Imogen shook her head. "I'm no one, Ami." She tried to pull her hand away, but Amahle wasn't letting go. "I'm nothing."

"You couldn't be more wrong." She stepped closer and pushed her fingers into Imogen's hair, scraping her fingernails gently over her scalp. "You've already become everything to me."

She tugged Imogen's head down to hers and pressed her lips against Imogen's. Every hair on Imogen's body stood up and reached out to Amahle. She desperately wanted to pull her closer, but she couldn't seem to move her limbs. The smell and feel of her was so intoxicating she felt as though she had no control of her body. She felt as though every atom of her being was ripped asunder and re-created in that moment.

"How did you do it?" Amahle whispered against her lips before tugging the lower one between her teeth and sucking on it.

"Do what?"

"Make me feel again."

"I didn't do anything."

"Yes, you did." Amahle leaned forward and cleaved her body against Imogen's. "You brought me back to life." Amahle cradled Imogen's face in her hands and stared deeply into her eyes. "I'm sorry."

"For what?"

"For hurting you. I did it on purpose because I knew it was the only way you'd leave me. I promise I'll never do that again."

"It's okay."

"No, it isn't. But I'll work on that."

Amahle kissed her again, and Imogen felt tears on her cheeks again. "Why do you always cry when we kiss?" Imogen asked.

"I'm not crying, Immy."

"I can feel it."

Amahle softly wiped the tears away from Imogen's eyes and then leaned in to kiss her eyelids, the tip of her nose, her cheeks, and her forehead before seeking out her lips again.

"Please say you'll stay here. I have plenty of rooms for you to choose from, or…"

"Or?"

"There's plenty of space in my bed."

There was nothing Imogen wanted more, but her pride wasn't quite ready to let go without some kind of fight, regardless of her heart, body, and soul being ready to follow Amahle like a puppy dog. "What about your career?"

"I guess we'll just have to see how much my voters really care about my sexuality. It's a risk I'm willing to take."

"Why now?"

"Because I can't stop thinking about you. Because I can't stop wanting you. Because I can't stop wanting to know what you're doing, thinking, feeling, every second of every day. Because I hope to God you feel the same way." Her kiss lingered as Amahle's fingers explored the skin at the nape of Imogen's neck. "Do you?"

Imogen didn't say a word. She couldn't. She pulled Amahle's body tight to hers, smiling against her lips as Amahle devoured her mouth. She ran her hands up Amahle's back, enjoying the way her muscles moved under her hands as her hips undulated while their desire bloomed.

"Mmm hmm."

Amahle tore her mouth from Imogen's with an audible pop. Her arms still wrapped around her neck, Imogen struggled to turn her head and see who had interrupted them.

"Julius just called from the airport. He'll be here in twenty minutes," Laura said. "Sorry to interrupt." Imogen could hear the smirk in her voice. "Carry on."

Imogen chuckled and clasped her hands around Amahle's waist. "Perhaps we should continue this conversation later?"

"Probably a wise idea." She leaned down and kissed Imogen's lips once more. "Not a good idea." And once again. "But a wise one."

CHAPTER FORTY-SEVEN

Hey, boss, his dick didn't drop off yet, but I'm pretty sure it won't fucking work again." Tsotsi chuckled at his own joke.

Sipho tried not to move. Every time he did it only hurt more. Every nerve felt like it was on fire. There were brief moments of numbness, and he prayed those would last. But then the Professor would touch some part of him. He didn't think it was with the crocodile clips, but it didn't matter now. At least the heat and electricity had cauterized his mangled ankle and stopped him from bleeding to death. When he considered that, he wished it hadn't.

"Has he said anything yet?"

"Just cried."

"So you're a hard man, eh." The man crouched down, and Sipho was able to see his face clearly for the first time, and he hoped like hell that he didn't realize he wasn't unconscious. "I was a young man when my father-in-law, Johan, taught me this technique. He brought this guy in, already had the shit kicked out of him, and he showed me how to wrap 'em up. Like cotton on a bobbin, he said. Just keep wrapping it around." He tapped Sipho's cheek. "Know who that was, boy?" He gripped Sipho's cheek and turned his head from side to side. "You've got a look of him after all."

The words made sense, but at the same time they didn't. He opened his mouth to demand what he was talking about, but the words never made it.

The man laughed. "You want me to make it easy on you? Okay, I can do that." He leaned in close and whispered, "I was there when they did this to your father, boy. Me and my father-in-law, my fucking hero, lit your pops up like a firecracker. Sang like a fucking canary." He stood up straight and laughed. "Since he's not saying anything to us let's send him back to his sister. There's more than one way to skin a cat. Cut out his tongue and dump him on her doorstep." He sniggered. "By the time she sees him she'll wish she kept her nose out of other people's affairs."

"Right, boss. You got a delivery address?" The door closed and Sipho could hear the Professor giggling gleefully as he held Sipho's nose until he opened his mouth to breathe.

"Not here, you dumb shit. He'll bleed all over my fucking car, man. We'll cut it when we get there."

They grabbed his legs and arms and the agony was too much. Liquid fire flowed over his body, through his veins, and escaped through his screams. The rough carpet on the bed of the boot prickled at his over sensitive skin. His body shook, his control gone.

"Fuck, man, he pissed all over your car, Tsotsi man."

"Fucking pussy." Tsotsi's fist thrust his head into the floor and Sipho let go and allowed the comforting blackness of unconsciousness to envelop him.

Jostling brought him round untold minutes or hours later. It didn't matter. With awareness came pain, and he tried to conjure up the blackness, the numbness, once again.

"Wakey, wakey, boy." Tsotsi slapped his face and grabbed his flaccid jaw. "One last gift to remember me by." He laughed as he tried to grab Sipho's tongue. He was quick to clamp his teeth, protecting the muscle. Instead he tried to scream without opening his mouth, he tried to kick out, punch, anything.

"Tsotsi, someone's coming."

"Fuck. You got lucky, boy. He told me not to kill you."

A flick of his wrist and Tsotsi was gone. Hot, thick blood ran across his lips, down his throat, and dripped audibly onto the concrete beside his ear. Giggles and laughter accompanied the sound of a car engine roaring into life.

Sipho tried to get his arms to work enough to press on his cheek, to stem the flow of blood, but they wouldn't work. He tried to roll onto his side so he didn't swallow the hot blood running across his lips, but he couldn't coordinate the effort. Then he forgot why he was fighting at all, and stared up at the wrought iron gate, the razor wire, and the perfect blue sky above. A plane carved a white line into the blue hundreds of feet above him. *I never got to go in a plane.*

CHAPTER FORTY-EIGHT

The automated buzz on the security gate alerted them to activity outside. Amahle checked her watch.

"I thought you said twenty minutes till Julius got here?" she said to Laura.

"That's what the man said."

"He must have gotten the fastest taxi in Cape Town." She stared at the transcript Imogen had given her of the Truth and Reconciliation hearing of Colonel Johan De Villiers. She knew she needed to know what was in here. She knew it was vital to proving the link between Wilson and PharmaChem was deeper than simply signing a piece of paper, but for the life of her she couldn't force herself to read it. She'd grown up on the stories of the horrors contained in reports like this, and she'd been at the trial itself. She knew about the beatings, the torture, the rapes, and the necklacing. On both sides, people had confessed to their most heinous deeds in the hope of amnesty. Some confessed with no more thought than to retain or regain their freedom, some in the search of something more elusive, something even more precious and much harder to find. Redemption. Forgiveness. To reclaim their humanity, perhaps even their souls.

"What the hell is that?" Laura scowled into the monitor.

"It isn't Julius?" Amahle asked.

"Not unless he's IDing himself with the foot of a coloured man. Josh, Greg, go and take a look." She glanced over her shoulders. "No chances, boys."

Greg took his gun from his waistband, checked it, and held it ready. "Not one."

Josh opened the door and Amahle stood over Laura's shoulder, staring at the monitor as she switched the feed to as wide a shot as she could.

"What is that?" Amahle pointed to the screen. "It looks like rubbish."

"No. That's a foot there," Laura said, pointing. "But that should look the same if it was a foot. That looks like a lump of meat or—" She punched keys on the laptop and zoomed in closer. "Oh fuck."

"What? What is it?"

"Boys, make sure we're clear out there, but I'm calling for medical help. We've got a casualty out there."

"Roger."

"Who? Who is it?"

"You can see as much as I can, ma'am."

"We're clear out here," Greg said. "We need medical attention, fast."

"On my way. Who is it?" Laura said as she jumped to her feet and grabbed the medical kit they'd brought with them. When they'd first arrived, Amahle thought they were being ridiculous with the amount of supplies they brought with them. Now she only hoped it was enough to help whoever was out there. Whoever had been left as her next message.

"It's Sipho," Josh said.

"No." Amahle grabbed the door handle and dragged it open, Imogen and Laura right behind her. Her heart pounded in her chest as she cleared the driveway and rounded the gate. She stopped and pulled a huge breath into her lungs. "That's not Sipho."

"Are you sure?" Josh asked. "From the pictures I saw I thought it was."

"No, it can't be." She stared down at the bloody, mangled body. Greg and Laura had rolled the man—she was sure it was a man—onto his side and held thick cotton pads to his cheek. They were talking so fast she couldn't make out any individual words. He was naked. The lump of meat they'd seen on the monitor was all that remained of his right foot, and the plethora of cuts, bruises, and wounds told their own tale of everything the poor man had suffered.

"It is Sipho," Imogen said from beside her.

"No, it's not. Sipho's got—he's not—he's…" Amahle stared at the body on the ground, and slowly, the swollen and indistinct features began to swim into focus. The scrapes on his knuckles, the ones she'd seen at the hospital, were almost healed, but every other wound was bleeding freely or seeping blood slowly onto the concrete. The flesh around part of his ankle looked charred, as did his fingertips. A long, thin cut along his cheek ran from the corner of his mouth up to his ear.

"It is him," Imogen said.

Josh nodded and continued to scan the area. The knowledge didn't change his actions or his demeanour at all. He just stood there, looking up and down the street.

"Why aren't you helping him?" Amahle shouted. "Why are you just standing there? Help him."

Imogen wrapped her arms around Amahle's shoulders and spoke quietly into her ear. "He's doing his job, sweetheart. Laura and Greg are helping Sipho."

Amahle tried to shake her off. She wanted to push Josh. She wanted to grab his arm and drag him to Sipho's prone body, to make him do something.

"They don't need Josh getting in the way. They're doing everything that can be done for him. Josh's doing the best thing he can right now. He's making sure they're safe to help Sipho, and that you're protected while you're out here." She turned Amahle's face until she had no choice but to look at her. "He's going to be okay. Trust them. They're an amazing group of people, and they know what they're doing here. Let them do it."

Amahle wanted to get away from her. She wanted to kneel by Sipho and tell him it would be all right, just as she had when they were younger. She wanted to tell him that she was sorry they'd hurt him because of her. She wanted to take all the pain he had suffered and feel it herself, suffer it herself, to save him from it. But she couldn't. She felt impotent. Just as she had when she had lain on the floor of her home and watched as Grace had been ravaged.

The paramedics arrived and were quickly into action. She could see the movement but couldn't make out any individual moves. She knew she was helped into a vehicle, and she knew she was led down a corridor to a hospital room. She knew she was surrounded by people, but the only one she could see was Imogen. Imogen holding her hand and telling her that she'd be okay, that Sipho would be okay. She wasn't sure how long she sat listening to Imogen's voice, no longer hearing her words, just her voice. The low tones, slightly husky with emotion, and filled with caring as she glanced over frequently.

All Amahle looked at was her hand. Their fingers entwined. Black and white. She'd always found the contrast so striking when they were little. Nothing more than that. Just another beautiful thing about her friend, her golden hair and skin that turned pink when they played on the vineyard for too long. She spread her fingers and slid their palms together before turning Imogen's hand over in hers. She needed to know every millimetre, every line and crack on her skin, every hair and follicle, every vein that pulsed with life just under the skin.

"What do you think, Ami?" Imogen said, her question dragging Amahle from her trance.

Amahle shook herself as she surfaced and took a breath for what felt like the first time since she'd seen Sipho lying on the ground.

"About what?" She frowned when she noticed who Imogen was talking to. "When did you get here?"

"I arrived at the house before the ambulance left, Amahle." Julius stared at her. "Are you all right?"

She waved her hand. "I'll be fine. What do I think about what?"

"Julius thinks we need to strike while we have the element of surprise on our side. Gather a press conference and present them with the results of our investigation now. Get the public on side," Imogen said. "All he wants is an exclusive interview with you later in return. Isn't that generous?"

"Very. What about the police? They need to investigate."

"I know someone we can trust. He's almost here. We can brief him while I get my cronies over here. We'll do it outside here. I know you won't want to go anywhere while we wait for news about your brother," Julius said.

"Where is he?"

"Still in surgery."

"In surgery? What do you mean?"

Imogen grasped her hands again. "Amahle, you signed the consent forms."

She tried to remember, but it was all a blur. "What's wrong with him?"

Imogen frowned. "Do you want to go somewhere else while I tell you?"

"No. Just tell me."

"Okay." She took a deep breath, and Amahle readied herself for the details. "He has many injuries that they'll have to deal with, cuts that will scar his face and so on, but they aren't life threatening. There are two major issues for them. His right lower leg, they're pretty sure they will have to amputate, but they don't know if it will be at the ankle or mid calf."

"Oh God." Amahle put her hand over her mouth, remembering the bloody lump of meat.

"Are you okay?"

"There's more?"

Imogen nodded solemnly. "Do you want me to stop?"

Amahle shuddered. If he could go through it, the least she was going to do was listen to what the bastards had done to him. "Go on."

"The doctors are also trying to assess the damage to his penis and testicles. They aren't certain, but they found wire wrapped around them and burn marks under the wire. They think he was electrocuted."

"What do you mean assess the damage?"

"They're doing all they can to save it."

"Amputate his penis?"

"They hope not."

"Jesus Christ." She closed her eyes, and bile rose in her throat. She put her hand to her mouth.

"Bathroom's here." Imogen tugged her to her feet and pushed her the ten feet into the room. She held Amahle's hair back while she bent over the bowl and threw up.

Imogen rubbed circles over her back. "You feeling better?"

"No."

"I love that honest streak of yours." Imogen held out a packet. "Here. Mint."

"Thanks. Did they say how long it would take?"

"The surgery? They didn't know. Lots of complex procedures going on. Lots of potential for things to go wrong."

"But they think he'll be okay, don't they?"

"They didn't make any promises, Ami. And they wouldn't commit to anything with regard to what shape he'd be in if they could save his life." She pulled Amahle into her embrace. "I know this probably scared the shit out of you again, but please, please don't try to send me away again. I'm not going anywhere, and I don't want to have an argument with you here."

"I wasn't going to."

"You weren't?"

"No. You're right. It has scared the shit out of me, but having you here with me helps. You help." She twined her fingers with Imogen's and smiled. "Thank you."

"Shall we go back out there and see if there's any news? The doctors did say that they'd keep us up to date when they could."

"You're just full of good ideas, aren't you?"

"Come on." Imogen wrapped her arm around Amahle's shoulders and led her back to the waiting room. Julius stood as they approached him.

"Get on the phone, Julius. If we're doing this, we're doing it all the way."

"If we do this there's no turning back."

"I know."

"Any sign of Claudia?"

"None. Her house was empty and there's no sign of her at the office. I've got Laura's people looking into any potential minefields she's planted on the evidentiary trail, but so far they haven't found anything."

"They haven't exactly had long to look, Ami," Imogen said.

"I know." Amahle turned back to Julius. "Call your cop friend—"

"I already did." He pointed to the doors. "He just walked in."

"Sergeant Solongo. That's your contact?" Amahle asked.

"Sergeant? No. This is Lieutenant General Solongo."

Amahle whirled around to look at the unassuming man walking toward them. "It looks like you have some explaining to do."

"My apologies for the misinformation, Minister. I have been working undercover. I want to reestablish the anti-corruption unit, but I've been stonewalled at every turn. I decided to go undercover and bring irrefutable evidence to the government to force the issue."

"I can certainly understand that thought process, Lieutenant General."

"I'm very sorry to hear about your brother. Julius filled me in. I had a few leads back in Stellenbosch but nothing concrete. Just the link to a local thug by the name of Tsotsi, as I mentioned to you."

"I remember. The good news is I have a lot more for you. And it will do your case for a new anti-corruption unit no harm at all."

"I'm all ears."

"I'll just go see if they have somewhere a bit more private for this," Imogen said. "It's going to take a while." She wandered over to the nurses' station.

"One of those stories, is it?" Solongo asked.

"More than you can possibly imagine." Amahle ran her hand through her hair. "How much do you know about the HIV treatment programme?"

"More than I wish I did. My brother and his wife have HIV. They have two children who were born with this despicable virus."

Amahle reached out and gently touched his arm. "I'm so sorry, Lieutenant General."

"Please, call me Dingane."

"Dingane, what I have to tell you will directly impact your family. And for that I am very sorry. We've worked as quickly as possible."

"I'm sure you've done all you can."

"There's a family waiting room we can use over there." Imogen returned and pointed a little way down the hall. "The nurse said she'd find us in there if there was any news on Sipho."

They followed Imogen to the small room and took seats on the uncomfortable plastic chairs. The bright colours hurt Amahle's eyes under the harsh fluorescent lights, but she pushed her discomfort aside. It was nothing compared to the pain and suffering of so many others. There was a jug of water and some plastic cups on a table. Imogen poured them all glasses and indicated for Amahle to start the story. It took almost an hour for her to cover every detail, and when she finished, Dingane whistled.

"That's one hell of a story. I take it you have proof?"

"The proof is right here in this hospital. There are evidence stores where rape kits and so on are kept. All Dr. Marais's samples are in there. It's in the pills your brother and his family are being prescribed, I have no doubt."

"You certainly know how to get a man's attention."

"I don't want a man's attention, Dingane. I need the whole country's attention, and I need good officers to take care of business."

"I know enough officers with affected family to be able to make the arrests we know of now. But if this is as big as you say, I can't guarantee we have enough people to make sure this shit is properly taken care of. We're talking a massive recall of medication. Coordinating the collection and redistribution of medications to those with contaminated supplies alone will be immense."

"I know."

"The people will be outraged. There'll be riots."

"I hope not."

"How do you plan to start getting the information out to those who need to coordinate the response?"

"I'm having my office send out emails to all hospital administrators, executives, and pharmacies within the hour. Detailing which hospitals need to test their stock. We're also organizing collection points in affected areas for people to dump their bad medications. Emergency stockpiles of Combivirine are being gathered as we speak and will be distributed as soon as they reach the hospitals."

"And how are you going to tell the people? Send them letters from the hospitals?"

Amahle shook her head. "Too long. Too many people won't see them or be able to read them, or they will ignore them. We're taking this out there straight away." She glanced at her watch. "I'm holding a press conference in twenty minutes."

"I can't possibly coordinate multiple arrests in that time."

"Dingane, it's amazing what we can do when we're motivated and fighting for what's right."

"It would be a lot safer to send out letters and give me the time to pick these bastards up."

"It might be. But I refuse to betray the people any longer. We have the means to help those in need. We have the medications to help them stay healthy and fight AIDS. Greed has stolen that from them. I refuse to hide what has happened and skulk in the shadows while people die. I will not do it. I will not live the rest of my life ashamed of this. I—we— have been trusted with the care and protection of our people, Dingane. I will not betray that trust as others have."

Dingane looked her in the eye, and she hoped he couldn't see her shaking.

"Very well. I have some calls to make, Amahle." He held his hand out to her and shook it firmly. "It is a pleasure and an honour to serve and protect our people alongside you." He left the room, his phone already in place, barking staccato words to the person on the other end.

Amahle turned to Julius. "How many did you manage to get in touch with?"

"Every media service in Cape Town will be there and all the major national news services who have representatives in Cape Town. I'll go and make sure everything is set up outside for you. I'll see you down there."

"Good. Are you ready for this?" She looked at Imogen.

"You want me there with you?"

"Yes. Like I said before, I'm done with skulking in shadows. I've never made a secret of who I am. I'm not ashamed, and I refuse to behave as though I am."

"You sure?"

"I just said so. Come on. Let's go." She stopped at the nurses' station. "Is there any news about my brother?"

"I'm sorry, no. Nothing yet," the woman said, a piteous smile on her face. "Would you like me to put my head in and see if they can tell us anything before you go?"

"Please."

"I'll be right back."

"Thank you." Amahle waited until she was gone. "Do you think they teach that smile in nursing college?"

Imogen chuckled. "Probably. At law school we have a whole term dedicated to the appropriate look for every occasion. From the smile that instills fear to the one that eviscerates."

"You'll have to teach me that one."

"I think you've got that one down, Minister."

"Minister?"

Amahle turned to see a doctor approach her. "Yes."

"I'm Dr. Stephanie Sisulu. I'm one of the team working on your brother. So far he's hanging in there, but we still have a long way to go. We weren't able to save his foot. The damage to the tissue was too great and there were already signs of necrosis as we debrided the wound. There was also substantial capillary damage to the lower leg and we've had to amputate just below the knee."

"And his other injuries?"

"The damage to his penis is extensive. We are doing all we can, but it isn't looking good."

"What does that mean?"

"We won't amputate unless we have to. There is substantial burn damage to the tissue, and the wire that was wrapped around it has fused both to itself and in places to the flesh."

"Oh, God."

"We will have to perform skin grafts to try to rebuild some areas of the flesh and muscle. It won't be possible to do all that needs to be done right now. We need to ensure there is no infection before we can consider the grafts." The doctor shook her head. "It's been years since we've had to treat injuries like this."

"What do you mean?"

"The last time I was part of a surgery with a penile injury like this was before apartheid was abolished. It was a technique used by the police back in the day."

"The police?" Imogen asked.

"Yeah. They'd shock the poor soul until it literally dropped off."

"That really happens?"

"I'm afraid so. I have to get back in there. I'll keep you updated."

"Thank you, Doctor."

Imogen ran her fingers through her hair. "Well, that was more information than I needed to know."

"Me too. Come on. I've got a press corps to talk to."

"You sure? You can take a few minutes if you need to."

"I just need to get this over with."

"Okay, but just remember, whatever happens next, you're the good guy in this story. You're doing the right thing."

Amahle nodded and pushed the call button for the lift. "I'll try to remember that when someone starts calling for my head."

"Head of state, more likely."

"I thought you were a barrister, not a comedienne."

"Now look who's being funny."

They stood side by side in silence until the doors opened at the lobby. Amahle pulled a deep breath into her lungs and led them out the door.

"Jesus, how many people?" Imogen said.

"Looks like a couple hundred." Bulbs flashed as she took her place on the makeshift podium. Julius stood off to the side, camera on a tripod, peering down the eyepiece. He looked up as she turned to him. He held her gaze for a moment before looking back at his camera, but it was long enough for her to recognize the pride, faith, and the fire of righteousness burning in his eyes. They were committed and there was no turning back now. This was the right thing to do. She cleared her throat.

"Ladies and gentlemen of the press, thank you for joining me today. Make sure you've got your recorders on, your notebooks out, and your brains in gear. I have a lot to get through, so please, no questions until I'm finished.

"When I was a little girl my grandmother told me a story. Some of you may know it, the Curse of the Chameleon. I see some of you nodding. For those who don't, in short, it is the story of how the Creator made new skins for the people of the earth in order to prolong life. He gave the gift to the chameleon to deliver, but he was tricked and the new skins were stolen by the snake. After this, the chameleon was so ashamed that he vowed to hide from people for eternity and humans died.

"Well, my friends, today's story has something in common with this tale. The HIV programme that we have built in South Africa is something I have been immensely proud to be a part of. To be a part of its inception, its implementation, and in guarding it for as long as it is needed. And, my friends, we need it more today than we ever did before." She looked directly into the camera, knowing that the feed would be projected into the homes of millions of South Africans.

"Over the past two years the statistics for our programme have been developing a worrying trend. Our numbers for those in treatment going on to develop full-blown AIDS have been considerably higher than the global average. Why? Do we have worse poverty than countries like Nigeria, Mozambique, or Liberia? No. Do we have worse sanitation than India? No. Do we have worse lifestyle situations than any other country in Africa? No, we do not.

"So why? Why were our people dying when we were using the same treatment regimens that all the other countries were using? A short time ago, I got a call from Dr. Derek Marais, the CEO of this very hospital, and he'd been asking himself the very same questions. Fortunately, the doctor was an exceptional man in the position to start finding the answer to his questions. I'm here today to share those answers with you all.

"Dr. Marais managed to isolate the areas performing worst in the trials. He managed to obtain samples of the medications they were prescribing, where they were getting their drugs from, and then obtain samples directly from the source. He was able to test those samples and determine that the drugs being prescribed as Combivirine was in fact aspirin. Nothing more."

A roar of outrage and questions erupted from the crowd of reporters. People wanted to know where Marais was, who was selling the counterfeit drugs, how many people were affected, how many hospitals, how were they going to stop it. So many questions, so many voices that they all ran together as each member of the press stood and stepped toward her, trying to ensure their question was the first she had to deal with. She felt a presence beside her on the podium. Two, actually. She glanced over her shoulders and smiled as Imogen stood to her left, and on her right, Lieutenant General Solongo.

"They're in custody," he said.

"All of them?"

"Not quite. Still no sign of Claudia De Villiers, and we haven't arrested the minister yet, but PharmaChem won't be trading anymore."

"Thank you."

Amahle held her hand up and waited, silently requesting they stop and let her continue. It took several minutes before the noise level was manageable again.

"Thank you, thank you. Let me finish, and if I haven't answered your questions, I'll do so then. I promise. So, where was I?"

"Aspirin," Julius shouted from the crowd.

"Thank you. With a little digging, Dr. Marais was able to ascertain who the supplier was for the hospitals who were unknowingly prescribing aspirin, and he even managed to get samples from them himself to test. When he brought this to me, we expanded the testing to uncover just how many hospitals were being defrauded in this way. The results were shocking. The company in question supplies almost half of the hospitals across the country. Only the private hospitals supplied by this company have been receiving genuine drugs.

"The company involved is called PharmaChem, and I've just been informed that three of the four directors of the company have been arrested. The fourth will be apprehended very soon, I'm sure. Everyone else involved in this conspiracy will also be brought to justice.

"We have evidence, hard evidence, of the other people involved in this, and there are officers on the way." She looked directly into Julius's camera. "No one involved is getting away with this. Everyone involved will be charged with the mutilation of Thambo Umpala, the murder of Dr. Derek Marais and his wife, the torture and attempted murder of Sipho Nkosi, and the attempted murder of more than three million South Africans.

"You have all been given a list of known hospitals where their supplies have been contaminated. As I speak to you, they are already in the process of removing them from circulation, and my office is coordinating with them to get them emergency supplies of the correct drugs. Everyone watching, if you are taking Combivirine and your medication looks like this"—she held one of the white pills up so that every camera could focus on it—"then it is more than likely that you have been given the incorrect medication. My office is arranging collection depositories as we speak. Everyone here today has been given a list of those locations. Please, please, display those lists on your screens now. If you have these pills, go to one of the depositories, take your medication with you, and we will give you an emergency supply to get you through until we can get normal supplies to every hospital and pharmacy within affected areas.

"Give the volunteers your name and we will arrange blood tests for you. We want to ensure you are getting the correct dosages of medications and that your health has not suffered. For your health and your peace of mind, I encourage every single South African who has HIV to go to one of these depositories as soon as you can. There will be queues, and I know you will be scared, for yourselves, for your children, and you have every right to be angry. I'm angry too, my friends.

"I know you all think we politicians sit around doing nothing but lining our own pockets, and keeping away from the rest of the population, that your problems are not our problems. I wish I could disagree with you. I wish I could tell you that you're wrong to think that, but I can't. What I'm going to say to you instead is this.

"You all know me. You all know my story. I fought for this programme from the very beginning. Trust me. Trust me to fix it. Trust me to do what is right for us. What is right for South Africa, and what is right for everyone who is suffering. Because I suffer with you. My mother is HIV positive. She has been given these pills. And like you, we don't know how long she has had them, or how that has affected her health.

"I am angry that it was possible to perpetrate this crime. And there will be steps taken to ensure that it can never happen again. I will not play with peoples' lives. I will not play with the health of the nation. And I will not stand by while anyone else does. Trust me. Be patient. And please go peacefully to the depositories for help. I will not let you down. We have been deceived, but unlike the chameleon, we need not feel ashamed. Do not hide away from this. Come and let us help. Thank you."

The barrage of questions that followed felt like a wall of sound hitting her. It was hard to pick out individual voices, it was hard to keep track of who was asking what, and it was exhausting. Amahle wished she could sleep for a week, but the hard work was just beginning. There would be a reshuffle in the Ministry of Health, there would be outrage up and down the country, and there would be calls for compensation, retribution, and justice. Then there was her mother to deal with, Sipho's rehabilitation, Thambo's. God, the list was just never ending. Imogen threaded her fingers through Amahle's and squeezed gently. One step at a time.

CHAPTER FORTY-NINE

Y ou're still on every channel." Imogen handed Amahle a glass of
wine and sat on the sofa beside her.

It had been a week since her press conference, and Amahle's
image was still plastered on every newspaper and TV across the
country. It was the first time they'd been back at the house since Sipho
had been left on the pavement to die, and they were both exhausted
from sitting by his bedside and trying to coordinate the efforts of police,
hospital staff, volunteers, and local aid agencies in the cleanup and
redistribution. A week where they had spent every moment together. A
week where Imogen had offered her comfort without asking anything
in return. A week where they'd touched and talked, cried and held each
other, and every second, Amahle had felt herself fall more and more in
love with her. Despite all the distractions, despite all the pain, fear, and
uncertainty, she wanted nothing more than to be with Immy. To touch
her and not have to stop. To hold her and never let go. A week in which
every aspect of her life had changed, morphed into something full of
colour and life. She knew now that there were many incarnations of her
grandmother's tale, about the curse of the chameleon, and that shame
manifested itself in many ways. She wasn't hiding anymore. Not from
life, not from people, and not from herself.

"Did you hear about that news broadcaster who tipped you to be
the next president of South Africa?"

"I don't want his job."

"Really?" Imogen tugged Amahle's foot onto her lap and pressed
her thumbs against the sole, kneading until she elicited a purr from
Amahle's lips.

Amahle shrugged. "Not all it's cracked up to be."

"Some of the pundits are saying this scandal will cost him his presidency."

"Still don't want it. I've got enough on my plate with my own job, thanks." She sipped from her glass and closed her eyes, obviously revelling in the contact. "I'll give you a week." She pushed her foot further into Imogen's hands. "Okay, two. Then you have to stop that."

Imogen chuckled. "Yes, ma'am." She switched feet. "I want to talk to you about something."

"What?"

"Sipho."

"What about him?" Amahle opened her eyes, a look of near panic set upon her face. "Did the hospital call? Is he okay?"

"I'm sorry. I didn't mean to scare you. I haven't heard anything new. I was meaning about everything that happened at the vineyard. The stolen money."

Amahle closed her eyes again. "I don't want to talk about it, Immy. I know he's going to go to jail for it. The evidence is—"

"That's what I want to talk about. I don't want to press charges."

"What are you talking about?"

"The only person who was really hurt out of that was my dad, and he's not here to worry about it anymore."

"Why would you do that?"

"Sipho's been through enough. He's more than paid for his mistakes. And I really do think he had good intentions."

She couldn't disagree. They knew now that he would survive his injuries. But at what cost? Scars marred his face and body, his leg amputated mid calf, and he faced many months of surgeries to reshape what they'd saved of his penis. Yes, he'd paid a price for his mistakes in ways the authorities would never be able to exact from him. But that didn't mean they wouldn't still come after him. And even if Imogen didn't press charges, there was still the matter of the destruction of Dr. Marais's office, the assault on Thambo, and the murders of Dr. Marais and his wife. There were still so many questions about his role in those acts that he would have to answer for, despite the deal she knew he was being offered—amnesty for his testimony. "He still broke the law." And she knew her brother well enough to know that his actions, the decisions he made, would haunt him for the rest of his life.

"No, he borrowed money from me. We'll work out something like a repayment plan so that the accounts can be ratified, but I think you'll find the repayment terms are pretty reasonable."

"Payment plan?"

"Yeah, I was thinking one rand a month. Sound okay?"

Amahle chuckled. "I think I can manage that."

"Why would you have to manage it?"

"Well, he doesn't have means to support himself."

"Sure he does. He has a job at the vineyard as soon as he's up to it."

"You're still going to employ him?"

"Sure. He's the manager at the vineyard."

"How can you trust him?"

"I think he's learned his lesson. Don't you?"

"You have a point." She settled back to enjoy Imogen's ministrations again.

"Any news on your mum?"

"Yeah." Amahle closed her eyes again. "And in other joyous news, she hasn't been taking a cocktail. Ever. It seems like Sipho did it all for nothing. Her blood is so thin from all the aspirin, the doctor said it took hours for the needle wound to heal when they took her blood."

"And?"

"She has AIDS. With all the drinking, cirrhosis, too. He doesn't think she's got long left."

"I'm so sorry, Ami." Imogen shifted so that she could pull Amahle into her embrace. She might have been a rotten mother, but she was still her mother, and you only got one of those.

"I still don't understand why they didn't go to a clinic, why they didn't tell me, why they just tried to hide it."

"Because they were ashamed."

"It's an illness. There's no shame in being ill."

"Oh, sweetheart, you're not that naive. Whether you want to admit it or not, there is still a huge stigma attached to HIV and AIDS sufferers here. People who don't know much about it are scared, and those who do, well, they look down on those who have it as sluts, junkies, and degenerates. I'm not saying it's right. Far from it. But I am saying that's what people think. And you know that."

"It's not right."

"I already said that."

Amahle sighed as Imogen's hands worked on a knot at the base of her skull. "I got a call from Dingane a little while ago."

"And?"

"Fred Pugh sold out James Wilson. You were right on the money about all of it. Pugh was also the one in control of the thugs that Sipho was involved with. He's been in and talked to Sipho. He's willing to testify, in exchange for amnesty. And now they're all singing like canaries. Solongo was on his way to arrest Wilson when he called."

"And Claudia?"

A shadow passed over Amahle's face. "Nothing yet. Her picture is at every border crossing, port, and airport. They'll find her eventually."

"Are you more pissed or embarrassed?"

"It's a pretty even split if I'm being honest. I thought I was a good judge of people. Thought I had good instincts." She shook her head. "I feel like a fool."

"Don't be. She fooled everyone. I never suspected she was in on it. She seemed like she was your friend."

"That's the most humiliating part. She was a friend. A good one."

"It's not your fault, Ami."

"No. But it certainly makes my judgement questionable, and your pundit is calling for me to run for the presidency." She chuckled. "They'd be laughed out of the studio no doubt."

"I think you're wrong. But I don't want to argue with you." She pressed her thumb into a particularly tender spot, and her breath caught when Amahle bit her lip. She cleared her throat. "What about Roland? He's the only one I can't figure out. Was he in on it or not? Did he know what was going on with Beth?"

"He says not."

"And?"

"Well, so far no one has implicated him, and they're pointing their fingers in every direction that will deflect it from them, so I've got to say no. He's not involved."

"Poor man. It looked like he doted on her at the ball."

Amahle saw the look of relief flitter across Imogen's face. Probably glad her own instincts with the man hadn't been so far off that he was another bad guy. She only wished she had the same instincts, and she felt terrible for what he was going through. "Yeah, his name was leaked to the press and they have his home surrounded. The police are watching too."

"Why? In case Claudia shows up?"

"Yes."

"Not going to happen. She's too smart. I'd be amazed if she's still in the country."

"You think she was the brains behind the whole thing?"

"Well, let me put it this way. If I was the barrister for any one of them, she's who I'd be pinning it all on. You name it—coercion, blackmail, threats—anything I could think of to get the jury to believe she was the one behind it and my client was her puppet."

"Because she isn't there to defend herself."

"Exactly. With a case like this it won't get them acquitted, but it might get them a reduced sentence."

Amahle snorted a laugh. "Not likely. The country is baying for blood."

"True."

"I don't want to talk about it anymore. People are getting the help they need. The bad guys are going to jail."

"Yeah. I'm glad they got that Tsotsi chap." Imogen shuddered. "Did you see his picture on the news? Christ, he gave me the creeps."

"I did. Now stop talking about it." Amahle wanted to stop thinking about everything they'd seen, and everything that was still to be dealt with. It seemed never ending, and she needed a break. From both the situation and her own doubts. She'd spent a week wanting and waiting. It was time to forget it all for a little while and let her soul come home. "Let's see if you can put that mouth to better use."

"I think I can do that."

Amahle grabbed her shirt and tugged her close. "So stop talking then."

Imogen let her close the last of the distance between them and place light kisses along her lower lip. She licked it delicately with her tongue before claiming it fully. Amahle's mouth opened beneath hers, allowing her inside, and she sighed when she first slipped her tongue inside. The heat of her kiss set a fire in her body, her heart, her soul, and she had no idea how she would survive without it ever again. The touch of her skin was more vital to her existence than air. Her kiss more life giving than water, and her caress as nourishing as food. She pulled back and looked down into Amahle's eyes. She trailed her fingertip from her temple to her jaw and along to the point of her chin.

"Do you have any idea how I feel about you?"

"Horny?"

Imogen chuckled. "That too."

"I'm sorry. Tell me."

"No, no. It doesn't matter." She pushed Amahle back until she was on top of her, stretched out on the sofa. "I think I'll just stick with horny." She leaned down and kissed her again, moaning as Amahle threaded her fingers into her hair and scratched her fingernails over her scalp. The soft wanton noises Amahle made were driving her crazy, and all she wanted to do was elicit more of them. She wanted to hear every moan, taste every sigh, and feel every tremble as Amahle let go of her control and just felt. She ran a hand along Amahle's ribs, over her collarbone, and round the back of her neck, easing her head closer as she deepened the kiss.

Amahle tore her mouth from Imogen's. "You're driving me insane."

"It's entirely mutual."

"Take me to bed."

"You don't need to ask me twice." They laughed as Imogen clambered to her feet and helped Amahle up. They held hands as they walked into her bedroom, smiled as they pulled the blinds together, and Imogen's smile widened as Amahle pushed her back onto the bed. She raised her hands to the first button of her blouse and teased it through the hole so slowly that Imogen could focus on nothing else. As the tiny plastic disc was finally freed from the cloth, she heard herself gasp. Each button was released in similar fashion until Imogen was leaning up on her elbows, her breasts bobbing up and down as she panted, and she shifted awkwardly on the bed, her panties so wet they stuck to her uncomfortably.

Amahle's shirt hung open, a red lace bra peeking from beneath the cotton fabric as she dropped her skirt to the floor. Hold-up stockings with lace trim, and red lace panties covered her as she knelt on the side of the bed.

"Do you always wear sexy underwear like that?"

Amahle nodded. "Makes me feel confident. Like I know a secret that no one else does."

"Except me."

"Except you." Amahle gripped her shirt and tore the buttons open before leaning in to cover Imogen's skin in kisses. Her chest, breasts, and stomach were lavished with hundreds of fluttery little kisses, her tongue darting out occasionally to trace a path around a nipple or her navel. She gave up the idea that she had any sort of control under Amahle's skilful ministrations. She trailed her hands up Amahle's thighs, loving the textural change between the silk of her stockings and the softest skin she had ever felt. The high cut of the panties left her with plenty of skin to explore, but it wasn't nearly enough.

She slipped her hands under the tails of the cotton shirt and over the scarcely covered backside. The muscles quivered under her hands, flexed as Amahle moved, and broke out in goose bumps when she scratched her nails over the taut flesh.

Amahle worked her belt open and tugged her pants and underwear off her legs, tossing them off the bed along with her own shirt. Imogen groaned at the sight of Amahle's full breasts spilling over the top of the constraining fabric. She sat up and wrapped her arms around Amahle's waist, pulling her in tight and burying her face between her breasts. Kissing, licking, sucking them into her mouth. She tugged the fabric down so that she could suckle one nipple and pinch the other to a stone hard peak. She could smell Amahle's desire, feel her thrusting against her stomach in search of contact, but she never wanted the moment to end. She wanted to spend the rest of her life touching her, loving her. She wanted to be everything Amahle would ever want or need, and she needed her to know that before they made love.

"Ami, I—"

Amahle covered her mouth with her own, stealing the words as she pushed her back down onto her back and straddled her hips. Imogen wrapped her arms around her back and rolled them over until she was lying between Amahle's legs and ground against her. She tore her mouth from Amahle's and gazed down at her. She slipped one hand between them, unable to wait any longer to touch her. She pushed the lace to one side and slid two fingers easily inside her.

"Look at me." She thrust her fingers gently, rocking her hips against her hand, pleasuring them both. "Ami, look at me."

Amahle opened her eyes and gazed up at her.

"Keep looking at me." She angled her fingers to hit the sweet spot inside her and watched as Amahle fought to keep her eyes open under the onslaught of pleasure. "I love you." Amahle's inner walls clenched around her fingers as Imogen's declaration seemingly caused a chain reaction inside her that pulled Imogen over the edge and into her own orgasm.

"I love you too."

EPILOGUE

As we commit this body to the ground, we remember that it is not our loss that we should look to on this day. But instead look to the peace and joy Mbali will find in the presence of our Lord." The minister stooped to pick up a handful of dirt. "Your suffering is over, my child. Go in peace." He dropped some of the dirt on the casket. "Ashes to ashes." He opened his palm and let the rest of the red clay soil fall. "Dust to dust."

Imogen squeezed her hand as they each followed the minister's actions and slowly filed away from the cemetery.

The crowd was small. The two of them, the minister, and Sipho were the only ones who came to pay their respects. Amahle snorted a sad laugh. Wrong phrase. She had long since come to terms with having no respect for her mother, perhaps saying good-bye was the better option. Either way, there were few people who cared enough to show up, and given how hard her mother had made the last six months of her life, Amahle wasn't sure she blamed them. She'd barely wanted to come herself.

Sipho came up behind them, moving awkwardly on his crutches. His prosthetic was due to be fitted in a couple of weeks. His recovery was well under way, even though there was still a long way to go. Physically, he was recovering well. Mentally, emotionally, not so much. A suicide attempt had led to a hefty dosage of antidepressants, but Amahle was determined to see him through it. Losing their mother was particularly hard for him. The futility of all he went through was thrown in his face as her casket was lowered into the ground.

Amahle rubbed her hand up her arm, trying to ward off the chill as the sun disappeared behind the clouds. She glanced at Imogen and wondered how she was doing. "You okay?" she asked.

"Me? I should be asking you that question."

"Well, I'm fine, thanks. Glad she's no longer in pain. You look like there's something on your mind."

"The last time I was at a funeral was my mother's."

"Ah." She tugged her to a halt. "Want to go and see her?"

"I don't need to." Imogen put her hand to her chest. "She's always here. Always was." She leaned down and kissed Amahle softly. "I was just too stupid to realize that all the people I loved were always here."

They walked back to the vineyard, through the rows of vines down to the orchard. They sat under their tree and watched the sun set over the mountains, arms wrapped around each other, backs pressed against the bark.

"We've got a long week ahead of us, sweetheart. Perhaps we should make a move?" Amahle said quietly into the fading light.

"Yeah. Should be fun." The trials were due to start on Monday, and the country was on tenterhooks, waiting for the truth to be revealed.

"Fun? Are you serious?"

"Yup. A case like this is a once in a lifetime thing, babe."

Amahle snorted. "Wish it wasn't in my lifetime."

"I know. But it is, so…" Imogen shrugged.

"Yeah, yeah. Suck it up and get on with it."

Imogen chuckled. "Something like that." She stood and held her hand out to tug Amahle to her feet. "Let's go home."

Amahle kissed her softly. "I already am."

❖

She bit into her energy bar without dropping her gaze from the binoculars she held. She watched as the two women clasped hands and wandered toward the armoured car waiting for them, door open, guards looking out vigilantly. She smiled as they got into the car. Always the second one in the convoy. She made a quick note on her tablet before opening another app and checking her camera feeds. She was pleased that they were all working clearly. She wished briefly that there was something going on there so she could check sound levels, but there would be time for that later.

Her eyes flittered back to her binoculars, and she was more than a little peeved that she'd missed the cars actually driving off. It didn't matter though. She had what she needed.

Time to put the next stage of her plan into action. She opened her laptop and hacked her way into the government's computer servers through the backdoor programme she'd left. She squinted at the lines of code scrolling across her screen as she searched for the sequence that would drop her into Amahle's computer.

"Gotcha." Claudia started typing. "You should have taken care of me when you had the chance, Minister." She added files and lines of code where she wanted them. Seemingly hidden, but not nearly hidden enough. She opened her email programme and attached a couple of juicy pages before addressing the missive. "Now it's my turn to take care of you." She pressed return.

About the Author

A native of Stockport (near Manchester, UK), Andrea took her life in her hands a few years ago and crossed the great North/South divide and now lives in Norfolk with her partner, their two border collies, and two cats. Andrea spends her time running their campsite and hostel to pay the bills, and scribbling down stories during the winter months.

Andrea is an avid reader and a keen musician, playing the saxophone and the guitar (just to annoy her other half—apparently!). She is also a recreational diver and takes any opportunity to head to warmer climes and discover the mysteries of life beneath the waves.

In 2013, Andrea was awarded an Alice B. Lavender Certificate for *Ladyfish* and followed up by winning the 2013 Lambda Literary Award for Romance with her novel *Clean Slate*. Her third novel, *Nightingale*, was a finalist in the 2014 Lambda Literary Award for Romance and the 2014 GCLS Award in the Traditional Romance category.

Books Available From Bold Strokes Books

The Chameleon's Tale by Andrea Bramhall. Two old friends must work through a web of lies and deceit to find themselves again, but in the search they discover far more than they ever went looking for. (978-1-62639-363-9)

Side Effects by VK Powell. Detective Jordan Bishop and Dr. Neela Sahjani must decide if it's easier to trust someone with your heart or your life as they face threatening protestors, corrupt politicians, and their increasing attraction. (978-1-62639-364-6)

Autumn Spring by Shelley Thrasher. Can Bree and Linda, two women in the autumn of their lives, put their hearts first and find the love they've never dared seize? (978-1-62639-365-3)

Warm November by Kathleen Knowles. What do you do if the one woman you want is the only one you can't have? (978-1-62639-366-0)

In Every Cloud by Tina Michele. When Bree finally leaves her shattered life behind, is she strong enough to salvage the remaining pieces of her heart and find the place where it truly fits? (978-1-62639-413-1)

Rise of the Gorgon by Tanai Walker. When independent Internet journalist Elle Pharell goes to Kuwait to investigate a veteran's mysterious suicide, she hires Cassandra Hunt, an interpreter with a covert agenda. (978-1-62639-367-7)

Crossed by Meredith Doench. Agent Luce Hansen returns home to catch a killer and risks everything to revisit the unsolved murder of her first girlfriend and confront the demons of her youth. (978-1-62639-361-5)

Making a Comeback by Julie Blair. Music and love take center stage when jazz pianist Liz Randall tries to make a comeback with the help of her reclusive, blind neighbor, Jac Winters. (978-1-62639-357-8)

The Price of Honor by Radclyffe. Honor and duty are not always black and white—and when self-styled patriots take up arms against the government, the price of honor may be a life. (978-1-62639-359-2)

Soul Unique by Gun Brooke. Self-proclaimed cynic Greer Landon falls for Hayden Rowe's paintings and the young woman shortly after, but will Hayden, who lives with Asperger syndrome, trust her and reciprocate her feelings? (978-1-62639-358-5)

Mounting Evidence by Karis Walsh. Lieutenant Abigail Hargrove and her mounted police unit need to solve a murder and protect wetland biologist Kira Lovell during the Washington State Fair. (978-1-62639-343-1)

Threads of the Heart by Jeannie Levig. Maggie and Addison Rae-McInnis share a love and a life, but are the threads that bind them together strong enough to withstand Addison's restlessness and the seductive Victoria Fontaine? (978-1-62639-410-0)

Sheltered Love by MJ Williamz. Boone Fairway and Grey Dawson—two women touched by abuse—overcome their pasts to find happiness in each other. (978-1-62639-362-2)

Searching for Celia by Elizabeth Ridley. As American spy novelist Dayle Salvesen investigates the mysterious disappearance of her ex-lover, Celia, in London, she begins questioning how well she knew Celia—and how well she knows herself. (978-1-62639-356-1).

Hardwired by C.P. Rowlands. Award-winning teacher Clary Stone and Leefe Ellis, manager of the homeless shelter for small children, stand together in a part of Clary's hometown that she never knew existed. (978-1-62639-351-6)

The Muse by Meghan O'Brien. Erotica author Kate McMannis struggles with writer's block until a gorgeous muse entices her into a world of fantasy sex and inadvertent romance. (978-1-62639-223-6)

No Good Reason by Cari Hunter. A violent kidnapping in a Peak District village pushes Detective Sanne Jensen and lifelong friend Dr. Meg Fielding closer, just as it threatens to tear everything apart. (978-1-62639-352-3)

Romance by the Book by Jo Victor. If Cam didn't keep disrupting her life, maybe Alex could uncover the secret of a century-old love story, and solve the greatest mystery of all—her own heart. (978-1-62639-353-0)

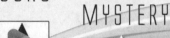